Pathways

Pathways

All-New Tales of
Valdemar

Edited by
Mercedes Lackey

DAW BOOKS, INC.

DONALD A. WOLLHEIM, FOUNDER

375 Hudson Street, New York, NY 10014

ELIZABETH R. WOLLHEIM
SHEILA E. GILBERT
PUBLISHERS

www.dawbooks.com

First Printing, December 2017
1 2 3 4 5 6 7 8 9

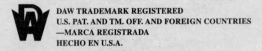

Contents

Silent Storms
Brigid Collins

The Collegium had dumped a Trainee on Herald Selte.

Even with Haven an hour's ride behind, Selte still twitched in her saddle. The distant voices rumbled like thunder at the horizon's edge. Thunder told tales about lightning, and lightning could drop with little warning to those who didn't understand the language of the weather. Selte did understand it—at least, as well as she could. She'd studied the weather all her life.

What left her floundering was conversation with people. She hadn't had to find a way to communicate with anyone other than a few Heralds since being Chosen, and what little she did with those Heralds barely qualified anyway. Being alone with her understanding Companion in the wilderness, where she didn't have to listen to spoken words or Mindspeech, kept her from feeling her losses too much.

Cerilka's sides buzzed against Selte's legs. Selte dug her knees inward before the Companion finished soothing her. Too hard, she realized, but nothing to do about it now.

Cerilka tossed her head, but she did not repeat her buzzing.

But her Companion was right. The storm cloud existed only in Selte's head. Sunlight beat down upon the dry, cracked dirt road. Even under the mottled shade of browned and curled leaves, the heat of high summer barely lifted. The air tasted of dust rather than ozone on the scarred remains of Selte's tongue.

The weather had whispered the same tale for three months now, until there could be no mistaking it: parched, choking, much of Valdemar a dried-out, crumbling husk in the continuing drought. Selte had included as much in the written report of her weather studies upon her return to Haven and had received in exchange a new, uncomfortable set of orders.

Ride Circuit through towns and villages rather than the wilderness. Ensure the people of Valdemar have the knowledge and tools to protect themselves from fires while the drought continues. Take this Herald Trainee and somehow, without the use of voice or Mindspeech, teach her to read weather.

Selte didn't have any power over the weather. She could do nothing to affect when the rains came or how hard they fell. But she tried to be a good listener, and the weather offered no judgments on Selte's lack of replies. It simply confided in her, and she interpreted its meanings as her limited abilities allowed. Sometimes she got it wrong, and that was on her.

She didn't blame the weather for the things her village had done to her in anger.

Selte felt her buttocks tighten against the too-stiff leather of Cerilka's fancy saddle, and Cerilka's tail swish reply came more tentatively than usual. Selte brushed her fingers through her Companion's mane in a soft apology.

She wished she could have ditched the fancy saddle back at the Collegium for the broken-in one she didn't have to be afraid to use, but their assigned Circuit meant they had to adhere to the official Herald and Companion uniform. She couldn't even scramble out of her own fancy Whites.

But a pleasantly worn saddle and comfortable clothes wouldn't override the invasive presence of Herald Trainee Marli and Companion Taren behind Selte and Cerilka.

"I can't believe how I've gotten used to the Collegium. It's so quiet out here." Marli's voice rippled with ingrained laughter.

Selte tensed. Was the girl laughing at her? Sounds

abounded out here, with birds singing and the wind rushing, and these ridiculous bells chiming on the saddles
with every step the Companions took. The only quiet one
was Selte, since Marli apparently couldn't go even part of
a candlemark without saying something. Selte had yet to
give any kind of response to the girl's prattle, hoping
she'd get the hint and keep quiet eventually.

No such luck yet.

"It really reminds me of my hometown, you know?
Like life is at a slower pace outside of the city."

Trying to parse the chatter made it hard to focus on
the subtleties of the weather, so Selte did her best to ignore the conversation she couldn't participate in anyway.

"Not that I dislike the city. I thought I would, you
know, when I first came here. If it weren't for Taren, I'd
have been completely terrified out of my skull leaving
home. But Haven isn't really so different."

Taren whickered, and Marli laughed again.

A thin breeze wound across the road, gossiping about
tomorrow's wind and flapping Selte's sweat-soaked
Whites. Then it blustered into the brush off the road and
disappeared into the wild.

Selte sighed after it, a silent curse on her new, con-
stricting Circuit.

"I know, right? The other Trainees say I'm still a country bumpkin, but I—"

Selte twisted around, her pants squeaking against the
fancy saddle, and glared at the Trainee. With one hand
she covered her own mouth, and with the other she
pointed at Marli.

Marli stared, eyes wide and mouth open, but no more
sound came out.

Satisfied her point had finally been received, Selte
righted herself. She let Cerilka take over following the
road, tipped her head back, and watched the thin, teasing
shreds of cloud drift overhead. They were too high and
too thin to shed even a single raindrop onto parched
Valdemar, but at least they were something. They were
the weather hemming and hawing over the idea of
maybe changing course sooner than later. Unless they

weren't. She could never be entirely sure of the weather until it happened.

There wasn't much Selte could teach anyone, really.

A brief pressure flared in her mind, Cerilka's sign for Selte to emerge from her solitary musings. The Companion knew better than anyone Selte's preference for silence, and she always kept their mental contact gentle and unobtrusive, reserving actual words for emergencies.

Taren had moved up beside Cerilka, and Selte glanced over to see Marli smiling at her.

"So, do you think it'll rain?"

Selte bit back a groan and focused on the long, tortuous road before them.

Marli had never run into a person she couldn't talk to. Before Taren had Chosen her, she'd been the peacekeeper in her hometown, which was no small feat, considering how the farming families back home mistrusted the Heralds that tried to solve their long-standing grudges. At the Collegium, she'd solved a multitude of disputes of varying degrees of seriousness. She'd made tons of friends throughout her training, getting people excited about working together no matter the task. People just felt comfortable opening up to her.

Herald Selte, however, had given her the cold shoulder at every turn, except when circumstances forced them to interact. Then she'd either glare at Marli or shy away, until Marli felt guilty for even opening her mouth.

The situation had her feeling cramped and constrained.

:*How am I supposed to learn anything if Herald Selte won't talk to me?:* she asked Taren.

They were riding through the cobbled streets of a lakeside town, checking that the people had followed the fire safety instructions another Herald had left a few weeks earlier. From here Marli had a view down the hill to the lake itself and the enlarged strip of rocky beach the drought had exposed. Small boats lay stranded on the stones, and the breeze carried the odor of rotting fish from where the carcasses lay baking in the unrelenting sun.

Taren snorted. *:The Collegium told you Herald Selte was mute. What sort of miracle do you expect her to pull off?:*

:That's not what I meant,: Marli replied. *:She clearly has a way to communicate with Cerilka. Why can't she try something like that with me? Or she could write. All Heralds learn that.:*

:Perhaps she is not comfortable having someone listen to her.:

Marli supposed that must be true. At each stop along their Circuit, whether the stop was a check-in like this one or a full teaching session for the fire-safety guidelines, Selte had stepped back and let Marli lead the discussions. While Marli enjoyed the process of working through people's issues with the new codes, she was still a Trainee. She could use a little help every now and then. But once they were back on the road, Selte's prickly silence reigned, and Marli's plans to confront her would-be mentor fizzled away. The woman looked ready to bolt every time Marli asked for guidance.

:There must be something I can do to put her at ease,: Marli said. She could find common ground with anyone. She wasn't an Empath or anything, her mental gifts being Farsight and Fetching, but she didn't need a supernatural enhancement to pick up on people's signals. Usually, anyway. The only signal she got from Herald Selte was "leave me alone," and it came through like a clap of thunder.

Marli wrapped up her inspection of the last row of houses, marking them on her list as "compliant." As Taren turned them away from the lake view and back toward the center of town, Marli tilted her head back the way she'd seen Selte do time after time. Not a single cloud drifted above today, but the harsh sunlight leached the sky of all color until it looked oppressively overcast. Marli hardly had time to feel the moisture of her own sweat before the thirsty air wicked it away.

Mimicking Selte once more, Marli sniffed, grimacing at the fish odor. She wondered what Selte read of the coming weather from the weak breeze. Not that broaching the topic of the weather had a different effect than any other conversation Marli might start. Herald Selte seemed content to bristle and sulk her way through this Circuit.

Marli and Taren arrived at the town's main gate in time to see Selte and Cerilka plodding up from the opposite side of town. Both Herald and Companion moved as though they had burrs under the saddle but were too burned by the sun to care. The creases in Selte's weathered face were etched deeper than they'd been this morning, and her rumpled Whites masked her wiry frame, making her look older than she was.

Marli erred on the side of caution, as well as conserving her own energy, and merely raised a hand in greeting. Selte rewarded her with a short version of the stink-eye.

"Shade?" Marli said when Selte drew closer. The path out of town would soon take them to a stand of oak and birch, as well as the Waystation the four of them were utilizing while they worked with this town.

Selte nodded curtly and proceeded to share all kinds of gestures with Cerilka as they all moved along the road.

:*She's certainly comfortable with Cerilka listening to her,*: Marli said. She didn't begrudge her own plaintive tone. It was hot, she'd had a long day, and Herald Selte simply wasn't being fair. When they reached the Waystation, Marli would confront Herald Selte. No more letting guilt silence her.

:*You can't solve everyone's problems, my love,*: Taren said.

:*I'm just not trying hard enough.*:

Taren chuckled, and Marli let the affectionate sound soothe her ruffled feathers. He always indulged her need to grope for a solution, even when she hadn't been asked. *Most* people were grateful anyway.

At the station, Marli and Selte settled the Companions as comfortably as could be expected in the shade of a tall oak before heading inside.

A layer of grime coated the floor and fixtures, mostly dust blown in by the hot wind. This Waystation didn't have the homey, welcoming feel of the one by Marli's hometown, but it was stocked with what they needed for a couple of nights, and it was serviceable as a shelter from the elements. Of course, rain would have been the more usual worry, but the Waystation provided a bit of relief from the unending sun, too.

Selte moved to where her saddlebags lay on the floor and, without any shame, stripped out of her Whites.

Marli averted her eyes. So much for a confrontation now. Even after all her time at the Collegium, she hadn't been able to let go of her small-town breeding. A person deserved privacy while naked.

Instead, she grabbed her own saddlebags and went back outside to sit in the biggest patch of shade she could find. Dry grass crunched under her as she got comfortable. The heat still beat down too much to be pleasant, but she'd endured worse on this trip. She removed a piece of dried meat and the map from her bag.

She liked tracing her finger along the roads of the map, liked charting the course from one stop on their Circuit to the next. She liked imagining the conversations she could have with a more willing companion on the long stretches between settlements.

Her finger paused at the upcoming turn the road would take once they moved on from the lake town. If they took the northern fork, they would reach her own hometown within a day and a half. Instead, their assigned Circuit directed them to the southern fork.

Homesickness and relief warred within her. It was becoming harder to pretend she'd simply been too busy to use her Farsight even once to check in on her family and friends back home. The possibility that they had denounced her for becoming a Herald always drifted through the back of her mind. She missed everyone so terribly, but they might want nothing to do with her now.

She'd never had to grow accustomed to loneliness.

Fighting the burn behind her eyes, Marli tore a bite from her dried meat. She had to chew a while before her throat loosened enough to swallow. Taren was with her, she reminded herself. He would never leave her. But her Companion simply didn't understand how her family's rejection would hurt her. He wasn't as reliant on other people's approval as she was.

Something rustled in the dry grass behind her. Unchecked, hope welled that Selte had noticed Marli's need for another friend, that the Herald who was supposed to be her mentor had sidled over to finally allow a connection between them.

A glance over her shoulder showed that Selte, dressed in fresh clothes, was laying her soiled Whites by the door to dry in the sun. When she finished, she went straight back inside without looking in Marli's direction.

Marli stuffed the rest of her dried meat in her mouth and chewed with vigor, swallowed too early, and replaced her map in her saddlebags. Then she stood, brushing dirt and grass from her pants.

:You up for settling a few of the townsfolk's disputes?: she sent to Taren.

If she couldn't solve her problem with Herald Selte, there were plenty of others waiting for her attention.

Cerilka had been warming to Taren, and Selte knew the two Companions had taken to chatting as they traveled. With Cerilka distracted, Selte didn't know what to do with her comments about the weather. Anytime she considered sharing her thoughts on the patchy clouds or the strengthening wind, she hesitated. Cerilka wasn't completely ignoring her; she gave Selte wordless mental touches now and then. But Selte still felt a bit abandoned.

Which stung all the more since they'd veered south. Selte had as much power over their assigned course as she did over the weather, but that didn't make the fact that their next stop was the place she'd been born any easier to stomach. Then again, maybe a visit to the village she could no longer call home would be good for her.

She could do with a reminder of her lack of teaching qualifications.

Trainee Marli had kept quiet since they'd left the lake town behind. When Selte glanced her way, the girl didn't seem to be engaging in the Companions' conversation. She simply rocked along with Taren's gait, her head tilted back, her face a mask as it had been this entire leg of the journey. Something was bothering her, and if even Selte could pick up on it, it must be something big.

Selte kept her muscles loose, lest she accidentally interrupt Cerilka, but it was hard with all her failures running through her mind. She knew she ought to reach out to her Trainee. Communication wouldn't be impossible, they had options. At the very least she had to impart some weather knowledge before their Circuit wrapped up. Surely she could use the building clouds as a lesson in rainfall probability. She could point out how these clouds looked as if they might drop rain but how other factors negated the likelihood. That was simple enough, right?

But the closer they came to Selte's village, the more the voices echoed from the past.

How could you have missed the signs of such a storm? All this destruction is your fault!

Silence would be better than your false security.

The memory of heat and copper filled her mouth, and she swallowed. No, no, she had no business teaching Marli a thing about the weather.

So instead of opening any form of dialogue with Marli, Selte flipped her hood up to shadow her face.

Once they crested the next hill, the defensive walls surrounding the village came into view. The last time she'd seen them, a storm of unprecedented strength had blasted them clean of all ivy and caused damage by smashing some uprooted trees against them. Now they were repaired, and tendrils of yellowed green were snaking their way upward once more. The people wouldn't take kindly to Marli telling them to clear the new growth away, but it was too much of a fire hazard until the rains came more reliably.

Signs of long-standing repairs shone beyond the walls, too, with shingled roofs she didn't recognize bearing the dull sheen of many seasons' worth of high winds. In the distance, the strip mines that pulled iron ore from the mountainsides seemed to have returned to full working order.

Nestled at the entrance to a long valley, this metal-working settlement made an ideal place to study rapidly changing weather patterns, though not many could read those patterns accurately, as Selte well knew. The strong winds set the flags on the observation towers flapping and snapping and drove much of the summer heat away down the length of the valley. They also carried the smoke from the forges away from the Heralds' northern approach, for which Selte was grateful. She didn't know if she could handle the smell of hot metal now. She groped for the clasp of her hood, holding it in place against the breeze.

Motion drew her eye to the high top of the weather reader's tower, where she had spent every spare moment of her childhood. Someone stood beside the barometer, apparently ignoring the way the wind yanked on his student robes. The boy was young, but his face already bore the effects of long candlemarks enduring the elements.

He noticed their approach and hailed them, then rang the bell three times to signal the arrival of a Herald to the village.

Marli perked up the moment the four of them passed through the gate. A scattering of people came to greet them, children fawning over the Companions while their parents scolded them halfheartedly. Smiles sprouted on every face, which Marli returned in spades.

Selte huddled deeper into the shadows of her hood. They hadn't recognized her yet, but it was only a matter of time.

She tightened her fingers in Cerilka's mane and pulled back gently. These people didn't want her here, and rightly so.

Cerilka twitched her neck in counterargument. She took the sting from her disagreement by swishing her tail against Selte's legs. Things would play out as they were meant to, according to the Companion.

By the time a decent crowd had gathered, Selte was swimming in her own sweat. She recognized a handful of faces, and though they wore cheery grins now, Selte's memory saw them twisted with fury.

Cerilka swished her tail again, and Selte took a deep breath. She pulled on her own time as a Herald Trainee and grounded herself. The past was in the past. She could deal with the fallout only if she stayed in the present.

Beside her, Marli radiated confidence as she brought out the fire safety codes. No other Herald had stopped here before them, so the full education was in order. Marli excelled at teaching people. Selte had seen copious evidence of such at each town they visited. The girl addressed concerns without trivializing them, and she always took the time to ensure all of her students had a base understanding of the material before moving on.

But it didn't take long for this group to challenge her.

"What do you mean, we have to shut down some of the forges? That's our livelihood, woman!"

Marli didn't back down. "I understand we're asking you to make a sacrifice, but you have to weigh the cost of cutting your iron production against the very real chance of a stray spark sending fire sweeping through town. This temporary measure is designed to keep everyone safe while we wait out the drought."

"The clouds have been building for weeks," one man grumbled. "The weather reader says the rains will fall any day now. Maybe there's no need to shut down any of the forges."

Selte lifted her head to glance at the sky. True, a bank of clouds hovered near the peaks to the east, but the wind that currently blew from that same direction had been whispering of changing course all morning. When that happened, the clouds would disperse, and the weather would hold its dry pattern for a while longer.

But she could have misread those signs. Here at the site of her most catastrophic failure, what right did she have to question the interpretation of their current weather reader?

She tilted her face down again, only to find Marli watching her. The Trainee nodded, then turned to address the people again.

"Herald Selte thinks the rains will not fall for some time yet. You can trust her judgment. She has read the weather throughout Valdemar for many years."

Selte wasn't certain how to process this revelation. How had Marli known what she was thinking?

Marli's statement affected the gathered people, too. An angry muttering broke out, and many faces pointed toward Selte where she sat astride Cerilka.

Cerilka stomped her rear left hoof, but Selte barely registered the Companion's attempt to calm her.

Blood pounded in her ears, and her throat constricted as she met the stares of the very people who had condemned her to silence.

There was the matron of the stables, who'd lost her best horses when the roof crashed down in the winds. Behind her came the man who used to oversee the mine operations, the lines on his face not enough to disguise the long, jagged scar across his cheek where he'd been caught by flying debris.

Standing closest to her now was the master of the forges. His eldest son had worked in the strip mines and had been struck dead by lightning before he could reach shelter. The master's grip had the strength of tempered steel as he'd held Selte down and brought the red-hot tongs toward her to carry out her punishment.

Liars should be silenced!

But she hadn't lied. She'd been young and brash, and she'd made a mistake. But the punishment had been carried out, and the trauma had taken more than just her physical voice.

Selte fought to catch her breath through the haze of memory and fear.

The forge master pointed at her, his eyes like flaring embers. "Selte? They'll let anyone wear those fancy uniforms these days, won't they? But we know how to keep our people safe. We'll not listen to 'advice' from one we already know has designs for our destruction. The forges will run as usual. You *Heralds* had best be moving on."

"Wait, friends," Marli cried. "We have only your safety in mind with these codes. Please hear me out."

"We'll hear nothing if it comes from *her*," said the stable matron. "She bears the mark of a liar."

Others joined her, pointing and spitting at both Heralds and Companions now, until the Companions were forced to back toward the gate.

Marli continued her attempts to soothe and placate, but as more people became aware of what was happening, her words fell on deaf ears and were eventually drowned out.

"—Liars!—"

"—Take your false advice elsewhere!—"

"—*Fire!* A fire at the mines!—"

The call rolled over the rest of the rabble like thunder even though the crier gasped for breath from his dash. And like thunder, it made everyone freeze in their tracks with paralyzing fear.

In that motionless moment, the wind shifted as it had told Selte it would. Traces of smoke drifted through the village. Selte tasted ash.

By the time the student in the observation tower caught up with the emergency enough to hammer the signal bell in the double peal of "fire," Selte had envisioned multiple ways for the air currents to fan the flames directly at the vulnerable settlement.

She couldn't let them get that far.

Beside her, Marli trembled astride Taren, her face pale. Even Taren remained stock still except for the agitated swishing of his tail. In all the time they'd been riding this Circuit, trying to prepare the citizens of Valdemar for the event of fire, they themselves had yet to run into even a single errant ember. Having knowledge of the codes was one thing, but applying them was quite another.

Selte grabbed her Trainee's sleeve and shook her. Once she had Marli's attention, she pantomimed dumping a bucket of water repeatedly.

Marli's face remained pale, but she nodded and turned to address the people in a calm, commanding tone. "Form a bucket line. Use what water you can spare."

By now the village leaders, the stable matron and the

forge master, had regained their wits, too. They barked orders to those nearby, and people scrambled to form up. Some ran to collect buckets, others descended upon the water pump.

They would waste a lot of water in their panic.

Selte tapped her heels against Cerilka's sides. Marli could stay behind to direct the bucket line, but someone had to control the fight at the flames. She would go to the mines and help the men cart dirt and sand back up the hill.

Cerilka signaled her agreement and shot away at a gallop for the southern gate. Selte trusted that the Companion had informed Taren of their plans.

The smoke grew thicker and grittier as they hurtled down the main road, but Selte didn't see the flash of fire until they reached the gateway in the southern segment of the village wall. The men who watched for bandits were gathered along the walkway at the top, either dashing around aimlessly or standing motionless and staring at the oncoming destruction. Nobody seemed certain what to do.

Cerilka thundered through the open gateway, then skidded to a halt. The fire had already crept partway up the grassy hillside separating the mines from the village, binging on the feast of dry fuel and growing into a gluttonous inferno. As Selte had feared, the wind fanned the flames directly toward the village.

Her stomach churned. The path to the mines was already cut off.

She'd never dealt with a firestorm before, but she had weathered plenty of other storms. A change in the situation necessitated a change in the plan of action.

She couldn't access the dirt and sand at the mines; therefore, a fast trench would have to do.

Cerilka pivoted to face the village wall and the people standing atop it. Rearing back, she flailed her front hooves and let out a shrill scream.

The maneuver worked, and all eyes turned down to the two of them.

Selte swept her arm out to indicate a line running

parallel to the wall, and Cerilka pawed at the packed dirt hard enough to make a deep gouge.

A few of the men caught her meaning, and their calls soon had everyone running for their shovels and picks. Selte leaped off Cerilka's back and accepted the shovel one early responder pushed at her. Cerilka returned to her pawing, and Selte dug the point of her shovel into the hard packed soil.

Together, alongside men who once thought her the least trustworthy person among them, Selte worked to cut the trench. The flames drew closer and closer every time she looked up, until she simply decided to stop looking. She didn't need the evidence of her eyes to follow their enemy's progress, not when the crack and roar of it filled her ears, and the stinking fumes it kicked up smothered her nose and mouth. The searing heat grew and grew, until the shovel's handle slipped in her sweaty hands.

She and the men sweated so much together it seemed to turn the ground they were rushing to break into sloppy mud.

Selte blinked ash and salt from her eyes. The ground really was muddy. Had the bucket line arrived? She wiped surprisingly cool sweat from her brow, and caught fresh raindrops on her forehead when she tilted her face up.

The fire hissed and guttered mere paces away from the ragged trench as the rain intensified. Soon, the inferno that had swept up from the mines was reduced to only so much smoke, which the wind tore to shreds.

Selte dropped her shovel and slumped against Cerilka's side. She ran her fingers through her Companion's mud-streaked coat, not saying anything, just exchanging comfort.

She'd been wrong about the weather again. But this time, her village had benefited from her mistake.

Selte and Cerilka didn't rush ahead for solitude as the four of them rode away from the village, and Marli and Taren didn't lag behind in uneasy silence. They traveled side by side like old friends.

Still, Marli waited to speak until they'd gained some

distance from the villagers, who had followed up their expressions of gratitude with a firm request for the Heralds' rapid absence.

"I don't know exactly what history is between you and your village," she said, "but how can you be so calm with them rejecting you like that? You used to be one of them, didn't you?"

Selte wondered the same thing. As they climbed out of the valley, she found the continuing drizzle unexpectedly reassuring. It smelled fresh, like a day in a new spring rather than a summer growing old. With each cool drop, the fear and self-doubt that had haunted her in the years following her punishment washed away, and for the first time she rode with her shoulders held back and a sense of contentment growing in her heart.

She'd been wrong about the rain, but it hadn't mattered. Her training and experience in the years since she'd left home had taught her how to prepare for the worst, and she knew without any need to second guess herself that her expertise and quick action had saved the village from the inferno.

The villagers knew it too, but the scars of the past would never fully heal for either party. No sudden acceptance from the forge master would give Selte back her voice, just as no amount of now trusted storm-proofing advice from Selte would bring the master's son back from the Havens.

Uncertain how to communicate that feeling to her Trainee, Selte shrugged and made a gesture she hoped implied *it was a long time ago*.

Marli sighed and looked forward. "It wasn't that long ago for me. Can people really be so judgmental about one fork in your path?"

Selte saw the pain writhing within her Trainee. The storm Marli foresaw hadn't landed yet, but she feared it all the same. She saw what little she now knew of Selte's past as good data to judge by.

But sometimes, even predictions made with the best data didn't come true. All a weather reader could do was look at patterns and prepare for any inevitability. In the end, the destruction didn't come from being inaccurate. Selte knew that now.

She lifted her head so the raindrops fell on her unprotected face. Then she reached over and plucked at Marli's sleeve. Once the other woman shifted in the saddle, she gestured up at the gray clouds.

See those? She indicated with a flick of her fingers and a raised eyebrow.

Marli glanced up, shrugged, and returned to her not-quite-slouch. "So you were wrong this time. I know you can't always say for certain what the weather will do. I *have* picked up a couple of things from watching you."

Selte let the slight sting in Marli's voice roll off her, let her Trainee have a moment to voice her dissatisfaction. Then she asked Cerilka to relay her next message.

:When I'm reading the weather, all I do is sit back and listen. I let it tell me whatever it wants to say, whisper its secrets, gossip about the land, or complain about the wind. From those tales I can make a good guess as to how it will behave. I imagine that's similar to what I've seen you do with people, though I . . . have a hard time figuring out what people mean when they say this or that.:

Marli blinked, then smiled. It was a tentative gesture, not the easy, open grin she used with the people of Valdemar. "People aren't that hard to figure out. They're just . . . well, I suppose they kick up their own kind of storms."

Selte nodded, pointed at herself, then shrugged. *And if I can manage to weather the storm from my harsh past . . .*

Marli's smile widened. Along the rainy trail to their next destination, Herald and Trainee conducted the first of many weather lessons in a silence that spoke volumes.

Traded Places
Kristin Schwengel

"I'm no fine lady from the Fifty made of spun sugar, Capin! I won't melt from a few drops of rain. I've been cooped up in this carriage for the three days since we left Mornedealth, and I need to *move*."

Suiting action to words, Valia pushed open the door of the large traveling coach and stepped out into the light drizzle. The maidservant her mother had insisted on remained crammed in her corner, pursed lips radiating disapproval of her mistress' boyish apparel and behavior.

"Your brother will have my head if anything happens to you, my lady," the guardsman replied, but he moved back to allow her space on the narrow ledge of road.

"My brother knows better than to stand in my way," Valia said with a grin that softened her sharp words. "Besides, I'm sure Tenna could use some exercise while we wait for his return." She gestured to one of the other two guards, who hurried behind the coach to the picketed horses.

Capin managed to conceal his sigh. "You won't find a safe place in these steep forests to let her run like you did at your parents' estate."

Valia's only response was a shrug, and moments later the guard returned leading two saddled horses: Capin's heavy chestnut gelding and Valia's athletic bay mare.

The two mounted in silence, and Valia nudged Tenna off the bare excuse for a road and up the slope into the forest, angling back along the ravine they had followed for most of the day.

Stretching her legs into the stirrups, Valia inhaled the pinewood air and felt her mind clearing, even as the rain tapered off to nothing. She had no particular objection to her approaching betrothal, but she had no enthusiasm to race toward it, either. Despite her words, she *was* a lady of the Fifty Noble Houses of Mornedealth, and arranged marriages were the rule for women of the Fifty. She could not be married against her will, but she was expected to honor her family's concerns first, and until now she had felt no calling that would change her choices. No Mage Gift, no religious devotion, no previous attachments drew her from her familial duty, so she and her brother and the bare minimum of guards that could be considered respectable were traveling to the city of Llyrida, where her parents had negotiated a match with the local Duke.

Tenna shook her head against the sudden tightening of the reins, and Valia sighed and relaxed her fingers' grip on the leather. Not for the first time, she wished she *had* shown some sign of magery or desired to join one of the religious houses that dotted Jkatha. Without Mage Gift or a spiritual vocation, it was next to impossible for her to move beyond the constrained roles of the nobility. She certainly had no aspirations among the social elites; the idle prattling of gossip bored her, and the eternal fussing about clothing and jewelry was even worse. Her mother had years ago despaired of turning her into a "proper" lady, insisting only that Valia know how to comport herself respectably when she had to and otherwise allowing her to ride and train in swordplay with her brothers. Of all things, she most hated being idle and useless—and it seemed to her that a lady of the Fifty was destined to be exactly that.

Loosening her grip on the reins again, Valia pulled Tenna to a halt in a small clearing and turned to Capin, who had ridden close at her heels.

"How many marks do you think it'll be before Seb and Rall come back? How long can we ride?" *How long am I still free to make my own decisions?*

Capin thought for a moment. "It's only been a candle-mark since he left, my lady. Maybe two marks? They weren't planning to go all the way down to the plains, just through the steepest portion of the downhill slope to make sure the way was clear for the carriage. Rall knows the area from his visit on your father's behalf, and he figured we'd be in Llyrida before dusk."

Valia's reply was interrupted by a low rumble down the mountain, making their horses dance and half-rear, the whites of their eyes showing and nostrils flaring. Dismounting, the two understood the animals' nerves as the ground trembled beneath their feet. The rumble grew to a roar, the earth shaking and causing Valia's stomach to turn, and it took all her strength and weight on the reins to keep Tenna from breaking free in terror. Crashing sounds of rending trees and falling rocks echoed around them.

It seemed to last forever, yet in mere moments the ground stilled and uncanny silence settled over the forest. Eyes wide, Valia looked at Capin.

"Landslide," he said. "All this rain must have loosened a portion of the mountain, and it went down into the ravine."

"Might it have blocked some of the road ahead of us?" On this side of the mountain, the road had closely followed the cliff edge.

"Only one way to find out."

With a last soothing pat on Tenna's sweat-damp neck, Valia gathered the reins and hoisted herself back into the saddle. Capin had already mounted, and he led the way down the slope.

The return through the forested slopes was silent until Capin pulled up his horse with a muffled oath. Distracted, Valia barely noticed in time to rein in Tenna.

"What—" Her voice died into nothing as she looked past him, to where the coach and the other guards should have been awaiting them. The road now vanished into a steep drop, and a crazed pile of boulders and shredded trees leaned straight out over the edge.

As one, they dismounted, securing the horses to one

of the still-standing trees before picking their way with careful haste to the new edge of the ravine.

Valia's stomach churned and sank as she stared down, seeing just enough around Capin's bulk to confirm her worst fears. The crushed body of one of the carriage horses, its head at an impossible angle, drew her eyes to the mud-covered carnage of what remained of the vehicle itself, lying half buried on its side with a great boulder squarely on top of it. A horrified gasp escaped her, and she held a hand to her mouth against sudden nausea. If she had stayed in the coach like the poor lady's maid . . .

"The other guards?" she whispered, her voice trembling into the too silent air.

Capin shook his head, shifting his position to further block her view of the ravine, and a hoarse cry from the sky above drew her attention to the circling of carrion birds overhead. Valia bit her lip and turned away, the blood drained from her face, her stomach in knots.

"We need to find Lord Sebasten, and Rall," Capin said at last. "Come." He turned to the horses, and Valia followed in a numb silence.

"We'll have to backtrack up and go deeper into the thick pines, to circle around the weak area. The rockfall took out a fair slice of the mountain, and it might still be unstable."

Valia nodded as she untied Tenna and mounted, strangely thankful that he made no effort to comfort her. His short words instead kept her mind practical, focused on the reality of their situation without dwelling on the horror behind them in the ravine.

It was nearly two candlemarks before they returned to the road, much lower down the mountainside from where they had left it.

"Should we go up to find Seb or down?" Her brother would know what to do.

"Up to make sure he isn't behind us. He must have heard the landslide and would have started back to find you."

Before they'd gone a dozen paces, Valia grabbed at

the pommel of her saddle, a strange vertigo washing over her. "Seb," she gasped, her stomach churning as it had before, when the earth had dropped away. Fear flooded her veins, paralyzing her, and a vision of falling rocks passed before her eyes. In almost the same moment, the mountain rumbled again, the sound echoing down toward them.

The ground around them shook less with this slide, and they were better able to manage the horses, who stood with legs splayed for stability, tossing their heads, but not attempting to throw their riders. Valia folded forward in the saddle, clinging to Tenna's neck and fighting waves of nausea, her vision spinning between the road beneath her and a nightmare of collapsing rocks and trees.

When all was once again calm, Capin turned to Valia, his brows raised in question at her white face.

What was that I felt in the moments before the tremor? What did I see? All her thoughts went to Seb, and she bit back a moan. This second slide had shaken the earth less than the first, yet she had *seen* what was not before her, had *felt* the ground moving more. Her heart sank to her churning stomach. Somehow, she knew that what she felt was what happened to her brother.

Valia shook her head, tears filling her eyes. "Let's go to Llyrida," she said, her voice shaking. "I could *see* the rocks falling, and I felt Seb's fear . . . I don't think I could bear to see . . ." She let the stumbling words trail off, then turned Tenna's head. Whatever reply Capin might have made was soon lost in the cadence of hooves.

Along the way, her imagination filled her mind with the pictures she dreaded seeing in reality: her brother's fiery gelding instead of the coach horse, her brother's blond head instead of the guard's, all crushed, buried by falling, sliding rock. Her vision swam with tears as Capin nudged his mount past Tenna to lead the way down the mountain.

Two riders made better time than the carriage had, and all too soon the two were near the edge of the forest that swathed the foot of the mountains. The distant walls of Llyrida were a hazy darkness splashed against the pale green of early spring growth on the plains ahead.

Capin looked over at Valia, then reined in the chestnut, using the horse's big body to slow Tenna and guide her to the side of the road.

"We need to lay plans," he said, the brusque edge in his voice bringing Valia back from her stricken mental wanderings.

"What do you mean? Should we not just find the duke and explain?"

"My Lady, I do not know these parts. I don't know whether a woman with only a single guardsman will be safe. Whether you would be safe without your brother and the others. I think we should use some sort of disguise, for a day or two, until we learn if we can trust the Duke."

Valia blinked back tears at the mention of her brother, her thoughts slow. "Disguise? As what?"

Capin studied her, his eyes narrowing in thought. "You're slight enough, if you cut your hair and wear the right clothes, you'd pass for a lad. Your riding gear will do with the help of dusk and torchlight. If we need time, I can look for a job as a guard, at least for long enough to hear what rumor tells of the Duke. I say we wait until dusk to approach the gates, just before they might be closing for the night."

Valia nodded, her gaze focused blankly at the ground ahead of her.

"Come, milady," he said, his voice suddenly gentle. "Let us set up a little camp off the road here so we can get you ready."

After cropping Valia's blond hair to a boyish length with his knife, Capin stared at her. "With your hair short, you're the image of my lord Sebasten," he blurted out, then snapped his mouth shut as the threatening tears spilled down her cheeks and she curled into a ball of misery, buried under her cloak.

The rest of the slow afternoon passed in the silence of gloomy thoughts until they broke camp in the early dusk, riding out onto the plain for the last candlemark of the journey to Llyrida.

A light drizzle started as they neared the north gates, and the guards barely glanced at the cloaked Valia as Capin spoke with them. Lost in grief, she didn't even hear their conversation, and she numbly allowed Tenna to follow Capin's chestnut down the main road through the city. The drizzle thickened to a steadier rain, and the crowds on the streets thinned rapidly, everyone finishing their business in haste to get to the comforts of their own homes and fires—or that of the nearest tavern.

"I've got enough coin for a few nights," Capin said, guiding the horses down a side street of buildings that looked rather like the people around them: not fancy, but well-maintained. "We should know enough to take our next steps before the coin runs out."

He turned off the street into the well-swept yard of an aging inn. Glancing up, Valia saw a hanging sign with a strange blue-winged blob, and she looked at him in question.

"Gate guard said the Blue Gryphon was a fair and honest inn—none too fancy for the size of my purse, but reputable."

Valia dismounted in silent assent, and they gave their horses over to the care of one of the stable-lads, who eyed the fine animals with awe.

The innkeep standing at the bar looked to be a good fit for his location: grizzled but tidy, his figure only just starting to thicken around the middle, as though he had led a more active life than one would expect of a townsman. He greeted the two of them with respectful welcome, and again Capin took the lead.

"A room for me and m'cousin, and stabling for our horses," he said, gesturing at Valia, who had pushed back her hood but kept her head low, her damp hair shielding her red-rimmed eyes. "Three days standard?"

The innkeep, Master Sarcen, nodded, and the price he named met with Capin's approval. "That includes breakfast and use of the steam baths," he added. "Other meals can be had here in the tavern room if you're not off working." Although he didn't raise the inflection of his voice, his expression made a question of the last sentence, and Capin nodded.

"We've got no fixed plans," he said, "but I might be looking for guard work if we're here longer than a sennight."

"Th' lad, too?" The innkeep tilted his head in Valia's direction.

Capin shook his head. "Messenger, perhaps. He can take care of himself with a sword, but he's not trained hard enough for full guard duty."

"If you decide to stay, check at the Great House. His Lordship hasn't kept a large household, but with his coming betrothal to the lady of the Fifty from Mornedealth, word is he'll be hiring. All kinds of jobs need doing when there's a wedding to be planned."

"Thankee for the suggestion, Master. Now, if we might have a bit of supper to warm us, we'd be most grateful."

They ate in silence, letting the comfortable babble of the common room float around them until Valia began nodding over her half-empty plate. Capin tapped her arm to rouse her, leading her up the stairs to the tiny bunked room that the innkeep had allotted them.

"That's right good news," he said as they settled in. "Means the duke isn't keeping quiet about the betrothal, and at least the common folk here in the city expect good to come of it. I'll go out in the morning and get some more boyish clothing for you, and see what else I can hear."

"Capin, I—" Valia stopped, spreading her hands in a gesture of uncertainty. "You're spending your own coin to take care of me, and . . ."

"Na, milady," he replied awkwardly. "'Tis my job to care for you until we know whether you stay here or return to your parents."

In the morning, while Capin went off to the shops, Valia returned to the stables to check on Tenna and the gelding. The horses had been well-tended the night before, so she brushed them until their coats gleamed. She wondered what the stable-lads thought: anyone staying here would not have too much coin, but their horses were of far superior quality to any others in the yard.

The grooming session was interrupted by Capin, who rushed into the stable carrying a wrapped bundle. "Mi— Val," he said, catching himself and shortening her name to something passably masculine, "His Lordship is hiring this morning. If we hurry, we might get there in time."

"I hadn't thought we'd look for jobs right away," Valia replied, pitching her voice low and fighting off a surge of panic. *It's too much, too soon. I don't know if I can pull this off.*

"Better to have something now than to inquire in a few days and only hear, 'if you'd have come yesterday, I might have had something for you.' If we need to, we can still leave." He gestured impatiently, and Valia put the brushes and combs back in their rack on the wall and scurried to their room to change into the not-quite-livery he had found for her.

"Capin Jensdar and m'cousin, Val Shabony. I'm fully guard-trained, but the lad has only got a bit of sword-and-knife experience. We're new to town, staying at the Blue Gryphon, and heard His Lordship was hiring."

The man in charge looked the two of them over, then gestured to a nearby serving-lad.

"Gevin, take Capin to Guardsmaster Rawson." He tilted his head back to Capin. "The guardsmaster will test your skills and training. If you meet his approval, he'll offer you what position he thinks is best.

"As for Val," he continued, "I'll have the house steward do much the same for him."

Capin followed the boy out of the servants' entrance down toward the stables and guardhouse at the other end of the great courtyard, leaving Valia to wait with a handful of young men dressed in similar not-quite-livery. She kept to herself, trying to appear shy rather than nervous, hoping the steward's interview wouldn't expose her deception. She and Capin had created a simple history for her that wasn't too far from the truth—somewhat genteel birth, family fallen on hard times, and an attempt to make a new start—but it would not stand up to intense scrutiny.

As it happened, she needn't have worried. The house steward asked only the most basic questions, mostly about a footman's duties. Having seen those duties from the other side of the table, and with her mother's training in running a household, her answers satisfied, and midday found both of them in the Duke's employ, with Valia waiting on the duke in person.

Duke Orrin was clearly unused to having a large household, so he was more free with his new staff than most nobles, even conversing with those far beneath him in rank. He took a liking to Valia—Val, as she was now known—and soon had her running errands all over town and reporting straight to him rather than to the house steward. The Duke himself was younger than she had anticipated, and handsome enough to meet the standards of most young ladies of the Fifty, but something about him made Valia uneasy. Not as though he was dangerous, but as though something didn't match up about him.

It wasn't until late in the day, when she noticed him standing near her while refilling his wine goblet, that the pieces fell into place. He was standing as close as a young suitor might at a dance or a fête—but to him, she was a young man herself. *He's—oh, what's the word the Hawkbrothers use, shay'a'chern? Like Seb is—was.*

Valia stifled a gasp as the sense of loss flooded over her anew. In the busyness of the day, she'd had no moment to think of Sebasten, to miss him, to mourn him. To keep the tears from springing to her eyes, she forced herself to concentrate on the Duke, handing him his glass without allowing their fingers to touch and stepping away to return the decanter to the sideboard.

If he thinks to play those games with me, I've had more experience dealing with flirting men than anyone in Llyrida, she mused. *But why is he marrying a woman, then? Does he need to sire an heir himself? Or is it just to keep up appearances, with his lady taking discreet male lovers as well as he?*

Thoughts like these kept her mind occupied until his Lordship retired. She was able to maintain a prudent distance without revealing that she knew the duke was trying *not* to do so, but it was an exhausting dance of subterfuge on top of her other deceptions. She was glad to be released from service for the day, although she had been surprised to find that she mostly enjoyed the activity of employment. Before she left the estate to return to the Blue Gryphon, she had only a moment to speak with Capin in the guard-house. Surrounded by other guardsmen, she dared not say much, just letting him know that the Great House wasn't ready to fit all of the new staff in the servants' quarters and she had been given leave to stay at the inn.

The next day, anticipation hummed in the air throughout the Great House. The steward expected that the 'fine lady of the Fifty' would be arriving that day, and there was also a rumor of an unexpected visitor: a Herald-Envoy from Valdemar. It was astonishing to Valia—and to everyone else—that a Herald in peace-time had traveled this far south, all the way through Rethwellan.

Early in the day, as he had the day before, the duke sent Valia to a jeweler not far from the northern gate to enquire if the welcome-gift he had ordered for his to-be-betrothed was completed.

"Lad, the gem merchant isn't back yet from Kata'shin'a'in, the only spot where he can get those cat's-eye gems in the color and size his lordship wants. He planned to be back two-three days ago, but with the spring rains as heavy as they've been—" the jeweler shrugged, "—small wonder he's delayed. I've offered his lordship smaller stones, or different colors, but he's refused every time."

Valia returned the message to the Duke, resuming the careful dance of avoidance until a flurry of activity at the estate's gatehouse summoned the duke and some of his household to the front receiving porch of the Great House.

The faint, delicate chime of silver bridle-bells drew all eyes to the Herald-Envoy and her Companion, and Valia

was hard-pressed not to gape openly, as were so many of
the other servitors—and even the handful of other nobles that were hanging about the duke to see what they
could. The Companion was unearthly in its—no, his—
beauty, glowing in the midday sun. Valia felt the eyes of
both the Herald and the Companion drift over the assembled crowd.

Weren't they supposed to be able to read minds? If so,
surely they could tell that she was no boy. *Don't you dare
give me away,* she "thought" at the two of them. The Herald made no response, but the Companion's brilliant
blue eyes rested on hers for a moment, and she felt her
mind spinning at the intensity of his gaze.

:I wouldn't dream of it.: Astounded, she "heard" the
voice inside her head, a rich male tone that sounded
both surprised and amused.

"Herald-Envoy Ardra, at your service, Duke Orrin,"
the Herald announced, dismounting and dropping a
brief bow to the Duke. She straightened and stepped forward as the duke came down the stairs to take her hand.

"Gods, where am I going to put her? The best guest
rooms are reserved for the Lady Valia, and we've heard
no word yet of her approach." The house steward's anxious muttering caught Valia's ears, and she turned to the
older man, ignoring the diplomatic exchanges in the
courtyard in front of them.

"Give the Lady Herald those rooms anyway. I'd lay
odds no lady of the Fifty travels without a retinue so
large it takes three times as long to travel any distance.
For a day or two, until more rooms are in order, you'll
not be needing them for the Duke's betrothed." *Especially not as the Duke's betrothed is already staying at the
Blue Gryphon,* she added silently. *We'll just ignore the
fact that this lady of the Fifty had to be forced into taking
any retinue at all.*

The house steward cast her a look grateful for the
suggestion and hurried back into the house to give the
orders while she returned her attention to the duke and
the Herald-Envoy, stifling her grief and regret over the
fate of those who had accompanied her.

"No, my Lord, I didn't see signs of a traveling noble as I came down from the north, but Feste and I didn't keep to the main road. There was a landslide a few days ago, I think, and a portion of the road got washed into the ravine."

Valia felt the blood drain from her face, a sick dread mingled with grief roiling her stomach. *Please don't mention the carriage, please don't mention the carriage, please don't mention the carriage—*

The Herald paused, her brown eyes darting over to her Companion's astonishing blue ones, then continued. "You'll need to send a land crew out to re-cut the road higher up the slope, maybe build something to shore it up. It's a good thing that almost no one is traveling the roads this time of year—between the weather and the spring planting, most everyone is staying close to home. Even when we were on the main roads in Rethwellan, Feste and I saw few other travelers."

Clear relief lit the Duke's face. "Surely, that must be what delays my to-be-betrothed. I will send men out this afternoon to assess the damage and plan the repairs."

Polite conversation and compliments duly exchanged, the house steward led the Lady Herald to her guest suite, while her Companion was taken to the open paddock where he could graze or seek shelter under the lean-to roof as he chose. As the Herald-Envoy departed, she sent a subtle inquiring glance in Valia's direction, which *she* pretended not to observe. A slight smile quirked the Herald's lips, and she gave her Companion a *look* before entering the Great House.

Later that day, just before shops would close, the duke again sent Valia to the jeweler.

"Look, lad, the gem merchant didn't come in today!" she snapped. "A quartermark since the last time you were here wouldn't be enough time for me to set the gems even if he *had*. Off with you now, and don't pester me three times tomorrow!" She all but pushed a baffled Valia out of the shop, closing the door in her face. She could count the bolts as the jeweler loudly shot them home behind her.

"I only stopped the one other time, first thing this morning," she whispered to the solid doorposts, then turned and made her confused way back to the Great House to find the Duke.

The house steward seemed surprised to see her when she came to him, but he gestured toward the Duke's inner courtyard garden when she asked where his Lordship might be found.

The courtyard garden was a carefully tended retreat of a few paths circling through trees and shrubs groomed to conceal one path from the next. Now that dusk was falling, the pages had lit torches throughout, casting a soft glow while the night-blooming flowers filled the air with their heady scent and gentle gittern music from the minstrel's corner teased the ear.

Rounding one corner, Valia spotted the duke in an embrace with a blond young man in dark clothing that seemed vaguely familiar.

Her first thought was relief that she would no longer have to keep up the dance of avoidance, and she backed away, intending to make some noise farther down the path to give the couple a moment to disengage. Before she lost sight of them, though, the pair turned so she could see more of the other's features, and all thought of discretion vanished.

"*Seb!*" she shrieked, and the two sprang apart, the young man turning to stare at her, the same stunned disbelief she felt written across his face.

"Lia?" he responded in wonder, then opened his arms and she flung herself into them, sobs of relief shaking her body. Sebasten's own tears dampened her hair, and he held her as though afraid she would vanish. It was long minutes before the two of them recovered some semblance of coherence and straightened, smiling at each other through misty eyes, hands clasped.

The Duke stood awkwardly nearby, his gaze going from one to the other in confusion. "Val—Lia?" Sudden comprehension dawned. "I think that this is going to be a long night," he said at last, and gestured to a path that led to a pair of benches beneath a gently drooping willow tree. "I have many questions, and even the answers I see already are . . . complicated."

The siblings followed him, sharing a single bench while the duke sat opposite them.

"So," he continued, "you must be my betrothed, the Lady Valia, who somehow survived the landslide your brother told me of." He tilted his head at Valia, who nodded. "But why did you come in disguise and take employment in my household?"

"The landslide buried the carriage and all the guards but Capin, who was riding with me a little farther up the mountain," she replied. "Seb and another guard had gone ahead to make sure the road hadn't been too washed out for the carriage to pass. When the second landslide came, I felt it as though I was falling into it myself, even though we were further away. I believed it meant that Seb and Rall were trapped in the rockfall, and so we came to Llyrida." Her voice trembled at the memory.

"The second slide happened just in front of us, and we barely escaped being caught up in it. But Rall and I were sure that you had been in the carriage," Sebasten interrupted, his hand on hers tightening in comfort. "We spent all yesterday and most of today at the ravine, trying to climb down, but it was so steep and unstable we had to give up."

Valia smiled at him, tears of mingled joy and relief glistening in her eyes, then continued her recounting. "Capin and I didn't know how—" she paused, choosing her next words carefully, "—safe I would be with only a single guard. So he suggested I disguise myself as a boy. Then we found out that your lordship was expanding your household and decided it was the best way to see things first hand. The rest of my story your Lordship knows."

"And since you and your brother look almost alike enough to be twins, everyone treated him as your disguised self when he arrived." The Duke looked over at Sebasten. "Small wonder you were so confused when I told you to pour me a drink the moment you walked in!"

Sebasten nodded. "After Rall and I left the ravine, I came immediately to seek you out to share the terrible news. Rall stayed with our horses, and when I asked at a shop near the gates where the duke might be found, the owner gave me a message to pass on about some jewelry." He smiled in apology. "Which I of course forgot until this moment—she doesn't have it finished yet."

"Oh, that explains why the jeweler was so sharp with me!" Valia exclaimed, then subsided into silence while her brother went on.

"Not knowing what else to do, I found my way to your estate, and the guards and the steward just waved me into this courtyard, and—" Sebasten flushed red. "Well, the rest you know."

The Duke smiled slightly, looking from one to the other. "Which is how we got to this place. But how do we go forward?"

Sudden inspiration struck Valia. Building up a picture of the Companion in her mind, she "thought" at him, *:Feste?:*

The voice in her mind was at once startled and appraising. *:. . . Ye-es?:*

:Can you ask the Lady Herald to come to the inner courtyard garden?: She felt a sense of assent without words, and turned her attention back to her brother and the Duke, who were discussing the landslide and the work needed to restore the road.

"I have an idea, but I don't know if the Herald-Envoy will be willing to help," she finally said, when she heard a subtle scrape of shoes in the gravel on the nearby path.

"I have a suspicion that I am here specifically to help," the Herald's voice preceded her as she rounded the corner of the path and smiled at the two startled men.

"I don't know what you know of the Heralds and their Gifts," she said, "but one of mine is a strange kind of Foresight that sometimes sends me traveling far out of my way, without knowing *why* until a problem arises for which I happen to be the solution. And my Feste suggests that this young lady might be the, er, problem this time."

She sat on the bench beside the Duke, who briefly introduced the siblings and sketched out the facts before them. She turned to Valia. "Although you were intended to do so, I take it that you no longer wish to wed his Lordship?"

The Duke and Sebasten blinked at the Herald's insight, but Valia nodded. "No one would force me to, but there would be a significant loss of dignity for my family if I did not, and they were looking forward to alliance with his Lordship. We are not directly in line to inherit the wealth of our House, so this is a way to maintain our family's status." She looked at the duke and smiled. "It is not that I have taken a dislike to you personally, my Lord, but—" her eyes flicked to her brother, "I would wish for a true pairing."

The Herald had followed the quick movement of Valia's eyes, reading the expressions on all three faces, and she nodded in understanding. Then her brow furrowed, and she turned to the Duke. "Were you needing to wed for the purpose of siring an heir, my Lord?"

The Duke sighed and shook his head. "Mostly to secure an inheritance from a distant cousin, who left it to me with the stipulation that I must be wed before I was thirty. Which is two moons from now."

"What will happen if you do not?"

"The estate in question will be given to the Sisters of Hebra."

Valia giggled at the Duke's pained expression, and the Herald gave her a perplexed look. "Hebra is a noted goddess of families in this area," she explained to the Envoy, "and the Sisters of Hebra often expound upon the many virtues and benefits of the married state and fertility within the married condition. It is a very *pointed* bequest."

The Duke nodded. "My cousin did not approve of my being—well, as I am."

"Do you *need* this inheritance?"

"Not really—my estates are fruitful enough. And I am able to choose my own inheritor, so I don't have to sire an heir myself." He sighed again. "It would have been nice to tweak Cousin Agadrew's nose one last time."

The Herald rolled her eyes. "So, if you can stomach your discontent enough to listen to the occasional preaching from the Sisters, you have no obligation to wed the Lady Valia?"

Duke Orrin shook his head, then smiled at Valia. "As you said, my Lady, it is not that I have a *personal* dislike for you, but . . ." His eyes went back to her brother.

"Here is my idea, then," Valia said. "What if we simply continue the pretense that I was in that carriage? No disgrace will fall on our family, or on you, for a failed alliance when the lady in question is buried in a landslide. Capin can return to our parents and tell them the truth of things." She gave her brother a sidelong glance, recognizing the near-besotted expression in his eyes when he looked at the Duke. "Perhaps Seb can stay here for a while, representing my family's friendship with you."

"But what of you, Lia?" her brother asked.

At this, the Herald smiled. "That, I think, is why I was drawn here," she said. "We can put it about that I am in need of a servitor for my return journey, and the duke will generously offer one of his footmen, and there will be no trace of either Val or the Lady Valia remaining in Llyrida."

"If you would like that, Lia?" Sebasten was frowning, but Valia nodded at him, a sudden excitement blooming inside her.

"You know I have never wished to be a great lady of the Fifty. Traveling as an aide to the Herald-Envoy will suit me better than anything that was available to me in Mornedealth. I will miss you, of course, but at least I can write." She smiled, her heart lighter at the prospect before her than it had been since she left her parents' estate.

:And you have a latent Mind-Gift that's now emerging,: Feste's voice filled her head. *:That's why you 'felt' and saw what your brother did during the second landslide. Ardra can't help you with it—she doesn't Mindspeak with anyone but me—but I can. And will.:* She had the sense that he meant something more and that he found

something in the situation very funny, but he didn't elaborate.

"And once we get to Valdemar, you can make your next, er, choices from there. There are more opportunities than you might expect that may interest you, which you could not find among the nobility of Jkatha." There was something both sympathetic and welcoming in the Herald's brown eyes, with a trace of amusement to match Feste's.

Valia blinked, then relaxed and leaned against her brother while they planned her departure. For nearly the first time in her life, she felt that her future held something to look forward to. *At last,* she thought as the conversation swirled around her, *I will be able to do something.*

Reborn

Jennifer Brozek

Lia couldn't get the boy out of her head. She'd dreamed of him for weeks. First it was just flashes of brown hair and brown eyes. Then it grew with a shy smile and joyful laugh. She had the impression of soft clothing and rich fabric. She couldn't tell why, but she liked this boy. A lot.

Last night the dream had turned dark and strange. A sense of motion, of running, of fear. Her boy—her *Chosen*—was in trouble. She needed to help him. She needed to find him—

:Lia?: A nip to her flanks.

Lia turned on Kalin and snapped at her neck. *:Let me be!:*

:Thinking about your Chosen *again?:* The other filly danced out of range of Lia's half-hearted kick.

: Leave me alone. Go play with the rest.:

:You'll always be alone if you act like that.: There was no teasing in the other Companion's mental voice as she trotted toward the rest of her playmates.

Lia knew Kalin was right, but she couldn't shake the fact that the boy was important—to her, at least. No, Companions didn't usually get the call this young, but that didn't mean it didn't happen; after all, there was a first time for everything. She thought about going to see the King's Own Companion again. Then she remembered what he'd said to her:

:I know you think this boy is special to you, but more likely, you are having flashes of Farsight or Foresight. No,

you're too young to hear the call or to recognize your Chosen. You have at least another year. The boy you describe is too young to be Chosen. Perhaps, in another year or two, if you still dream of him, then we'll do something about it.:

But a year or two would be too late. It was time to take control of the matter before it was too late for her and for the boy.

Someone would come. They had to. Or he was dead. It was the one thing Owen was sure of. Even as he blinked in the darkness of the hood over his head, he could still see the blue eyes of the filly reassuring him that she *would* come, *would* save him. He'd never seen a filly the color of snow and with eyes the color of the sky before, but he was sure she existed. Perhaps on his uncle's estate.

Uncle Briden. He wouldn't know the carriage was late for at least another day or two. He wouldn't know to send help.

"Boy!" Ernst, the lead bandit, yanked open the carriage door. "Where's the treasure your father sent with you? I swear by my hand, I'll kill your man if you don't tell me."

Owen shook his head. "I'm sorry. I—" He winced as the bag was ripped from his head.

"Don't you lie to me." The hissed words promised pain.

"I'm not. I don't know about any treasure. I'm to be fostered. All I have with me is my clothing." It was the truth as far as Owen knew. His father had given them enough provisions to survive on the road with no need to resupply.

The big man with the grizzled beard glared. "Then your man dies."

Owen tried to look past Ernst to the household guard sent to protect him: an old man who was a friend as well as a guard. The bandits had already killed the other two guards. Arvin was alive now only because he'd been in the carriage with Owen at the time of the attack. "Arvin? If there's gold, please give it to them."

"There's no treasure, milord. I swear it." The guardsman cried out in pain.

Owen couldn't see what shape Arvin was in, but he didn't sound good. "Please, all we have is yours. Let us go."

Ernst barked a laugh. "Naw, boy. Gotta make our money somehow." He eyed Owen's clothing. "Fosterage, eh? Who to?"

"Lord Briden, my uncle."

"The one with the castle in the hills? I know him. Bet he'd pay a pretty coin for you." Ernst paused, his voice taking on a contemplative tone. "Bet both your uncle *and* your father would pay to get you back."

Owen didn't say anything. He didn't know what to say. Ernst shoved the black hood over his head. As the bandit did so, the man's knuckles grazed Owen's cheek, and he heard Ernst's thoughts in his mind, *"Two ransoms and a shallow grave for the pair of them. Good bit of gold if I play my cards right."*

As the carriage door closed, Owen knew he had to escape before Ernst put his plan in motion. He just hoped he could figure out a way to save both himself and Arvin.

Lia considered her options: Jump the fence at Companion's Field. Steal away in the dead of night. Kick over a lamp and start a small fire and escape while everyone was distracted—she rejected that last one as too dangerous as soon as it came to mind. There were too many problems with all of her plans.

As she considered, she wandered into the stable. On the other side was the road out to the rest of the castle area and Haven proper. The guards kept those from the other collegia from "accidentally stumbling" into the Companion and Heralds' territory, but they didn't seem to stop anyone from leaving.

She considered making a run for it. Everyone knew she was too young to leave on her own. Maybe—

"Hello there." A young stable boy interrupted as he walked in and smiled at her. "Nara, right?"

Lia didn't stop to think about what she was doing. The

boy was new and young. He probably wouldn't get into trouble . . . much trouble anyway. She nodded and nickered to him. Then, with an imperious stomp of a hoof as she'd seen Nara do, she gestured to a light saddle with her nose.

"Ah, need to get ready, milady?" The boy put down his tools. Without another question, he fitted her with a blanket, saddle, and bridle. She nickered her thanks as he finished and patted her shoulder.

Heart pounding hard, Lia held her head high and trotted down the way, past the guards, and out the gate. No one stopped her. No one shouted a warning. Still, she continued at a good clip until she was out of sight. Slowing as she moved into the twisting thoroughfare of the city, Lia followed the mass of people heading in the direction of the main gates.

She hadn't thought it would be this easy, and most of her planning had been around getting out of the Palace grounds and Haven itself. She hadn't figured out what to do next other than "save the boy."

The very thought of him brought both pleasure and fear. She had to find him now that she was free.

Owen dreamed in stutters and stops. The blue-eyed horse—*Lia, her name was Lia*—was in trouble. Angry voices yelled at her like thunder from the sky. Her body was pounded by hail and branches. It was as if the land itself chased her. He reached out to her. *Be careful. Be safe. Don't hurt yourself for me.* Those blue eyes came closer as she seemed to hear him.

The carriage rocked and the door slammed shut, yanking Owen from his dream. He sat up as Ernst settled himself in the seat on the other side of the carriage. "Good carriage. No leaks. I think I'll keep it after I return you home."

Owen didn't say anything. He kept his body and hands still. He'd worked to free himself from his bonds, but he hadn't succeeded yet. The rope was looser, however. Now that he was awake and the dream of the horse—*Lia*—faded, he could hear the spring storm all around them. It raged hard, with heavy drops breaking through the trees to crash against the carriage's roof. "Where's Arvin?"

Ernst scoffed. "Care for your man, do you?"

"Yes." He worked to keep the offense out of his voice. Of course he cared. The men and women who worked for the family were extended family in a way. "Please. Is he well?"

"Well enough for now. Under the carriage. We'll see when my men get back if your kin think you're worth the price. We should know soon enough."

Owen relaxed. Arvin might still get wet, but at least he was somewhat protected from the rain. "Thank you."

:How dare *you pretend to be me!:*

Lia stumbled in surprise. Nara's mental fury was almost physical. She'd been so intent on getting out of Haven, she hadn't considered what would happen when she was discovered missing.

Right now, Lia was concerned with heading to one of the new fiefdoms in the hills. She was glad she'd taken the time to study the map when the accordance was drawn up. *:I did not. He called me you. I didn't—:*

:Don't you quibble with me, young lady! You get your tail back here immediately. We're going to have a talk about this.:

:No.:

The older Companion radiated surprise and shocked disapproval. *:What did you say? Don't make me get the Heralds involved.:*

Heralds or not, Lia refused to be swayed. *:My Chosen is in trouble. You do what you think you need to do. I'm going to do what I* know *I need to do.:* She shut Nara out of her mind and continued to run.

There was no real road to follow in the direction of the boy, just a trail through the hilly woods. The sky opened up in a torrent of rain that beat against her, causing the swaying branches to slap at her face and her body as she pushed through them as fast as she could. Now that she'd shut out Nara, Lia wasn't sure what the

Companions would do. She had almost a full day's head start. She would make the most of it.

Even as her visibility dropped to a few feet and she shivered with every step, Lia could feel the boy. Feel which direction she needed to go. If she were blind, she'd be able to find him. Awake, she could easily sense him, even in his darkness and fear.

As the hoof beats drew closer, Ernst sat up, and Owen's heart soared. *Lia is here. She'll help!* He didn't know how she'd help, but—

His heart plummeted at one of the bandits, Pitor, calling out, "Ernst!" With it, his stomach sank. It wasn't rescue. It was his doom. Or the first part of it.

Ernst left the carriage without a word. Owen strained to hear the men while he worked his wrists against the rope and the rope against the metal of his coat's buckle.

"Well?"

"Success. The brat's father paid after he saw the flag from the carriage."

"All of it?"

"All of it."

"Were you followed?" Ernst's voice took on a strident note.

Owen listened hard, trying to figure out what the concern was. A moment later, he heard more hoof beats. Again, his heart soared. "Lia," he murmured.

Again his heart broke as the hoof beats revealed themselves to be the other bandit.

"It's Dev." Ernst sounded relieved. "What's the word?"

"Lord Briden don't believe we got the boy. 'Anyone could steal a tabard,' he said."

Owen worked the rope harder against the metal. He didn't know what the bandits would do now. One person had paid. One hadn't. Part of him was grateful his father thought that much of him. Part of him understood where his uncle was coming from.

"Well then," Ernst said. "Let's see if Lord Briden will believe a dead guardsman."

Owen froze. The bandits had left Nicholas and

Camlin dead by the side of the road. Would they go back to get the bodies?

Arvin cried out in pain.

Owen ripped the hood from his head and was out the carriage door before he'd realized he'd moved. Through the squalling rain, he saw Ernst twist the sword piercing Arvin's chest. Arvin's mouth moved in apology to Owen as the older man breathed his last breath and died.

:May I ask what you're doing?:

Startled, Lia snorted in and almost tripped over a tree root. The new voice was familiar in an uncanny way, but she couldn't place it. *:??:*

:I'm Herald Sarah with my Companion, Tavin. Tavin tells me the other Companions are very worried about you, and I'm the closest Herald to you. He doesn't have Mindspeech. I do.:

:I'm not going back!:

Mental amusement flooded the link. *:I didn't ask you to. I just asked what you are doing.:*

Lia felt forward. She was *close*. So close to the boy— Owen, his name was Owen—and he was in pain. So much pain. *:Rescuing my Chosen. I don't care if you think I'm too young. He needs me now. Right now, or he's dead.:* The rain came down in sheets as lightning flashed through the sky, and thunder crashed so loud she feared she'd be deaf when she regained her senses.

Half blind from the storm, Lia galloped through the forest, heedless of the dangers, to reach Owen. Breaking through a line of trees into a small glade, she couldn't understand the scene before her.

Owen didn't scream his dismay at Arvin's death. Instead, he let his fury take over. It was the fury that had grown in the back of his mind since the bandits had first attacked.

Without understanding how he did it, Owen pulled that red fury into himself before directing it at his enemies. A lightning strike next to Dev knocked him from his horse as he yelled his shock. The next lightning strike hit Pitor, still holding the dead guardsman.

Ernst whirled on Owen, his mouth opened in a small O of surprise. It quickly morphed into something neutral and infinitely more dangerous. "Boy!" He pointed his sword at Owen, its blade dripping blood and rain.

"No." The word and every other word after it was lost to the rain. "No. No. *NO!*" Owen chanted the negation as if it would bring Arvin back. With each step towards the old man, the two surviving bandits moved away, circling behind, out of line-of-sight.

Owen reached Arvin and knelt. One touch told him the old guardsman was not coming back. He looked up and threw all this fury at the two bandits still circling. The force of this fury took the shape of a gale that knocked them back. Both hit the sturdy carriage.

Lia didn't know what power Owen had used to blast the men back, but she knew she needed to get him away. She pushed through the rain to his side. *:Owen, to me. Owen, get on my back.:*

Turning blank brown eyes up to Lia's flashing blue ones, Owen stared. "You came," he mumbled. "You're real."

:Yes, Chosen. I came. We must flee. On my back, now.: She kept a cautious eye on the men. They recovered faster than she'd expected, scrambling to their feet. They were still armed—one with a sword. The other with a bow.

Owen looked down at his wrists. They were free of the rope. He didn't know when that happened or how. He was exhausted, drained of everything except for grief at the loss of his guardsman who'd also been a friend.

"Boy! That's a pretty horse there. Don't want her to get hurt, do you?" Ernst called from the cover of his horse.

Lia saw the nocked arrows before Owen did. *:Mount up. Please! Mount up!:*

The fear in Lia's mind-speech broke through the pain. Owen did as he was told. Only when he was in the saddle with Lia already galloping away did he see the danger as both Dev and Ernst let arrows fly.

Lia screamed as one arrow glanced off the top of her

back and the other lodged in the muscle of her left haunch. Neither hit the boy. Both spurred her into a gallop. She knew she was better and faster than a normal horse. She'd never had a reason to test that until now.

As Owen pressed himself close to Lia's neck, he felt an echo of her pain. It was a throb in his left butt and hip as if he was lying on a rock. The pain, while distant, was familiar. The sound of a bow string snapping pushed him into that familiarity. *:Run. Run!:*

He'd run like this before, on the back of a horse . . . a Companion . . . who was not Lia. But he knew her into the depths of his soul. They'd fled the enemy, the darkness that had come for them.

Lia traveled back along that path with him. She'd fled at Owen's side. Not as a Companion . . . but as his sister.

The moment of realization lasted a thousand years. They once had been brother and sister. Twins. Chosen by twin Companions. And hunted by demons . . . Killed by monsters. They'd each died alone. Reborn separately. Recast as Chosen and Companion. Reunited at last.

And hunted once more.

:No!: The word was a declaration as one.

Owen pulled Lia's bridle up, stopping her. The pair fed their current and past loss and fury into the power Owen had used before. Lightning struck all around them. This time, the lightning did not miss Dev. He and his horse died screaming. The scent of charred flesh filled the air.

Lia reared up, her hooves slashing the air in challenge. The other horse reared and bucked in fear, dumping her passenger. Ernst turned to run, but Owen swept him up in a whirlwind, throwing him into the trees as the bandit's horse fled.

:Enough.: A voice intruded.

:Let the storm take him.: Owen demanded as Lia grounded herself once more.

Whiteness entered the battleground. A shining whiteness with blue eyes and a familiar gaze. *:Enough, younglings. Enough. He's down. There will be justice.:*

Lia recognized the voice as Herald Sarah. As the

same time, another name came to mind: Sorcha. Her Companion from that doomed life. Her Companion who had sacrificed herself in a vain attempt to allow Lia—*Milla*—to live.

Owen stared at the pair standing between him and his quarry. The Companion, he knew in the deeps of his soul. "Torin?"

"Tavin. In this life, he's Tavin." Herald Sarah moved closer. "Can you stop the storm? Either of you?"

At the same time, the young pair realized that Owen had created the storm and Lia fueled it. Owen looked at the dead horse and man to one side, remembered the dead man in the glade, and saw the senseless man behind the Companion he'd once been bonded to. He'd killed men. Just as they'd killed Arvin, Nicholas, and Camlin. He was a murderer. He was no better than the darkness that had hunted them a lifetime ago.

The rain came again in torrents, the wind whipping about their faces. Lightning flashed close again. Lia neighed wildly, a cry of fear and regret, her eyes rolling. She knew she had played her part in this tragedy. She'd fed his fury, reveled in it. Encouraged it in pain and fear for her Chosen.

This realization struck them both in a mingled thought as fiercely as the lethal lightning strike: Neither of them deserved the second chance they'd been gifted. All around them, they felt unseen eyes watching and judging them. They were as guilty as Ernst.

Before they could call the lightning down upon themselves, Sarah and Tavin were there. Sarah embraced Owen as Tavin pressed himself to Lia. *:If you go, we go with you.:* Sarah's mental voice was calm and filled with understanding.

The younglings, tense and filled with the overwhelming realization of who they once were and what they'd just done, resisted. The more they tried to pull away, the tighter Sarah and Tavin held on, until something within the children broke and they relented, keening their fear and sorrow. This only made the older pair hold on all the more, soothing the stricken pair as best they could.

As the four embraced, Tavin shielded them all from the storm and their raging emotions. The bonded four, once torn asunder, were together again.

Sarah and Tavin stood vigil over the sleeping pair, despite the safety of Lord Briden's stable and the curious stable hands who sought a look at the newly Chosen noble son. In sleep, both Owen and Lia looked peaceful. The older pair knew otherwise.

Sarah rubbed her temples as she finished explaining to the King's Own what had happened on her ambassadorial trip to the new fiefdom. The fact that one of theirs had been immediately Chosen was both a point of pride and consternation. It had taken half the night to convince Lord Briden that the Heralds of Valdemar were not child thieves.

:I notice you didn't mention the connection between the four of us.: Tavin's mental voice was filled with mirth.

:Of course not, you silly thing. Reincarnation isn't well known amongst even the Heralds. We only know because of our special circumstance. There is no need to make their training that much harder.: Sarah considered the pair with a troubled frown. *:They're going to have a difficult enough time as it is. I don't think their reunion was supposed to be like this.:*

After a moment's pause, Sarah bowed her head. *:Do you think what Owen did was magic? Do we have the first Herald-Mage since Vanyel?:* She tried to keep the hope out of her thoughts.

:I don't know. I truly don't. It could be a different talent. It probably was *a different talent. But even I will admit it could be Mage talent. It's been twenty-five years since Vanyel's death. Would the Heralds know how to train a Herald with Mage talent?:*

She shook her head. *:I don't know. Even if it was Mage talent, there's a good possibility he burned it out of himself in his rage and grief.:*

:True. But what a burden to bear on top of everything else.: Tavin snorted, then nibbled Sarah's hair *:You know*

what we should do.: The shape of his idea floated between them.

She looked her Companion in the eye. *:Can you do
that?:*

:Yes. With your help.:

Sarah considered the idea longer. *:Then we should do
it. I'll write up a report for those who will need to know.
In time, when they've grown together, when they can control their powers and their emotions, we can reveal it to
them once more.:*

The memory block took less time but more energy
than they thought it would. For now, Owen and Lia
would remember most of what had happened, but not
their previous lives. They'd still feel the kinship with
Sarah and Tavin with the thought that the older Herald
and Companion had rescued them from the bandits . . .
and from themselves.

In time, as all of them grew together, the truth would
be revealed. For now, it was time for them to heal, learn,
grow, and enjoy this life without the burdens of the previous one.

"Do you think my father will be proud of me?" Owen
rode next to Herald Sarah in front of the jail carriage, the
ambassadorial carriage, and the accompanying contingent of guardsmen.

"For being Chosen? I would think so. Only the best
and brightest are ever Chosen. You're a special boy—
even without your talent, which can be as useful as it is
formidable."

"Do we need to tell him about . . . about . . . ?" Owen
hesitated.

*:About how we lost ourselves to our fury and need
Herald training now more than ever?:* Lia supplied.

:Yeah. I guess.: Owen sighed. He looked up to Sarah.

The older Herald looked to the horizon. "Tavin believes that you should tell him if you feel he needs to
know now. Otherwise, it can wait. I agree." She glanced
at the boy. "However, he is your father. He will have
questions. Follow your heart."

Owen nodded. "I hope he's proud of me."

"I'm proud of you. Both of you. You were able to pull yourselves back from the brink. This is a hard thing to do in the face of such grief, rage, and destruction." Sarah clapped him on the shoulder.

Owen's furrowed brows did not change. He stroked Lia's mane. When he spoke again, his voice was barely above a whisper. "But how can I be a Herald when I've killed people?"

Sarah drew in a long slow breath, searching for the right words. Tavin helped her find them. "Heralds and Companions are not perfect beings. We strive to do our best. That is all we can do. There is only one time in all the history of the Heralds that a Companion repudiated her Chosen . . ."

:Never!: Lia interrupted.

This declaration cleared some of the storm clouds in Owen's face.

The Herald continued, " . . . And in the end, even he was given another chance. It was a strange, hard road to walk for the young man." She paused, musing. "There's an old and well-regarded bard who could tell you the tale much better than I could. Master Bard Stefan stays close to Haven and the Palace these days. He works closely with us. Someday, he'll tell you the story of Tylendel."

Sarah tapped Owen's shoulder, forcing him to look at her. "What's important for the here and now is that you understand what you did and why. That you look deep into yourself and you make sure something like that never happens again. Heralds are not infallible, but they must strive to be."

Owen nodded. "I understand. I promise, I'll never let it happen like that again." He looked forward at a call from someone up ahead. His grin reappeared. "It's Edric! One of my father's men." He urged Lia forward, waving. "Edric!"

Sarah watched them go, both pleased and concerned. The young Herald and Companion had a long and strange road before them. She only hoped Stefan would be willing to tell them his whole story when it came time to let Owen and Lia remember their past—as he had before to another young pair who had needed to hear it more than they'd realized.

For now, she would guide and train them the best she could. It was all a Herald could do.

The Girl Who Rejected the Ordinary
Janny Wurts

Kaysa awakened, groggy and travel sore. The heat on her face carried no whiff of wax to suggest a lit candle. The cot beside hers was empty, without the telltale sound of a sleeper's breathing. The chatter of grooms from the stable yard outside meant sunrise flooded the room's only window.

No mending the shortfall. She had overslept. Her fellow travelers and their Companions would be waiting to depart. Arif's exclamation drifted upward, the clipped bite to his phrases fuming at the delay.

Kaysa flung off the quilt with none of last night's reverence for the quality cloth. The embarrassment burned; she shared the inn's best, as befitting a Herald in royal service, when in truth she was not Chosen, and the inconvenience of her blindness posed a liability. The mission she accompanied sought to resolve a threat that had already killed one Herald and damaged the mind of his surviving Companion. Today's inadequacy came a week's travel from her home and a day's ride from the main road to Haven. She had spoiled the early start needed to reach the town of Exodus before dark.

Kaysa's rushed feet hit the floorboards. Determined hands felt for the wall she required to guide her in the strange room, where she had left her clothing and boots in careful order the evening before.

Her toe hooked on a footstool that should not have been there. Kaysa crashed to her knees, tears pricking her lids. Not from the pain, though her rapped shin bled. What boneheaded folly led her to believe she could behave as if sighted, or, worse, expect others might handle her disability as smoothly as the family she had left behind?

Truth heightened her disgrace. Her handicap hampered the Heralds, again.

She had expected to pull her own weight, sure her duty lay with their urgent need to report to the Queen's Council at Haven. The murdered Herald's Companion had been rescued by her intervention. She possibly held some vital detail to solve the mysterious death.

Right or wrong, inconvenience or worse, she wrestled fresh doubt. Everyone might have been better off if she had stayed in Ropewynd, spinning yarn in her mother's loft.

Regret came too late. She could only go on, groping on all fours to recover her orientation, when careful steps and measured use of her senses should have avoided the lame-brained tumble to start with.

No question of her rank incompetence now. Arif's curt impatience sent someone's rushed step up the stairway. Lara's, by the bang of her heeled boots as she leaped the risers two at a stride.

Kaysa's fingertips brushed the wall. She stood just as the hinge squeaked and the door barreled open.

Silence, not scolding, filled the awkward pause.

Lara puffed a vexed breath. "You tripped on that foot stool? Oh, Kaysa, I'm so sorry!" Contrition, sprung from the able-bodied embarrassment of forgetting the drawbacks of Kaysa's condition. The predictable surge of humility followed, as pity strove to amend the lapse. "My thoughtlessness made you late. Here, I'll help."

Kaysa gritted her teeth as her clothes were passed to her like a baby. Haste forced her to accept the demeaning grasp steering her to the wash basin to splash her face. She gave her hair a cursory brush, pride sacrificed for expediency.

"I'll skip breakfast," Kaysa said, at last ready to leave.

"Nonsense." Lara dashed to the open casement. "Arif! My stupid mess delayed Kaysa. Could you send word to the kitchen to bring something for her?"

Arif's rumbling bass called, "No problem!"

"Please, no extra trouble." Kaysa's cheeks flamed that Lara had shouldered the blame, as if the fault had not been her own for missing the early wake up call.

"No bother!" Lara seized Kaysa's hand. "The inn's reputation won't let the Queen's Own go hungry! The landlady's already packing provender. Honey buns, boiled eggs, and some cheese should do nicely. Lark won't need the reins. You can snack in the saddle."

Because she was guided over the threshold, Kaysa did not have to click to interpret the echoes, or slow to navigate the strange hallway, or inch forward until her foot found the head of the stair. Smell, touch, and sound marked the bounds of her world and honed her awareness to a keen edge.

Outside, the clear morning's brisk wind brought the scents of fresh puddles and greenery. Jess's banter chaffed the lisping groom who delivered the victuals for their journey: hefty portions, by his grunt of effort as he lashed the pack to his saddle rings. Valdemar's Heralds were often supplied beyond what the realm's tokens paid an inn's coffers. As part of their company, Lark was led forward, already saddled and bridled.

Too rushed to stroke his nose, Kaysa quickly mounted. The boy passed her a slice of hot sesame bread. She left the bridle reins draped on the Companion's neck, took a bite, and trusted herself to his guidance.

Jess set off in the lead, whooping over the prank that had Arif wearing his shirt inside out.

"You'll check next time you dress in the dark," Lara chided, not about to draw rein for anyone's rumpled dignity. "You can set your clothing to rights when we pause, and meantime, your gaudy taste won't terrify the wildlife."

"With luck?" Jess's chuckle reverberated off the stone pillars of the stable yard gate. "He'll find himself beating for cover in bushes cropped short by browsing sheep. Forget the wild game. The goose girls' eyes will be drawn to those colors like a beacon!"

Lara snorted, amused. "Rub it in, and Arif will toss salt in your beer at Hanniker's Tavern."

"If we reach Hanniker's," Arif groused. "We have to clear Pelagiris Forest first. Till then, watch your back. The Shin'a'in stalk beasts in bright clothes as an art form."

"Hot air," Jess dismissed, not to be rattled. His saddle squeaked. Likely, he'd twisted to see whether Kaysa could manage a quicker pace. But the food in her hand held them back, a disappointment Jess hid by heckling his partner.

"Time aplenty to set you on your rear, Arif, perhaps before we get to Exodus."

Kaysa gulped her last bite and dusted off the crumbs, unable to share the joke behind the current bout of ribbing. Before Arif seized the last word, a mock scuffle broke out to see who could unseat the other.

"Eyes in front!" Lara snapped, not amused by the horseplay. "We're not in safe country!"

That doused the jocularity like cold water and spurred the party to a brisk trot. Surrounded by jingling bridles, Kaysa minded her obligation to keep up. On her own, Lark's gentler gaits had reassured her. Now, wind in her face and buffeting her ears, she must leave her well-being to luck.

She diverted her nerves by listening to the Heralds' speculation, which rehashed Tarron's unlucky fate. They had already dismissed the commonplace perils to travelers in the deep forest. Freak storms and attacks by dangerous animals could not have damaged Lark's use of Mindspeech. All had shied from the subject of rogue magic, until Arif slapped a stinging fly on his Companion's neck and said, "He could have encountered a Change Circle. Truly."

Kaysa urged Lark forward. "Not likely. No such dangers lurk near Ropewynd. Though my gran described rare outbreaks of mage storms to scare us children into good behavior, nothing uncanny has troubled the region since before her grandparents' time."

"Not saying your elders were wrong," Jess responded. "But village folks as a rule don't venture far into the wood. There might have been a small anomaly hidden in a difficult place."

Kaysa allowed that stretches of the ravine were impassable, but if trappers could not surmount the terrain, neither could Lark or his rider. Bloodstains and furrowed scars marred her saddle, still fresh when she had found the Companion entangled in a fallen tree. Something vicious had brought Tarron down. But unless Haven's healers could restore Lark's mind, Kaysa possessed the only witnessed details, no matter how insignificant.

Lark shivered under her. She stroked his silky neck, afraid the discussion in some way distressed him. If only she had been his Chosen! Incapable of responding through a Herald's bond, Kaysa murmured to calm him.

Yet her mount's tension only increased, his back stiffened to a choppy stride.

"Something's not right," she announced, uneasy.

"Do you think?" Lara paused. The others drew rein. Bunched together, Heralds and Companions, everyone listened.

The surrounding forest seemed ordinary, loud with birdsong and fragrant with the last dew drying under the early sun's warmth. Insects buzzed. A foraging creature scuffled in the brush, and a squirrel jumped, rustling through the canopy. Jess's trail-wise experience perceived nothing wrong, and Lara's best judgment agreed.

Arif pressed his Companion ahead, eager to redress his muddled shirt and level his outstanding score.

"It's all right, Kaysa," Lara consoled, perhaps with sincerity. "Better to alert us for a false alarm than say nothing." Nobody admitted her blindness might lie at the root of her jumpy unease. Humiliation flamed Kaysa's cheeks. Too well, she recognized tolerance masked under the trappings of courtesy.

Long since, she had learned to weather the cool

isolation when folk chose to gloss over her inconveniences. Unwilling to ruffle the seamless partnership shared by the three Heralds, she patted Lark's neck and said nothing more.

The forest in fact sounded peaceful around her. The play of warm air carried no untoward scents. But the unsettled moment gnawed at her. As if for a split second, a wrongness had *almost* suspended all sound and movement in the surrounding trees. Perhaps she fretted over a phantom conjured by imagination. Yet Lark's tension under her touch had been real enough, an event without precedent, even amid the vulnerable uncertainty of the days she had traveled alone.

Kaysa focused on her innate perceptions. Nothing disturbed her sensitive ears. Lark's demeanor stayed docile. Reason argued she had cause to be anxious, days removed from familiar ground. Plunged into unknown territory with strangers, she did feel displaced, challenged at every turn by new trials. The Heralds could not fully grasp what she faced. Untroubled, they lapsed back into their habitual camaraderie. Jokes led to teasing and fond reminiscences of former assignments. Kaysa followed a half-step behind, while Arif's gravel bass described settling a knife brawl between two drunks in a tavern, and Jess topped that anecdote with another, funny enough to fold them in their saddles, about being trapped in a sheepcote by a raging bull.

"I thought Lara was going to wet herself," Jess claimed, though she insisted he'd been the one to soil his breeches dodging a charge. Talk turned to the pleasure of the dark beer shared in the aftermath.

Kaysa smiled wistfully, left out as Arif related the hilarious story of steering Jess's unsteady step from the Halfway Inn's tap room, then his Companion's concern, and the well-meant head bump to prop him erect that knocked them both sprawling into a pigsty.

The exchange of adventures and spirited quips beat the tedium of winding yarn and rope. The workaday task of weaving paled beside the richness of lives led beyond any backwoods villager's upbringing. Kaysa ached with yearning. Could a blind girl ever be Chosen? Was she even capable? If she could not evade a mad bull, or stride fearlessly into a fight to defend Valdemar's peace, did she deserve the privilege of being a Herald? How could she manage the responsibilities of the Queen's justice in the wider world?

Truthfully? She could not find her way home! Without Lark's guidance, she would have been utterly lost, unable to leave the bounds of her village. Now en route to Exodus on a rough trail, she battled the dismal likelihood that she was incapable. Lark's presence had admitted her into the company of the Heralds dispatched to ascertain Tarron's fate. What business had she impeding their mission on the *chance* she might recall an overlooked clue of significance?

Kaysa swallowed, inwardly shamed by the possibility that she had been selfish.

A chill raked her to gooseflesh. Lark shuddered, and this time, she *almost* caught the fleeting sense of the disturbance that seized the forest. So brief an impression, she could have assumed her perception was playing tricks on her. Already Lark steadied. Ahead, Arif's growled repartee upbraided Jess until Lara's brisk interjection cooled their roughhousing.

Nothing had distressed them. When Kaysa broached the incident, they listened. But since their Companions remained untroubled, no credible evidence supported her experience.

"Lark might be responding to your stifled fear, a reaction to having been traumatized," Jess pointed out. Patronizing, perhaps, but who knew better than the Chosen how Companions related to human minds?

"Lark's been damaged, besides," Lara qualified, a practical effort to salve insecurity. "Since none of our Companions can read him, we have to assume that Tarron's loss left him badly shaken. For all we know, the pair might have been savaged by brigands. Our report to the Queen's Council will determine the course of further investigation. If worse trouble brews farther west, prompt word could be crucial."

To that purpose, Lara and Jess forged ahead. Only Arif hung back. Perhaps more sympathetic to humiliation while wearing an inside-out shirt, he lent Kaysa's concern gruff encouragement. "We're not saying you didn't catch something we missed. Keep your ears pricked and shout out if it happens again." Against her self-conscious uncertainty, he added, "Promise you will."

Kaysa nodded, too upset to speak. She trailed the party of Heralds, too aware of the dampened morale suppressing their carefree conversation.

Maybe they took her precaution seriously, the rapt quiet a sign of attentive communion with their Companions. Riding behind in bleak isolation, Kaysa whispered to Lark, "Better hope we were wrong. I'd gladly take the embarrassment."

For if danger pursued them, she would be dead weight, reliant on the Companion to flee if protection required a fight.

Yet the fair weather morning passed without incident. Arif snatched the moment to right his shirt when they stopped to eat. Kaysa perched on a boulder, munching her share, while Lark browsed beside her. The placid rhythm of his jaws and the dry warmth of his hide told her all was well. Birds chirped overhead, the same songs that filled the forest at home in the moist scent of greenery under noon sun. She might have paused to rest with the lunch basket she carried to her father and brothers at work at the rope walk, had she not parted ways on the irreversible journey to Haven.

The Heralds enjoyed their cold meal with the purposeful air of folks short of time on a mission. Only Jess's quick laughter showed nerves, doubtless because he had a vengeful dig coming from Arif.

The Heralds remounted promptly and set a brisk pace into the afternoon. But their scheduled plan met obstruction again, when a washout entangled by a wrack of deadfalls forced them off the narrow trail. Kaysa clung to Lark's mane through the impasse, her senses overwhelmed by the rattle and swish of thrashed branches. Nothing bothered Lark's poise. No queer gap disrupted the tranquility of the forest. Frogs croaked from the reedy banks of a creek, silenced only by their splashed passage. Nothing but birds' wings whirred through the whisper of boughs overhead.

The Heralds rejoined the trail without mishap, speculating about which of two preferred taverns might still have rooms: the one the bards favored, with comfortable beds, or the hunters' lodge, which served heartier fare.

"Not tonight, anyway," Arif grumbled, morose. "Unless you want to risk traveling past dark, we'll have to camp in the wild."

"I have no difficulty with riding late," Kaysa ventured.

But Lara dismissed her effort to make up for the morning's slow start. "The inns will be full by sundown. Better to rest the Companions than to spend the night in the hayloft scratching fleas with the barn cats."

Jess added, breezily cheerful, "Rise early and ride, and we'll snag a late breakfast and a hot bath before we move on."

No one berated Kaysa, although a blind girl in a rough campsite had little of worth to chip in. Reliant on the Heralds, she could only stay mindful as the day cooled toward dusk. Her attentiveness detected nothing amiss, even when Lark turned his neck for a prolonged glance behind.

"Do you see something?" Kaysa listened, intent.

But the fallen hush as the birds roosted was normal, and the place selected for their overnight stay was a pleasant hollow set in the curve of a brook.

"A Herald's favorite," Jess confided cheerfully as he helped Kaysa remove Lark's saddle. His steps marked by the scuff of his heels, he ran on, "The stones for the fire pit have been here for as long as anyone can remember."

No shed with stored provisions graced the site, however. "Bears," Arif admitted on inquiry. "Nothing built here would withstand the hungry marauders."

But there was a lean-to with a thatched roof, sufficient to keep the dew off their gear while they spread their blankets under the stars.

"Who knows?" Lara added, unpacking the last of the

generous fare bestowed by the inn's kitchen. "The Herald-Mage Vanyel may have slept here. He and Stefan could have toasted their supper under the summer sky, just as we are. Here's Arif. He'll find you a seat."

"I just need a walking staff to find my own way." But Kaysa's preference was disregarded as Arif took the suggestion and guided her to a log by the fireside. She settled there, aware the gesture aimed to bolster her spirits. Even though Jess cut the stave she requested, she could not gather kindling or contribute much beyond aimlessly stirring a readied pot. While she could smell meat if it burned and poke a potato to tell if it was done, such skills were scant use among three sighted folks, efficiently busy. She became the loose end, her offer to scour the cooking utensils politely turned down. No one belabored the reason: that a dropped a knife or pan might drag someone else from their rest for a tiresome search.

She was not faulted for her shortcomings. But when Lara assumed the duty of clean up, Kaysa followed, determined to dry and stow the gear in the saddle pack. She found Arif at the streamside ahead of her, engrossed in conversation with Lara.

Their voices were too low to be overheard. Yet the sudden silence that met Kaysa's approach spoke plainly.

Her parents and her brothers broke off that way when she caught them in discussions of her disability. Too well, Kaysa recognized the stiff embarrassment, then the familiar, bright tone of pretense as nervous reaction prompted a swift change of subject. The evasion struck her keen ear like false notes.

Arif would have been questioning her sorry misjudgment. Arguing, surely, against her concern, that her outspoken alarms were a worthless distraction. Her awkward intrusion would be brushed aside, the delicate problem deferred until later. The Heralds would shelter her feelings before the inevitable decision to relieve themselves of the hindrance.

Nothing Kaysa could do eased their straits. She had come too far. The Heralds could scarcely abandon her in the Pelagiris Forest. Likely, once they reached Exodus, she'd be handed over to a paid escort and sent safely home.

Miserable, Kaysa spun on her heel. She spread her blanket and tucked up to rest, while behind her Jess admired a rising, full moon she could not see. At Ropewynd, she would have swept the yarn loft and locked up, then laid the kitchen fire for the next day while her brothers finished their chores. On familiar ground, she was self-reliant, not a trial to everyone's nerves.

In daydreams, her yearning for challenge beyond the horizon had never included the setback of wrestling with her incompetence.

The Heralds banked the fire and turned in at length. Kaysa listened to their breathing deepen with sleep. Yet she could not settle. While the other Companions kept watch, Lark reclined, legs folded, his relaxed contentment a comfort to her anguish. All seemed well. Nonetheless, her worry persisted, chafed by the unhappy suspicion the Heralds could not relieve themselves of her presence quickly enough.

Time passed. The croaking frogs in the brook and the hoot of a hunting owl joined the whispered drip of dew that marked the depth of the night. The woodland rhythm lent her no grasp of the hour. At Ropewynd, caught wakeful, she listened for the rattle of the baker's boy's handcart as he fetched wood to light the bread ovens in the wee hours. The bells of the dairy cows, come in for milking at sunrise, broke the still calm of daybreak, soon followed by the delightful aroma of the first baked loaves, set out to cool.

Here, the crickets' chorus rasped unchanged through the buzz of Jess's snores.

Kaysa's eyelids drooped when the change came again: a fleeting, gapped moment, not quite like silence, as though a ripple of shock had crested and passed. She shoved erect. Her hand sought Lark, tucked behind her. His coat was warm to her touch, without any trace of a tremble.

Uneasy, afraid, Kaysa dared not believe her senses played tricks on her. If she distrusted her instincts, too timid to rely on herself, what in the wide world did that make her to anyone other than a helpless burden? Fear threatened to define her. The blind girl who startled at nothing became the nuisance the able-bodied dismissed with innocuous kindness.

And yet *something* was not right. Kaysa stroked Lark's shoulder again. He suffered no tremors, no damp, breaking sweat. The Companion lifted his head, lipped her hair, then blew a soft snort. Unlike yesterday, he displayed no alarm.

Kaysa swallowed. She could put her faith in Lark or in herself. Rouse the Heralds, perhaps for *nothing*, and suffer redoubled disgrace as they humored her. Or she could act *now*, because Tarron may have died because he had recognized his dire peril too late.

Nothing did not kill. Reproach harmed no one, truly, but her. Only cowardice shrank from hurt pride.

Kaysa kicked off her blankets and grabbed her staff. She groped past the firepit, guided by its radiant warmth, until she encountered a form in repose. Lara's, by the faint scent of sausage grease ingrained from cooking their supper.

"Get up," Kaysa whispered as she prodded the Herald.

Lara stirred, quickly wakeful. "What's wrong?"

"I don't know. Not for certain." Braced for ridicule, Kaysa pushed on, "But I've noticed something not right, maybe stalking us. We ought to leave, *now*."

"You heard something?" Lara's query seemed forbearing, though her alert movement suggested she listened.

Kaysa strove to explain. Not about what she had heard but what she had not: W*hat was missing*.

Lara did not wait for justification but gently roused Arif and Jess. "Trouble, maybe," she said softly. "Kaysa thinks so. My Companion's not bothered, but better if we aren't caught napping."

Arif fumbled for his boots, perhaps planning to scout. Maybe Jess would have lingered for questions. But the oppressive grip of the forest closed in until the air bore down like a weight.

Not silence at all, Kaysa realized, but a dense pressure that dampened her eardrums. As she labored to breathe, the invasive scent struck her like a damp cloth in the face. A rank smell, atavistic, saturating the breezeless night with such potency that she exclaimed aloud.

"What smell?" Arif demanded, short of sleep and transparently irritable.

Kaysa answered with bone-deep certainty, no matter that her experience set her apart. "Like a wet dog with bad breath, only worse."

That moment, a Companion snorted. Hooves stamped in the darkness. Lark surged to his feet and joined the jostling herd.

"Boar, maybe," Jess remarked, his lanky frame arrived at her shoulder with a fragrant armload of split birch. "Not likely to trouble us near a fire." He set to, fanned the stirred coals to life and built a fresh blaze from the embers.

Not a boar, Kaysa realized. At Ropewynd, the musky scent only lingered where the creatures wallowed in the wood. Whatever approached raised a reek strong enough to cause nausea. Through Arif's crack inviting the odds on whether they'd have fried pork for breakfast, Kaysa realized, chilled: the frogs' croaks in the brook had swelled at regular intervals, trailing raggedly off into silence. But this moment, their singing did not return. More, the crickets were quiet *on all sides*, not just where the dank odor wafted on the breeze.

"Now," Kaysa cried, urgent. "We need to leave *now!*" She bent, scrounged two sticks of kindling, and cracked them together. The echo bounced off the lean-to. She moved that way, swinging her stave until she banged the support pole. Behind her, the huddled Companions stopped milling. Jess stopped joking in favor of lighting a torch, expecting to drive off a wild animal or, better, to speed its departure.

"Hurry!" Kaysa fumbled through the piled strap leather. "Leave the bedrolls and packs."

"Lark's uneasy, not panicked." Lara's reproof stayed exactly patient. "If it's only a boar ..."

Kaysa barked her knuckles against a saddle, hopefully hers. An exploratory sweep of her hand sought the scar on the seat, stained yet by the coppery tang of Tarron's dried blood. Contact scorched her fingers. No surprise encounter with spark or flame, but a poisonous scald that seared her bare skin like acid. "Magic!" she shouted, "The marks left by Tarron's killer are burning my palm!"

That shattered indulgent pretense at last.

One of the Heralds jostled against her side. Arif, by the pungency of the bracken cut to pillow his head. "Let me see."

"No!" Kaysa pushed him away as the puzzling details slid into place. "Don't touch! For Chosen, the residual taint may be deadly." No longer hesitant, she qualified swiftly, "That's why Lark trembled! Other stains on his saddle blanket did not wash clean. The residue seems to react to the magic used by whatever's tracking us. Nothing bothered my village or me until Lark and I joined your company. The Companion remembers what destroyed his Chosen. With the blanket in direct contact with his skin, the sting as the spell engaged would trigger his traumatic memories."

She had missed the uncanny sensation before, while her clothing protected her.

"We have to leave. *Now!* I'll ride bareback." Freed of his tainted tack, Lark would not feel the goad that panicked him. But Kaysa could not abandon the evidence needed as proof to inform the Queen's Council. "The saddlecloth stays with me. Find a blanket. I'll bundle it."

Fearing Arif's doubt, she begged, "Hurry!" The heaviness strangling her faculties was no quirk of her imagination. "Do you hear the quiet? We're being hunted. Lark's saddlecloth carries a poisonous taint. Something unspeakably ugly may happen if one of you Heralds should touch it."

Arif did not hesitate. "All right. My saddle goes on Lark."

"No time." Kaysa tried to prod him along, surprised by an arm slighter than the gruff voice suggested. "I'll stay astride somehow." Though Goddess help them all if she failed. A misstep at this pass would be fatal.

Movement to the left pressed the scratchy sensation of wool into Kaysa's hand: Lara, with the requested blanket. "Lark's saddlecloth's a short reach to your right. Roll it inside. Once it's covered, I'll help you tie it."

Jess's warning arose from the fireside. "Trouble's coming in fast!" The staccato snapping of sticks spun him toward the lumbering charge of whatever approached. "Get Kaysa on Lark. Stay with her. I'll follow with my Companion."

But the inbound threat came in too swiftly.

"Run!" Kaysa gasped, chilled by the tightening quiet and cruel certainty that the Heralds were targeted prey.

The monstrous predator hurtled out of the woods: not a boar. The vibration shocked through the ground carried the weight of not one creature but three.

"Change-Beasts!" yelled Arif.

Flame fluttered. Jess, defending his ground, swung his torch and backed against the firepit. "Run! Get Lark and Kaysa out of here!"

No time left for Lara to secure the wrapped saddlecloth: Arif's wiry grip hurled Kaysa astride Lark with the bundle clenched in her arms.

The Companion bolted when she straddled his back. Lashed by his mane, knees clenched to his sides, Kaysa clung, whipped by low hanging branches. Arif galloped to her left, with Lara beside him. Neither dared slacken the breakneck pace. The least move to cater to her disability would bring ruin. All relied on their Companions in flight.

Night impaired human sight. Worse, unaccustomed to living in darkness, the Heralds' ears overlooked the use of echoes, as reflected hoof beats gave notice of tree trunks before their Companions swerved in avoidance. Or maybe sighted instinct cued them to look back as the aberrant monsters burst from the wood and took Jess, armed with naught but his sword and a torch.

For Kaysa, the nightmare unfolded in sound: from

behind, vicious growls rasped through tearing flesh as Jess fell without a cry. Blood and horror sowed panic among the Companions. Kaysa endured the thunderous tumult of hooves and the battering onslaught of whipping twigs and rushing wind. Agonized for Jess, fleeing terrors that blindness could never imagine, she ached for a sweet kindness forever lost: the lilted laugh, the considerate touch bestowed from the heart as Jess checked her gear, and his joyful horseplay that enlivened the tedium of travel.

Kaysa's only tribute for a lost friend was to stay astride. Through tears, she begged that the salvaged cloth clenched to her breast could unmask the murderous enemy.

Riding for her life, she used what she had, listening behind in the hope that Jess's bereaved Companion had miraculously won free. Instead, she heard the ominous crash of pursuit, closing on their lead from both flanks.

"They're cutting us off," she called out. "Trying to stop us." Whatever foe terrorized the Pelagiris Forest, the force worked the Change-Beasts with intelligence. The assault was driven by magical means for who knew what ugly purpose.

"Only two," Lara disclosed from the partnered awareness of her Companion. "Jess maybe wounded the other before he fell."

But no such heroic last stand had occurred. Kaysa knew, heavy-hearted. Jess's brief struggle had ended alone. If Bards' verses one day memorialized the courage of his final moments, he had not left the world on his feet, battling to save their company.

Clearly, Kaysa had picked up the hideous evidence: sounds of teeth rending lifeless flesh and the ripe tang of slaughter assailing her nostrils. The Change-Beast had paused only to gorge on its kill and, too likely, to shred the carcass of the loyal Companion.

Arif faltered, choked speechless by grief, which stung Lara into a tirade. "Don't you dare pull up! Yes, I know what Jess meant to you! But our mission is paramount. We must survive to reach Haven!"

To that end, they fled, harried by a ruthless hunt that

seemed tireless. The Heralds' battled the odds with their woodcraft, twisting and turning through the dense green-wood. Kaysa hung on without sense of direction, lost if she fell behind. The ordeal lasted until dawn, which drove the Change-Beasts to lair up under daylight.

Surrounded by birdsong, shown respite at last, the Companions heaved with exhaustion.

"Goddess protect us," gasped Arif. "No one's seen Change-Beasts like that since the Mage Wars. They never course in packs unless a Dark Adept controls them." His apology addressed Kaysa directly. "You were right. I was wrong. There is evil afoot."

"Ill magic," Lara agreed. Unspoken, the sorrow none cared to broach: that Tarron must have fallen afoul or been lured by the same nameless horror. That Jess had also been felled by such malice posed a deadly threat to the realm.

"We cannot turn aside," Arif resolved against the ap-palling stakes. "Our duty demands action, no matter the cost."

Kaysa was left to point out the disturbance, thrashing its way through the greenwood. "Listen up! Something follows us."

The Heralds paused. Both responded. "Companion!" Then, in detail Lara supplied through their bond, "She led the Change-Beasts down a false trail and helped draw them off before sunrise."

Shortly, Jess's Companion arrived in their midst. Scraped and stricken by her brutal loss, she was nonethe-less whole. Her witness of the arcane attack confirmed Kaysa's theory. The fell power had tried to suborn her beloved Chosen before he died.

Lara's shock blazed with outrage. "This rogue power wants to warp Heralds for a nefarious purpose!"

Arif explained to Kaysa what had been shared through their mind-linked Companions. "Jess went down as Tarron did, assaulted by magic designed as a snare. He threw himself into the jaws of the Change-Beast rather than be overtaken. By his final wish, his Companion es-caped what appears to be a plot aimed to discredit

Valdemar." Sick with loathing, he paused, leaving Lara to frame the conclusion.

"Because of you, Kaysa, we were not caught asleep. Jess died grateful for your timely warning."

Day brightened around them. Kaysa marked the subtle warmth as the sun reached the crowns of the trees: no unsettled sign marred the morning, and no eldritch presence bespoke an intrusion. But if no hostile force seemed in evidence, the moment's reprieve could not last.

Charged with Lark and the evidence critical to the realm's security, she spoke with the honesty she ought to have embraced before leaving Ropewynd. "You must drop me at Exodus." Henceforward, she must not impede the Heralds or further endanger their critical mission. "Better I make my way home with the traders than jeopardize your duty to the Queen's Council."

"That's risky business," Lara objected. "The beasts tracking us will hound our trail into Exodus. We cannot expose innocents to such peril, and besides, our most direct route to Haven lies straight across country, not by the road."

The Heralds firmly resisted Kaysa's bid to part company. "You provided our only warning last night. Yesterday, if we'd paid closer heed to your sensitivity, Jess might still be alive."

"That course might play into your enemy's hands," Kaysa cautioned. "Keep to the wilds, and the spelled attack that snared Tarron and Jess could also destroy you."

The stiff rustle of Arif's objection preceded his spoken word. "Not quite. We could have been baited days before this, or driven into disaster. But whatever conspires against the Queen's Own did not plan for our surprise advantage."

Kaysa braced for the hardheaded conclusion. Two Heralds were unfit to fill Jess's shoes. Her parting at Exodus was inevitable for the greater good of the realm.

But sensible Lara overturned the blind girl's expectations. "We had you and Lark in our favor. If the saddlecloth in that blanket lends warning only you are fit to discern, we must rely on your senses to see us through."

"Will you come?" Arif pleaded. "For Jess, and for Tarron. Could you keep watch, even though the path may be dangerous?"

Kaysa lifted her chin. "Yes," she said, at last sure of her place. Because she was a girl who stepped outside the ordinary, she could do her vital part to serve Valdemar.

Unexpected Consequences

Elizabeth A. Vaughan

Dearest Father,

We have come through winter as well as one could expect, and spring is starting to show its fair hand on my lands. To my delight, the woods and fields are filled with wildflowers, most of which are strange to me, but their sweet scents and colors soothe my anxious soul.

Anxious? Yes, for I have learned that the greatest risk to my people is the time between winter and spring, when our stockpiles are at their lowest, and the new crops have yet to come in.

· But if spring brings me these worries, it also has brought new hope to my people, who do not fear hard work. The able-bodied are in the fields, seeing to the herds, planting the crops. My fear is that our crops will not be sufficient to feed us, much less provide for surplus. Embroidery, the herds, these can only go so far to sustain us. I remember your lessons, Father. 'Wise is the man with more than one color of wool in his shop.'

Added to my worries is that, as the Lady of Sandbriar, it is my duty to see that the tax records kept for the accounting to the Crown are true and accurate. My Steward, Athelnor, fulfilled these obligations for

*my late husband, and the Old Lord before him. But
he is of advanced years, and he caught a chill this
past month. So, as a result. . . .*

"I'll go," Cera said firmly, hoping to end the argument.

"Lady, you can't." Athelnor coughed, a racking, painful sound. He'd insisted on coming to his office, trailing
blankets and handkerchiefs, a knitted cap perched on his
old head. "The risk—"

"You can't go, you old fool." Marga, his wife, hovered
over him, scolding as she pulled at his blankets. Athelnor
batted her away.

"I will take Gareth and a few of the other lads," Cera
said soothingly from her usual chair.

Gareth looked up from tending the hearth fire with a
grin, his face lighting up at the thought of escaping his
grandfather's office and its endless paperwork. "I can
bring my boar spear."

Marga rolled her eyes at her grandson, clearly still upset. Cera knew she hadn't forgiven him and his friends
for going boar hunting without permission.

"I miss my cousin, the Old Lord," Athelnor's voice
was the merest whisper, tired and pained. "I see him in
Gareth . . . in that smile."

Marga gave Cera a worried look as she knelt at Athelnor's side. "I know," she said softly.

"Forgive an old man his memories." Athelnor took a
ragged breath.

Cera smiled gently. "This will give me a chance to see
what my people need."

"And be seen," Marga said. "You are always telling
her she needs to be seen more."

Athelnor gave them all a gimlet stare. "Wildflowers
brings wild men," he recited the old proverb. "The bandits will be out, lurking in the woods. No place for a
lady."

"No place for a man with the ague, either," Marga
said tartly.

"You have been explaining all winter how it works,"
Cera said. "You go out in early spring to check the

records of the towns and villages so that when the Heralds come through to certify the accountings, all is in order. Then, after that, the Guard comes through and collects the actual tax money, yes? And it's only Headman Ondon's figures that look wrong this year."

Athelnor slumped in his chair. "It wouldn't even be necessary, except Ondon is horrible with numbers. Good with people, but poor in his sums."

"It's settled then." Cera rose from her chair and headed the door. "Ondon is close enough that we can be there and back again in a day. I won't be carrying any more than my normal purse. Queen Selenay has confirmed me in these lands after the tragic death of my late lord. I would insure that all is done well and properly so that she knows of our devotion to our duty and the Crown." Cera paused in the doorway. "Gareth, let's plan to leave tomorrow, earliest."

Athelnor was still muttering against it as she left the room, but she pretended not to hear him.

Cera went to find Alena, her handmaiden. They'd be there and back without staying, so there was no need for Alena to go with her. That would have horrified Alena in the day, but she was adapting to the ways of Valdemar just as Cera was. Perhaps even faster, now that they were both out from under the restrictions imposed on them by her late husband.

Cera found her in the old solar, now the heart of industry, with embroiderers working around the clock. Children, too, learned to spin and sew the basics for an hour or so every day after their regular lessons. Elderly grandmothers taught the delicate patterns to the younger women.

The women all smiled and nodded, but none paused to rise from their work. Cera had no time for wasted curtsys, and they knew it.

And in the center stood a man on a stool, his shirt pulled up under thin arms, struggling to hold up a pair of thick work pants three sizes too big while being scolded by a woman with pins in her mouth.

"Hold still, hold still," Alena scolded as she tucked and pinned along one leg.

"I am, woman." Ager struggled to keep his balance and hold up the heavy cloth. "Quit pokin' me."

"Big strong man like you." Alena glanced over, and then dipped a quick curtsy to Cera. "M'lady."

"M'Lady." Ager bobbed his head, blushing beat red.

Cera ignored his embarrassment. She didn't come any closer, for she still wasn't completely comfortable around the man. Still, she could feel some sympathy for him. She focused on the pants. "Those are awfully big to be taken in. Maybe start with something smaller?"

"Nothing smaller to be had." Alena smiled through her pins, reaching for an inner seam.

"Here now, woman, don't be doing that," Ager let go with one hand to bat her away. "Least of all here." He blushed harder, looking around him.

"I need to take an even amount from all the seams, or do you want to chafe?" Alena demanded, ignoring his struggles and pinning away. "You'll need heavy pants, working with the herds. Was it something important, m'lady? I can leave him standing here a bit if you need me." Alena turned her head, and winked at Cera.

"Later is fine." Cera tried to keep her laughter out of her voice as Ager protested again. "Come find me when you are done."

"As you wish, m'lady."

Cera headed back out with a light heart. Alena hadn't looked so cheerful in a long time, hadn't had that sparkle in her eye even before they'd left Haven. She knew that look; it was joyful and happy and filled with the possibilities of—

Oh . . .

Cera stopped dead in the hall.

Ohhh.

Alena and Ager? That wasn't wise. It would only lead to pain and heartbreak, and if he so much as raised his hand—

She stood there for a long moment, caught by her own thoughts, her heart racing unexpectedly in her chest.

No. No, that was wrong. She made an effort to take in air. One long breath after another.

Love could lead to heartache, Cera knew that well. But that was her own experience. Alena had every right to think on her future. If her eye fell on Ager, well, so be it. It would not be Cera's choice, but it was not her choice to make. All she could do was wish her loyal handmaiden the best, and see to it that Ager treated her well. Or he would answer to the Lady of Sandbriar, with all the power of Valdemaran law behind her.

Her heart calming, Cera continued on to her chambers. She would not sour another's joy.

But she would ask Athelnor to refresh her on the applicable Crown law. Just in case.

Ondon had been welcoming, and it had taken her less than two hours to correct his errors. To her relief, he'd not been resentful of the correction, just grateful and a bit embarrassed.

"My thanks, Lady Cera." He'd brushed the few gray hairs that remained over his pate. "Can I offer you the hospitality of my home this night?"

"No, Headman, but thank you." Cera knew they'd not much time to spare. "If we leave now, we'll be back before supper. And the boys were promised a berry crumble for their efforts."

"Best eaten hot," Gareth chimed in.

Ondon had seen them off with effusive thanks. Now the sky was clear, the air crisp, her cloak warm, and the road open ahead. Even her steady mule seemed to be enjoying the day.

Wildflowers danced in the breeze on both sides of the road, their scents lovely but strange. Perhaps different was the better word. As lovely as Sandbriar was in springtime, it was not the same as her childhood home in Rethwellan.

The boys rode ahead of her, talking and laughing, no doubt planning another hunt.

Leaving Cera with only her thoughts for companions. She took another breath of crisp air and tried to be grateful to the Trine for their blessings. But spring was bringing with it the anniversary of her unlamented husband's death. When she'd learned of his participation in the attack on Queen Selenay, she'd thought her life would be ended as well. But thanks to the mercy of the Queen and her Companion, Cera found herself with a new home and new responsibilities.

Athelnor and Marga had been silent on the issue, but that anniversary would soon be upon them. So far, all had respected her official mourning of a year and a day, but that would soon end. Well, all but Lord Cition, who had sent his second son Emerson early, to "get in first" as Emerson had put it.

Thankfully, Emerson's goal had been far different from his father's. She smiled to think of her weaver suitor, writing letters to his father about her stubbornness while weaving his tapestries in every spare moment he had. He'd soon have the first finished and she looked forward to having it displayed in her Great Hall. Emerson was already muttering about his second project, one he was keeping a massive secret.

Cera sighed and considered her options. She thought of keeping others at bay using Emerson, but that hardly seemed fair. Or honorable.

In her heart of hearts, Cera admitted she wasn't sure how she felt about marrying again. In the beginning, her marriage had been good. Better than good, it had been lovely. There was joy with a spouse who shared secrets, goals, and plans, an intimacy that went beyond their bodies. She missed that.

But when it went bad—and it had gone bad quickly—it had been a nightmare. The yelling, the blows. Cera shuddered. At the time she had thought she had been at fault, not him, that she had caused his anger and flareups, and there were still moments—

A gentle cough brought her back to the present. Gareth had slowed, bringing his horse next to her mule. "A copper for your thoughts." He grinned at her.

She grinned back.

"So how bad were Ondon's sums?" he asked, sitting

his horse easily, carrying his long boar spear balanced in one hand.

"Bad enough." Cera chuckled. "He was embarrassed but happy when I discovered that the error was in the village's favor." She tilted her head. "You could have checked it for yourself, you know. Your sums are better than mine."

"Shhh," Gareth said. "Grandfather is trying to keep me indoors as it is. He finds that out, and I will never hunt again!" His face was filled with youthful horror at the idea.

Cera laughed, then gasped as her mule suddenly backed and kicked. She kept her seat, looking back—

A man lay sprawled on the road behind them, his head bloody. What had—?

More armed men appeared from the woods all around them, intent and silent.

Gareth cried out a warning to the two lads up ahead. With one swift move, he stood in the saddle, and thrust down at his attacker with his boar spear. There was sickening crunch, and the man fell back, taking the spear with him.

Cera's horror paralyzed her, but not her mule. It kicked again, sending two men skittering back, clearing the area around her.

Her heart pounding, Cera slid from her saddle and darted to the side, away. There were four against the boys, and they were trying to pull them from their horses. The boys were giving as good as they got, but if she could lure some away, even the odds—

Cera let out a loud whistle, the kind she used to summon herds back home.

Heads turned.

She held out her coin purse and jingled it once. The sound of coin on coin sounded oddly loud to her ears. Not a plan really. More of a desperation.

It caught the attention of the bandits. "Get her!" cried one.

Cera turned and ran back along the road, cursing her skirts and swearing never again to look like a lady.

She could hear footsteps behind her, but she didn't dare look back. Around the curve ahead was a crossroads, and if the Trine was with her, maybe aid, or at least a moment to hide in the tall wildflowers, thick along the road.

The sounds of fighting faded, but the heavy breathing behind her grew closer. Cera ran faster. A distraction, she needed something, anything.

She threw the coin purse to the left, into the underbrush. He'd want the money, he'd stop and gather—

He didn't stop. "Got ya—" was muttered in her ear.

Cera cried out at the feeling of heavy fingers brushing against her skirts. He'd lunged and missed, heavy feet stumbling. She leaped forward, her breath ragged, running for her life. The road curved, the crossroad came into view.

Cera ran right into the middle of a herd of wooly, fuzzy horses. At least that was the impression she had before the animals scattered, making odd chirping noises.

There were other noises as well, deep sounds of outrage all around her, but all Cera knew was the tug on her skirts from behind. Her attacker forced her down, yelling at her, pinning her to the ground, his hot breath on her cheek, a hand on her breast.

Cera screamed, hot white rage flooding through her. She couldn't see, didn't know anything but the weight on top of her, and fury.

She lashed out, bucking the man up and off, rolling, beating, and clawing at his face. Without thought, she kept punching, scratching, pummeling. Maddened, desperate to injure, desperate to hurt him, to prove he was wrong. She *was* enough, *was* good enough, pretty enough, smart enough, damn him! Cera screamed again, lost in a blood-red mist of wildness.

"Easy," a voice spoke close by, an easy rumble. "Easy, girl."

Cera paused and gulped air, raising her fists and looking around wildly for other attackers.

There weren't any. All she saw was the legs of animals and men all around her. Cera blinked up into the light;

one of the wooly horses stared back at her with wide
eyes, floppy ears, and a rabbitlike face.

The rough voice spoke again. "I think he's had
enough, girl. No need for any more now."

Cera looked down.

She was straddling a man, his head rolled to one side,
his eyes closed, his face bloody and beaten. She sucked
in a breath as she saw her own hands, covered in blood.

"It's okay." The voice was closer now. She looked up
again at a broad-shouldered man towering over her.
"Can I help you up?" he asked, as if hesitant to touch her.

Cera nodded and felt a strong hand at her elbow, lifting her to her feet, drawing her slowly away from her
assailant.

"Are you well?" the man asked, keeping his distance
once he had her on her feet. "Did he harm you?"

"No," Cera almost reached to check her hair but
stopped herself at the sight of her hands. "I think . . . it's
his blood."

"Good," the man said. "We are on our way to the
manor house of Sandbriar. We can take him and you to
the Lady and—"

"Cera!" Gareth shouted in the distance. *"Where are
you?"*

"Here," Cera croaked faintly.

"A friend?" the man asked, and at her nod, he bel-
lowed for her. "Here. She's here!"

The sound of galloping hooves approached, and then
a frantic Gareth was in her arms, pale and trembling and
hugging her for all he was worth.

Cera clutched at him just as tightly, shaking in her
own right. Through her tears, she wondered when he had
gotten so much taller than her. "The others?" she asked.

"Guarding the bandits," Gareth blinked away tears as
he pulled back. "We got the best of them, but the one,
the one I struck with the boar spear, he's—" Gareth
gulped, turning paler. "He's dead."

"Oh, Gareth," Cera whispered, and hugged him again.

"Not like killing a boar, is it?" the man asked quietly.

Gareth pulled out of Cera's arms, his eyes hard. "And

who are you?" he asked, suspicion in every line of his body.

"I'm Withen Ashkevron, second son of Lord Ashkevron of Forst Reach." There was no offense in his voice or manner. "We—" He gestured at his companions, who were looking down at the bandit with grim expressions— "We are bringing this herd to Sandbriar at the request of its Lady." Withen frowned. "Seems there's a need here about."

Cera caught her breath. "These are *chirras*?"

"Aye," Withen said. "You know of them?"

"I sent for them," Cera breathed, staring at the animals. Tall, with a longer neck than a horse. Delight rose in her heart at the sight of the animals sniffing at the wildflowers. One of them looked right at her, an oddly familiar blossom trailing from its mouth, bobbing as the animal chewed the stem.

"Lady Cera?" Withen asked.

Suddenly aware of her torn and dusty state, Cera tried to hide her hands in her skirts. "Yes," she said. "You are very welcome, Withen. My thanks for the timely rescue."

Withen smiled. "You didn't appear to need much in the way of rescue, Lady."

"We had them in hand," Gareth said stiffly. "Why did you run? We could've handled all of them."

"My fear got the best of me," Cera said.

"But—" Gareth protested, but Withen interrupted.

"We should see to the Lady," he said gently. "Gather up the living and the dead and continue on. My men will aid you, Gareth. We have water if you wish to clean up, Lady Cera."

"That would be best." Cera glanced at Gareth and saw they had both realized the kind of reception they were going to get from his grandparents.

Gareth and a few of the others headed back along the road, taking a *chirra* to haul the body. Withen's men bound the one at their feet as Withen brought Cera a waterskin and cloths. It was then that she noticed his limp.

Withen noticed her look. "The war," he said shortly. "Tore my knee right up. Healers did their best."

Cera nodded, washing her hands under the stream of water he poured. "The others?" she asked softly.

"All men looking to be needed," he said, his voice just as low. "Not all the injuries are on the outside, Lady Cera."

She glanced up at his pained brown eyes, then looked away. She was embarrassed at her outburst and wondered what she'd said in her madness. "I know that well."

"I suspect you do," he said. And to her relief, he left it at that.

Athelnor and Marga were horrified at what had happened and at the same time thrilled at the arrival of Withen Ashkevron. Once the dead bandits had been buried and the living ones secured, Withen and his men were given a warm welcome and a tour of the manor house. Cera had to keep herself from rolling her eyes as Athelnor asked more questions of Withen's heritage than Cera was comfortable with.

"I was named for a great-great-great-too-many-to-remember grandfather," Withen explained. "But my elder brother is the heir, and well-suited to the position. I was always happier with a plow in my hand rather than a quill pen."

"Well, you are most welcome." Athelnor had hustled himself out of bed to greet them, and now he was sagging with fading energy. "Perhaps Lady Cera will finish the tour." He coughed, looking very pleased with himself.

"I'd be happy to," Cera said, sharing a grin with Withen. She waited until she had closed the door to Athelnor's office. "He is not very subtle, is he?"

"No worse than the matchmakers back home," Withen said.

"Down here is the solar," Cera said. "We are training the young ones to embroider."

"Da said something about that." Withen gestured for her to lead the way. "Afraid it's kinda lost on the Ashkevron men, but the women—"

"Lady Cera." Emerson dashed down the hall toward

them, his arms filled with balls of wool. "You have to help me. These dye lots don't match, and the sky is—" He slid to a halt, staring at them. "Oh, excuse me. I didn't . . ." He trailed off.

"Withen Ashkevron, I'd like you to meet Emerson, second son of one of our neighbors, Lord Cition . . ." Cera started, but then realized that no one was listening to her.

Emerson was blushing. Withen stood blinking. Staring.

Cera paused.

No one said anything.

"Withen and his men brought *chirras*, Emerson. They will be staying for some time, hopefully permanently." Cera looked at Withen. "Emerson is our resident tapestry weaver."

Silence.

"Would you like to see my tapestries?" Emerson blurted.

"Y-Y-Yes," Withen stammered, but hesitated. Then his face hardened, and he stepped forward.

Emerson didn't even blink at Withen's limp. He waited until the other man was even with him, and then headed off, taking a mile a minute about colors, patterns, and his idea for a new design.

Cera blinked, taken aback to be left alone. The look on Emerson's face. It was—

Oh.

Ohhh.

Something deep in her chest relaxed. Cera started to smile.

There'd be assumptions made, but it was fairly clear as she watched Emerson and Withen stammer and avoid each other's gaze, that her newest suitor was not truly sincere.

To her astonishment, she felt only relief. No shame, no offense. Perhaps she needed to admit the truth to herself. She'd no wish to remarry. At least, not right now.

Still, she wouldn't close her heart to the possibility. Nor could she ignore the needs of her people. Part of her honor as Lady of this land was the responsibility to see to her people. To ensure their lives were held in good hands long after her own life had ended.

But that knot in her chest was gone, and she felt lighter somehow. Summer was coming, and with it the potential pleasure of watching young lives come together.

A dance, she thought. A summer dance for all, to celebrate the end of her mourning period and the new season.

Cera smiled, and then turned to go back to Athelnor's office. She'd have him start planning the celebration, something he could do from the comfort of his office.

Then she'd put on her barn boots and go check on her *chirras,* and—

Memory hit then, of her kneeling in the dust with bloody hands, staring at a *chirra* eating a wildflower with a strong, familiar scent.

Cera paused.

She needed to walk her fields.

The *chirras* seemed to enjoy their new home. Cera watched from the barn door as Ager and some of Withen's men checked the animals over carefully.

She wasn't alone. Some of the single women and younger widows were admiring ... well, maybe it wasn't the *chirras* they were looking over.

"Still not sure they'll survive the heat," Old Meroth grumbled. The old shepherd, grizzled and gray, had seen her walking through the yard and hailed her. He sat in his usual spot outside the barn, in the sun, his three elderly sheep dogs at his feet. Even with his right arm lifeless, and the sag to the side of his face, he still ruled the yard.

"The Old Lord's herd had been here years," Old Meroth continued. "They'd gotten used to it. These soft northern ones, they'll die of heat stroke, sure enough."

"We'll care for them," Cera said. She'd already felt through the pelt of one animal, marveling at the triple layered fur, and examined their clawed, dog-like feet. "The others adapted. These will too."

Old Meroth snorted, grumbling under his breath.

Cera straightened away from the doorjamb. "I've a mind to look at that ram," she said. "See if the pizzle rot cleared."

"Young Meroth's off checking the lambs. I'll walk with ya," he said, rising slowly to his feet. "Walk'll do us all good."

His dogs didn't looked like they agreed, but they rose with tails slowly wagging, as if warming to the idea.

They followed the fences, some of which clearly needed attention. Cera mentioned that, more to make a mental note, but it set Old Meroth off on young'uns and their laziness. The dogs were content to walk with them, occasionally slowing to sniff the world. But Cera was watching the side toward the forest too, checking the flowers. Looking for—

"There he be," Old Meroth stopped and leaned on the fence.

The ram was in the clover, tearing at the plants. He lifted his head, grass hanging from his mouth, and observed them calmly as he chewed.

"Wanna check his nethers?" Old Meroth asked, leaning on the fence as the three dogs flopped down in the grass at his feet, panting. "I could have the dogs roust him."

That decidedly did not please the dogs.

"There's no need. The stench would tell us," Cera said absently. She took a deep breath, searching for a familiar, sweeter scent. Of a flower she'd seen dangling from the mouth of a *chirra*.

"Aye, aye," Old Meroth looked over his shoulder as she wandered into a patch of wildflowers. "Lookin' for sumthin' else?"

"Yes." Cera smiled as she bent over. "See this? This green flower? You have to look hard, but here at the center—" She opened the flower with her fingers. "See the deep purple?"

"Aye, it's a weed," Old Meroth grumbled.

Cera pulled a trowel from her bag. "Oh, no, not just a weed." She knelt. "In Rethwellan, it's called wild kandace. Valued for its healing properties."

"Kinda like people sometimes, eh?" Meroth was looking out over the field.

"What?"

"Overlook it, until you see into the heart of them."

Cera sat back on her heels. "Meroth, are you complimenting me?"

"Aye," Meroth said. "But don't be tellin' anyone. Ruin me reputation, it would."

With a laugh, Cera turned back to her work. "I'm going to move this to the herb garden and see if I can—"

"Don't see why," Old Meroth grumbled again. "There's a whole fallow field full of 'em over north of the lambing sheds. I'll walk you there, if you've a mind to."

"A field? Full of them?" Cera rose, and put her trowel away. "Why yes," she said, trying not to laugh out loud. "I've a mind to."

To the Honorable Apothecary Reinwald, Capital of Petras, Kingdom of Rethwellan

Dear Reinwald,

I am going to impose on the friendship between your Trading House and my Father's. I trust that you are aware of the change in my circumstances. Sandbriar has a need for more avenues of trade, and I wished to inquire of you if you ever found another source for that rare herb named wild kandace?

I have a source for dried leaves and flowers, and I plan to use enfluerage to create oils next year. I hope to have a fairly ample supply this fall, and wondered if you had an interest? If so, please let me know, for it would delight me greatly to trade to the benefit of both your House and my Land.

With all respect and great affection,
Lady Cera of Sandbriar,
In the Kingdom of Valdemar

A Herald's Duty
Phaedra Weldon

I'm sorry, Herald Emil, the Queen had written in her missive to him, a rather impersonal response, given his standing as Herald Bard. *Though we are gravely worried about the position and fate of your son, Ferris, all of those capable of riding out in search are busy with their own Circuit or on errands for the throne.*

Emil stared at the messenger, the Healer Phallon and a friend of Ferris. "That's all she had to say?"

Phallon's expression showed the grief he felt. It was one of his failings as a physician and his greatest asset, which lent itself to trust. His patients could always rely on him not to lie or mask the truth. "Emil ... many Heralds on Circuit are sometimes ... out of touch. Other Companions can't find them, but usually there is little cause for alarm. If something happened to Ferris, Syr would let the other Companions know."

"*Something* can happen to *anyone*, and the Companions wouldn't know," Emil protested as he carefully set his lute on his bed. He'd just finished restringing it but hadn't tuned it yet. He was too angry, too ... disappointed. "That doesn't mean I shouldn't worry. I didn't want him going to begin with."

"The Queen commanded it."

"I didn't agree with her decision to send a single Herald." He stared at Phallon with pleading eyes, trying to make sense of it. "The conflict with Karse may be ended, but the war still rages for those who do not know. He went into an area to look into reports of rogue Sun-priests. And though Solaris might have granted them sanctuary, they are corrupt ... they ... might remain ill-informed."

Phallon stepped forward and hesitantly put his hand on Emil's shoulder. "Ever the optimist, even when speaking of a former enemy, eh? The Queen knows all of these things, Emil. But she can't spare anyone at this moment. Word will come soon, and Ferris will be fine."

Emil didn't answer and instead put his hand on Phal-lon's and squeezed it. "I hope you're right."

Phallon returned the squeeze and then removed his hand, turning to leave Emil's rooms. "Oh, and one more thing."

"Yes?"

"She also commands you don't go off on a fool's er-rand to look for him yourself. You are scheduled to per-form during her dinner in a fortnight. She requires your soothing Bardic Gift."

Emil lowered his shoulders. "I understand."

"I hope you do. I will see you at dinner, Emil." With that, Phallon left.

And within an hour, so did the Herald Emil Ains-worth.

The people of Chapel Hill were kind and helpful once they were filled with drink and sweet music. It didn't take much for Emil to set them at ease with his Bardic Gift. A few choice songs, just a slight push in the emotion of the music so they would understand his plight. Some remembered a Herald with good looks and a sweet dis-position. He'd healed a few cuts and scrapes during his stay with them and had asked the same questions about Sunpriests.

Many agreed there had been stories of Sunpriest raids in the area and told him as much. But those had stopped in the past month, before the conflicts with Karse were ended. The town itself had only recently received word of this, and all were surprised.

The barkeep, a rough-looking man who boasted to be

of Karse blood, as were many of the people in south Valdemar, instructed Emil to travel to Lisle and seek out The Wayward Son inn. Ask for Innkeeper Shea Merridens. This was the same instruction he'd given Ferris before he departed.

:Your mood seems much improved,: came the lilting voice of Emil's Companion, Nythil, as they headed down the road to Lisle the next day. The day was cool and pleasant, with birds chirping under the bright sun overhead.

"Aye. But don't let that fool you. I am still worried."

:Ferris and Syr yet live. I can just . . . sense Syr.:

"You can?" he nearly pulled her reins to stop. "In Lisle?"

:No. I sense she isn't speaking for a reason.: Nythil sighed. *:Perhaps we should learn more first?:*

"You sound like Phallon."

:He is a wise man. You should listen to him more often.:

When the village's tallest spire appeared over the trees, Emil released the reins and the direction to Nythil, knowing she would take him where he wanted to go. He pulled his lute from its secure place and made himself comfortable as he began tuning it. He sang now and then, listening to the notes, cringing when they clashed, and adjusting his voice and pitch to accompany the instrument and not drown it out. A Bard's voice and his instrument should work as a team, or the enjoyment is lost for all.

This wasn't something he'd learned during his years at Collegium but something he believed in his heart. He'd been able to pluck a tune from the moment he touched his father's lute. Jasson Ainsworth had been a master at crafting instruments and loved listening to them, but he never had the talent or skill to play them. Even so, he'd been the first to instruct Emil not to shout out lyrics, but to move with them, listen to them, and, most important of all, *feel* them.

Music and song worked as one. Always.

So did he wind this magic as he strolled into Lisle, singing a small dancing song he'd learned on his last

Circuit, which had been ... ten years ago? When he retired from traveling to help raise his son after his wife
passed away. The lyrics were light and made of nonsense,
which brought the curious to him as chores were paused
and work was put aside.

He continued singing with a smile, spreading his mirth
to those who followed his Companion and he to the center of town to a central well. Slipping off Nythil's back as
she bowed to the children who *oooh*ed and *awwww*ed at
her beauty, he stood on the highest of the flagstones surrounding the well and finished the tune with a flourish.

"Sing another one!" came a shout.

"Do you know the one about the Grandfather's
knees?"

"No no, sing that one that's got the wailing ghost!"

:I think you have them.:

He did too, and he held up his hand so the crowd
would quiet and listen. "Please, dear people of Lisle. I
know all these songs and have performed them well.
And though this has been a nice distraction from the day,
chores must be done and work tended too. If there is a
place I might set up to perform this evening, I would play
them and many more."

There was disappointment for a moment, until a
woman's voice rang over them all. "Aye, you have the ear
of my establishment."

He looked to the right as the crowd parted and a
handsome woman, close to his own years, approached.
She wore work leathers and breeches, and her graying
hair was pulled back in a tight knot at her neck.

Emil bowed to her. "And who do I have the honor of
speaking with?" Though he already suspected the name.

"Shea Merridens. And you might be?"

"Herald Emil Ainsworth."

He noticed a few looking at each other. They had
heard this name before.

A new voice spoke up, belonging to an elderly man,
late in years. "There was another Ainsworth here, also a
Herald. Can't recall his name, though."

"Ferris Ainsworth," Emil said. "He is my son. I had

hoped to catch up with him on the road, but alas, I've had no luck." He sensed hesitation in the crowd, not so much as a feeling but by their body movements. The hesitation and nervousness alarmed him, and if he had not already used his Gift to win them over, he might have been instantly shut out.

The elderly man held up his hand and snapped his fingers. "Nice fella. The girls really liked him, and he—"

"He's not here," Shea Merridens said in a calm voice. A smooth interruption.

Emil smiled at her. "Do you know which direction he went? He was on the Queen's orders."

All eyes were on her, and only her.

Interesting.

"I'm afraid I have bad news for you." She put her hands on her hips. "But your son was taken by Sunpriests."

:Hmmm.:

:Don't 'hmmm' me when a stranger says something like that about Ferris. Is she lying?:

:There is a truth within a lie. Don't trust her.:

Emil strummed a few melancholy chromatic notes to relay his sadness to his audience. Several of the men removed their hats in respect. He wasn't sure whether that was good or bad. "But the conflict with Karse is over."

The reaction wasn't what he expected. There wasn't a gasp or even a surprised cry. In fact, he was pretty sure everyone here knew this, even though the town farther north had just learned the news themselves. So Lisle knew before Chapel Hill?

"Aye, it is," Shea said. "But those priests are corrupt devils. They consort with the wicked and steal our food and horses. They don't care to know the truth, nor when they are told, believe it." And as if to make a point, she spit to the side.

Several nods. Hats back on heads.

"So you have told them?"

"We've told the ones we've caught—" said the elderly man, the one who didn't know Ferris' first name.

"Drum." Shea looked at him. "Don't you have something to do?"

He backed down and then backed out of the crowd. Emil made a point of watching where he went as he spoke. "My dear Lady Merridens. I do hope I haven't intruded on bad tidings. But I am very distressed to hear this about my son. May you and I speak in private?"

"Certainly. Please follow me. And about your horse—"

"My Companion." Emil stepped down to find he and Shea stood eye to eye. "She's not a horse."

She looked back at Nythil, the Companion's bright white flank shining like white marble. "If you say so."

"Nythil can take care of herself."

With that he removed his bag and started to remove the saddle.

:Leave that on. I'm going to have a look around the area. You might need it if we have to make a hasty retreat.:

:You think that's warranted?:

:Let's say I'm . . . wary.: And with that she trotted out of the crowed and back through the gate.

"Aren't you worried she'll run off?" asked a small child beside him who'd been staring at Nythil the whole time.

Emil smiled and knelt down beside her. "Companions are Companions for life, little one. She will always return to me, and I to her."

"She's pretty."

:She has good taste.:

Emil made a face. "She *is* pretty, but she does lack humility."

Nythil made a rude noise.

A young man took up the pack Emil removed, and they followed Shea to her inn, just behind the city's main council hall. It was a tavern and an inn, and a few patrons lingered in the bar area as they entered. They raised their tankards to Shea and cheered as she waved at them to stop.

One of them spotted the lute in Emil's hand and begged for a song. Shea told him to come back tonight and ask again. More cheers.

They stepped into a back room with a fireplace, a

large table, a few chairs that had seen better days, and another door. Shea opened the room's only window beside the door, and Emil assumed it led outside, perhaps to an alley. She gave the young man a key and a number and told him to put the Bard's bag in the room.

While he was away, she grabbed a pitcher and two cups and set them on the table. "I'm sorry I had to be the one to tell you about your son."

"You say this as if he were dead."

She sat down, and he took a seat facing her, the table between them. "Once the priests take you, you don't come back."

"Why would they take a Herald?"

"Magic," she said as she filled each cup with drink. He wasn't sure what it was, but he didn't like the smell. "They hate all magic. Claim it's devil's work, and yet they summon devils themselves." She looked at him but didn't drink. "I'm sure they burned him."

"And his Companion?"

"Companion—he had a horse like yours?"

:She sounds genuine. It is possible Ferris kept Syr away from the town.:

:Yes . . . but, why?:

"Yes, he did. My Companion would know if something happened to Ferris. I'm more than sure he's alive."

"Not for much longer." Emil gave her a sharp look. "It's been four days since he disappeared. I'm sure he'll be dead soon."

He licked his lips. He had his lute in his hand and sat back, strumming. "Tell me about these Sunpriests. You said they stole your food and your horses?"

The slight touch of his Gift was subtle enough that he saw her relax. A little. "They came up from Menmellith about two months ago. I heard talk of them hitting the outer settlements. They came to take us back to Karse."

"Us . . . you are a Karsite?"

"Most of us are, or our parents are or were. Not all of us are magic; some just came with those who possessed it. I'm familiar with it. My mother had Foresight but was never properly trained."

"She could have gone to Haven—"

"No. She did her duty and stayed here and protected our town." She looked at the table. "I don't have the Gift, so I can't see when trouble is coming. But when I heard of the Sunpriests nearby, I did what I had to do."

Emil stopped strumming. "And what was that?"

Shea didn't answer. Instead she stood and nodded to the cups and pitcher. "Drink. Relax. Tonight, you will play. And maybe by tomorrow, you will know of your son's fate." With that parting shot, she left the room.

Emil sat forward, shaken, but determined more than ever now to find Ferris and solve what had become a dangerous mystery.

Nearly an hour passed before Emil found the elderly man Shea called Drum. He was inside the local Healing House, surrounded by books and thick reading glasses, along with all manner of drying herbs, glass bottles, and several sizes of mortar and pestles. He appeared to be looking for something on a shelf when Emil approached him and cleared his throat.

The man jumped with a short bark and turned to face him. He narrowed his eyes, and it was then that Emil saw the whiteness in one of them. The man was half-blind.

"I'm sorry ... but I'm not seeing anyone today."

"It's me, good sir. Emil? We met in the square."

The man looked confused, then his expression changed. "Oh, yes. You've spoken to Merridens. Please ... be gone with you." He turned away.

"Yes, I have spoken with her, and she gave me distressing news about my son, remember? The Sunpriests took him?" Emil walked around the room so he could see the man's face. "You know Ferris."

"Yes," the elderly man answered. "I am called Drum. Your son ... very Gifted. And his horse, quite the beauty."

Emil gave up on correcting people about the horse misconception. "When was the last time you saw him?"

"As was said ... he left five ... maybe four days ago."

"Left ... but Shea said he was taken."

"Shea has her own truth." Drum looked around as if he'd said something bad and someone was listening. He gestured for Emil to come close. "You have to talk quietly here. We don't want the Sunpriests to hear." He put his hands on a loosely made line of vials and picked up each one in order, from left to right.

Emil had worked enough with Healers to identify certain medicines, herbs, and roots. He came closer and put his hand on Drum's. "May I see those vials? Can you put them back the way you took them?"

He watched as Drum did so, and Emil recognized the markings on the bottles themselves. "These are some rather dangerous powders, Drum."

"Yes, they are. Put together in the order I have them, from left to right, they make a very good common remedy for lots of things. I don't see as well as I used to, so I put them here like this so I know how to put them together."

Emil focused on one vial in particular and another vial just behind it. The one behind was an all-purpose crushed herb, but the one in front was a poison. If this ingredient were added, it would make a potion that would cause a slow death. "Drum—" he began.

But Drum was already talking. " . . . Always like this, you know. Before the Sunpriests came, we lived in relative peace and quiet. But something happened, you see, and Shea's never recovered. It hardened her . . . and I wish . . . I always wished I could have helped."

Emil removed the vial of poison and pushed the healing vial forward. "What happened, Drum?"

"Shea's daughter, she was a sweet and lovely child, she had a fever . . . it was just before your son came to us. I put together the medicine . . ." he looked at Emil with a stricken face. "And she died."

Emil put his hand to his face. "Did . . . was her death slow?"

"It was terrible," Drum said, and he wiped his eyes. "The Sunpriests had raided us a few days before. They were hitting us every week, it seemed. Stole fabric, clothing, came in here and stole medicine and books . . ." He sighed. "They took food from the inn and things from people's rooms. Word was sent to the Queen—" he shook his head. "But then little Jenita died, and everyone was so sad."

"Shea blamed the Sunpriests."

"Yes." Drum looked away. "It was after Ferris came and helped me straighten everything out that the raids stopped. A few of the Sunpriests came into town, but they died. They were struck down with the same malady that killed little Jenita. Shea called it justice. Their bodies were burned."

Emil stepped back as he started putting some very terrible pieces together. "And Ferris?"

"He was horrified when they burned the bodies. Argued with Shea, and then he . . . just wasn't here anymore. Shea said the Sunpriests took him, so it was time to cull the rest of them."

"And?"

"No one's seen a priest in a while. Sorry about your son . . . I'm sure he wanted to help them, and they killed him."

Emil doubted that very much. In fact, he was pretty sure he knew where his son was. "Drum—"

:I found Syr!:

He stopped in midsentence and put his hand to his temple. *:And Ferris?:*

:I'm coming to get you. Meet me at the front gate!:

"Are you feeling well, Emil?"

"Yes, yes I'm fine. I think I'm going to rest before tonight's performance. Please . . . do come to the inn tonight?"

"I will. I enjoyed what you did before."

With the vial in his hand, Emil left the House of Healing and headed straight for the gate, making sure he kept close to the village walls and their shadows, so no one could see him. Once he was with Nythil, they rode like the wind southeast of Lisle.

At first, Emil thought Nythil was wrong as she trotted through a dense area of the forest and then stopped along a brook. The low branches blocked out most of the sun, creating a twinkling effect overhead. Flowers grew in abundance, tickling Emil's nose as he dismounted and took a look around, hands on his hips. "I'm not really sure . . ." he whispered.

"Father!"

The sound of Ferris' voice banished all doubt and sadness from his heart. He turned to see his son standing beside a tree—no, he was leaning heavily against it!

Emil ran to his son and caught him before he fell forward. Ferris was warm in his arms—too warm. He was feverish and shaking. "Ferris? What's wrong? Did the Sunpriests hurt you?"

"Sun . . ." Ferris's dark brows drew together over his bright blue eyes, now dulled with fever. "The Sunpriests?" Then he laughed. "There aren't any Sunpriests. Not here. There never were."

"I'm . . . I don't understand."

There was a movement beside him and Emil looked up to see Syr come into view. She looked a bit worn herself, her coat not as shiny and white. Worry swirled in her indigo eyes, and she dipped her head, nudging Ferris's foot. His Whites were soiled and showed wear and tear.

"What's going on?" Emil asked. "Why are you ill?"

"My malady isn't as life threatening as theirs, Father." He swallowed and made an attempt to stand on his own. He managed it after two tries and then reached out for the tree once again. "In the cave there, are . . . were . . . three families. All escaped from Karse, coming from Menmellith. They started with fifteen in their group, hoping to come to Valdemar for a new life."

"Magic?"

"*Was* . . . of the families, two possessed Gifts. One had the ability to Heal to a much greater extent than me. The other, the oldest of the three fathers, had just a bit of Fetching. Not very strong, but enough to pull or push a cart out of the way when he really tried. Of course, the effort exhausted him. Smaller things were easier. I can only retell the tale I was given, I'm afraid. They are both dead." Ferris put his hand on his Companion's nose as she nuzzled his side. His dark hair was in disarray and hung over his brow. "Poisoned."

Immediately Emil thought of Drum. "The innkeeper, a woman named Shea—"

"Merridens," Ferris finished the name with a sneer. "Insisted there were Sunpriests raiding them. They stole things—attacked townspeople. I know. That's why I was sent here, remember?" He coughed and gave his father a smile. "They were starving and came to ask for food. They met with the local Healer first, who told them to speak with Merridens. But she denied them anything. She recognized their clothing, knew they were from Karse, and sent them away."

"That's ... when they started stealing."

"Small things at first, yes. To survive. Halided, the father with Fetching, was good at remaining unseen as he pulled and pushed things to his children. He made a game of it, to cheer them up. They took materials from a few of the merchants, the ones who routinely ripped up surplus, and from Merridens' inn. They didn't steal her pantry stuffs, Father. They stole what she left out." He closed his eyes. "Until they started getting sick."

Emil tightened his jaw.

"The children succumbed first, and the Healer could mend or fix physical breaks. But not internal illnesses, not like that. Shortness of breath, sweats, lack of appetite. They couldn't eat or drink water ... they needed medicine."

"So they stole from Drum."

"Aye. They were able to take some before one of them was caught. He was only twenty, with no magic and no intent to harm, only to help. He was killed and buried in the woods by some of the villagers; Shea told them he was a Sunpriest. But then Shea's daughter became ill, and she brought her to see Drum. Drum gave her medicine ... but she died within twenty-four hours." He sighed. "I came too late ..." Ferris looked at his father, the rims of his eyes red. "All of this had occurred, and I only had what Drum and Shea said. That the Sunpriests had brought their demons with them and her child had died."

:You know the truth, don't you?: Nythil said.

Emil nodded. "She wasn't wrong . . . but she wasn't right, was she?"

Ferris looked away. "When Tikal, the young man who made the last run for the medicine, took what he thought he needed, he . . . messed up Drum's order. Drum can't see that well . . ."

"And he had his vials set out to make his potion."

Ferris nodded.

Emil reached into his robes and retrieved the vial. "This is what he made the medicine with."

Ferris took the vial and looked at the marking. "Yes, but . . . where did you get this?"

"It was on Drum's shelf, and it wasn't where it should be."

"Then she's still doing it!" Ferris hissed.

Emil touched his son's arm. "Son . . ."

"She's poisoned them, don't you see? Shea was poisoning the scraps, knowing these people were taking them. When I saw that vial and read the contents, I started asking questions. I found out they only took medicine after Shea realized they were stealing from her . . . stealing refuse!" He took his father's arm. "I found dead animals in the woods, Father. Animals that had also fed from the tossed food. She poisoned them, and they came looking for medicine that should have been freely given."

Emil closed his eyes. *:And inadvertently caused the accidental poisoning of Shea's own daughter by moving Drum's medicine around.:*

:Yes.:

It was a tragedy within a tragedy, and if Emil had the gift of writing a song he would. He doubted he could put into words the sorrow he felt. The uselessness of what had happened.

"Does Shea even know why her daughter died?"

"I tried to tell her," Ferris said. "After I found them here and heard their story. But she wouldn't listen to me. She gave me fresh water for them and refused to believe me. Told me I was no longer welcome if I was going to help the Sunpriests." He shook his head. "I'm such a trusting fool, Father. She poisoned the food . . ."

Emil's eyes widened. He shifted onto his knees and took his son by the shoulders. "She put something in the water?"

"Yes. Luckily only I drank it. I poured it out when I noticed the taste, but not before I'd had enough to take hold. I know the poison, I know what she combined. The remedy is with Drum. But I haven't the strength to ride into town and fight for it."

"Well, I do." Emil stood and helped his son to his feet. "You'll ride with me on Nythil. Syr can follow behind—"

"No, Father. I can't leave them."

Emil looked around when his son nodded to something behind him. There, standing only a few feet away, were four children, ranging in ages from twelve to perhaps seven. The youngest had her finger in her mouth, her other hand clutching the hand of a boy who was probably her brother. Emil gasped and looked back at his son, understanding everything now. "They're . . . they're all that's left?"

Ferris nodded. "I was able to take just enough medicine to heal only a few. They voted to save the children."

Emil looked at the children. How long had it been since they had bathed, or had a decent meal? "I'll be back with medicine and food, Ferris. You'll get well, and then we'll take the children and leave this place. I have to tell the Queen what's happened."

"The Queen has more pressing troubles now, Father." Ferris smiled. "As Herald, I have the power to address this grievance myself and to right it. These children, and their parents, were not priests. They were just refugees, fighting to survive." He looked at the children. "Abandoned and forgotten."

A plan, a decision was made in Emil's mind, and approved by his Companion. He wasn't sure how much of it was his and how much was Nythil's. Either way, he needed to get back to Lisle. The sun was setting, and it would be dark by the time he arrived.

He gave his son a hug, then gave him what few sup-

plies he had, including a few apples he'd been saving for
Nythil. "Rest, be ready." With a last look at the children,
he tousled the hair on the oldest and mounted Nythil.

The waning moon was high when Emil came into the
side gate of Lisle. The guard there seemed happy to see
him, explaining that Merridens had been looking for him
and wanted a report the moment he returned.

"Did she say why?"

"I assumed because the tavern's crowded—they really
want you to play. I think everyone in town is there."

Emil cursed in his mind.

:You could use this to your advantage.:

He looked at his Companion. *:Oh? Do tell?:*

After Nythil explained the advantage, Emil smiled
and put a hand on the guard's arm. "Yes, I am indeed to
play for your wonderful town. But I do need a few favors
beforehand—think of it as a surprise. Do you think you
could help me?"

"I'd be honored—but shouldn't I tell Miss Merridens?"

"Oh, no, no. That would ruin the surprise!" Emil gave
the guard a list of things he needed, and the guard assured him he could have everything in a half-hour. Emil
made plans to meet him back at the gate at that time.

Nythil remained outside the gate, trying to be as in-
conspicuous as possible, which could be difficult for a
bright white Companion. Emil headed to the Healing
House and found the powders his son needed. Once he
had everything neatly and securely packed into a canvas
bag, he returned to the gate.

The guard showed up just before time, with two packs
in tow. Emil checked the contents. "And you're sure
these did not come from the inn? Wouldn't want to spoil
the surprise."

"Positive."

"Good man." Emil strapped the packs and the medicine to Nythil's back and kissed her neck. *:Be careful.:*

:You as well. I have the easy part in this.: And she took
off into the night.

"Did your horse just run away?" The guard looked and sounded surprised.

"No. She's finishing an errand. Now," he patted the guard's back. "I have a performance to give."

"Where were you?" Shea asked in a low whisper after Emil entered the tavern to cheers and raised tankards. He'd changed into his performance clothing. His graying hair, held back in its silver band, added to the colors that made his blue eyes stand out.

"I went looking for my son," he said as he removed his lute from its wrapping. More cheers.

"And?" Her eyes widened.

"Listen and learn," he said as he waved at the crowd.

Emil sat on a stool set out by the hearth and tuned quickly before he jumped right into his old repertoire of bawdy tavern songs. The mood in the room joined in raucous laughter and cheer, in camaraderie and happiness. When he was done with the list, he could feel them united, their prejudices and petty differences put away. They were ready. Primed.

Even Shea Merridens, whose previous apprehension seemed to have dissolved.

"Now, if you will all indulge me," he returned quickly as he spoke. "I have an old song—the first one I learned when I started my lessons at the Collegium. Many of the songs we're taught there are in themselves parables. Teaching songs. Stories set to rhythm and verse. Since it's been . . ." he rolled his eyes, "a very long time since I played," laughter from the audience, "I'd like to play it once again."

"What's it called?" said one of the patrons.

"A Herald's Duty." Emil began picking the strings with his fingers and then closed his eyes as the tune flowed from his heart, to his fingers, and through the music.

The song spoke of an injured man on the road, his clothing filthy, his body covered in sores and festering wounds. Those traveling the road recognized him as a thief and moved away from him.

Several travelers saw him and refused to help. First

was a merchant whose wares this man had taken. The second, an innkeeper whose food he had stolen. And the third a Healer whose medicines he'd removed.

There was a fourth man, a Herald, who also recognized the man as someone who'd stolen his lute. His emotions at the loss of his most valuable possession ran high, but as a Herald, the Queen had tasked him with the highest of priorities. The Kingdom and her subjects, first. Know and exhibit kindness, forgiveness, and charity.

So the Herald turned back and helped the man—and thus learned the truth.

The man had a family, deep in the woods, but had no job, no means of making the coin to provide. So he'd stolen the merchant's cast off fabrics so his wife could sew their daughter clothing to keep warm. He took the scraps thrown out by the innkeeper to feed his wife and child. And when his daughter became sick from the rotting scraps, he stole medicine from the Healer to make her well.

"'And what of my lute?' the Herald asked." Emil sang to an enraptured audience. He looked up to see the door open behind Shea. The innkeeper stepped aside as Ferris, pale and slow-moving, but already looking better, guided the four children into the tavern.

The audience looked in puzzlement at the children and then back at Emil, who finished: "'I took the lute so my child could sing.'" He ran through an emotional riff of notes before he looked at them all and said, "Before you stands what is left of the alleged Sunpriests, people of Lisle."

Ferris stepped forward, and to Emil's surprise, Drum stood and joined him as he addressed the people. Ferris told of the plight of three families, their need addressed to the innkeeper, the merchant, and the Healer. Of how their parents stole to protect their families.

And how the food taken from the inn was poisoned.

All the while Emil played his lute, keeping the emotions even as revelation could sometimes be volatile.

And when Ferris was done, and Emil ended the song, the people stood and surrounded the children. They spoke to them, hugged them, and then as a group, took them away from the inn until all that was left was Shea, and Drum.

Emil put his lute away and joined his son, giving him a hug.

"I—I didn't know ..." Shea said, her voice faint and shaken. "I was so angry at my daughter's death ..."

Did she understand her true role in her daughter's end? Emil didn't know. He made the decision to leave things as they were now and guided his son out of the inn. Drum followed them, and together they walked into the House of Healing.

But it would take much more than what the Heralds could do for the village of Lisle.

It would take compassion, forgiveness, and time.

Woven Threads of Love and Honor

Dayle A. Dermatis

Her boots crunching with every step, Syrriah carefully picked her way across the hard-packed snow covering the path between the stables and Heralds' Collegium. It was cold enough to snatch her breath away. The heavy wool coat she wore over her Trainee Grays protected her from the worst of the chill, along with the knit cap pulled low on her head, the scarf wound around her neck and face, and the fur-lined deerskin gloves.

Yesterday the weather had warmed slightly, and then the temperature had dropped again last night, leaving everything covered with a slick sheen. After weeks of gray skies, the sun had come out today, and she squinted, half-blinded, against the glittering world of white while carefully placing each foot before moving forward.

At her age, a fall would take time to recover from. Not that she was old, exactly, but nearing fifty years meant her body just didn't heal as fast from injuries, and her hip was already bothering her anyway. Still, in less than a year since she'd been Chosen, her body had changed, thanks to the physical practice required of a Herald Trainee. She'd always been active, although in her previous life as the lady of a manor holding, she hadn't had much need for intense physical labor. The challenges here had brought her to a new level, and she'd become more toned, gained more stamina and strength. The new curve of muscle at the back of each arm was a revelation.

The winter air was crisp and clear, carrying murmurs and occasional shouts from the students streaming in from different directions: the dormitories, the stables, the salle. Syrriah could still smell the warm, comforting, horsey scent of her Companion, Cefylla. (Not that Cefylla would ever stand for being referred to as a horse; Companions might be horse-shaped, but they were so very much more.) She'd lingered too long with Cefylla, making sure her mash had been warmed, running the currycomb over her coat, and just . . . *being*.

With Cefylla, she never felt lonely.

Ahead, Syrriah saw her daughter Natalli, her head tucked so close to her friend Keliana's that their hair seemed to mingle, blond curls with short, dark brown waves. Her son Benlan was also there, striding without fear of slipping in a group of three other boys, laughing. She resisted the urge to call out to them. They would always and forever be her children, but here they were fellow Herald-Trainees.

Both had made every attempt to welcome their mother when Syrriah arrived, still stunned to be Chosen at her age, after the full life she'd led. But she didn't want to get in their way. They already had friends, habits, lives here, and so Syrriah had gently declined invitations to sit with them at meals or otherwise keep company with them. She might be a fellow Trainee, but her age made socializing with the other students awkward for them and her.

She reached the wide, double-doored entrance to the Heralds' Collegium and filed inside with the rest of the students. The hallway echoed with the sound of snow being stamped off boots and called farewells as friends split to go into different classrooms.

Syrriah and Natalli shared more than one class; this one was a review of the current political climate of Valdemar in relation to the neighboring countries as well the various regions within the kingdom itself.

The bright morning sun streamed through the tall windows. The room was warm from a well-stoked fire, and students left their outerwear in relatively neat piles by the door, making the room smell faintly of sheep, sweet and comforting, and smoke, sharp and comforting.

Syrriah's curriculum at Collegium was different from the other students', thanks to her age and circumstances. She didn't need basic instruction in subjects such as etiquette, logic, or even history, except for the most recent history being touched on in this class, the events that had been happening in Valdemar since her husband had died and she'd stepped down from running Traynemarch Reach. She hadn't ignored the news coming from around the kingdom, but she'd paid it less mind.

Her studies now were more focused on the gaps in her education, the things she hadn't needed as the lady of a manor: upper-level law, survival skills, weapons, some of the finer points of judgment as it related to a Herald's job of handling disputes as the voice of the Queen. In some cases, she was allowed to do an independent study, mentored by a teacher and researching in the Library.

But for now, politics.

Syrriah's head was bent over her notes when a rustle and murmur cascaded through the room.

A third-year student, standing in the doorway, said the Dean of the Collegium wished to speak to Keliana.

Two rows in front of Syrriah, Natalli, eyes wide, put a hand on Keliana's arm. Syrriah watched as Keliana shook her head, gently touched Natalli's hand, and pulled her arm away.

Her face pale, Keliana rose, nodded to the teacher, and kept her eyes straight forward as she turned and walked to join the third-year, while the rest of the classroom sat in silence, watching her go.

Waves of apprehension and concern poured out of Natalli, so much so that Syrriah had to raise her internal shields to block the emotion. Six months ago, she hadn't known how to do that, and she was gratified that it came easily now, automatic and swift. The skill of blocking out emotions was almost more important than sensing them for an Empath.

She knew Natalli and Keliana were friends, but the depth of Natalli's concern surprised her.

Keliana, an unaffiliated student well on her way to becoming an Artificer, was a whip-smart girl, from what Syrriah had seen. Rather serious, rarely laughing . . . although when she did smile, her blue eyes shone with light.

Once Keliana and her escort were gone, the room buzzed with whispers again, until the instructor called for order and went back to the current lesson.

Syrriah found it hard to concentrate, knowing her daughter was upset. Natalli clearly had known something was wrong even before the third-year had come to collect Keliana.

And Keliana had walked out of the room as though she were being led to the gallows.

Syrriah's Empath Gift was new to her, having broken free in her head less than six months ago, like a dam bursting, and only the support of her Companion, Cefylla, had kept her from being swept away with it.

She'd learned to shield, but not with her own children. Never, she thought, with her children.

She would never pry into their personal thoughts or feelings, but she would always be available if they needed help. She was, after all, a mother first and foremost, before she'd been Chosen, and being Chosen didn't change her love for her children.

It was a strange situation to be in, really: to have been Chosen when she was solidly in middle age, after a full (if unremarkable in comparison) life as the Lady of Traynemarch Reach, after all four of her children had been Chosen, after her husband had died, too young and much missed, just as they had been considering retiring and passing the work of running the manor and holdings to Syrriah's sister.

Strange—and wonderful—to forge the bond with dear Cefylla.

Only the Companions knew how or why someone was Chosen, and that wasn't information they shared or explained. If Syrriah was to have a whole new life as a Herald-Trainee and someday a Herald, it was not for her to question.

Her Empath Gift might have had something to do with it.

And now that gift, along with a mother's intuition, showed her that Natalli was deeply unhappy. It didn't take any special gift to know that her unhappiness had something to do with Keliana.

Information traveled fast in a small, enclosed space like a school, and it took only a few hours for the gossip to solidify into fact: Keliana had been caught cheating.

All students, whether Herald Trainees or unaffiliated, were held to a high standard of honor. Keliana likely would be expelled.

Syrriah knocked on her daughter's door. The other students sitting on the floor in the hallway had fallen silent when she arrived. She knew some of them—a few even smiled a greeting—but they all watched unspeaking as Natalli opened the door.

The fine blond hairs that had pulled out of her braid wisped into a halo from the static of pulling off her knit cap. That she hadn't smoothed them down spoke volumes to Syrriah. Her pretty daughter, while practical and efficient and not prone to affectation, was normally fastidious.

She had dark circles under her eyes, too, like bruises marring her naturally pale skin, and her mouth was thin, drawn. Syrriah wondered how much she noticed because of her Empathic Gift, and how much simply because she was, now and forever, a concerned mother.

Natalli glanced past her to the common room, then held her door open so Syrriah could enter.

Herald-Trainees' rooms all had the same furniture: bed, wardrobe, desk, bookcase. Natalli had decorated hers with some pictures her older sister, a full Herald currently riding Circuit, had drawn. Syrriah had some of her own; Riann was a talented artist who frequently used her family as models in her sketches.

A woven rug brightened the room with its reds, yellows, and blues. Syrriah had made it for her daughter when she was a baby, and she was glad Natalli had brought it with her.

Natalli's coat was a crumpled heap on the floor. Syrriah automatically picked it up and hung it on a peg by the door. When she turned back, her daughter said, "I'm studying; I have a logic test coming up. So . . ."

"I just wanted to make sure you were all right," Syrriah said.

"I'm fine," Natalli said, even though everything from her body language to her tone of voice said otherwise. Her chin was jutted, as if she was daring her mother to contradict her.

"You're worried about your friend; that's not only understandable but commendable," Syrriah said gently.

"She's innocent!" The words burst from Natalli.

"The honor extends to everyone, including instructors," Syrriah said. "You believe she's being accused unjustly? Is there proof?"

"They say there is."

"What does Keliana say?"

Natalli scowled. "She isn't saying anything. But that's not your problem, Mother." She gestured at the book open on her desk. "I really do have to study."

There was a time, not so long ago, when Natalli would have poured her heart out to her mother. That she didn't now, hurt.

Or maybe it was something else—something more?

"Natalli . . ." But no. She couldn't say what she was thinking, because if she was wrong, her daughter would be devastated. So Syrriah pushed her fears aside and said simply, "You know I'm here if you need me. I want only the best for you."

"I know, Mother. Thank you." Natalli submitted to a hug, but her entire body was tense.

And Syrriah left, her heart heavy, more concerned than she'd been when she arrived.

*   *   *

Her next stop was Benlan's room. He was in the common area with some of his yearmates, and unlike Natalli, he didn't feel the need to speak in private. He also was more willing to hug his mother, although she felt a hint of embarrassment from him.

His head was nearly at the same level as hers. When had he grown so tall? How had she not realized? He was still slender, lanky, the rest of his body not quite caught up with his height.

It would soon, though, she knew. He wouldn't be a boy much longer.

"I don't want to get involved," he said, holding up his hands, when she asked. "Natalli's business is her own. None of us really know Keliana, either," he added, indicating the other boys sitting in chairs or on woven rugs in front of the fire.

They were a year apart, but at this age, a year could be a chasm.

"I know her sister, Keysa," one of them said. "She's nice, and she says Keliana is the best sister a girl could have."

"Keliana gave me good advice when I came here," another boy said. "I was homesick, and she noticed and talked to me. I'm fine now," he added when another boy scoffed at him, and he genially hit the scoffer with a pillow, no malice behind it.

Boys expressing their friendship; Syrriah was familiar with it.

"I'm just worried about her," Syrriah said. "She seems to be taking Keliana's situation personally."

"She's a *girl*," Benlan said, brushing the hair out of his eyes. "They take everything personally."

The others chorused their agreement of the blanket statement. They'd be men soon, yes, but for now they were still children, and girls—even their sisters and friends—were like a different species to them.

"Does Natalli's Companion have anything to say about this?" Syrriah asked Cefylla as she walked back to her own room.

:Nothing he's willing to share, dove,: Cefylla said. *:It's a private matter.:*

"Of course; I wasn't prying," Syrriah said.

:No, you weren't,: Cefylla agreed with warmth. *:You're understandably concerned about Natalli. I'm sorry I cannot help.:*

If there was an emergency, Syrriah trusted that the message would be shared; the Companions would never allow their Chosen to be harmed if they could help it.

Syrriah spent a restless night, the concerns tossing and turning in her head almost as much as she tossed and turned in her bed. She'd always told her children when they worried about something that the problem would seem smaller in the light of day, but when she finally slept, she woke still chewing on the problem.

Keliana wouldn't be sent home just yet; the weather was too harsh for her to safely travel.

Syrriah told herself that if Keliana was innocent, as Natalli insisted, then she'd need an advocate.

She told herself she was helping Keliana, even though she knew she also wanted to understand Natalli's reaction.

She soon found out there were quite a few people willing to advocate for Keliana.

Although many of Natalli and Keliana's friends were wary of speaking with an adult, the fact that Syrriah was Natalli's mother helped pave the way for her. To a certain extent, anyway.

Those students genuinely praised Keliana, swearing to her kind nature, her honor, her commitment. Everyone attested to her commitment to learning, her love of education, and Syrriah heard story after story of Keliana going out of her way to help other students, especially new arrivals.

Yet they all hesitated about . . . something. Something that apparently had to do with Natalli—and that was where being Natalli's mother was a hindrance rather than a help.

Syrriah had trouble believing Natalli could have

anything to do with the cheating, but the tiniest hint of concern crept in, no matter how hard she fought to keep it out. Concern . . . and guilt for even thinking it.

But if not that, then what was Natalli and the other students unwilling to talk to her about?

There was only one with whom she could share her fears: Cefylla.

"I feel as if I'm betraying her even by thinking it," she fretted. Even as a small child, Natalli had taken the concepts of right and wrong very seriously. Syrriah remembered Brant, her husband, having to teach Natalli the idea that nobody was perfect all the time.

:There's something, clearly,: Cefylla said. *:But you know Natalli's Companion would never stand for her cheating.:*

Syrriah felt a glimmer of hope. "That's true," she said. "But if not that, then what?"

Even at a distance, she sensed Cefylla's shrug. They both knew Syrriah hadn't expected an answer to her question.

What bothered her most, really, was that she felt more distant from her children than she had when they'd been Chosen and left Traynemarch Reach for Haven. Her loving, trusting daughter had pulled away from her, hiding her misery instead of asking for help or comfort, and her son . . . she barely recognized him now.

She hoped they knew she would do anything for them.

The only physical thing Syrriah truly missed at Collegium was her loom.

When she was the most homesick, she'd go down to the weaving studio where they made the cloth to clothe the Heralds and students—gray for the Herald-Trainees and white for the Heralds, rust-brown for the Bardic-Trainees and red for the Bards, pale green for the Healer-Trainees and dark green for the Healers, and blue for unaffiliated students.

The looms were larger than the ones she'd had at the manor at Traynemarch Reach.

Syrriah's old looms had been only wide enough for her to pass the shuttle from one hand to the other. Here, the looms were so wide that younger students were employed to shoot the shuttle through the shed—the separation between the two layers of thread created when the weaver raised and lowered the heddles.

This created wider fabric, which in turn meant patterns were easier to cut out and assemble.

Syrriah missed weaving the intricate tapestry designs she'd been known for in her area, but she still found the simple repetition of weaving the plain fabric soothing, meditative. It was her best time to think.

The clunk of the heddles, the swish as the shuttle slipped between the threads, all created a peaceful rhythm. The threads were fine, soft, expertly spun without slubs, the random thick areas that could occur if the spinner wasn't proficient. Syrriah was equally impressed by the dyers, who managed to create the same shades of color every time.

She let her mind wander as she raised and lowered the heddles, as she tamped down each row of weft. The more she pondered, the more she was sure she was missing something.

She was probably missing something because her mind kept circling around to her own children, rather than focusing on Keliana.

The threads that wove everyone together, one tapestry. She loved her children. Benlan loved his sister, even if he chose not to get involved in whatever was going on. Natalli cared for her friend Keliana. And Keliana . . .

Syrriah gradually became aware of silence in the room. The two children who'd been shooting the shuttle back and forth were staring at her, patiently waiting for her to continue. Without being aware of it, she'd stopped weaving.

She thanked the children as she rose from the stool.

She had to talk to the Dean of the Collegium.

It was another brutally cold and bright day. The sun glinted off the snow to a degree that made Syrriah's head ache. She squinted as she moved carefully between the buildings of Collegium. The icy air bit through the layers of clothing she wore.

At her knock, Dean Elcarth rose from his desk and came around to greet Syrriah, telling her to hang her coat on an already overflowing rack by the door. A crackling fire warmed the room, and she stood by it for a moment, savoring the feeling of the heat returning to her bones.

Elcarth's office seemed small because it was crowded with a large desk, piles of books, a large slate board and bowl with pieces of chalk, and several chairs. A row of herbs in pots on the windowsill gave a fresh scent to what would have been an otherwise stuffy room. Syrriah had been here once before, to present her project to help the solitary students who eschewed crowds, a project the Dean had endorsed. She suspected that was why he'd agreed to speak with her on the current matter.

He was a tiny, gray-haired, elderly man with a surprising energy; he reminded her of a bright, observant bird, taking in everything around him through bright black eyes and processing it swiftly. He was also, in her experience, patient and thoughtful.

"Yes, I'd heard you were asking questions about Keliana," he said when she'd broached the subject. "If it had been anyone else, we might have put a stop to it, but given your other work with the students, I was rather curious to see where you were going with this."

"I appreciate that," Syrriah said sincerely. "Everyone has said Keliana is intelligent, kind, helpful—a model student."

"Other than this incident, I agree with you wholeheartedly. Her parents frequently write to ask about her progress—almost too frequently." He rolled his dark eyes ever so slightly. "But it's always been my pleasure to tell them how well she's doing and that they should be proud of her. I can only assume they are, given their attentiveness."

The Collegium had sent reports about her children, but Syrriah had never asked for additional information, trusting the missives she'd received. It hadn't meant she was anything less than proud, though.

She refocused on the current issue. "Were there any other indications Keliana was cheating, any other dishonorable behavior?"

He shook his head. "No, but she will neither defend nor explain her actions."

"May I ask how she cheated? What exactly did she do?"

He leaned back in his chair and considered. Then he leaned forward again. "She was found in Herald Lurias's office, looking at a test he had prepared."

Syrriah hadn't taken any classes from Lurias, but she knew who he was; most of his subjects were for the younger students, subjects she hadn't needed instruction in.

That fact solidified her suspicion.

"Was Keliana taking any classes from Lurias?" she asked.

Elcarth sat back again, this time with surprise and then clarity shaping his expression. "I . . . don't believe so."

"Was her sister, Keysa?"

A slow nod. "I believe she was."

"And how is Keysa doing in *her* studies?"

He drew a deep breath in through his nose. "Like Keliana, she's very bright. She does very well, but . . . she's solidly in the middle of her classes, I would say."

"Not in danger of being asked to leave because of poor performance?"

"Not at all. She's a fine student, just not a remarkable one."

They didn't have to discuss the proposition that lay in the air between them: that Keliana had been looking at the test for Keysa's benefit.

"Well," the Dean said thoughtfully, the word rolling in his light voice, "I think we need to speak with Keliana again."

"No," Syrriah said quickly, and then realized she'd spoken as if he were her peer, which despite the relative closeness of their ages (closer to her than the average student, to be sure), he wasn't. She flushed. "I'm sorry. I'd like the opportunity to speak with her. I think she might be more willing to open up to me, because I'm not an authority figure. My daughter is also a good friend of hers, so . . ."

"This is very unusual," Dean Elcarth said.

Syrriah smiled. "I'm a very unusual Trainee."

In the end, he agreed.

Natalli was less agreeable.

"I'd hoped you'd stay out of this," she said.

"I'm on Keliana's side," Syrriah said. "I think I know what happened, and if she's willing to tell the truth, her place here at the Collegium may be reinstated."

Natalli chewed on her lip, a habit she'd recently picked up, if the chapped condition of her mouth was any indication. "I'll ask her if she'll speak with you," she said finally.

Keliana was willing. To talk, at least. What she was willing to say, well, that would make all the difference.

Despite the cold, they walked outside. Everyone else was smart enough to stay inside, in the warmth, so they had privacy.

Keliana's dark eyes were red-rimmed but dry, and her mouth was set, as if she'd accepted her fate and would face the consequences with dignity. She had a mien that seemed above her years, Syrriah mused.

"I've already told the Dean I have nothing more to say," Keliana said. "I went into Herald Lurias's office to look at the test. It was against the rules and dishonorable, and I know I should be expelled." Her voice was tight. She was clutching something inside, something she was terrified of letting out.

Syrriah still had much to learn about her Gift of Empathy. Shielding herself had been the first lesson, the most important one. Now she focused on what else she'd been taught, and did what she could to encompass Keliana and herself with a feeling of safety. She knew she couldn't change someone's emotions, but hopefully she could help Keliana feel she could speak freely.

"But you didn't look at the test for yourself, did you?" Syrriah asked, her voice soft.

Keliana's breath hitched—surprise and then a sob. She turned to Syrriah, the sudden movement making her foot slip on the icy path, and she caught herself with a hand on Syrriah's arm. Her fingers squeezed. "Please, whatever happens to me, tell them to let Keysa stay here. She didn't know what I was going to do—she's innocent— she needs to stay."

"I believe you," Syrriah said. "I may not have much influence, but I'll do what I can."

She was about to add that Keliana ought to explain everything to the Dean, when the girl's defenses shattered. Tears spilled, and she flung herself into Syrriah's arms, nearly knocking them both down.

"Natalli told me how wonderful her parents were, but I didn't believe it," she whispered. "I had no idea . . ."

And slowly, the truth spooled out of her, a trembling thread she'd kept so tight it had nearly snapped.

Her parents weren't proud, exactly—they were difficult taskmasters . . . to the degree that Keliana was punished any time she deviated from perfection. Because of how well she'd been doing, she'd been safe here from their wrath . . .

Keysa was another matter. As the Dean said, she was bright and hard-working but not spectacular. The fact that you had to be exceptional just to secure a place at Collegium as an unaffiliated student apparently wasn't enough for her parents.

So Keliana had hoped to give Keysa some support. She'd been tutoring her younger sister, and when that hadn't been quite enough, and she'd known Keysa was faltering, she'd chosen to put her own honor at risk.

"I just don't want Keysa to be sent home," she said, her voice trembling. "My parents had put their focus on me, and they'll be angry enough at me. If Keysa's there, too . . . if they think she's failed, too . . ."

Syrriah couldn't imagine putting that kind of pressure on her children, much less punishing them if their honest efforts didn't lead to perfection. Perfection was impossible.

That they tried, and that they were loved, was infinitely more important.

"We need to talk to the Dean," Syrriah said, but she didn't push. Her hands and feet might be numb from the cold, but this was a decision Keliana had to make on her own.

A hesitation, and then Keliana nodded. She pulled away, swiped at her nose. Some of the tears had left frozen tracks on her pink cheeks.

As they walked back, Syrriah saw that they hadn't been alone after all. Standing by the doorway to the dormitories—well out of earshot but watching from the distance—was Natalli.

The moment Keliana spotted Natalli, she broke into a run. Not quite a full run, given the treacherous ground, but as close a gait as she could.

When Keliana reached the building, Natalli hugged her, then cupped Keliana's face in her hands, her thumbs swiping at the tear tracks.

Syrriah stopped.

The realization, the understanding of what Natalli and all the others had kept from her, swept through her ... a breath of a moment before she watched her dearest daughter kiss the girl who meant far more to her than just a friend.

Syrriah and Natalli walked from the stables together. The weather had warmed—not enough to melt the snow; they were still in full winter—but enough that they could not be bundled up as tightly.

The previous afternoon, after hearing Keliana's explanation (which she told with Syrriah's presence and support), talking to Keysa, and then consulting amongst themselves, the Dean and the instructors agreed that while Keliana had gone against the rules of Collegium, there had been extenuating circumstances. She would be censured but not expelled, and the information would not be shared with her parents.

She had shown not only honor but courage in trying to help and protect her sister.

"Thank you," Natalli said again to her mother now. "I'm ... I'm sorry I didn't talk to you. I just ... I didn't think you would understand."

Syrriah squeezed Natalli's gloved hand. "You don't have to apologize anymore."

"I thought ..." Natalli took a deep breath. "I thought you'd say I was too young for a relationship."

Ah. Despite all the talking they'd done while grooming their Companions, they hadn't gotten to the real heart of the matter until now.

"It's not about your age," Syrriah said. "There are other, more important factors that determine whether you're ready for a relationship. Most importantly, I want you to be happy and safe."

"I am—I am now," Natalli amended. "We know things will change when I leave to ride Circuit. A Herald's life isn't easy, and we don't know what will happen. What we have is enough for now."

Despite her words, Syrriah felt the twinge of fear and sadness Natalli still hid, deep within herself. The first broken heart is the hardest, even if the girls parted as friends and the circumstances of their lives kept them apart.

A pairing between a Herald and non-Herald was possible, but it was far from easy.

They were near the Collegium building when the sweet ringing of bells filled the courtyard.

The throng of students parted, creating a pathway for a riderless Companion, its coat winter-white but warm.

A Companion that walked, sure-footed and deliberate, to stand before a dark-haired unaffiliated student.

The expression of pure joy on Keliana's face was a beautiful thing to behold, more radiant even than the sun sparkling on the snow.

"It looks like you have less to worry about right now," Syrriah said.

Then she felt arms around her, and gathered Natalli into her embrace.

"Thank you," Natalli whispered again, and Syrriah, content, rested her chin on her daughter's head and smiled.

Her children were growing up, becoming the adults they were meant to be, and she loved them all the more for it.

Patterns

Diana L. Paxson

Deira jerked around at the sound of a child's cry, shrill with fear. As she caught her breath, she heard hoarse shouting from the Exile's Gate, which she had just passed through herself a minute ago.

Was it another riot? The campaigning season had begun, and a new influx of refugees from the Tedrel Wars was pouring into the confusion of suburbs that spread beyond the Old City's walls. Valdemar's capital was called Haven, but it was becoming a city of fear, where suspicion was the enemy.

Deira's rooms were in a safer neighborhood just below the first wall near the gate to the South Trade Road, but the market on the eastern side of the city was a place to find bargains. This had been her last chance to buy washed fleeces from the spring shearing. She had made a down payment on a wagonload to be delivered the next day.

She hoped it would arrive. When every day brought new tales of Karsite agents and Tedrel atrocities, Haven vibrated like an overstressed thread on the loom.

She shifted the sack of Rethwellan lambswool roves she had bought and looked back up the narrow street. At their old home in Evenleigh, the raw materials of her trade were available at the nearest farm, but two years ago, her daughter Selaine's thirst for knowledge had proved stronger than her love for the village, and she had been admitted to the Healer's Collegium here.

Fortunately, Deira had found a market for her more am-
bitious rugs and tapestries in the capital as well.

The street was emptying. Two leaning houses shadowed the lane, flaking plaster exposing weathered beams.
As the noise increased, a small figure darted into the
light, tripped, and sprawled at her feet. An instinct
swifter than thought brought her forward, full skirts
swirling, as the first pursuers appeared.

"Get'em, get'em!"

"Where's the rat got to, then?"

City toughs, thought Deira, dropping the bag of wool
on top of the child. *Youths not big or skilled enough to go
to war, but dangerous to a woman or a child.* There were
six of them—hair spiked and slicked in a clumsy imita-
tion of a recent court fashion, faces red with exertion
and nasty glee.

"Hey, Nanny—seen one o' them Southron ratlings
scuttle this way?" said the first, looking her up and down
with an insolence from which her nearly forty years and
status as a master weaver usually protected her. For a
moment the years fell away, and she was a girl scarcely
older than this lad, pregnant and fleeing her burning
home.

"Thieves, ever' one of 'em," a second boy chimed in.
"Th' men take our work, and the littles lift what's not
nailed down!"

"Do your mothers—" Deira began, gathering her
forces for the tongue-lashing they so richly deserved.
She closed her lips as a quiver at her feet reminded her
there was more at stake than her pride, and as the child
pressed against her ankles, bent her knees so that her
skirts brushed the ground.

"You talk kinda funny, maybe you one o' them South-
rons what say the Sun's th'only god?"

"I am a respectable widow from Evenleigh," she said
coldly. *And there is no One True Way in Valdemar!* Her
thought ran on, but this was no time to argue theology.
"I see no fugitives here—"

The other toughs were already moving on. With a last
glare, their leader hurried off to get in front of them.

Deira stood for several long moments before lifting the bag of wool. A boy of three or four years with fluffy, fair hair crawled from beneath her skirts and stood, staring around him like a startled owl. For a moment her gaze was caught by the complex pattern bordering the scarf around his shoulders. As the child gathered himself to run, she grabbed him.

"Carry this so it hides your face, and stay close!" she hissed. "Do you understand?" The roves were light but loose, and the bag was as big as he was. She thrust it into his arms.

She felt the tension in the small shoulder ease and loosened her grip, but she did not release it until they had turned the corner. Then she took the bag from the boy's arms and tipped up his chin to get a better look at him.

"Mis'tess! I not bad boy, not steal!"

Deira nodded, relieved that she could understand him. Many peoples had gone into the making of Valdemar, and some of their dialects might as well have been foreign tongues.

"What is your name, boy? And where are your mother and father?"

"Name Affi—" he replied, his flushed face crumpling in grief. "Boys chase me. Mata lost, Vata lost . . ." He shook his head in despair.

Somewhere there was a mother in anguish. *As I fear for Selaine.* Deira thought. *But at least my daughter is studying to be a Healer, not a Herald.* Far too often the wind brought an echo of the tolling bell that announced the loss of another Herald in the Tedrel Wars.

In upper windows, lights were beginning to glow. From down the street she could hear raucous laughter as the Blue Boar opened its doors. The days were getting longer, but it would be full dark soon. Night was no time for respectable folk to be abroad in this part of town.

"Do you smell that sausage?" she asked softly. "I have some at home. Will you help me eat it? We can look for your Mata and Vata in the morning."

The boy sniffed, but after a moment, he nodded. Deira held out her hand.

*　　*　　*

Deira and Affi were sorting yarn when she heard footsteps on the stairs that led to her second-floor studio. Two days had passed since they had gone back to the market to search for his parents. There had been many with the brightly patterned clothing of folk from the southeastern borders, but none whose garments bore that odd, meandering pattern she had seen on Affi's scarf. All she could do was leave word as to where he could be found.

Affi had wept silently all the way home, but he seemed to be bouncing back with the resilience of the very young. Deira shuddered to think what might have happened to destroy that sunny nature had she not been there.

Leaving Affi to hold the yarn, she went to the door.

Below the woven awning that identified her house and her trade stood a man with the lean build of the hill folk and a smaller woman swathed in a woolen wrap whose borders matched the one Affi wore. Deira stepped quickly aside as the boy galloped past her and into his mother's arms.

"No need for introductions," she said, smiling. "Be welcome here!"

Presently she had them seated at her table, and Affi, presented with a fresh scone, fell silent at last.

"Mistress, we be thankin' you," the man said with dignity. "We been losin' our home, but we still live—not so if we losin' our child."

"You are from the southeast?" she asked.

"From near Cebu Pass. I hight Jilander Thornsson, my wife, Shireie. I have sheep, 'til t' Tedrel came." Bitter memories darkened his eyes. "They kill all. Don't even *eat 'em*. We run, but noone needin' sheepherder with no sheep. Folk say in Haven the men all go fight, they wantin' folk to work, so we come here. . . ."

While her husband spoke, Shireie looked around, her dark eyes bright as a bird's. Deira had gotten the place cheaply because it was a single large room. Her rolled bedding and a chest filled one corner, but the

room was dominated by the standing loom Affi's
mother stared at now.

Deira looked back at the woman's shawl, whose border, like the one worn by her son, was woven into the
selvage of the cloth.

"Is that your work? If so, *you* have a valuable trade—"

"What good a weaver got no loom?" Shireie asked
bitterly. "We be livin' now in shed by stable. I cook oats
the horses spill. Jilander clean stalls."

If any of the patrons left him a tip, thought Deira, noting his lean cheeks, *it's clearly going for better food for
the boy*. She had done the same herself in the days when
she was a refugee, scrubbing pots in an inn to feed herself and her child. She winced, visualizing what would
become of Affi, growing up in the slums. If he survived
the bullies, he would become one himself and trade that
sweet smile for a snarl.

"May I?" she gently turned the fabric to look at the
underside, where the images appeared in reverse. "This
is tablet-weaving, yes? I've used it to cord an edge, but I
have never tried such a complex design."

The other woman's thin features lit in a shy smile. "Is
bein' for protection."

Deira nodded. She had heard that some of the hill-
folk patterns were actually spells.

"This path go round to guard—th'eye watch out for
danger." Shireie indicated the lines that wound in an angular spiral around the central figure, a diamond shape
like the God's-Eye amulets children made with crossed
sticks and ends of yarn.

"It reminds me of the Main Road." Deira laughed,
remembering her frustration with the route that spiraled
around the Old City between the first and second walls.
There was no direct road to the Palace, a hindrance to
any enemy, but an annoyance to those with business
there. "I work on large pieces—" She nodded at the
loom, which held the first half of a rug in the subtle
shades of the hills around Evenleigh. Decision crystal-
ized as she looked back at Shireie. "One of the Court
ladies made my rugs the fashion here. Now I have more

orders than I can fill. Would you consider helping with the work and living here with me?"

Shireie sent a startled look at her husband as Deira gestured around the room. "You will have to roll up your beds every morning, but we can set up a second loom." She paused. "It would be better for the boy. . . ."

It was only as she spoke that she realized how far Affi's presence had gone to fill the gap in her life left by Selaine's departure for the Healers' Collegium, and how much she had dreaded seeing him go.

"You not be knowin' us—" Jilander replied, suspicion warring with pride.

"Knowing your child, I know you," she answered.

"Mother! Who *are* these people?"

Selaine stood in the doorway, her pale green Healer Trainee's uniform glowing like spring leaves, the sunlight making an aureole of her golden hair. Jilander leaped to his feet, the chisel with which he was shaping a base for an inkle loom poised in his hand, and Shireie turned pale. Only Affi, playing with the sweet-smelling curls of wood, greeted the newcomer with his usual sunny smile.

Deira fought down annoyance. "May I introduce Jilander Thornsson and Shireie and Affi. They hail from the Cebu hills. This is my daughter, Selaine."

Selaine looked back at her mother. "I heard there was rioting at the Exile's Gate. I know you go to the Wool Market there. I was afraid for you."

"There was a fire at one of the taverns. People are looking under their beds for Karsite spies," Deira replied, "but we have been quite safe."

"*We?*" echoed Selaine. "You mean these people are living *here*?"

"Since you are not, it can hardly matter to you," Deira snapped in return. "Now sit down, remember your manners, and I will make a pot of tea. If it will sweeten your temper, I might even find a honey cake to go with it."

Blushing, Selaine pulled out the bench and sat down, and Jilander began to work on the wood once more.

"Now, tell me the news from the Collegium." She winced as her daughter's smiling lips thinned.

"I don't know how much the City hears about the wars ..."

Too much and too little, thought Deira. The last two summers had brought incursions by the Tedrel mercenary horde hired by the Sunpriests of Karse, breaking through the border in a different place each year. The goal of Karse had always been to weaken its northern neighbor, but it was said that the Tedrels wanted a homeland.

"Rumors," she answered. "Some of our neighbors have lost kin."

Selaine sighed. "The wounded who survive the first few days in the field hospital are sent here. We Trainees help as we can." She grimaced. "It turns out my Fetching Gift is precise enough to draw bits of bone and wood and metal out of wounds. Two Trainees have resigned already—I suppose it's just as well they find out they cannot face it now, before wasting more of the instructors' time—but all of us have bad dreams." Stress had worn the last childish softness away from her features. Deira could see the face she would wear as a grown woman now.

"I wish you didn't have to—" she began, but Selaine shook her head.

"You've always been afraid I would be Chosen as a Herald! I've never felt called to ride out to bring justice to the world. But when I see pain, I want to fix it. And I'm *good* at it, Mama, can't you understand?"

Deira nodded slowly. If other women's children were dying, she could not grudge the help her own child could give. "Well, my love, even the Karsites cannot keep Midsummer from coming," she said bracingly. "We'll all feel more cheerful after the festival."

"If there *is* a festival," her daughter replied. "I doubt the King's Council realizes how much of their business the students get to know. Some at Court are saying Karsite agents are behind the troubles in the City—" her gaze moved to Jilander and then away, "—infiltrating Haven disguised as refugees."

"When you were born," Deira said in a cold voice, "*we* were refugees. I lost my family when the Karsites burned Westerbridge. Don't you remember what it was like to have no home? And even at Evenleigh, there were monsters," she added, remembering the Spider that had attacked the town.

Her daughter straightened. "When the wounded are fevered, they talk ... there are worse things in human form than the creatures that escape from the Pelagiris hills."

" 'Tis truth, Mistress," Jilander said suddenly. "Nobody pay attention to man muckin' out stalls. I hear men talkin'—*not* refugees—men with money. They get Haven lowlife to start trouble, maybe at Festival."

"At Court they are saying the Festival should be canceled because of the danger," Selaine said somberly. "Some even say that to praise the sun will strengthen the enemy."

"That makes no sense!" Her mother exclaimed. "Karse may have hired the Tedrels, but if those bastards worship anything, it's not Vkandis but their dream of a homeland."

"Be that as it may, the Council is talking about imposing a curfew and martial law."

"With what?" Deira shook her head. "Half the constables are off at the war. No—if fear prevents us from celebrating life, we have already given in to the enemy."

"That is what the King said," her daughter replied, "when he visited the Healer's Hall."

Shireie's eyes rounded. "You see t'King?"

Deira suppressed a smile. To someone from the borders, King Sendar must seem as remote as the gods. Even she had taken awhile to get used to the possessive pride with which their rulers were regarded by folk in the capital.

"He is a good man. He *cares* ..." Selaine said. "Selenay does too. She comes to help us when she can." She looked back at her mother with a sigh. "Maybe it's a good thing you have somebody with you. I was worried about you, living alone."

"If you are worried, come to see me more often—"
Deira replied, lips twitching.

"I will," said her daughter, but she did not smile.

From then on, Selaine seemed to turn up every few days,
usually with a few of her friends in tow. Deira had wavered between amusement and resentment at the idea
that her child was trying to protect her, but gradually she
came to understand that the students found her big
room, where each day the pattern grew on the loom and
Affi chattered as he played on the floor, an affirmation
that hope and order still existed in the world.

One evening a week before the Festival, two students
from the Healers, a fledgling Bard and a gray-clad Herald Trainee, sat at her table. The sun had just set, and a
golden afterglow shafted through the high windows and
the open door. Deira had set the visitors to work carding
fleece while she put together a platter of flatbread and
smoked meat and cheeses with some early vegetables
from the countryside.

"If only we had a Herald-Mage!" exclaimed Donni, a
fourteen-year old with hair the russet of his bardic tunic.
"We're studying the ballads of Vanyel Ashkevron now. If
he were here he'd flatten those Tedrels with a spell!"

"Magic fights magic . . ." Lisandra said slowly. She was
eighteen, a Herald-Trainee who was often told she
looked like Princess Selenay. "Our Gifts and Talents are
only good against mortal enemies. Herald Vanyel was
given his powers to stand against supernatural foes."

"What the Tedrels have is lots of very natural spears,
arrows, and swords," said Garvin gloomily. "Every time I
go into the Hall of Healing, I am reminded exactly how
much harm they can do." Tall and lanky, he had a kind
face and clever hands. He had been one of their more
frequent visitors, and Deira was beginning to wonder if
he was interested in Selaine.

Little Caren, clad like him in green, sighed agreement.
"If we can't blast them, I wish we could at least ward our
own fighters with a protective spell."

"We got no Mages, in t'hills." Shireie spoke up suddenly. "But my old Mata teach me yarn magic. Can't guard sheep an' goats, but Tedrel scum leave our house alone."

"Is that the pattern you wove into Affi's scarf?" Deira asked.

"Can we see?" asked Caren eagerly, but Affi was already running to the corner where his bedding was stowed and pulling out the scarf. Caren passed it to Lisandra, whose Gift was Psychometry.

The Herald Trainee closed her eyes, moving her palm back and forth a few inches above the cloth.

"I feel *you*, Affi," she murmured, smiling, "like a little star—"

"His name *mean* 'star' in old speech of the hills," Jilander said, his voice soft with wonder.

Lisandra nodded and began to trace the design with her thumb. "And I feel *you*, Shireie. A mother's love is a powerful protection . . ."

Shireie bent her head, but on her cheeks Deira saw the glint of tears. Her own eyes were prickling as she remembered how often she had feared for her own child. *And will again,* she thought grimly, *when Selaine leaves the Healers' Hall and goes out into the world.* Perhaps she should ask the hill woman to make a scarf for her— for all of them—for in the past weeks Selaine's friends had become like family.

"But there's more—" Lisandra went on. "The pattern moves, keeps moving, winds back and forth, pauses in little points of light—what am I feeling here? It's like a fence, a running fence with lights to guard and guide. . . ." She opened her eyes. Her thumb was on one of the crossed-diamonds.

"Like a God's-Eye!" exclaimed Donni.

"So that's why you asked to hang one over our door . . ." Deira nodded as the other woman's face lit in one of her rare shy smiles.

"Pretty—" Garvin sighed. "Wish we could wrap it around Haven!" There was a murmur of agreement as the scarf was passed from hand to hand.

"Well, why not?" Selaine asked suddenly. "I don't

mean a woven ribbon—that would take years—but we could wind yarn back and forth along the streets and hang God's-Eyes on those statues they keep putting up at crossroads!"

They all stared at her.

"You need t' spell—" Shireie said. She murmured something in the old dialect. As Jilander tried to translate, Donni closed his eyes, lips moving.

"Around, around, it's wound—" The others fell silent as his Talent kicked in and his voice took on the ring of incantation. "On every road and way. Eye of Light shine bright, go safe by night and day!"

"Still, that would take an awful lot of yarn—" Caren said as the boy fell silent. One by one the stares moved from Donni to Deira, whose thoughts had become a tangle of exasperation, disbelief, and an odd thread of excitement.

"Even if we spin up all the wool I have, it wouldn't be enough," she protested, "and how would you get it around the town? Would the Constables even give permission?"

"The race—" Garvin said in the silence that followed. "The sun-torch race through the City is already part of the Festival. I'm entered to run this year. Once it starts, no one will be surprised to see people dashing around the town."

"We'll collect yarn from all over—we can tell people it's for decorations!" Selaine said.

"I know how to get more!" Donni exclaimed. "There's an old song about a priestess who wanted land for a temple. The king said she could have as much as her cloak would cover, so she unraveled it and laid the threads end-to-end."

"And I know *where!*" Lisandra laughed suddenly. "There's a room in the Palace where they've been stowing ancient hangings for generations. I bet Selenay could get us in."

Deira looked up, met her daughter's challenging gaze. *They have the energy, but they need me to focus it. She is waiting to see if I will do the right thing.* Whether it *was* the right thing was another question, but she could not deny the appeal in those hazel eyes.

During the next two weeks, there was scarcely a moment when Deira did not hear the hum of a spinning wheel. Fortunately, for their purposes yarn spun with a single twist was good enough, and the strands did not have to be plied. Deira heard that humming in her dreams. She would wake wondering if the spirits had spun more while she was sleeping, as they did in the tales from her old home. Sometimes there was indeed more thread in the morning than she remembered having spun the day before, though she suspected the work had been done by Shireie. Perhaps the compulsive labor was a way to fight her fears.

As it is for me, thought Deira, looking at the bags that were beginning to fill with balls of yarn. Affi had gotten quite good at winding them. In a life of dislocations, she had learned that doing *something,* even if the purpose was unclear, felt better than to simply wait for an outcome one could neither stop nor see.

They had spun up the wool Deira had bought at the Exile's Gate and undone the rug that had been on the loom. Now the cloth from the Palace storeroom was coming in, the faint reek of mold mingling with the scent of the herbs with which it had been packed away. It was a measure of the preoccupation with the war that no one in authority seemed to have noticed, much less objected to these nocturnal forays. The enthusiasm with which everyone had responded to Selaine's plan had amazed her mother, but perhaps Deira should not have been surprised. You fight to defend the things you love, and where you love, you belong.

The table was covered by a map of Haven on which they had marked the neighborhoods where each runner would lay the yarn, and the route he or she would follow to create the pattern. Or try to—the major roads were laid out according to a plan, but the lanes and alleys between them were as unpredictable as ripples on the Terilee.

Deira picked another length of yarn from the basket

of odds and ends and began to work it carefully around
the crossed sticks of the God's-Eye she was making now.
The students had decided she should place the final ornament on the Palace Gate, as if she had been the organizer
of this plot instead of, perhaps, its enabler. This strand
was red for courage, next to the blue of honor. Each color
carried a prayer, a blessing came with each twist of the
yarn. The rich brown earth of Valdemar was already
there, and the green of forest and field. In the center
gleamed the golden threads representing the monarchy,
and at intervals, a length of pure white for the Heralds
whose labors united the land.

"I bind this thread to the pattern with my blessing,"
she said softly, reaching for a piece of white cord.

Midsummer Eve . . . It was a night when the strength of
the Sun was at its height—and the moment when balance required that it decline. The Lord of Light was honored in Valdemar, but it was hard not to see in this
moment an opportunity to bind the ability of the Karsite
Sunpriests to support the Tedrel enemy.

Beyond the open door, dark rooftops bordered a
golden sky. Crows called to each other as they flew home,
and from somewhere near the river came the deep beat
of a drum. With the approach of night, the temperature
was easing to a comfortable warmth with a hint of cool
breeze. It should have been a peaceful scene, but Haven
vibrated with tension. The country folk held that at such
times wild powers were abroad. What pattern would this
night's weaving leave on the loom?

"Around . . . around . . . it's wound. . . ." The words of
the spell echoed in her brain. During the day, what
seemed like most of the students in the Collegium had
come by to collect their bags of yarn. Deira picked up
the God's-Eye, said farewell to Shireie and Affi, and
started down the stairs. She was wearing her own best
clothing, a long vest of forest green velvet embroidered
and trimmed in the Westerbridge style over a full-
sleeved, lightweight linen gown with flowers woven into
the fabric around the hem.

She stiffened as a distant roar echoed across the town. The official runners would be heading up the Southern Trade Road now, and all over the city, students from the Collegium would begin laying a winding trail of yarn through their assigned neighborhoods, connecting at the crossroads until all of Haven was joined. Her task was to go to the Palace Gate and complete the spell.

Her neighbors were lining up along the avenue. Deira hurried past them, shivering as she passed through the gloomy tunnel beneath the massive outer wall, and turned left along the Main Road that spiraled around the Old Town. A continuous line of shops and dwellings for the more prosperous classes fronted the curve of the road that ran along the wall. A trail of yarn already lay there. She followed it down an alley to the Pig Fountain, one of the more notable monuments on the next round of the Main Road. The rotund gentleman whose statue smiled smugly from the top had made his money selling sausage, but the student who was yarn-binding this neighborhood had hung the God's-Eye around the neck of his pig. A second line of yarn was already knotted to it.

Deira took a deep breath, feeling an increase of tension in the air. If evil was abroad, would it sense the pattern meant to contain it? Would it respond? As she realized that the magic was working, elation warred with fear.

"Around, around, it's wound, on every road and way . . ."

The yarn should have been invisible in the fading light, but to her eye, that wavering line seemed to glow. It led her down another intersecting lane. Behind the buildings were yards with warehouses and stables, and workshops for those who practiced luxury trades. Beyond them lay walled gardens and the mansions of city leaders. Deira was moving into the realm of the wealthy now, a district where she had always felt like an interloper, even when she was delivering a rug to one of the fine ladies who lived there. It was worse now, as if some power were resisting her purpose here.

"You will have the easy part," Selaine had told her.

*"The racers must spiral all the way around the Main
Road. All you have to do is stroll through the alleys in the
nice part of town."*

As Deira forced herself to continue forward, she wondered if, in their focus on the Gifts and Talents, the Collegia had forgotten the rules of Magic. The country folk
knew that as with any other force, the use of such power
evoked its opposite. If there *were* Karsite agents at work
in Haven, how would they be reacting now?

Darkness was falling. She had reached the third round
of the spiral without incident, and found more yarn to
follow, but the air vibrated with strain. By now she had
worked her way around to the East side of the Old City.
Going downhill, over the rooftops she could see the towers of the Palace beyond the inner wall. The fourth spiral
of the Main Road brought her to the river. Beyond the
bridge, the road rose again in a final swirl to the gate in
the inner wall that was her goal. She moved more quickly,
following the glimmer of thread on the ground.

At the edge of the river stood a semicircle of benches
shaded by a silver-leaf tree. The yarn wound around
them, and a God's-Eye swung among the shifting leaves.
At the head of the bridge two Constables conversed
with a man whose gray leather uniform made him almost
invisible in the failing light.

As she neared the bridge, Deira heard footsteps behind her and stepped aside. For a moment, she thought
it was one of her yarn-runners, for he carried a pack, but
this man was dressed like a highborn. As he strode past,
the man in gray spoke, and one of the Constables, spear
at the ready, moved to bar his way.

The fellow glanced around him, and before Deira
could respond, stepped back and pinned her with his left
arm while he threatened her throat with the knife that
suddenly appeared in his other hand.

"You let me across or she dies!"

It had been a long time since Deira had needed to
fight for her life or her honor, but she had not forgotten
the moves. As her attacker spoke, her wooden heel came
down on his foot, and twisting, she thrust upward at the

arm that held her, the God's-Eye still in her hand. He cried out and reeled back, releasing her, his other foot landing square upon the yarn that crossed the road. The Constables leaped to block his escape, but instead of running, the man dropped his knife and turned to follow the yarn back to the benches and around the silver-leaf tree.

"*Eye of Light shine bright*..." Deira cradled the God's-Eye against her breast, wondering if anyone else had noticed that it was when the ornament touched her assailant that he let her go. Everyone was staring as the man walked round and round. Then a constable seized him, and the gray man began searching him with grim efficiency, collecting another dagger and throwing the pack to the ground.

"And what is it here we have?" he asked as a round clay vessel stopped with wax bounced out and rolled across the ground.

"Burning ... to burn, no, light I was making ..." said the prisoner, still trying to follow the yarn. Blinking, he pointed to the lantern the other Constable was holding.

"It's full of oil!" one of the onlookers exclaimed, pointing where light gleamed from a spreading pool.

"Smash that against a wall and throw a torch, and you'd have light, sure enough—a Midsummer blaze to remember!"

"To the Guardpost take him!" the man in gray ordered. His stern gaze searched the crowd that was gathering. "Go home! The race from behind your own walls you should see."

Deira flinched as those keen eyes met hers. His strong features were marred by old scars, but he seemed more harried than unkind.

"You did well, Mistress. Living here you are?"

"My daughter is a student with the Healers," she said. "She invited me to watch the end of the race with her there."

"This night strange folk are about. Not safe, the dark places. On the Main Road stay."

"Yes, sir." Indeed, to follow the great spiral over the

river and up the hill to the wall was now the only way to reach her goal. Deira dropped a curtsy and started across the bridge, heart pounding in mingled elation and fear.

She was just in time.

As Deira climbed the hill, she heard shouting and saw the flare of torches rounding the curve of the spiral behind her. Their ruddy light gleamed on the smoothly flowing water as they crossed the Terilee.

"Around, around, it's wound, on every road and way." With every step she chanted the spell. Before the Inner Wall a crowd of folk were waiting, most of them in white or red or green. Deira saw only Selaine, the end of the yarn that ran down the road in her hand. She held out the God's-Eye so that her daughter could tie it on.

"Eye of Light, shine bright—" Light danced across the gate yard as the torchbearers raced toward them, Garvin in the lead.

On the pillar of the gate there was a hook where a banner could be hung. Deira slipped the loop of the God's-Eye over it and fell back, feeling a kind of mental click as she let it go, like the sound when the last thread has been beaten up against the weft and the weaving sword is laid down, the pattern complete, the work all done.

From around the city, she sensed little explosions of dismay as other plots were foiled. She could *see* the network of spirals laid across the buildings, the God's-Eyes glowing like the stars above. There was wonder in her daughter's face, in a few others a dawning comprehension, and speculation in the gaze of the man in gray.

It didn't matter what he thought of her now. The Tedrels were still out there, but Haven and its people, old and new, would stand.

"Go safe . . ." she whispered. "Go safe by night and day!"

Out of the Pelagiris
Ron Collins

Nwah held her breath as a ramshackle delivery wagon rumbled past. Its driver screamed complaints at the mule pulling it, and its wheels clattered roundly against hardened ruts in the dirt.

It was late morning. Overcast was rolling in, and thunder had been grumbling since they arrived, so on top of everything else it felt like rain.

She looked at the hard-packed streets, imagined them muddy, and held a paw up to inspect the spaces between her toes. The city was disgusting. Just thinking about cleaning herself here made her pelt crawl.

:Isn't this amazing?: Kade said.

The intensity of his excitement was like a smithy's blast.

:Yes,: Nwah replied. *:Amazing is one word for it.:*

She hoped the distractions kept him from noticing exactly how unamazing she thought the city was. Coming to Oris—and specifically its capital—was her choice after all. Kade hadn't cared a whit where they went as long as they got out of the Pelagiris, but Nwah wanted to see where her first pair-mate had come from. It wasn't the boy's fault the city's incessant barrage of movement, sound, and smells was driving her mad. Her reaction was embarrassing, actually. Her mother had raised her to be a brave pup, but now her only thought was to get out of town before Kade could see how unhappy it made her.

Before she was killed, Rayn had said Oris was a quiet place.

Until now, that had been true.

The kingdom as a whole was mostly rolling grasslands and sparse woods filled with wildlife that made Nwah happy. The open sky and wide horizon helped her recognize ley-lines of power as they came into range. It was easy to practice her "magic" as they traveled the plains, and she found herself playing idly with her Gift along their journey.

It was almost fun.

This was unusual because, unlike Kade, who enjoyed teaching himself new things with his Healing Gift, Nwah was unnerved when she toyed with magical powers. They felt dangerous. Fluid. As if the magic were a thing of its own, and she was just tagging along. She didn't like being out of control. She had problems enough just staying alive.

Kade nagging her didn't help.

It is my Gift, she thought. *I can leave it be if I want.*

But the open skies over Oris made her feel safer somehow. At one point she even changed a rabbit's fur from brown to gray, though she had no idea how she did it.

:You're a natural,: Kade said.

She wished he would stop.

The two of them were not connected in the same way she had been linked to Rayn, but, though she could not say why, this connection they shared was stronger. It had been five years since Kade had healed her. Five years that had deepened everything. Now they were like brother and sister, only more. At one point she thought she knew everything that could be known about Kade.

But leaving their home woods and walking across the land had changed things yet again.

Everything was new.

There was so much to learn, so much to absorb, and the two of them were so different in some very important ways.

Kade was not *kyree,* and Nwah was not human.

She felt that even more strongly when they came

upon a *kyree* pack the morning prior to arriving at Tau. They were traveling through woods. She sensed the alpha male from a distance, but since this wasn't her time of heat, she ignored him.

:There are kyree here,: she said to Kade.

:Do you want to find them?:

Nwah considered the idea.

She hadn't known her kind were anywhere outside the Pelagiris, and suddenly finding others made her ears twitch with curiosity. On the other side, she didn't know how she would fit in with this clan, and they were so close to the city. Beyond even that, she was feeling the edges of a ley-line in the distance.

The juxtaposition of Tau, these unknown *kyrees*, and a line of magic made her think the world was asking her to choose something important.

It added up to pressure.

:No,: she finally replied. *:We're so close. Let's go on.:*

:When we come back, maybe?: Kade asked.

:Maybe.:

So they went on.

They walked through those woods and over clearings of farmlands and ranches. They spent a last evening sleeping under open skies in the protected calm of Tau's outskirts. It was quite lovely, really.

But the city itself was different.

Less than an hour here, and already her nerves were shot.

Flashing wheels made her afraid she might lose her tail. The strident swing of soldier's boots and the sharp hooves of horses racing up the street made her tremble for fear of being kicked. Clouds of strange perfumes rolled over the city: Cooked meats, baked breads, and spices that made her sneeze from a street away all combined to make her dizzy.

Worse, Nwah and Kade had just found the market, a place where absolutely nothing stood still.

It was too much.

Realizing Kade hadn't replied to her, she craned her neck.

He stood still as a stone, his hand gripping the walking stick he'd picked up when they left the Pelagiris. His angular chin was slack, his gaze oddly distant. His lips had an upward curl that made him look as drunk as Nwah felt.

:Are you all right?: she asked as she followed his gaze.

It was a girl, standing at a weaver's stall across the way and running her hand over finely woven fabric. She was more athletic than slim, more graceful than soft. She wore a simple day dress that flowed to the ground and was cinched tightly around her waist. Her movements spoke of a pragmatic, if not sensible, nature. Her hair was dark, and her skin was a middling shade of brown. Her eyes reflected the green of the dress, and her lips had been blushed with something rose colored.

Two other girls stood by her side, a pair of guards followed.

She was arguing with the weaver.

:We need to find a place to stay,: Nwah said, hoping to forestall what was going to happen. The last thing she needed was for Kade to go on the rut.

Kade said nothing, though, just shouldered his travel bag and stepped across the street, nearly getting run over by another cart. He showed no reaction, but he moved so quickly Nwah broke into a trot to keep up.

"Hello," Kade said to the girl.

She stopped in midsentence, then grimaced. "Do you see I'm working a deal here?"

"I apologize," he replied.

"Oh, he's quite the fair one, isn't he?" one of the girls said. She was taller and thinner than the target of Kade's attention.

Nwah did not like her tone.

"Not fair enough for Winnie," the other replied, twisting a lock of dark hair around her finger, "but I fancy him well enough."

The two broke into laughter.

Kade ignored them. "What's your name?" he asked the bargaining girl.

"That's none of your business," she replied, returning

to the weaver, who stood with one knobby finger lifted as if to make a point.

Nwah noticed, however, that the girl had turned her face so she could glance at Kade from the side of her eyes, that the shade of her skin darkened, and that the her essence shifted to an aroma that suggested something beyond attraction.

This was not going well.

Kade put his hand on the girl's shoulder. "Pardon me, but—"

With rapid speed, one of the guards grabbed Kade by the collar, lifted him up, and pushed him hard against a heavy post that had been driven into the dirt to mark the corner of the marketplace.

"You'll keep your hands off the lady," the guard said through gritted teeth as he ground his forearm against Kade's throat.

Kade's toes were barely able to touch the ground. He dropped the walking stick, gasped for air, and used both hands to balance against the pole.

Nwah growled and hunkered down to leap.

:Nwah!: Kade said. *:Stop!:*

She held up, barely. Muscles around her eyes tightened. Her whiskers rucked up, and her ears turned back. Every sense became intensely focused.

"Is that your pet?" the guard muttered.

"She's my compatriot."

The guard gave an amused smile and glanced at the other man, who had his hand on his sword. The armor they wore was similar but not quite uniform: leather uppers with pads at the thighs, weapons looped into belts. The one element common to both was the blue chevron each wore on their shoulders. Their boots were old but cared for. Their hair was longish but tied back. Neither had bathed for a few days, and the guard whose forearm was grinding into Kade's throat could use a good cleaning of the teeth.

"You hear that, Lag?" the guard said. "The boy says this shaggy *kyree* is his compatriot."

"No worse than what I've seen you bring home," the other guard replied.

"I'll cut you for that," the first guard said.

The girl broke in, stepping forward.

"Release the young man, Hivenswirth," she said. "He's done nothing wrong."

The guard hesitated, but he relaxed his grip enough that Kade settled back to the hard-packed dirt. The cherry-red flush that colored his cheeks faded to something a bit healthier. The guard kept a fistful of Kade's cloak grasped up against his chin, though, and he held Kade firmly to the post.

"The young man's grimy hand touched my sergeant-at-arms' daughter," the guard said to the girl. "That's wrong enough for me."

"Your sergeant-at-arms' daughter can take care of herself."

"Your daddy would disagree."

The guard pressed harder on Kade's collar and put his face into Kade's gaze.

"Who are you, boy?"

"My name is Kade. I'm a Healer from the Pelagiris."

"From the wildlands, you say? A Healer?" The guard raised his voice across the way. "Did you hear that, everyone? We've got a man of medicine from the dark woods here with us today." The pressure on Kade's collar grew even tighter. "Maybe he can whip us up a little brew, eh? A little medicinal wort of the liver, as it were?"

Nwah stifled another growl. The ruff stood up around her neck and down her back.

The fresh ozone of power came to her, then.

The ley-line.

Not far away.

She could sense it now, feel the sizzle of its presence. It called to her. Its odor filled her nose and made her chest grow warm.

A thin growl came from her throat, and she thought she tasted blood.

:Nwah!: Kade's voice broke her thoughts. *:Don't do anything stupid.:*

"What do you say, Healer? Got any special potions for me?"

"No, sir. Nothing handy, anyway."

"That's what I thought," the guard said. "Sounds to me like what we really have here is a faker from the wilds—if that's even where he's from."

The guard threw Kade to the ground amid laughter from a crowd that had now grown around them without Nwah being aware of it.

City people are a strange lot, she decided as she looked them over. They were cleaner than the travelers in the Pelagiris, cleaner than the bands of Hawkbrothers and other independent raiders who stayed on the road for months at a time. Some of them Nwah could barely smell, yet they felt somehow lesser for that cleanliness.

Their numbers were great, but it was as if they didn't even exist.

"If you know what's good for you," the guard said, "you'll get out of Tau before you find whatever trash bones you and that animal are planning to scrounge for lunch."

Kade stood, repositioned his bag, and brushed road dust from his pants.

"Look at the blighter," the second guard joked. "As if takin' a layer of dirt from the outside is gonna make a difference."

:Come on,: Kade said as he grabbed his stick. *:We need to get out of here.:*

As they stepped away, the girl called out.

"Winnie," she said. "My name is Winnie."

Kade turned to her. "It's a pretty name."

:Come on, lover,: Nwah said, feeling strangely angry.

Watching Kade be threatened made her heart clench, but she felt his attraction for the girl—and while his ache for her was familiar to her own physical desires, his was different, deeper in ways she couldn't understand. His went beyond physical. Where her mating was not meant to last, she knew humans often mated for life.

That difference made her jealous.

The mere fact she had become jealous was embarrassing, which again made her angry.

It was a vicious loop that she could see was unfair even as she was thinking it.

Kade was her bond, but Kade was also human. He would have human reactions, just as she was *kyree* and could never be anything but *kyree*. Would he call her on the hypocrisy of slaking her own physical desires while being fearful of him doing the same?

:Thanks,: Kade said as they walked through the streets, nearing a corner.

:For what?:

:For being here,: he said. *:And for not doing anything stupid.:*

She gave the audible click that meant *You're welcome*.

But as they turned the corner, her ears were sensitive enough to hear the guards speaking behind them.

"Hey, Hivvy?" the second guard said. "What's with that white streak in your hair?"

:I don't care what the guards said, I don't want to leave,: Kade said. *:There's too much to learn here.:*

They were sitting in the quiet nook of an alley, Nwah lying on her belly, paws forward and facing the open mouth that looked out onto the road. Kade's back rested against a silvered slat that was the wall of a smithy shop. He ripped a hank of bread from the loaf he had purchased from the small collection of coins he had earned administering salves and root potions on their way across the land.

Nwah was hungry, but she didn't feel like eating.

:They have an apothecary here,: Kade said. *:I'm sure I could learn something from him. And I'm sure there are Mages here who could help you. Besides, we've barely had a chance to look for Rayn's old haunts.:*

Rather than encourage this direction, Nwah pretended to clean her paw.

The alley was narrow. Its smell wasn't too horrific. *It would be a good place to be alone in,* she thought. If they were going to stay in Tau, she could see spending time here.

Did all cities have such places?

They would have to, wouldn't they?

Otherwise people would go insane.

A pair of crates were stacked nearby. If she used them right, perhaps she could make it to the roof of one of the buildings.

The idea of being higher up was attractive.

Boot steps and the heavy sounds of leather-bound strides came from the mouth of the alley. The two guards from the market blocked the entrance. A third man, bigger and radiating more power, stood between them. His hair, complete with a beard, was curled, red, and in messy disarray. A heavy cape draped over his shoulders, and a large sword hung from his side. This man was older than the others, his face lined and weathered, though his body was still stout.

The guard who had accosted Kade pointed a dirty finger.

"Him," he said. "He's the Healer."

The new man stepped forward, his boots crunching on the loose debris of the alley.

Nwah growled and took a sideways stance. The essence of the sword was sharp against her mind.

Kade struggled to his feet, still chewing. "What do you want?"

"I am sergeant-at-arms of this city," the man replied. "I have need of your services."

"Excuse me?"

"You are a Healer, are you not?"

"I am," Kade replied, standing taller.

"Then come with me."

:Don't go,: Nwah said.

"Why should I come?" Kade said, not glancing at her.

"I have a sick man who needs tending. These two said you might be able to help."

:I don't trust him,: Nwah said again.

:Someone's sick. I have to go.:

Despite her fear, or perhaps because of it, the answer didn't surprise her. Kade was a medic at heart as well as by Gift. She remembered the touch of his hands and the strength of his Gift as he had mended her own broken bones years before. She had touched his essence. She understood the pure nature of his mind.

Kade was an idiot sometimes, but he was a man who cared about others.

:I understand,: she finally said.

"My name is Kade," he said, extending a hand to the sergeant.

The sergeant hesitated, but eventually took the hand. "Know me as Castigan."

The man led them to the royal palace, or what served as one here in Tau.

It was a castle at least—barely—built high enough that its three towers could look over the city proper. A stone wall barricaded it from the common people except for a main gate that was now open and guarded by more men with light armor and blue chevrons.

Stables were built to one side.

The manor yard seemed smaller than it probably was.

They went around to a building Nwah realized was a barracks for the guard.

The guard's command center was at its northernmost point, which is where Castigan took them. It had its own tower, which was connected to the castle proper through a stone corridor running above like a bridge.

"The animal will have to stay outside," Castigan said at the doorway.

"Nwah is my companion. I need her with me."

The sergeant appeared to be ready to argue the point, but his gaze flickered to the guards, who nodded. "It is acceptable," he said. "But you will need to keep her out of the manor itself. The king will not brook such nonsense as a wild *kyree* in his keep."

"Understood," Kade replied.

:Are you my keeper now?: Nwah said.

:They don't need to know better.:

This was the first thing Kade had said that made her feel better since they had entered the city.

:I don't like this,: she replied. *:But let's get it over with.:*

Castigan left the guards below.

They entered the command center and climbed a twisting stairway to the upper reaches of the tower.

Being inside felt stifling. The walls were tall and closed. She didn't like the feeling of stone and mortar, and the stairs felt sharp. Unlike the caves she and Kade had sometimes sheltered in, these stone corridors felt dead. It smelled empty.

:How can people survive here?: she asked.

:Humans are different,: Kade replied.

The room they stopped in was small, with a small slit of a window that looked to the south.

Outside, it started to rain.

Not a storm, Nwah thought, but a gentle rain that would be mesmerizing if she let it. Right now, however, she had no intention of being mesmerized.

Right now, she was focused on the man who lay on a well-aged cot and was covered by a thin linen. He was probably as old as Castigan, but where the sergeant-at-arms was muscular and powerfully built, this man appeared to be wiry and thin. His skin was ashen. Fevered sweat had once plastered his short hair to his forehead, but now there was no sweat at all. Now the man was dry, and his skin was reddened. The hair stuck to him in a crusted shell.

As they came into the room, a nursemaid rose.

Kade did a double take. "Winnie."

It was the girl from the market. She gave a sincere blush of surprise.

Of course, Nwah thought. The girl was the sergeant-at-arms' daughter.

"I told you to stay away," Castigan said to her.

"He's sick, Father. I can't just leave him be."

"I've brought a Healer," he exclaimed. "So you can leave now."

The man on the cot gave a pain-laden moan.

"What's wrong with him?" Kade asked as he knelt beside the cot and examined the now shivering man. A table at the head of the cot had wet cloths and a decanter of water sitting on it.

"He's been sick for a fortnight," Castigan replied.

"Fever," Winnie added as she leaned over Kade's shoulder to watch. "He won't eat and can't keep

anything down when he does. And he's delirious. He
doesn't do anything but sleep, dream, and moan."

"Who is he?" Kade said as he put the back of his hand
to the man's forehead.

"He is my second in command," the sergeant at arms
said. "Lincecum Hale's his name. Commander in the
king's service."

"He took sick after the planting celebration," Winnie
again added. "He hasn't fully recovered since."

Kade examined the man's eyes, which were yellowed.
He ran a hand around the man's neck and shoulders.
"He's still very warm."

"Is it the plague?" the girl asked, her eyes wide.

"I don't know," Kade answered. "He needs to drink,
though. He needs to get liquid into him, or he's going to
burn up."

Kade dug into his travel bag, looking for the kit he
kept his medicines in. He removed one of the pouches
he had made from squirrel's hide, and shook out a pinch
of the crumbled basil leaf he kept tucked inside.

:Is it the plague?: Nwah said, suddenly afraid.

:Please be quiet.:

Distracted or not, the rebuke hurt.

She padded over to the foot of the cot and sniffed the
sick man's feet. They reeked of death. She put her tail
between her legs.

:He smells awful,: Nwah said.

Kade shut her down then.

Or, rather, he put some clamp on his emotions that
made her know she was to remain silent. Their link
would always be there, but she felt the distance Kade
was putting between them. Worse, she felt the attraction
the human girl had on him even more strongly.

:Fine,: she said.

She snarled and sat down at the foot of the bed.

"Hand me that decanter," Kade said to Winnie.

She gave it to him, smiling in a way she hadn't while
at the market. Her fingers brushed his as they exchanged
the decanter, and she watched in fascination as he
dropped the crumbled leaf into the water and swirled it.

Kade glanced at her with an unspoken question.

"I want to be a Healer," she said. "Unlike my father, I admire them."

:She didn't seem to admire Healers so much back in the market,: Nwah snickered.

Kade's brow furrowed, but he ignored the comment. He looked at the sergeant. "You should probably leave us."

Nwah understood now that Kade was going to use his Gift. This was always a personal moment for Kade, one he didn't often share with others.

The man nodded, then clomped to the doorway. "Winnie?"

"I can use her help," Kade said.

Nwah's eyes narrowed and another pang of jealousy hit. This time it was totally justified, though. Why was he letting her stay?

"I'll not leave my daughter alone in the same room with you," Castigan said.

"Father!" Winnie glared. "I am going to be a Healer whether you like it or not."

His jaw clenched, and for a moment, Nwah thought he might actually lash out at her. Instead, his eyes narrowed into tight beams aimed at Kade.

"Yes," he said. "I think that will be fine."

The jangle of his belts clamored as he descended the stairs.

The room became silent, and Kade raised an eyebrow.

"He means well," she said. "But he is set in his ways."

Kade shrugged, then placed his hands on the man's chest. "When I start, I want you to pour a thin trickle of water into his mouth."

Winnie nodded, her dark eyes growing wide.

"I've seen Healers work before. Will this be the same?"

"I don't know. Everything I do is self-taught."

"Then it's true you're from the dark woods?"

"Sure. But they don't seem particularly dark to me. Just seem like home."

"Will you teach me what you know?"

He actually blushed. "I can try," he said. "But I've never taught anyone before."

Nwah flipped her tail impatiently. It thumped onto the floor.

Kade's interest in her had been so obvious that even the buffoon of a guard had called it, but now Winnie's interest in Kade grew more transparent by the moment.

Nwah wondered whether the presence of the other girls at the market had made a difference in Winnie's attitude, or maybe it was the guards' presence. She didn't understand why it would, but humans, as Kade had said, were different. They hid themselves in the strangest ways.

The man moaned again.

Kade put his hands on the man's chest, closed his eyes, and began working with his Gift.

Winnie began pouring.

Nwah watched the two of them work together, growing more angry at Kade's snub as the water dribbled from the decanter.

Kade's fingers worked along the man's collarbone.

The man swallowed.

"Come here," Kade said to Winnie. "Put your hands on mine."

She put the decanter down and did as she was told. Her fingers looped between Kade's. Their eyes closed and their breathing grew into a steady rhythm. The man breathed better, and a yellow aura seemed to ooze from him.

Nwah couldn't stand it anymore.

She got up, and padded down the winding stairs and out into the manor yard, where, yes, it was now raining.

She sat at the base of the doorway, listening to the rhythm of the drizzle.

She could stay here, but she didn't want to be anywhere near the manor if she could help it.

She could go back to the alley.

Yes, the alley. That's where she would go. She would climb the crates and look out over the city. Kade could find her whenever he was done doing whatever he was doing.

Nwah stood up and stretched.

A familiar voice came over the pattering of rain. Castigan, the sergeant at arms.

"When the boy's done, grab him and put him in the dungeon proper."

It came from around the corner, Nwah realized—or rather, from the office with a window open. The voices were faint, but her hearing was good.

She slunk along the wall to get closer to the window, being careful to keep from getting too wet.

"What for?" the guard said.

"He's killed Hale."

"Killed him? He just went upstairs."

"Well, he hasn't killed him yet, but he's going to."

"The boy couldn't kill a fire beetle," the guard replied.

"You're not hearing my meaning, Hivvy."

A brief moment of silence hung in the air.

"Ah. I see," Hivenswirth said.

"Do you now?"

"Yes, sir. We all know the commander was a spy for Hardorn and that you were trying to get him killed in a good and quiet way earlier."

"Who knew Lincecum Hale could handle his poison so well?" Sergeant Castigan said. "And worse, who knew my daughter, of all people, would nurse him back so near to healthy even with giving him another dose?"

"So we're gonna kill him for good and hang it on the kid?"

"No reason to wait any longer. A traitor can't be let free, and I can't let the king know we let such a man into our ranks like that. Wouldn't look right for any of us now, would it?"

Nwah could almost hear the smugness of the nodding heads.

"But a strange Healer from the Wild Woods comes to town with a lovesick eye for the sergeant's girl, and gets himself kicked around by the guard ... well ... I figure pretty much everyone'll be able to connect those dots. When they are done, you will both go upstairs and finish the job."

"What about your girl, Castigan? She'll know."

"Word will be that he jinxed her, but between us she'll get the point. I know how to keep my daughter quiet."

"I see," the first guard said. "Hale's gone, a Mage no one knows is responsible, and Winnie toes the line. That ties it all up."

"Yes," Castigan said. "Yes, it does."

Nwah had heard enough. They were going to kill Kade for nothing more than the crime of being a convenient scapegoat.

She should warn him.

No. It wouldn't work. She knew him better than to think he would leave the sick man—the *poisoned* man. And he wasn't really listening to her now, anyway.

She considered magic. The ley-line along the outer ranges of the city felt suddenly stronger, but the idea scared her. She didn't know what to do with it, and a scan of the yard showed her how outnumbered she would be if anything went wrong.

There had to be another way.

The sound of chairs scraping the floor echoed from inside the room.

Her time was gone.

Yes, she thought. *There is another way.*

Silently, she slipped into the rain.

Nwah raced through the city, ignoring flashing hooves and bitter exclamations.

News that Commander Hale had died was rolling through town before she made it to the front gate. News of Kade's arrest wouldn't be far off.

There was one place she could go, one place she wasn't outnumbered.

So she loped at a steady pace, feeling the power of the ley-line alongside her.

Its aura leaked into her. For the first time, she accepted it fully. She breathed it in and used it to fill her body, used it to drive her legs farther and harder than she could run on her own. The road became less of dirt and more of grass, then became merely hard-pressed grass and rock. She didn't know how long she ran, but she became aware that the skies were darkening, and the land around her was filled with trees and the pure smells of moss and peat and other things: deer and elk, squirrel and hawk, denizens of the forest like her.

Kyree.

The male's scent was bold in the clean night air.

It spoke of her place in the world.

No, it spoke of the world itself: big and broad, noble and harsh, powerful beyond understanding.

She felt the aura of other *kyree*, too, dozens upon dozens of her kintype, no less present, no less bold. She merged with the power of her magic, forming it into a single message, a single plea.

:Come with me!: she sent to them all. *:Save my pairmate!:*

And they came.

The woods erupted with a cascade of movement, sounds, and scents of a hundred kinds. Boar beasts came through brush and briar. Ring-tailed bears and athletic elk came out of the woods with a scouring rustle that rose over the land. Muscled cats, coyote dogs, rabbits and rats, owls with the wingspan of cows, she called to the forest and the forest came to her.

:You are of us,: the alpha male said to her. *:We will do your bidding.:*

With that, her *kyree* cousins rode shepherd over this animal army as they turned toward the city proper and rolled over the land.

Nwah led them toward the city, feeling the true power of her Gift as she ran forward.

The ley-line was her life now. It was her purpose.

Its power raged through her army as they ran and flew and hopped and slithered toward the city. Her skin burned. The smell of clean fire overtook everything she knew as she raced ahead, her paws flying over the ground, her lungs burning with sweetness almost too great to bear.

:Save Kade!: she thought as she breathed in the world around her. *:Save Kade!:*

The night was dark when they arrived.

The ground was wet, but the rain had stopped.

The gate was closed, but walls are nothing to peregrines and owls, and gate latches can fall to the smallest of rodents when placed just so.

Nwah's heart pounded as she entered the city.

Her breath ached as her animal army raced past the guard and took the castle proper.

Her legs gave out then, and she lay in the manor yard, her tongue lolling in the mud.

She gulped last draughts of the ley-line.

Empty now. Unable to continue.

:The dungeon!: Nwah called, pulling at her Gift as hard as she had ever pulled and feeling it collapse over her. *:Find Kade in the dungeon!:*

It was the male *kyree* who took the command as she fell.

Nwah felt him, strong and bold in her stead.

Then the night went dark.

As with the city, there had been places to avoid in the Pelagiris.

Dark hollows, dangerous lairs, forces that tangled the land and oozed the essence of ugly magic.

The forest was her home, though, the place Nwah knew best. Her mother had taught her how to sense these places and how to slip through the brambles to avoid them. That was her answer when she asked herself how they survived in the woods, anyway. That was the story she told herself.

But in the darkness of this moment, Nwah could finally admit to herself that it was her Gift, too, that had saved them, that, unbidden and unthinking, she had tied into the wild powers of the dark forest and thrown protections over herself and Kade that kept them shielded while they lived under its canopy.

The Pelagiris was her home, though. It hadn't felt odd at all.

It was what she knew.

*   *   *

She woke to the smell of undergrowth and the sound of Kade's humming. The melody seemed somehow familiar. The pressure of his hand on her shoulder was like sunshine on her pelt.

A beetle scratched somewhere in the woodlands.

She opened her eyes to find herself in the cool shade of trees.

"She's awake."

It was Winnie's voice.

:Nwah?: Kade said. His voice was relieved, and so good to hear.

She rolled to her side, gave a grumble, and shook herself to remove debris from her coat. Every muscle in her body throbbed. *:Kade?:*

:I'm here.:

And he was there, beside her as he had always been, only this time the girl was also there. The expression on her face was more relieved than even Kade's.

Nwah felt another presence then. Masculine, noble, and very much *kyree.*

:The whole pack has been standing over you since we returned,: Kade said.

:Why?:

:I think you know.:

And she did.

Or, at least she almost did, which was good enough.

Life is long, she thought. *The world is big, and full of dangerous places.* If she had learned anything from their travels, it was that she had much more to learn about how the world around her really worked.

But she had even more to learn about herself.

She had to accept her Gift as part of who she was. Deal with it for being as real as Kade's was. She had to come to grips with what it truly meant to be *kyree* and to be paired with Kade in this strange way that was less than a Herald link but somehow so much more. They were lovers without being lovers, after all, friends who were more than friends, two people who circled each other like moons and planets, unable to exist alone but together pulling tides.

They were a strange pair, perhaps, but they were a pair.

And together they were going to make a difference.

"Is she going to be all right?" Winnie asked.

Kade put his hand on Winnie's shoulder and smiled in a way that said he'd followed everything she was thinking.

"Yes," he said. "I think she's going to be more than all right."

Trust Your Instincts

Dylan Birtolo

Fayne Jadrevalyn resisted the urge to wipe his damp palms against his clothing. He knew the gesture would be moot, since the sweat would just reappear within seconds. Despite the large gathering assembled here to witness the coronation of the new Queen of Rethwellan, the windows and open doors let in plenty of sun and allowed an occasional cool breeze to pass through. Fayne's perspiration had nothing to do with the day's temperature, but rather the duty that was soon to be passed to him as a distant relative to the Queen-to-be and one with the Mage Gift, even if he was yet to complete his training.

The trumpets sounded outside of the throne room, their echoes filling the chamber with a tune that made everyone stand a little bit straighter and hold their chins a bit higher. A few attending dignitaries went so far as to straighten their sleeves and pull them taut or smooth their dresses. For Fayne, he had to clench his hands tight to release some of the tension and resist the urge to shake them loose again. The time had come.

With strong, confident strides that were not matched within his heart, Fayne walked toward the small dais holding a weapon mount, on top of which rested the Sword That Sings. The hilt of the blade was adorned with emeralds set into the ends of the quillions, stones cut so perfectly that no matter how you looked at them, they caught and refracted the sunlight. The tip of the pommel housed a ruby the size of a child's fist, a gem that seemed to glow with its own light. Resting in the center of the hall to catch the slanted sun beams, the ornamental weapon was clearly a masterpiece.

But even that beauty paled in comparison to Fayne's senses once he curled the fingers of his right hand around the hilt. A warmth flooded up through his arm, not unlike the heat that came from resting in the field during a long summer day. The sensation was comforting, and in that moment, all his fears and concerns fled, leaving him with a sense of tranquility and peace.

Fayne reached out with his other hand and eased the weapon from its cradle, laying the bare blade against his palm. Turning around, he carried the weapon in front of him, his boots echoing off the stones with each step as he approached the Queen-to-be. She stood there, dressed in a gown that shimmered as if made from liquid silver, her hands clasped in front of her stomach. She appeared to be the picturesque definition of calm authority, but Fayne saw the tension in her hands. They didn't move, but the tendons were tight as she awaited her judgment. While her outward appearance was calm, she was nervous over what was to happen. In his opinion, that was an excellent quality for a ruler, but it was not his decision to make.

Even before he reached her, he knew how the sword would respond—he could feel it with every fiber of his being. The Sword That Sings had chosen her. She would be a good ruler. She would bring prosperity to his homeland, a realization that filled him with pride. The people would thrive and be well, and that was all he would ever think to ask for.

When he reached her, Fayne dropped to one knee, lifting the blade up high over his head with the hilt extended. At the edge of his sight, he saw the attendants holding their breath as they waited for the judgment of the Sword. It amazed him that they could not already tell what its answer would be.

She curled her fingers around the grip of the sword and lifted it to point at the ceiling. As she did so, it began singing, sending forth music that could never be matched or duplicated by human instrument or voice. It also began glowing, shining with a brilliance that made the sunlight itself seem pale by comparison. Those who had been looking on had to turn their heads or otherwise shield their eyes.

The Sword That Sings had made its choice clear. Queen Lethonel Jadrevalyn was the new ruler of Rethwellan. Long live the Queen!

"Don't you ever wish that you were named King, instead of your fourth or fifth cousin, or whatever our new Queen is?" Jhaeros brushed down a horse with exaggerated motions that made the animal snort and flick its tail at him. The thin man stood just out of reach and ignored the swat but did lessen his enthusiasm.

Dipping his hands in the water bucket, Fayne splashed some onto his face and used his wet hands to slick his short blond hair back, pushing it out of his face. A few trails of water dripped down his cheek until they lost themselves in his beard. The coolness felt refreshing on this inordinately warm autumn day—a nice break from helping an old friend with his stable chores.

"Not really. Sure, there was a time we used to talk about what we'd do once I was king, but those days are long past. They were nothing more than the flights of fantasy of a child anyway. Much the same as you pretending to be a traveling swordsman. I just became a Journeyman. That's good enough for me."

Fayne chuckled as he picked up his brush again. He walked to the next mount in the stable, a temperamental bay that flattened her ears and snorted at him when he came close. Only when he fished a treat out of his pocket and held it out to her in a flat palm did she lift her ears back up. He came down here often enough to visit Jhaeros that he'd learned the horses' temperaments almost as well as the stable hand.

"Yeah, just kids being kids, I suppose." Jhaeros paused and rested his hands on the horse's back. He was tall enough that he didn't even need to reach up to do so, even though this was one of the larger horses in the stable. "I just don't understand it. You had a chance for everything and never would've needed to work another day in your life. And you're okay with that because an artifact chose her over you?"

"You don't understand. It's not just some 'artifact.' It's the *Sword That Sings*." Fayne emphasized each word. He paused for a moment, savoring the memory of holding the blade in his hands. He'd thought about it off and on over the last year, but now it sprang to the forefront of his thoughts. After a shake of his head, he continued. "Even if it wasn't directly responsible for our prosperity as a nation, it's . . . alive and it knows things. I felt it."

"And it told you these things?" Jhaeros turned to face Fayne. Crossing his arms in front of his chest, he looked down at his childhood friend, one eyebrow raised. "It spoke to you? In a voice that only you could hear?"

"Well . . ." Fayne's motions slowed as he searched for the words to explain the sensation. Just thinking of it brought a brief shudder of comfort through his body. "It's not that it uses words or anything like that. It's more of a feeling. As I said, it knows things, and when I touched it, somehow it just shared what it knew with me. I knew it was going to choose Queen Lethonel. And I know without any doubt in my heart that she's the right choice. She's the rightful Queen. Besides, she's done well over the last year and change."

Jhaeros scoffed. "You sound about as convinced about that as I am. You sure you aren't having regrets?"

Fayne pressed his lips together and shook his head. His friend misread his tone, taking his distraction for a lack of faith. The more he tried to ignore it, the more his brain actively sought the memory of the warmth from the sword to calm his spirit. The mare in front of him swatted at a fly, the coarse hairs of her tail stinging his face as he got too distracted to remain at a safe distance.

That thought continued growing over the rest of the day, until Fayne found himself tossing in his bed and sweating, unable to find anything even close to resembling sleep. He tried meditation, but the Sword That

Sings invaded his thoughts even there, becoming a com-
pulsion and a need. He knew he had to feel its warmth
once again.

His mind made up, Fayne dressed and walked quietly
through the halls toward the throne room. The moon
was faint tonight, but it still cast enough light through
the windows to paint long white stripes across the
wooden floor. The rest of the palace was quiet, ignorant
of his nighttime wandering. Not even the guards were
awake at this hour, at least not inside the palace.

The hall looked almost more majestic when lit by the
moon and the stars. The banners hanging from the ceiling had an unearthly glow to them, and where the moonlight struck the marble floor here, it looked like ribbons
of silver. The throne was empty, but Fayne had grown so
accustomed to seeing his cousin in the seat that he
thought he caught a glimpse of her, causing a hitch in his
step. Next to the throne, the dais was back in its proper
place holding the Sword That Sings.

The moment Fayne saw the blade, it captured his entire focus. Nothing else seemed to matter. He moved
forward as if in a trance, bare feet shuffling against the
stones, his hand reaching out even before the blade was
within reach.

Before long, he stood next to the dais with his hand
hovering over the hilt, shaking with the anticipation of
gripping the magical sword. Fayne closed his eyes tight
and curled his fingers together around the hilt, anticipat-
ing the welcome, calming warmth.

The shock of bitter cold forced him to suck in air as
his entire hand felt as if it had just plunged into a glacier
stream from the mountains. The chill spread up his arm
through his chest until he found he couldn't even inhale.
His body swayed back and forth as he struggled to
breathe for what felt like an eternity. A sense of fear
flooded his brain, a sudden, irrational fear which had no
source nor reason, and seemed to come from nowhere.
He just knew he needed to run, but his entire body refused to listen to his commands.

With a surge of will, he managed to release his fingers

and jerk his arm back. Air rushed into his lungs in a long
gulp, and as soon as his legs would obey, Fayne ran back to
his room. He burst through the door and closed it, flatten-
ing his back against the wood, panting as he tried to calm
himself. The memory of what he had felt sent a shiver
through his spine, and he slid to the floor, wrapping his arms
around his legs and pulling them close against his chest.

Fayne had no concept of how long he stayed in that
position, but at some point, he fell asleep. His dreams
were plagued with the fall of his kingdom. He saw dis-
ease, famine, war. He saw a man sitting on the throne,
someone he didn't recognize but knew was of his blood,
growing wealthy while the people of his kingdom
starved. When he managed to wake, curled up on the
floor next to the door, Fayne could not shake the feeling
of dread threatening to overpower him.

Now his fear had a source, but that realization brought
him no comfort.

Trying as hard as he could to push the dreams away
seemed only to keep them close to the surface. Nonethe-
less, Fayne went about his duties for the day. As he at-
tended court, he barely registered the words that were
said, his eyes continuously drawn back to the blade. He
felt it watching him. Fayne didn't know how and didn't
know why he knew, but the sword was aware of his presence. It was asking something of him, almost as clearly
as if it had spoken. But Fayne didn't know what it wanted.
Was he being punished for touching it when it was for-
bidden? If so, it knew how to torture him and what images would cause the most pain.

Fortunately, court was blessedly short today, with no
matters that required his expert opinion or insight. As
the members shuffled out of the main hall, Fayne hesitated, his gaze lingering over the sword. Just as the first
beads of sweat formed on the side of his face, he jerked
his eyes away and strode out of the throne room without
glancing back.

That night, his dreams were no better. When sleep finally
came, the nightmares of the previous evening returned

with a vengeance. The people suffered under a cruel regime, crying to each other, and as they cried, Fayne felt his own tears warm his cheeks. At the end of it, the Sword That Sings was broken, shattered into fragments as he watched.

Fayne jerked to a sitting position, his breath coming in ragged gasps and his hand clutching his chest as he tried to shake off the remnants of the dream. When he was finally able to breathe normally, he knew what he needed to do. He didn't know how to explain it, and he didn't think anyone would believe him, but he needed to get the sword out of the capital.

Jumping out of bed, he shoveled clothes into his traveling pack, thankful for his Journeyman training which had sent him back and forth across the country, and instilled the instincts to travel light and ready at a moment's notice. Slinging his pack over his shoulder, he eased out of his room and crept to the throne room.

Once again, the palace passageways were empty, with everyone inside fast asleep. His feet carried Fayne to the base of the dais and he stood in front of the Sword That Sings. He reached up to grab it and paused, his hand stilled just a finger's width above the hilt. He took a deep breath and lowered his hand onto the metal, bracing for the shock of cold.

To his surprise, the weapon did not freeze his arm this time. It was chill to the touch, but there was a warmth underneath, like a fire in the middle of a snowstorm. The sword had spoken to him—this needed to happen. He knew that now.

Grabbing the sheath of the weapon, he tucked it away and fastened the belt around his waist. The blade felt oddly light compared to swords he had carried before, just a reminder that while it was enchanted, it was no weapon in the traditional sense. Even though he no longer held the hilt, Fayne found that he could still feel the magic, was still aware of its presence and the sensations it conveyed.

He ran out through the great hall and to the side door leading to the courtyard, opting for haste over stealth. If anyone saw him now, it would be impossible to explain why he was carrying the Sword That Sings. There was no reason for it to ever leave the main hall. This action doomed him as a traitor.

He eased the door open, wincing as the hinges groaned in protest, but the only sound that came in response was the chirping of crickets in the yard. Fayne didn't bother to close the door as he slid through and ran to the stables. He didn't want to take his chances going on foot. He needed to put as much distance between himself and the inevitable pursuit as possible. Plus, he needed help.

The small cottage house where Jhaeros lived was not even a stone's throw away from the stables, but no light emerged from the windows. Fayne wasn't surprised. Jhaeros would need to be up a few hours before sunrise to make sure the horses were fed and taken care of in case any of the lords or ladies wanted a morning ride.

Fayne knocked on the cottage door several times. Jhaeros groaned on the other side, but it was impossible to tell if it was a sign of him getting up or rolling over and going back to sleep. Fayne pounded on the door with the bottom of his fist, using a bit more force to add some urgency to his summons.

"Jhaeros! It's me. Get up. We need to go, now!"

After some unintelligible mumbling and a few heavy thumps, the door swung open and Jhaeros stood there, blinking several times, then knuckling his eyes as he stifled a yawn. His dark hair was disheveled and pointing in more directions than the thorns of a thistle seed. A cold burning sensation emanated from the sword and spread through Fayne's hip.

"Fayne? What the hell? The sun's not going to be up for a few hours."

"You remember what we were talking about in the stable? Well, looks like you get to live your dream. Traveling swordsman and all that."

Jhaeros reached up and pulled his hair back, tying it behind his head with a small strip of leather. He closed his eyes and took a deep breath. When he opened them, he focused on the man standing in front of him. "What are you talking about? Make some sense, or I'm going to shut this door in your face and crawl back into bed."

"You know how I said that the sword spoke to me during the ceremony? It did it again. And it told me that I need to get it out of the city as soon as possible. It can't stay here. Our entire future's at stake."

While Fayne spoke, his hand strayed over to the hilt of the sword, capturing Jhaeros's attention and pulling his gaze down. When he saw the bejeweled hilt, his eyes grew wide and any trace of sleep fled completely. His hand reached out for a moment, but he jerked it back well before it came close to making contact.

"That's . . . really it, isn't it? The legendary Sword That Sings? You realize that even taking it out of the palace is a crime. Leaving the city with it would be considered treason!"

"I know, but there's no other way. Look, I can't explain it, you need to trust me on this one."

Jhaeros hesitated, making Fayne pause. He needed to convince his friend—he couldn't do this alone. Fayne forced a smile onto his face, hoping his feigned exuberance would cover the blatant lie. "Besides, once we return, we'll have saved the nation and be heroes. Real honest-to-goodness heroes responsible for saving our country!"

Jhaeros stood in the doorway, his eyes darting back and forth from the sword to the stables. After a few tense moments of internal debate, he nodded and clapped Fayne hard enough on the shoulder to make the smaller man stumble.

"All right. I'll come with you."

Fayne shivered as the wind howled across from the Comb and bit through his clothes. A fierce gust caught the fold of his coat and ripped it from his hand, leaving him exposed to the fierce gale. After a brief fumble, he pulled the jacket closed, trying to shield himself from the elements. Not for the first time, he wished he'd the foresight to bring heavier clothing.

Their only remaining mount walked close enough

behind him that her head prodded him, pushing on him as he fought against the wind. Jhaeros sat in the saddle, leaning forward to hug the horse's neck, trying to absorb as much of the animal's heat as possible. His face was etched into a scowl that had become his standard look these past few weeks.

Ahead, the road bent around a small cluster of boulders arranged in such a way that they were clearly meant to be a resting spot for travelers. The blackened fire pit in the center of the limited shelter reinforced this theory.

Once they were out of the wind, Jhaeros slid out of the saddle, collapsing to a knee with a hand on the ground to steady him. Fayne walked over to help his friend stand up, but Jhaeros slapped his hand away.

"Why are we here? We should have gone east like I suggested, headed into Karse. At least then we'd be warm."

"The sword says—"

Jhaeros launched himself up and shoved Fayne hard enough to make the man stumble and fall backward. He instinctively reached for the sword, even though it was ceremonial. Ignoring him, Jhaeros stormed over to the exhausted horse, the animal too tired to eat, and began unloading gear from its back for the coming nightfall.

"I'm sick of listening to your damned sword! It doesn't talk, but still you know what it's saying and that it wants us to kill ourselves in these hills. There's not even enough food for the horse! I thought we were going to be heroes. Instead we're out here, on the border of Valdemar, just before winter, with almost no food. If that sword's even saying anything, it's been giving you the worst advice it possibly could!"

Fayne pushed himself up, dusting off the dirt after he did so. "And what about the times we tried ignoring the sword and what it wanted? Do you remember that? Do you remember the bandits stealing our horse? Do you remember the patrol from the capital that almost found us and would have killed us for traitors? Or how about the angry villagers in that town you insisted we stop at, despite the sword's misgivings? You just wanted to have a nice bed for the night, and instead we barely escaped with our hides intact. It seems to me that the sword isn't the one giving the poor advice."

Leather creaked in protest as Jhaeros tightened his hands around the straps holding their meager gear in place. Fayne noticed the tension and backed down, shrinking into himself as he walked to the firepit.

"I'll start a fire," he offered so softly it could barely be heard over the wind whipping around the rocks. Jhaeros offered no response but continued unloading their gear, tossing a bedroll to land near Fayne's feet. As he lit the fire with his magic, Fayne was painfully aware of how low his reserves were. Normally such an easy trick, now it left him barely holding on to consciousness.

They went about the rest of their preparations for the evening in silence. Words had still not been exchanged by the time they were seated and eating salted pork and apples. It was simple fare, but it traveled well.

Afterward, Fayne curled up in his bedroll, removing the sword from his belt and cradling it in his hands as he fell asleep. It felt cold enough to sting his hands, but he refused to let it go and was too exhausted to let it keep his eyes open.

Again, his dreams were troubling. He imagined he was trapped in a blizzard, walls of white surrounding him on all sides. Someone shouted at him, but the words were lost to the roar of the storm; all that was left was the sense of urgency and importance. Fayne couldn't even tell where the sound was coming from, nor could he see anything beyond the thick snows.

When he woke, he still clutched the sword, but something felt wrong—faint for lack of a better word. Sitting up and trying to shake the cobwebs of the dream from his brain, Fayne knew something was wrong.

He looked around, trying to put the pieces together. The fire was out, and only a few ashes remained, but that was to be expected. Jhaeros wouldn't have kept the fire going and would've wanted to get some rest himself.

Realization crashed over Fayne like a wave. Jhaeros wasn't there!

He scrambled to his feet and looked for some sign of his companion, but there was nothing. At first, he thought they might have been attacked, but then he noticed that all of the extra gear was missing, as was the horse. All Fayne had left was his pack and the sword.

He walked onto the trail and looked back, searching for any sign of Jhaeros, but it was too dark, and the hills obscured his vision. Maybe he could try setting out in the morning, hoping Jhaeros didn't travel too far before making camp.

Shivering from his exposure to the bitter wind, Fayne slunk back into the shelter. He thought to check his pack before curling back up, and was pleased to see that at least Jhaeros had not ransacked his personal supplies. Fayne tucked himself into his bedroll, savoring the fact that it still had some residual heat. He grabbed the sword and froze, breaking out into an immediate sweat despite the cool temperature.

He didn't believe it at first, so he checked again, feeling with his fingers and holding the hilt up to the sky so he could use the limited moonlight to verify his fear. Jhaeros may have left Fayne's pack intact, but he had pried loose the precious stones from the hilt of the Sword That Sings.

Fayne let out a wordless scream of rage, pain, and exhaustion that echoed off the hills and came back to him. Tears burned against his cheeks as he clutched the sword to his chest. As he curled up, lacking the energy to remain kneeling, a soft and gentle heat spread out from the blade, lulling him into a restful—if not comfortable—sleep.

With a grunt of effort, Fayne pulled himself across the ground into the shelter of a low cluster of rocks that blocked the wind. At their base was the only place he could see that wasn't covered in snow. Every muscle in his body was shivering. Where his clothes weren't frozen solid, they stuck to him with a damp cold that ate through his skin.

Once he was out of the snow, he rolled onto his side

and shrugged off his pack. The bedroll was damp too, but the inside was dry as he wrapped it around him. He continued shivering, but it did offer some small bit of comfort.

Once his trembling had calmed down enough that he could feel the exhaustion seeping into his bones, he considered his options. The bedroll wouldn't warm him enough without a fire, and his reserves were too depleted to magic a flame or provide a shield from the elements. He reached down and clasped the hilt of the sword. He didn't know if it could hear him, but he needed to try.

"I'm going to need your help. I could use some of that warmth of yours right now. Otherwise I'll never make it through The Comb."

The sword pulsed softly, issuing a gentle warmth that chased some of the chill from his body before falling still once again. Feeling invigorated from the magical assistance, Fayne stood and managed to trudge the couple steps to the edge of his shelter. Bracing himself against the rough rock, he leaned out, trying to see just how far he still had to go. It was a clear day, with a harsh wind that blew into his drawn face. But even here, near the top of a hill, all he could see was a barren, rolling, white landscape stretching as far as he could see in every direction. The trail was long lost, and it would take at least a couple more days to make it through The Comb.

Going back to his pack, he searched for food, but he found nothing. Upending it and spilling all his belongings out over the floor, Fayne saw he had no food left. He might be able to manage finding water, but nothing grew here that he could eat. His options were to starve, or head back and hope for the best.

He sat down and leaned back against the rocks, gazing out over his homeland stretching far to the south as far as he could see. His hand dropped down to the sword and rested on the hilt.

"I never was supposed to make it to Valdemar, was I?" he asked, his voice soft.

The sword was quiet for a long time before emitting a low, mournful sound that was beautiful enough to break hearts.

Fayne nodded and his lips curled up into a soft smile as he caressed the hilt with his thumb. "It's all right. I think deep down, I always knew that. But . . . this will help them? This will save my people?"

The Sword That Sings began to glow, emitting a light as bright as during the coronation ceremony a year and a half ago. Fayne's eyes had already closed of their own volition, but he could feel the light beyond them. And the song the blade released made Fayne think of his home, his people, and the country he loved. Fresh tears streaked his cheeks, with none of the sting of before.

"Then it was worth it."

Fayne drifted into an exhausted sleep listening to the song of his homeland, the song of hope and prosperity. The sword slowly faded into silence as Fayne passed from the world . . . the traitor who had saved his kingdom.

Discovery
Nancy Asire

The storm that had lashed the town had dissipated with the coming of dawn, but relief from the oppressive heat and stickiness that usually followed such departure was absent. By midmorning, the town began to swelter in the summer sunlight.

Perran, traveling judge out of Sunhame, representative of the Son of the Sun and keeper of the laws of Vkandis, sat by the open window that overlooked the garden behind the inn where he and his assistant, Levron, had rooms. The two guards that always traveled with Perran stayed in an adjoining room, ready to take any orders from their master at a moment's notice.

The scent of the flowering bushes in the garden wafted through the open window. Now that the sun had risen and the dampness of the rain began to evaporate, the perfume from those bushes grew even stronger.

"If it gets much hotter today, I swear I'll melt." This, from Levron, who stood by the window. "You'd think the storm would have brought some relief."

Perran nodded. "It's summer. We'll survive."

The judge sat clad in only a light white tunic, the black cloak of his judicial calling hanging by the side of his bed. He blinked and rubbed his forehead. The case he had been called to adjudicate appeared simple on the surface, but first impressions often led to misunderstanding. He caught Levron's eyes.

"So, what do you think? A simple case of one family

accusing another out of jealousy, or is there more here than apparent?"

Levron shrugged. "Hard to tell. The interviews I've conducted with their fellow citizens seem divided. Some favor the plaintiff, while others are strongly behind the defendant. As of now, I'd say the opinions are close to equal."

"Equal? At first glance, possibly. Did you sense any underlying evasiveness in anyone's answers?"

"I can't truthfully say one way or the other. But given the status of the defendant's family in the town, I wouldn't be surprised if some statements might be swayed by their position."

Perran steepled his fingers in front of his eyes. "So. What I need to know is rather simple on its face. Is this suit brought against Brock's family because the child has a bad reputation, or is the plaintiff asking for relief because Jerret's family suffered a loss caused by Brock? And what is the relief sought?" He glanced out the window and back again. "You've interviewed the majority of the townsfolk. Now I'll need you to take the statements of the mothers involved."

"Of course." Levron rubbed the back of his neck and stared at the ceiling. "Not a chore I'm looking forward to. From what I can tell, the two ladies aren't all that fond of each other."

"A fact evidenced by the other interviews you've conducted. You say this animosity has been brewing for years?"

"According to everything I've been able to discover. Even those who appear to favor Brock's family admit he's been in and out of trouble since he was little. The only thing that has kept him from stronger discipline is the fact that his family is more prominent than Jerret's."

"Well," Perran said, "not that we haven't run into that before." He sighed. "Do your best. And make certain the two ladies realize that you're my assistant, that what they say to you will be repeated exactly to me. Don't forget to pin your badge on your shoulder. That should be enough to keep what they say as honest as possible."

*   *   *

Who to visit first? Levron paused at the edge of the street bisecting the town of Zallow's Fork. This was the center of town, filled with the homes of the well-to-do, shops that catered to them, the inn where he and Perran were housed, and the town hall where the trial would take place. He looked to his left and right, considered tossing a coin to make his decision, then set off for Brock's home.

It was a lovely building, with a garden behind a low wall in front of the house. Levron took the stepping stone walk to the ornate front door and knocked.

"Yes?" A neatly clad man faced Levron. "May I help you?"

Levron bowed his head briefly. "I've come to interview Mistress Caromina on authority from Judge Perran, voice of the Son of the Sun and Vkandis Sunlord." As he said this, he gestured to the gold badge on his shoulder. "Your mistress has been informed that I will be here this morning to speak with her."

The man glanced at the pin and stepped aside. "Mistress Caromina will see you now. She's been waiting to speak with you."

Levron followed the man into the house, refusing to be impressed by the implied wealth displayed. Colorful hangings graced the walls, and the floor was covered with a deep-piled carpet.

Mistress Caromina received the two men seated in a high-backed chair. She was an attractive woman, her black hair gathered at her neck and falling across her shoulders. Her gown gathered light from the open window at her side, evidence that it was most likely silk.

She gestured to a chair facing hers. "Please be seated. I take it you wish to speak with me about the suit brought against this house."

"That is true, Lady," Levron said. "With any luck, our conversation should be brief if you answer the questions I have for you."

Her black eyes hardened. "I'm aware you are the judge's assistant. Have you worked with him very long?"

"Long enough so that he trusts me with my findings,

Lady," Levron replied. "Surely you don't question the authority I bring with me to question you."

Caromina drew a quick breath. "No. You must understand my position. My husband is a merchant of impeccable honesty. He would be here for this trial had he not been absent on business. Therefore, I stand in place of the head of household and will answer any questions you ask."

Levron nodded. "My thanks. I need to know more about your son, Brock. From what I've discovered, he has the reputation of being a troublemaker."

"Pffft!" Caromina lifted her chin. "He's high spirited, that's true. Sometimes the other boys in town find that intimidating."

"But he has been called to task in school, has he not?"

"He and other boys. It wasn't always his fault."

"I've been told that Brock was guilty of breaking a window in one of the shops a few blocks away," Levron said. "Is that true or not?"

"He was accused of that," Caromina acknowledged. "His father paid to have the window repaired but denied Brock was the boy who threw the rock."

"There have been other instances of Brock being accused of petty destruction of property, have there not?"

Mistress Caromina drew herself rigidly upright. "Who is spreading tales about my son? Who?" She darted a cold glance to her left, out the window at the neighboring house. "Is it that . . . that woman who is suing me? She surely is responsible for those statements."

"Not only her, Lady. Those statements have come from other people as well."

"I suppose she's behind most of those rumors. She's never liked Brock. For some reason, she has always looked askance at him."

"Has Brock fought with Jerret recently?"

Caromina eyes wavered. "They had a minor altercation."

"And this is the reason the suit has been brought?"

"It's bad blood between our two houses. A minor thing that's been blown completely out of proportion."

"But a broken leg is surely not a minor thing," Levron pointed out.

Lips thinned, Caromina looked away.

Sudden movement behind her chair caught Levron's attention. Two gold eyes caught the light as an orange tabby cat peered up at him.

"Is he yours?" Levron asked, pointing at the cat.

Caromina jumped to her feet. "Davan!" she cried. "Get in here! That ratty old cat is in the house again! I want it out of here now!"

Davan, the man who had greeted Levron at the front door, ran into the room with a broom and swiped behind Caromina's chair at the cat. A few prods with the broom, and the cat fled across the room and jumped out the opened window.

"That nasty thing!" Caromina said, her face flushed. "I wish someone would get rid of it!"

Levron stared at the window the cat had jumped through. "Who owns the cat?"

"No one! It comes and goes, though I hadn't seen it lately." Caromina sat down again and waved a hand at Davan. "You may go. Try, if you can, to keep that beast out of the house."

"Yes, Mistress. I don't think the cat will be back. Brock won't —"

"That's enough! Leave us!"

Davan bowed and left the room.

Levron cleared his throat. "If there's nothing else, Lady, I'll take my leave. You've answered most of the questions Judge Perran wanted me to ask. Thank you for the privilege of your company."

Outside, Levron wiped his forehead. The interior of Caromina's house had been more than warm. He glanced up, hoping to see a few clouds that might dim the sunlight, but the sky was a clear, uncluttered blue. Now, on to the next interview.

The house next door was slightly smaller than Mistress Caromina's, but it was well kept and also boasted a neat garden in front. Levron drew a deep breath and knocked on the door.

Instead of a servant, a tall woman faced Levron, her hair piled high in a bun. Her gown, while not as rich as the one Caromina wore, was still of quality.

"I'm Levron, assistant to Judge Perran. I've come to speak with the mistress of this house."

The woman nodded. "I'm Hannah. Please come in."

Levron followed the woman to a corner of the large entry room. Two chairs waited by an open window. Hannah gestured Levron to one and took the other.

"My thanks," Levron said. "Judge Perran wants me to ask you a few questions before we go to trial. Is your son here?"

"No. He's at school."

"Have the two boys, Brock and Jerret, been involved in fights before?"

"Hardly at all," Hannah replied. "You must understand, Jerret is not a fighter. He was sickly when he was young and never attained his full growth. Brock, on the other hand, is a big boy. Most of the boys in town are afraid of him."

"Why is that?"

"He tends to boss the other boys around. His family is well known, and if complaints are made to Brock's father or mother, they stand up for him."

"And your husband?"

Hannah glanced down at her hands, which lay crossed in her lap. "Reyard died more than a year past. Fortunately, we had enough savings and ties with other merchant families that we are not suffering."

"I'm sorry for your loss. Have you and Mistress Caromina been at odds for a long time?"

"I would say so. When we were young, she had eyes for Reyard, but he chose me to be his wife."

"And this caused animosity between you?"

"Yes. I think she's always held Reyard's choice against me."

"What is her opinion of Jerret?"

Hannah smiled slightly. "She doesn't care much for him. Says he's a bookworm and would blow away in a strong wind. It's true that he studies more than the other boys and that he loves animals."

"Oh? I saw an orange cat in Mistress Caromina's house. She didn't seem pleased that the cat was there. Is that your cat?"

"No. I don't know who he belongs to. He started coming around about a half a year ago. Jerret pets him and makes sure he has food and water."

Levron remembered a cut-off comment Mistress Caromina's servant had made regarding Brock. "Has Brock been mean to the cat?"

"It wouldn't surprise me," Hannah said. "He doesn't seem to have much regard for anyone or anything other than himself."

"The injury suffered by Jerret at the hands of Brock, was that something witnessed by others?"

"Yes. But Mistress Caromina swears the other boys are lying. She says Brock could not have injured Jerret." Hannah's face hardened. "That's the way it always is. Between Brock's father and mother, you'd think the boy was innocent as the first dawn."

"So, there have been complaints raised to them before that they deny?"

"I'm afraid so. If anything goes sideways in town, most folks look to Brock." She met Levron's eyes. "Please don't think that I'm saying these things to prejudice Judge Perran. I'm merely telling you what has happened in the past. It's nothing new that Mistress Caromina would defend her son. She does it constantly."

"I see. Why exactly did you bring suit against Brock's mother?"

Hannah glanced up at the ceiling. "I want that boy to be brought to justice. Jerret has a broken leg, suffered during that fight with Brock. I'm not seeking a monetary award; the Healer's fee was reasonable." She shook her head. "I'm fed up with the fact that Brock is never held accountable for his misdeeds."

Levron nodded. "I'll make certain Judge Perran hears everything you've told me. Nothing more can be done until the trial itself. I thank you for your honesty."

Perran watched Levron pace up and down the room, a troubled expression on his assistant's face. "What's bothering you?" he asked.

"Mixed feelings," Levron replied, stopping by Perran's chair.

"And by that you mean?"

"It's hard for me to set aside my personal feelings. Of the two mothers, I would not hesitate to grant truth of the matter to Hannah. Yet there was something about my interview with Caromina that didn't set right with me. Brock seems to be a bully. Evidently he's also been cruel to a cat that lives around Jerret's house."

"I see. And, of course, I can't let any personal feelings sway my judgment in any way. You know that."

"I do. I don't envy you. I would find it nearly impossible to ignore any opinions I have after gathering information necessary to make a judgment." A rueful smile touched Levron's lips. "That's why you're the judge and I'm not."

Perran laughed. "Wise of you to acknowledge that. However, there have been many times when I've depended on your observations. Truth can come clad in many colors. All I can do is judge the trial with information gathered by you and by questioning the two boys."

"We've not conducted a trial like this in ... well, it's been quite a while."

"Yes. However, I don't think having the two mothers come before me would be best. From what you've gathered, Brock's mother would defend him in any case. As you told me, Hannah isn't seeking a monetary award, which means she's not bringing the suit out of greed."

"I think she's more interested in stopping Brock's behavior. Even those who support Mistress Caromina have allowed that her son has been a problem."

Perran leaned back in his chair. "I'm not used to questioning children," he said. "But I suppose that's why I've been given the task of making judgments. I can't always be presented with situations I'm comfortable with."

"The trial is this afternoon," Levron said, stopping by the open window. A breeze made the heat slightly more bearable. "I don't envy you having to sit there in your robes. The town hall will be packed, I'm sure."

Perran raked a hand through his hair. "The perils of my position. Perception is important. While everyone is aware I'm the voice of the Son of the Sun when passing judgment, it certainly doesn't hurt to look the part."

Levron's estimation of the crowd gathered in the town hall proved correct. He stood behind the judge at the entrance to the large room, adjusting his own tunic and glancing at the gathered town folk.

Timar, Perran's senior guard, called out loudly, "All rise! Judge Perran is present at these proceedings. All honor to the Voice of the Son of the Sun and the words of Vkandis Sunlord."

The crowd stood and faced the aisle down which Perran walked, followed by Levron and the two guards. At the end of the room a large table had been placed, an impressive chair for the judge behind it, and a smaller chair set to one side for Levron. The two guards stationed themselves against the wall, arms crossed.

As usual, Perran's appearance caused a quiet sigh from the assembled crowd. His black robe made the heavy gold chain of his office appear even brighter. A handsome man, Perran's face held no discernable expression. From this moment on, he was speaking for the rule of law set down by generations of judicial representatives.

Two chairs sat opposite the judge's table. The boys had taken their places, and they now fixed their attention on the judge. Levron could immediately see the difference between Brock and Jerret. Brock stood nearly two hands taller than Jerret and outweighed the slighter boy. Jerret, his right leg encased in a cast, had leaned a cane against his chair.

"Today I stand as judge in this matter," Perran said,

his voice easily reaching the rear of the room. "The words I say will be based on my judgment of the case brought before me. Let me remind all present: The outcome of this trial depends on what has been discovered, what is said, and the answers I receive. I have been granted the power to make my judgment by the Son of the Sun and the laws of Karse. Once my judgment has been made, it is final."

A low murmur ran through the gathered town folk. Now it was more than apparent that the proceedings and its outcome were fixed by the laws of Karse and the power of the Son of the Sun.

"So." Perran leaned forward in his chair, his arms crossed on the table before him. "I'll outline the case brought before me. From eyewitness accounts, a disagreement broke out between the two boys before me: Brock and Jerret. No one can say for certain what instigated the conflict, though the outcome is undisputed. Jerret suffered a broken leg and had to be seen by a Healer, who set the limb and told the boy to rest the leg before trying to walk, using the cane you all can see that he brought with him. Now I'll begin my questioning. Brock, you will stand. And remember, anything you say had best be the truth. I'm sworn to Vkandis to hear only that."

Levron saw a slight change in Brock's expression. Until Perran had called out his name, the boy had appeared, if anything, bored by the proceeding. When the judge had called his name, a brief tightening of his jaw evidenced slight unease.

"You and Jerret are neighbors, are you not?"

"Yes, Lord."

"And from what I've been told, you don't think too much of Jerret, do you?"

"No, Lord." Brock squared his shoulders. "He's not anyone I would be friends with."

"Which doesn't mean you should fight with him, does it?"

"He annoyed me," Brock said. "Called me a bully."

Perran nodded. "Does the name ring true?"

"Just because he's better than me at school doesn't give him the right to make fun of me."

"And how does he do that? Does he call *you* names?"

Brock shook his head. "No, Lord. It's the way he looks at me. He's soft. He's always been soft! Doesn't like to play rough and tumble. Doesn't like the fact that I don't pay attention to books, art, and animals."

Perran caught Levron sitting up straighter in his chair, a curious expression on his face. What was it that Levron had said about Brock being cruel to a stray cat?

"I see. And because he's 'soft' and reads a lot, cares for animals, and likes art, you think he's less than you?"

"Look at him, Lord," Brock said, gesturing at Jerret. "What use is he going to be if he can't stand up to some teasing?"

"An interesting observation. It takes all kinds to make Karse great, young man." Perran leaned back in his chair. "Now I've been told you have quite a history of getting in trouble here in town."

"No more than anyone else," Brock replied, lifting his chin. "If anything goes wrong, I get blamed for it."

"And yet you have been disciplined because of recurring problems, haven't you?"

Brock's eyes wavered. "It's not always my fault. You can ask my father and mother."

"I'm sure they would speak very highly of you. I've also been told that you like to order other boys around and, when they don't do what you ask, you lose your temper."

"That's not true! If I lose my temper, it's because they don't listen to me."

"So, you took offense at what Jerret said and started a fight with him?"

"Why should I have to put up with someone like him questioning me?"

"I see. Also, it's been reported that you're not only lording over the other boys, but you've been cruel to animals."

"If you're talking about that mangy cat that Jerret takes care of, I might have kicked him a time or two.

Ratty old thing got in the house one day, and I didn't like it."

Levron noticed Jerret stiffened in his chair and shoot a dark look in Brock's direction.

"But kicking the cat isn't the only animal you've been cruel to, is that right?"

"My Lord! Please!"

A woman stood who had been sitting directly behind Brock. She glanced left and right, her face gone white.

"I assume you're Mistress Caromina," Perran said, his voice gone very cold. "By what right do you disturb these proceedings?"

"It's unfair, Lord, to ask my son whether he's been cruel to animals in the past. How does that have anything to do with this ridiculous suit brought against my son and my house?"

"Sit down, Lady," Perran snapped. "When you have attained a judgeship and have been given rights attendant to it, perhaps you might argue with me. Until that time, you will keep silent and refrain from disturbing these proceedings. Do you understand?"

This time, the murmur that passed through the crowd was louder. Caromina blinked several times, her cheeks flushed, and sat down, keeping her eyes lowered.

From where he sat slightly behind Judge Perran, Levron had a good vantage point from which to view the gathered town folk seated in the town hall. It gave him some solace to see that everyone appeared to be suffering from the heat as much as he. Several people had brought fans and were attempting to create a breeze. Another scan of the assembly revealed a mixture of expressions; some seemed amazed at Caromina's interruption of Perran's examination of Brock, while other faces held hints of anger.

As for Jerret, the boy had sat silent through the entire proceeding. His mother, positioned directly behind him, had remained quiet and composed. Once again, Levron thanked Vkandis that he held the position of assistant to a judge, for he grew more convinced that everything Hannah had told him regarding Brock rang true. He knew he would find it nearly impossible to render an unprejudiced ruling in a similar case.

He watched Brock's reaction to the continued questions Perran asked, the boy's face alternating between haughty assurance and slight confusion. He supposed Brock had never had to defend his past misdeeds.

As for Caromina, she could hardly sit still. Levron didn't need mystical powers to know what she thought. All the years of protecting her only son now fell under scrutiny, not only from her fellow town folk, but from a sanctioned judge straight out of Sunhame, granted powers by the Son of the Sun.

At last, Perran motioned Brock to be seated and turned his attention to Jerret. The boy's face went pale, but his eyes never wavered from the imposing figure of the judge.

"You do not need to rise, Jerret," Perran said, pointing to the cane the boy had leaned against his chair. "I understand it would be uncomfortable for you, and I need you to pay strict attention to the questions I ask. Be reminded that you, as Brock, are sworn to answer truthfully. Do you understand?"

"I do, Lord."

"All right. Please tell us briefly how you sustained your injury."

Jerret swallowed heavily. "I was out with a group of boys. We had finished school and had gathered by some shops before heading home."

"And you were doing nothing but talking?"

"That's all, Lord. And then Brock came up to us. He had several companions with him. My friends and I don't really associate with him or his friends. They tend to tease us every chance they get."

"Why is that, Jerret?"

"I guess it's because they're bigger and stronger than we are. They like to push us around. Anyway, he began teasing us again, calling us soft and useless. We don't play sports like they do, and I guess that makes them think we're sissies."

"What happened next?"

"There's an orange cat that has started living around my house. He roams a lot around town and has become affectionate. Anyway, we weren't all that far away from my house, so I wasn't surprised to see him. For some reason, Brock doesn't like the cat. He picked up a rock and threw it at the cat."

"Has he done this before?"

"Yes. But the cat's pretty fast and doesn't get hit much. I said something to Brock about him being mean to the cat and he didn't like it."

"Has Brock been cruel to other animals?"

"Yes, Lord. He kicked a puppy that belongs to Fora, a sister of a friend of mine."

Perran glanced at Brock. The boy's face had gone red, but his jaw still remained clenched. "I see. So, what happened next?"

"Oh, the usual, Lord. Brock called me nothing short of a wilted flower. I'm thinking I have to go home, get away from him. I turned to go and he pushed me. I almost fell, but I turned away. That's when he pushed me again, and I tripped over a low set of steps leading to one of the shops."

"Was this when you broke your leg?"

"Yes, Lord. It hurt awful bad."

Perran leaned back in his chair, resting his chin on his hand. He glanced at Caromina, who now sat motionless, her attention fixed on her son.

"Has Brock ever hit or pushed you before?"

"Several times. He doesn't like me."

"All right. So, your friends found some adults to take you home. And then the Healer came and set your leg, is that right?"

"Yes, Lord. He gave me something for pain, and it made me sleepy and confused."

Perran sat up straighter and drew a deep breath. "All right. Now, I'm going to consult with my assistant, who has questioned people regarding this case. I require silence in the room."

He motioned Levron forward. "Do the statements

made by Brock and Jerret ring true from what you've discovered?" he asked in a hushed voice.

"They do," Levron replied.

"Well, I think this might not be as difficult a judgment to render, then."

Sudden movement swept through the assembled town folk, a loud murmur arising from the rear of the room. Perran frowned, leaned forward and looked down the aisle, and saw an orange cat wandering toward Brock and Jerret. Total silence fell on the room then as everyone watched the feline visitor.

The cat looked around as if to get his bearings and came directly up to Jarret. With a soft meow, the cat rubbed up against Jerret's chair. Then he turned and stared at Brock.

Ears back, fur raised along his spine, and tail bristled, the cat hissed loudly, turned, and fled down the aisle toward the back of the room.

Levron found it difficult to keep a smile from his face. If evidence had ever been presented at trial, this intrusion was outstanding. He looked at Caromina, whose face had frozen in a distinctly horrified expression. Brock sat as if turned into stone, but Jerret turned his head to see where the cat had run off to.

From past experience, Levron knew judgment would be forthcoming. He felt certain he could foretell what Perran would say, but he kept his thoughts to himself, schooling his face into immobility. It would not do to give any hint as to what he hoped would be the outcome.

As for the town folk gathered at the trial, they sat silent, even their fans still, their eyes trained on the judge who sat behind the large table, ready to make a decision that could affect everyone.

Perran leaned forward, his attention locked on Brock and Caromina. Mother and son stared back, and it was difficult to sense what they felt. No matter. The judgment he would hand out was going to be distinctly different than what might be expected. As for Hannah and Jerret, they sat as silent as the rest of the gathered town folk.

"Hear me!" Perran said, crossing his arms on the table. "I speak now as the judicial representative of the Son of the Sun and Vkandis Sunlord. The judgment I render will be final with no appeal, and reported back to Sunhame.

"We're dealing here with a situation that I've seen in the past—a situation that, in many cases, goes unpunished. Caromina, will you please stand."

Brock's mother glanced left and right, squared her shoulders, and stood.

"You've heard the evidence presented and the testimony given to my assistant. It should be clear to you by now that you have a problem with your son."

"But, Lord," Caromina said, "Brock's always been a handful, but his father and I have tried to keep him in line."

"Not from what I've heard," Perran said. "Excuses made for him, over and over. No obvious punishment given him for any of his misdeeds. Do you realize that by withholding discipline of any sort, you're actually harming your son?"

Caromina shook her head slightly. "We only wanted the best for Brock. He's our only son, destined to follow his father as a successful merchant."

"If that is true," Perran said, "he won't do well as a merchant. Bullying in any form isn't favored among the merchant class. He may be able to hold sway over boys and girls in town, but I don't think other merchants would be pleased to deal with someone who won't listen to objections made against him. Eventually, they'll become exasperated and conduct fewer transactions with him. I ask you, what is one of the methods employed in dealing with goods to be transferred or sold? Is it trying to push others around, or learning to deal with different personalities that might not accept such actions and otherwise reach a compromise?"

Caromina glanced down at her feet, then looked in Brock's direction, but remained silent.

"The case before me has no request for a monetary reward. Mistress Hannah has raised the question of how her son was pushed by your son and consequently broke his leg. Jerret simply questioned Brock's meanness, displayed not only to him, but to other children in town and, by extension, to animals. If this behavior is not curtailed, it could become even more disastrous. Can you begin to see what the outcome could be?"

"I suppose, Lord," Caromina said in a small voice, "you have shown me another way of looking at things. We, his father and I, only wanted the best for Brock."

"And overlooked his bad behavior. Let me tell you a story. A few years back, I presided at a murder trial. The defendant had brutally killed three people. Now this might not seem to have any bearing on the decision I make today, but it does. From childhood, this young man had been cruel to animals, torturing them in any vile way you can imagine. This was not the first time I had been presented with a killer who began his life of crime by torturing animals. From those acts, he began to bully and beat other children. There seems to be some connection between that behavior that escalates into murder. This is a path I can see unfolding before your son."

"Murder?" Caromina exclaimed. "Surely not, Lord!"

"Yes, Mistress Caromina. It's a fact that I can give you more evidence of, that I've seen and passed judgment on. Bullies tend to go after anything and anyone they sense can't retaliate. It can start out as cruelty to animals that can't fight back, to going after younger children who are powerless to respond. This is also a behavior displayed when a bully sees ample opportunity to tease and push around other children." He looked at Brock, who had leaned so far back in his chair that it appeared he was trying to become invisible.

"Hear my judgment. I'm issuing an order that will be obeyed as if it comes directly from the Son of the Sun. For the act that broke Jerret's leg, there is no monetary award. Mistress Hannah didn't request one. What she did request was a review of Brock's behavior that resulted in her son's injury. My order will go to the instructors at the school both boys attend. The instructors will be ordered to pay special attention to Brock, to work with him in trying to turn his mind in a direction that doesn't promote the behavior of a bully. They will make periodic reports of Brock's progress. And let me make this clear: If Brock is unable to change his behavior, if any of his instructors see no improvement in him, there are schools in Karse that deal with bullies who are unable to change. I can see, Mistress Caromina, that you understand all too well what I'm saying."

Caromina bowed her head, her face gone pale. "I do, Lord."

"Then let it be my judgment. Brock will be monitored at school by his instructors. His friends, those who follow him in his bullying, will be held under scrutiny. This behavior will be brought to a halt. Today. Brock, you will stand."

Brock stood, his expression wavering between embarrassment and outright fear.

"You will now give your sincere apology to Jerret for causing his injury. And, believe me, I'll know if the words you say are true."

Brock turned and faced Jerret. "I'm sorry for what I did. It won't happen again."

Jerret nodded. "I hope not," he said in a steady voice. "I never held anything against you."

"So, then." Perran looked from Caromina, Brock, Hannah, and Jerret to the assembled town folk. "This is my judgment, sanctioned by the Son of the Sun and laws of Vkandis Sunlord. No appeals will be made. So I have judged, so let it be acknowledged."

Levron and Perran left the town hall behind, full of citizens who now were left to deal with the judgment rendered against Brock. Levron could hardly contain his appreciation for the judgment Perran had given. He had hoped the outcome would bolster his admiration for his master and had not been disappointed. It was a different trial from those he was used to, but the judgment had been, as far as he could see, correct to the last.

"Well, Levron," Perran said as they walked the short way to the inn. "What do you think?"

"What do I think?" Levron shrugged his shoulders. "Once again, you reveal yourself as a wise judge, one who takes all evidence into consideration and makes a proper judgment. I hope Brock can turn himself around."

"It's my hope too. I don't want to see a boy turn into a lawbreaker just because he thinks he can get away with it. Unless parents can truly see what their children are becoming, more cases like Brock's will surface."

Levron nodded as they approached the inn. "Vkandis protect!" he got out, pointing to the steps leading up to the inn. "Look!"

Sitting on the steps by the front door was the orange cat, tail wrapped demurely around his feet. He lifted one paw and gave his face a thorough washing, appearing totally unconcerned about what went on around him.

"I swear, it's the same cat that Jerret feeds," Levron said. "Perfect evidence offered at trial."

Perran stopped and cocked his head. "There's nothing better than direct evidence."

As for the cat, Levron could have sworn the cat winked once at him before he stood, arched his back in a liquid stretch, then sauntered off down the street, tail proudly erect, as if totally pleased with his participation in the outcome of the trial.

An Ostentation of Peacocks

Elisabeth Waters

"Lady Magdalena," the King asked, "what do you call a group of peacocks?"

"An ostentation of peacocks, Majesty." Lena's reply was prompt, as memorizing odd collective names for animals was a game at the temple where she lived.

"That's certainly appropriate," the Queen chuckled, looking up from her needlework. "I've never seen anything else so ostentatious in nature — only the clothing of some people at court is gaudier."

They were in the Queen's solar, relaxing before dinner. Lena suspected that the King and Queen would prefer to dine quietly in their rooms, and she would much rather be back at the temple of Thenoth, Lord of the Beasts, where she could wear a comfortable novice's robe, rather than the dress she was currently stuffed into.

Lena hated formal dinners, but, as the King's ward, she had to appear at court often enough that the other highborn didn't complain that the King was keeping her out of sight and unwed so that he could continue to control her lands and income. When she first became his ward at the age of ten, it hadn't been an issue, so he had permitted her to live at the temple, where she could learn to use her Gift of Animal Mindspeech. She was still allowed to live at the temple, but she was required to show up at court more frequently as she got older. She was sixteen now, and she feared that soon he was going to require her to go through an actual social season. She shuddered at the thought and thanked the god she was small for her age.

"Why did you ask about peacocks?" she asked the King. "Are you getting some?"

"I've lost some," the King replied, "and they were a gift from our newest Council member, so I do need to get them back."

"How did you lose them?" Lena asked. "And just how ostentatious was your loss?"

"They appear to have been stolen, and there were two peacocks and three peahens."

That's quite a lot to steal. "Do we know when? And do we have any idea who—or, in the god's name—*why*?"

"Politics," the Queen sighed.

"Oh, joy." Lena hated politics. "So the usual Council infighting just went up a level?"

"It looks that way," the King agreed. "It doesn't look good when the Crown can't keep a gift safe for even a few days."

"When were they last seen?" Lena asked.

"They were there at feeding time this morning," the King replied.

"Are we sure they're not still on the Hill?"

"We've searched, and we can't find them. We did find one peahen's feather near the gate the supply carts use, so we suspect they went out that way. The guards don't remember seeing anything unusual, but . . ."

"They don't know *everyone*, and a lot of supply carts look alike. Give me a minute." Lena closed her eyes and reached out with her mind. There were a lot of birds on the Hill, from hawks in the mews to lots of wild birds, but everything she touched was either contented on its perch or happily flying about under an open sky. Nothing felt unhappy, confined, or stifled—*and if they took the peacocks out in a covered supply cart, they'd be unhappy for certain!*

Wherever they were, they were not within her range. The most distant birds she could reach were crows ... the perfect spies, as long as they stayed interested. She sent a mental request, asking them to spread out along all the roads away from Haven—she didn't think anyone was going to try to drive peacocks across an open field, at least not close to the city.

Lena opened her eyes. "I've asked the crows to watch for them," she told the King. "It's a good thing it's summer; that will give them more time to look before the sun sets. And," she added, "it's a good thing you didn't send me on one of those visits to the country this year."

The Queen laughed. "He did make noises about it, but I'm afraid that there is some reluctance among potential hosts. Apparently there are rumors of dead bodies."

"Neither of them was *my* fault," Lena pointed out. "And the second one wasn't even from Valdemar—he just stumbled across the border before he died."

"Speaking of the late Lord Kristion," the King remarked, "his son Jasper has just arrived at court with Lord Teren."

"Has his widow managed to forgive Lord Teren yet? I could understand being angry with Lord Kristion—it's idiotic to wear brown leather and a deerskin jacket to go hunting. But she blamed Lord Teren for the accident." Lena sighed. "She got very angry when she found out that he had been named Lord Jasper's guardian jointly with her."

"I haven't heard one way or the other. You'll have to ask them when you see them."

When she spoke to them after dinner, however, they had other concerns.

"Are my dogs dead?" Jasper demanded fearfully.

"Of course not!" Lena replied. "Why would you think that? Did you not get the letters I wrote telling you how they were doing?"

"Yes, but—" He gulped. "The man in the kennels never heard of them."

"He must be new. When I came home packed into a coach with eight dogs and six puppies two years ago, I think everyone at court heard about it. Fortunately, I don't live here. I live at the Temple of Thenoth, the Lord of the Beasts, and that's where the dogs live as well."

"Can we go there now?" Jasper asked.

"Absolutely," Lena replied. "Just as soon as I get the King's permission to leave."

Lord Jasper virtually dove into the section of the kennel where his dogs lived, and he was quickly covered with them. It seemed that even the "puppies"—who really could not be called that any longer—remembered him. He looked up at Lena with a wide grin on his face. "Mother entered a convent. She's going to stay there and pray for my father's soul for the rest of her life. It's safe for me to take my dogs home now."

"We'll miss them," she said, "but I'm glad that your home is safe for them now." She grinned. "I hope you brought a bigger coach than I had! I barely fit in with all of them, and the puppies were *much* smaller then."

"We'll figure something out," Lord Teren said as Jasper looked anxiously at him. "If necessary, we can set up as a traveling show of trained dogs and give performances along our road home."

Jasper laughed. "That might be fun!"

Lena had reason to remember those comments when the crows reported back to her the next morning. The peacocks had been put outside to eat and stretch their wings, and they were quite visible. They were standing in a field where a traveling show was setting up; Lena could see tents being raised. They were also on the road that led to Lord Jasper's estate, and they weren't too far from Haven.

"We can catch up with them," she explained to a group that included the King, Teren, and Jasper. "The hounds have to take that road anyway, and Lord Teren did suggest turning them into a traveling show."

The King looked at the map on the table in front of him. "How do you plan to train greyhounds to do tricks in the two days it would take Lords Teren and Jasper to catch up with the show? They would have to have something special, would they not?"

"Easy," Lena said. "Animal Mindspeech. We come up with tricks, and I explain them to the dogs."

The King raised his eyebrows. "Were you planning on going with them?"

"Yes, of course. Remember, we have to get the peacocks back here, and I don't think stuffing them in a supply cart is going to work. Do you know how much space they need for just their wings? And the males need much more for their trains."

"You'll need a chaperone."

"Can't I just dress as a boy?"

"Not convincingly," the King said dryly. "You are, unfortunately, correct that you will be needed to bring the peacocks back here. I'll find someone to go with you." He turned to Lord Teren. "When do you wish to leave?"

"By midafternoon, if we can. Jasper and I have horses, but we'll need a cart—preferably a light one—for the dogs. And we'll need good horses for Lena and her chaperone."

The King sat silently with a look Lena recognized as "I'm having a word with my Companion." When he looked up, he said simply, "Your chaperone will be at the Temple of Thenoth with your mounts in an hour. Lena, go home and pack, and don't forget to tell the Prior where you are going."

Lena went back to the Temple and explained what was going on to the Prior. By the time she had packed what she thought she would need to join a traveling show, Teren and Jasper were in the courtyard. Jasper was holding their horses, while Teren tried to persuade the greyhounds to get into the cart and stay there.

"This is your horse, Lena," Jasper said excitedly. Obviously he thought this was all a wonderful adventure. "Isn't she gorgeous?"

She was gorgeous. She was also white, which would make it difficult to keep her clean on the road, unless . . .

Lena walked over to the horse and stroked her side. *:Hello,:* she thought at her. *:What's your name?:*

:Meri.: the mind-voice was amused. *:Don't worry; I volunteered for this. The King wants you safe, and lovely as the Companion's Field is, it can get boring. I don't have a Chosen yet, and Clyton says you're nice.:* Clyton was the Companion of one of Lena's favorite Heralds.

:Thank you. I hope you'll enjoy traveling with us.: Lena looked around, wondering if her chaperone had arrived.

:Amal and Kyra will be here soon—probably long before someone gets those dogs under control.:

Lena looked at the dogs playing "hop in and out of the cart" and gave a sharp whistle. That got their attention. "Listen up," she said, both verbally and in Mind-speech. "We're leaving Haven, and the first thing we have to do is catch up with a traveling show two days ahead of us. You *can* run beside the horses, but how long is that going to last?" Fourteen dogs jumped into the wagon, wriggled around to find reasonably comfortable places, and settled down, prepared to remain right where they were for the foreseeable future.

"Impressive." The female voice came from above her. Lena spun around to see a young woman, probably about five years older than she was, dressed in Herald Trainee Grays and mounted on a Companion.

"Thank you," Lena said politely. "You must be Amal. I'm Lena, and this is Jasper and Teren."

Teren looked pointedly at the uniform and the Companion. "I thought we were supposed to be disguised."

"We will be," Amal assured him. "This is just for tonight and tomorrow night, so we can stay in inns and use chits instead of coin. Then I'll change out of my Grays, and the Companions will disguise themselves."

"Companions?" Lord Teren asked. "How many will there be?"

"Just the two," Amal chuckled. "You didn't notice that Meri is a Companion, and she's standing right here."

"Lena rates a Companion?" Jasper asked. "I thought they only carried Heralds."

"Unpartnered Companions can carry people if they want," Amal said. "They're intelligent beings, and it's their choice. Meri volunteered for this mission—apparently Lena has a reputation in the Companions' Field."

Four days later, Lena stood on the back of a running "horse" while wearing tight trews and a colorful, scandalously short tunic. The costumes had been in Amal's packs, but Lena's planned dog show had been hijacked by the Companions.

:Nobody is ever going to expect Companions to perform in a show like this,: Meri had said, and she was right about that. She and Kyra, Amal's Companion, with Lena to translate, had quickly trained the dogs. Jasper was doing well as a performer, but Meri seemed to expect more of Lena. It wasn't enough for her to keep her balance while standing on a Companion galloping in a circle; Meri kept adding more tricks. She had Lena jumping through hoops, literally. Large wooden hoops, hanging from the rigging in the tent, which meant there would be trouble if Lena so much as brushed against one. Lena was once again thanking Thenoth that she was small for her age.

The next day they were traveling, and she decided to take a stab at both of her problems: Meri's nagging and her original mission. She left her group and went to the wagon that held Bram and the peacocks. "May I ride with you?" she asked. "Please? My family is driving me crazy!"

"Mine did, too," Bram admitted, moving over to let her hide inside the canvas shelter. He stayed on the driver's bench, but Lena noticed he was barely holding the reins, even when the procession started moving. He seemed to be paying much more attention to her than to the horses that pulled the wagon. "The birds are tolerating you, so you can hide in here. Funny, they don't usually like strangers."

"They must like you a lot," Lena said, "to tolerate being in such a small space."

"They know I'll let them out as much as I can," Bram replied, "and they've been my best friends for ages." Lena thought Bram was a year or two younger than she was, but she knew perfectly well that "ages" could be relative depending on one's surroundings.

"So," Bram continued, "why are you hiding from your family?"

The story was that Lena and Jasper, who both had light hair and blue eyes, were Teren's children, and Amal, with dark tan skin, brown eyes, and black hair, was their cousin. They claimed to be a family act, and nobody had questioned it. "They don't think I'm living up to my full potential," she grumbled. "They want me to do somersaults on Meri's back."

"*Can* you do somersaults?" Bram asked.

"Not even on the ground," sighed Lena. "Jasper gets away with little and cute—why can't I?"

"I'm friends with the flyers," Jasper said. "Maybe they could help you."

"Really?" Lena had seen the flyers practicing. They kept a net under them, but their act was done swinging between bars near the top of the tent, frequently with a person starting on the small platform on one side, grabbing a bar and swinging out before sailing through the air to a man she had heard called the "catcher" who swung upside down with the bar behind his knees. He would catch the flyer and toss them back to the bar they had left, and the flyer—usually—swung back and landed on the platform. If they missed, they landed in the net, moved to the edge, dropped down to the floor, climbed the rope ladder back up to the platform, and tried again. And again. The father of their family, however, seemed really strict and not likely to let anyone else use their equipment.

"Do you really think they'd agree to help me?" Lena asked.

"Yes," Bram said. "I've know them for five years. They spend winters near my old home."

"Have you been with the show that long?" Lena asked.

"No," Bram admitted. "This is my first season."

"Do you like it?" Lena asked.

"The people are nice, and they aren't trying to take my birds away from me."

"Why would anyone do that?"

Bram gave a long-suffering sigh. "My father thought the King would like to have them."

Lena gave him an incredulous stare. "Does the King have anyone who knows how to take care of them?"

"They say not."

:They didn't take proper care of you at the Palace?: Lena thought at the birds and stared at them incredulously as mental images of being fastened by jesses to perches in the royal mews came back to her.

"Someone put them in the mews?" she said in horror. "And put *jesses* on them? Didn't they notice these aren't hawks?"

"How do you know what happened to them?" Bram asked suspiciously.

"Animal Mindspeech," Lena explained. "You've got it too, don't you?"

"Is that what it means when I can hear them talking in my head?"

Lena nodded. "If your father really wanted to impress the King, he should have sent you with them."

"He doesn't know," Bram said miserably. "I didn't even know."

"Oh." Lena suddenly understood. "You've been taking care of them for years, and because you can hear them, you've been making it look easy, so your father thought *anyone* could do it."

Bram looked at her in surprise. "I never thought of it that way."

"Think about it now," Lena suggested. "Winter is more comfortable at the Palace than on the road, and the King would be glad to hire you."

"We're not on the road in winter anyway. But my father's going to be mad at me, and the King. . . ." His voice trailed off, and Lena decided not to pressure him further. *Let him think about it. With luck, he'll get used to the idea.*

*   *   *

To Lena's surprise, Bram did persuade at least one of the flyers to help her. Sofia was nineteen and laughed when Bram repeated Lena's complaint about not being able to get away with "little and cute."

"Oh, those were the days," she agreed. "Unfortunately, we grow out of them. At least you're small, and your weight is low on your body."

"Is that a polite way of saying I have no breasts?" Lena grinned at her.

"Yes, it is," Sofia laughed, "but that's a *good* thing." She looked appraisingly at Lena. "How old are you?"

"Sixteen," Lena admitted. "Seventeen next month."

"You may be one of the lucky ones then," Sofia said. "Let's see what we can do with you. Have you ever wanted to fly?"

Lena thought of all the birds she had linked minds with. "Oh, yes," she said fervently.

Sofia strapped her into a wide belt that fastened tightly around her waist, recruited two of the younger men from her act, and led Lena up the ladder to the platform. When Lena reached the top and looked down, she instantly wished she *were* a bird.

"Hold still," Sofia ordered as she hooked two ropes to the metal loops at the sides of the belt. The ropes stretched out to the sides, ran through rings above the net, and dropped to the ground, where the men held them. "Don't worry," Sofia said. "If you start to fall they'll make sure you don't land wrong."

"So I'll wind up hanging by my waist in midair?"

"Only if you totally freeze up," Sofia laughed. "Don't worry about it. The good thing about having your waist as the pivot point is that it's the easiest way to learn flips—what you call somersaults. From up here you can get multiple revolutions in before you land in the net."

"Uh—" Lena hoped she didn't look horrified, but she was afraid that she did, because Sofia chuckled.

"We'll start with learning to land in the net," Sofia said. "Hey, Bram," she called down. "Come up here, will you?"

Bram scrambled easily up the ladder, joining them on the now-crowded platform. Sofia unhooked a bar from above the platform. "This is called a fly bar," she told Lena. "All I want you to do is grip it firmly, swing out, let go of it, and drop into the net. Try to land sitting with your legs out in front of you and your hands to your sides. If you think your body is too far back, tuck your chin to your chest, and land on your back. Watch how Bram does it."

Bram gave them a big grin, grabbed the bar and swung out, releasing it at the bottom of its arc. He even brought his arms down gracefully as he fell to sit in the net.

"Does he spend winters practicing with you?" Lena asked suspiciously.

"Not seriously," Sofia said. "He comes to us when his father's not around." She patted Lena on the shoulder. "It's not hard, and the men holding the ropes won't let you fall." She grabbed a rod with a hooked end and pulled the fly bar back to them. "You saw what he did, right? Just copy it."

Lena took a deep breath, gripped the bar, and jumped. It went faster than she had expected, so she hung on until it swung back to the middle before she let go. Apparently she was doing all right, because she didn't feel any pulling at her waist. Falling felt slower than swinging had, so she copied what Bram had done with his arms, and landed in the net. "That was fun!" she exclaimed in surprise.

Bram had flipped off the edge of the net and was standing beside it. "Yes, it is," he agreed. "Now climb back up the ladder and do it again."

Sofia drilled her until Lena could land in the net as easily as she sat down in a chair. She could also bounce to her feet (the net was rather bouncy) walk to the edge of the net, hook her fingers in it, and flip off the side.

"Now," Sofia said, "watch this." She hooked the bar out of the way. "I'm going to jump off the platform and do a flip on the way down to the net. When you copy me, jump out and up to get a good start, and make sure you land sitting or on your back. Do *not* try to land standing up."

"I won't," Lena promised. "I have absolutely no desire to break an ankle."

"Good girl," Sofia said. "Watch me, give me time to get clear, and then copy what I did."

Sofia jumped, then leaned forward, tucking her head and holding her knees, revolved once, then untucked and landed sitting in the net. She got off the net and looked up at Lena. "Your turn!" she called cheerfully.

Her confidence was contagious, and Lena, rather to her surprise, managed a reasonable copy of the move. But when she swung over the edge of the net, her legs didn't want to hold her.

"Oops!" Sofia grabbed her. "I think that's enough for today." She unhooked the ropes and removed the belt from Lena's waist.

The man on their side of the net coiled his rope and retrieved the belt. "Good, job, kid," he said. "Keep training with Sofia; you've got natural ability." He walked off, and Sofia supported Lena as they walked back to the cart with the greyhounds.

"I hope you've also got some horse liniment," Sofia said, waving Amal over. "Get your cousin to rub it all over you before you go to bed or you won't be able to move in the morning."

Amal looked startled. "What were you doing?"

"Working on a somersault," Lena explained, "so I can do one on Meri's back."

"Whose idea was *that*?" Amal asked.

"Meri's."

"That's right," Sofia laughed, "blame the horse." She transferred Lena to Amal and added, "Make her walk around for a bit. She's got the makings of a flyer, and we were both having fun. I'm afraid she overdid it a bit. I apologize for returning her in this condition."

"We'll manage," Amal said. "Thank you for helping her."

"Anytime," Sofia said, "and I mean that. Lena, come back to me when you can, and we'll work some more. I don't guarantee you'll be able to do a flip on a galloping horse any time soon, but we'll try. Actually, I think you'll be a decent flyer first."

She walked off, leaving both girls staring after her.

"What's a flyer?" Amal asked, looking at Lena with concern.

"It's what she does in their act," Lena explained. "It's wonderful!"

"Tell me that when you can walk without help," Amal said dryly.

Sofia was right. Flying seemed to come naturally to Lena, and as they traveled toward Jasper's estate, Sofia's father started watching them practice, and then joined in so that Lena could learn to make the cross to the catcher and back. One day he invited Lena to join their act, saying it would be nice to have a cute little girl again. Sofia and Lena both broke out in giggles.

He and Sofia went with Lena to talk to her "father"; they pointed out to Teren that his act was at the beginning of the show while theirs was at the end, so there was no reason Lena couldn't change costumes and do both. When Lord Teren suddenly remembered that they were talking about the King's ward, whom he had promised to keep safe, he started making reluctant noises, but Amal took Lena's side. "Let her do it. She's worked very hard on this, and she loves doing it."

"I'd rather see her helping with the peacocks," Teren muttered.

"Bram doesn't need help with them," Lena said.

"I've seen you help feed them," Teren argued.

Lena shrugged. "I like Bram."

That did it. Lord Teren had no idea that Bram was anything other than a thief who was good with peacocks, so he decided letting Lena work with the flyers was a lesser evil, and by the time they approached Jasper's estate, Lena was spending more time with the flyers than with Teren and Jasper.

Amal called a private meeting one night. "If I'm right, we're getting close enough to your estates, my Lords, that both of you may be recognized any day now. You need to split off and take the dogs home, don't you?"

"Yes, we do," Lord Teren agreed. "But what are we supposed to do with you, and what about the peacocks?"

"I'd bet the flyers want to keep Lena," Amal said. "If you tell them that you and Jasper have to take the dogs somewhere to be bred or something, I'll volunteer to stay with Lena so she can remain part of their act."

"But you're two young girls," Lord Teren protested. "I'm supposed to be keeping you safe."

"I'll be in Whites next year, so it's not as if I'm a child. I have a tent that Lena and I can share, we'll pitch it near Sofia's, and the Companions will be with us."

:I wondered when you would remember us,: Meri said.

:I never forgot you,: Lena replied. *:Did you think I never noticed you in the back of my head helping me move my body the right way?:*

:Humph.:

"We were always going to have to split up," Amal pointed out. "Your job was to get us accepted by the show while you were taking the dogs home. Our job is to get the King's stupid peacocks back to Haven."

"They're not actually stupid," Lena objected.

"I don't care about their intelligence," Amal retorted. "I care about their location."

"Very well," Lord Teren sighed. "I'll talk to Sofia and her father, and see if they're willing to keep an eye on you two."

The flyers definitely wanted to keep Lena, and Papa assured her "father" that they would made certain that neither of the girls got into any trouble at all. Given the amount of time Lena spent practicing with them, there was no question of her having either the time or the energy to do anything improper. Amal admitted that she could both sew and embroider, and Sofia pounced on the idea of getting a new set of costumes.

Lena tried to spend her "free" time with Bram. The fact that he ate meals with the flyers—and now Lena and Amal—helped, because she really didn't have free time.

She also had no privacy; the nearest thing was when she and Amal were in their tent at night. Even then, they were limited to very quiet conversation.

"Try to spend time with Bram, will you?" she asked. "Get him to regard you as a friend, or at least as someone who firmly believes that he and the peacocks should stay together no matter what."

Amal thought that over. "You want him to have the two of us as friends in Haven."

"Exactly. I also want all four of us: you, me, Kyra, and Meri, to persuade the King that he should insist that the gift of peacocks include Bram to take care of them. I expect the Council member will be honored to have his son offered a position in the King's service—and if he's not thrilled at first, he can be told to be."

Amal chuckled. "I'm glad you're on our side. I'll do my part on the ground while you do yours in the air."

"I really do love it," Lena admitted. "It's not quite like being a bird, but it's as close as I can get."

With their division of labor agreed upon, both girls slipped into the routine of the show as it traveled on. Lena didn't think she had ever been happier in her life.

:Lena!: There was an insistent voice in her head, but it wasn't Meri's, and Meri knew better than to distract her when she was in the middle of a cross. Lena missed the catcher's hands and twisted to land on her back as she fell.

"What's the matter with you?" the catcher yelled down. "You don't lose focus up here—it can get you killed!" He added less angrily. "Are you injured?"

"I don't think so," Lena called back, gently and carefully testing her ability to move each joint. "Give me a minute."

:Lena!: This time she recognized the voice.

:Clyton? What are you doing here?: Clyton was the Companion of Samira, Amal's older sister, but they were out on Circuit somewhere. *Come to think of it, where are we?*

Two Heralds entered the tent. Samira was just behind

Robin. *Oh, right, it must be near the end of his first Circuit, so he's taking lead now.*

Robin ran over to the side of the net. "Lena! What happened?"

"Clyton Mindspoke me, and I fell."

"It was a pretty good save," Amal volunteered. "I looked up when I *didn't* hear the catch; she was falling, but she twisted in midair, and it looked like a good landing."

Lena groaned, more from embarrassment than pain, rolled to the side of the net, and checked the state of her hands and wrists before grabbing the edge and flipping out. Her legs and feet seemed to be uninjured as well.

Samira glared at Amal. "Why are you still here?"

"Uh—" Amal looked blank.

Robin burst out laughing just as Sofia swung out of the net and her father advanced on them.

"Why are you interrupting our practice?" he demanded furiously. If he recognized Heralds, he showed no sign of it. "Do you *want* to get someone injured—or killed? Who are you, what are you doing here, and what, by all the gods, do you think is *funny* about this?"

Robin sobered instantly. "You are correct, sir. I apologize for the interruption—"

"Clyton said she was falling," Samira said in an unsuccessful attempt at explanation.

Robin spoke hastily. "This is Samira; Clyton is her Companion. Lena has Animal Mindspeech, and Clyton spoke to her without realizing what she was doing, and I gather that caused her to fall."

"It's like having someone suddenly shout at you," Lena explained, "but I'm not injured." She shrugged. "Probably bruised, but that's nothing."

"And I was laughing because . . . I'm Robin, Chosen of Dathus, but I grew up in a family of traveling players. Lena, do you know what the date is? or where you are?"

"No," Lena shook her head. "I think it's still summer . . ." Her voice trailed off.

Amal looked somewhere between sick and faint. "Oh, no!"

"Just realized you're out of range, did you?" Samira said sardonically. Amal sat down suddenly on the ground and buried her face in her hands.

Robin continued. "They don't know the date or their location, but they know the next show time, the next rehearsal time, and the next meal time—probably in that order."

"Of course," Lena pointed out. "The show is the most important, followed by rehearsal. And we get called to meals."

"It's all my fault," Amal wailed. "I'm a total failure!"

"No, you're not," Lena argued. "Your job is to chaperone me, and nobody can say you haven't done that."

"She's right," Samira acknowledged. "It was Kyra's job to keep in touch with the King's Companion. Did she tell you she had lost contact?"

Amal shook her head. "I don't think so," she said weakly.

"Have a heart, Samira," Robin said. "It happened yesterday. It's not as if they've been missing for weeks!"

Lena started, "I'll go back if—"

"You'll go back if I have to drag you by the hair!" Samira muttered.

"You'd be pecked half-to-death if you tried it!" Lena shot back.

Robin sighed. "Sir," he asked Sofia's father, "could I ask you to call a company meeting? This is rather complicated, and it involves several members of your company." Papa sighed and nodded. One look up into the rigging had everyone there diving into the net, while Sofia ran out to round up everyone else.

It wasn't long before everyone was sitting around the fire where the midday soup was simmering. Lena sat between Sofia and Bram, with Amal on Bram's other side.

"Lena," Robin said, "perhaps you'd like to explain. I believe I heard you trying to set conditions for your return earlier?"

Lena nodded and turned to Sofia's father. "It's like this, Papa. It all started when Bram's father decided it was a good idea to give the peacocks to the King, without Bram to take care of them."

Papa looked slightly ill. "Those peacocks?" He gestured to the birds wandering around them. "They belong to the King?"

"Technically, yes," Lena admitted, adding hastily, "but he's not angry at anyone. He just wants them back before they're publicly known to be missing. When the peacocks went to the Palace, nobody really knew how to deal with them. Bram always cared for them at home, and he made it look so easy that his father didn't realize the job needed any special knowledge or abilities. Anyway, the birds were miserable, and Bram has Animal Mindspeech, so they talked to him, and he went to rescue them."

"And ran away to my show with them."

"Yes, but they're safe and happy here. They were missed, of course, and because I have Animal Mindspeech, the King asked me to find them, which I did. By then you were two days travel away from Haven, and this is where the dogs come in."

"What dogs?" Robin had apparently missed that part.

"Lord Jasper's greyhounds," Lena said. "It was two years ago, so you weren't with Samira then, but when Lord Jasper's father died, his mother ordered all the dogs killed, so they came to Haven with me for sanctuary. Jasper's mother just entered a convent, so he and Lord Teren came to Haven to take the dogs home. You were all heading in that direction, and the King wanted to get the birds back *quietly*, which meant not sending people who didn't know how to care for them to drag them back by force. So Jasper, Teren, and I came up with the plan of setting up an act and joining your show so we could find out who took the birds and why, and the King added Amal because he said I needed a chaperone."

"Where did you get your incredibly well-trained horses?" Papa asked suspiciously.

Lena took a deep breath. "From the Companion's Field. Amal is Kyra's Chosen—"

"She's a Herald?"

"No, sir," Amal said quickly. "Just a Trainee."

"And Meri doesn't have a Chosen, so she decided to come along for the fun of it," Lena finished.

Papa started chuckling. "So you all ran away to join the circus," he said. "But I'm guessing there's a problem now. Are you late getting back to Haven?"

"Very," Robin said. "Can you cancel the rest of your route and go straight to Haven to perform for the King?"

"We could," Papa said slowly, "but from what I hear, Companions can travel very quickly."

"Oh, they definitely can," Robin agreed, "and if all we had to do was get the girls back, we could do it in a few days of *very* hard riding. But Amal was assigned to this, and Lena lives at a temple. What we need to get back quickly is the birds."

"Who can't fly much at all," Bram said.

"He's right," Lena agreed. "They can barely fly. And we want to take Bram back so the King can give him the job of caring for them."

"Makes sense to me," Robin said. "So we need to travel by road. Amal, get the maps from my saddle, will you?" As Amal ran to do his bidding, he added, "It seems only fair, sir, that you and your troupe be compensated for your care of the King's ward and his property."

"Ward?" Papa asked.

"He means me," Lena admitted. "The rest of my family is dead, so the King is my guardian, but I've lived at a temple since I was ten. And I told the Prior where I was going, so they know where I am. Nobody's worried about me. Really."

Amal came back with the maps, and Robin and Papa put their heads together. "If we could take this road tomorrow morning," Papa said, "it would be much faster, but sometimes it gets blocked. . . ."

"Lena?" Robin held the map up. "Is this section of road clear?"

Lena reached out to Mindspeak the birds in the area. "It's clear now."

"Rain?"

"None in range."

"Vultures?"

Lena started laughing. "No, Robin."

"Insane magicians?"

"No!" She turned to the show folk. "Don't mind him. He's joking."

"Right," Robin said. "The vultures and the insane magicians were *last* year. All we have this year is a journey to Haven at our best possible speed."

"With a Royal Commission at the end," Lena said brightly. "It'll be fun."

Cobblestones
Fiona Patton

Fog was not common in Haven, and it had been an unusually foggy spring. The more religious citizens of Valdemar's capital city took it as a sign of flood, famine, plague, fire, or some other imminent catastrophe; the merchant class treated it as a trade-disrupting personal insult by Nature; and the working poor faced it as one more unwelcome challenge to lives already stretched near the breaking point.

The Watch, however, welcomed it. Most citizens, religious or otherwise, tended to stay indoors when they couldn't see their hands in front of their faces. That meant most of those hands were not getting into the kind of mischief that led to full cells and exciting shifts.

Tucked up beside his sister Kassie's pigeon coops on the roof of their tenement building, a two-month-old twin boy in each arm, Sergeant Hektor Dann of the Haven City Watch allowed that he had plenty of excitement these days without adding angry blacksmiths, suspicious shop owners, drunken students, and perennial pickpockets loudly protesting that they'd only just *found* the purse lying on the pavement. Stretching out his back, he peered blearily at what would have been a maze of city streets if he could have seen them and thought about the day to come.

The sun was coming up, and the quality of the fog was, if not thinning, then at least lightening. It would soon be time to return downstairs, give his children over to their mother, and spend another long day without them. He hadn't reckoned on missing them so much during Ismy's pregnancy, but now he understood the haggard smile he'd often seen on his father's face. He loved his boys, but they never seemed to sleep.

Edzel stirred fretfully in his left arm, and Hektor bounced him gently to settle him. The twins took it in turns to be colicky, and today was Eddie's turn. In his right arm, Ronald snuffled in his sleep. The twins also took it in turns to be croupy, and it looked like it was about to be Ronnie's turn at that. Both boys had already developed a healthy set of lungs and a clear opinion on when to use them, but at least up here on the roof, they wouldn't be disturbing anyone except Kassie's pigeons. And they'd seen it all before. Hektor remembered his father carrying his four younger siblings up here. Sometimes he had followed them, sitting with his back against the stairway wall, listening to his da's deep, rumbling voice as he'd sung first Jakon and Raik, then Kassie, then Paddy, back to sleep. Later, Aiden had carried Egan and Leila up here. Now with Thomar and Peston, new twin boys of his own, he and Hektor either passed on the stairs or shared the roof duty together, standing, looking out at the slumbering city and murmuring the songs their father had sung to them. He imagined their other siblings would do the same when it came time for them to start families.

"It's gonna get awfully crowded up here," Hektor noted. "But you two'll be all finished wi' this silliness by then, yeah?"

Ronnie yawned widely before turning to bury his head in his father's shirt.

"But not too soon, I hope."

As the town bells began to sound the hour, he straightened with a yawn of his own. "Well, that'll be all for today, I guess," he said, kissing each of his sons on the forehead. "Time for your da to go make a livin'."

He grinned at the word. Da had always been his own da or Aiden. But now it was him. He didn't think he was ever going to get tired of remembering that.

Ismy deftly collected both boys as he maneuvered inside the family flat a few moments later.

"Did you manage to get some sleep?" he asked, bending to kiss her cheek.

"A little," she answered with a smile. "C'mon you two, time for your breakfast. An' make sure to get yours as well, Hektor Dann," she added over her shoulder. "You can't expect to do a proper day's work on no sleep and no breakfast."

"Mm-hm. Love you. See you tonight."

Her eyes narrowed. "Yes, well, I love you too. Bring home some chamomile."

"I will." Hektor caught up his gray and blue Watchman's tunic with one hand while catching up a couple of currant buns from the plate his mother held out to him with the other.

"Where're Kassie an' Paddy?" he asked, wondering at the quiet. Aiden and his family had moved into a flat of their own one floor down a few months before, taking Jakon and Raik, who worked the night shift, with them. Kassie had been up to tend her birds an hour ago, but she and Paddy should still be at their own breakfast.

His mother smiled. "Kassie left for the Watch House early; some of the new messenger birds need special tendin' to, and Paddy's gone downstairs to spend a few minutes with Rosie before his shift. She's officially his girl now, you know."

"Really? Officially, is it? He told you that?"

"Of course not," she laughed. "Her mother told me that. So no teasin' him, mind, until he's ready to tell us himself."

"No promises."

"Well, at least tell him to be careful today. And you and Aiden be careful too. It's hay market day, and the streets will be filled with wagoneers who pay little enough attention on a clear morning."

"We will."

"And take another bun."

"Mm-hm. Love you. See you tonight."

She arched an eyebrow at him, but when he just grinned back at her, she smiled. "I love you too. Bring home some lavender."

The street was still thick with fog when he and Aiden headed down the tenement steps. Making their way along the ten long blocks to the Iron Street Watch House with the ease of long familiarity despite the weather, they walked in companionable silence until Hektor walked straight into an open shop door.

Aiden just shook his head. "You need more sleep."

"Yeah, that's not gonna happen anytime soon," Hektor answered, checking his nose for blood. "Remind me I have to stop at the herbalist's on the way home, will you?"

Aiden gave a snort of weary laughter. "We'll go together. You need blackthorn?"

"Chamomile. And lavender. You?"

"Blackthorn. And lavender."

"Colic?"

"Croup."

Yawning, Hektor rubbed a kink from the back of his neck before shooting his older and more experienced brother a slightly worried look. "You don't think they're actually sick, do you? Are all babies this fretful?"

"No. You were though."

The sound of a crash and a long string of invectives cut off Hektor's reply as both men took off running.

The wagon stood at an awkward angle, one wheel deep in a large pothole in the middle of the street.

"Is this the one out front of Linton's shop?" Hektor asked, bending his head to squint across the street as Aiden moved to calm the irate wagoneer.

"No. It's the one in front of Benj Grandstil's, an' it near broke my rear axle an' sent my load tumblin' into the gutter!" the wagoneer shouted, sputtering in rage.

Aiden raised both hands. "S'all right, Nev. Near broke ain't really broke. Hektor'n I'll push, you pull, an' we'll get you outta here in no time. Hek." He turned. "Hektor? *Sergeant*, what're you doin'?" He glared at his

younger brother who was crouched in the street, mea-
suring the pothole's span with the palm of his hand.

"I coulda sworn it was smaller," he muttered. "How
many cobblestones you figure woulda filled this?"

"What?"

"Eight, maybe ten?"

"Why does it matter?" Aiden jerked his head at the
wagon. "Quit fartin' about an' get over here."

"Yer brother needs more sleep," Nev noted with a
snicker, as Hektor rose reluctantly.

"So I keep tellin' 'im."

By the time they reached the Watch House, they'd
helped another three wagons on their way; one from another pothole, and two locked together when one had
tried to pass the other in the fog and misread the width
of the street.

"I hate market day," Aiden muttered as they made
their way inside. "Any market day."

Beside him, Hektor frowned at the street again before
heading into his office and the mountain of paperwork
waiting for him.

The fog cleared by midday but began to rise again by
evening. Passing Benj's shop on the way home, Hektor
paused to fix the size of the pothole in his mind's eye.

The next morning, with the fog no thinner, he frowned
accusingly down at it.

"That's bigger. I'm sure of it. An' so was the one in
front of Linton's."

"You think someone's stealin' cobblestones?" Aiden
scoffed. "For what? To pave their very own street?"

"I dunno, maybe." When Aiden shot him an exasperated look, Hektor shrugged. "Maybe not to pave their
own street, but maybe to repair it if they've got anythin'
like this." He crossed to the pothole, crouching down to
wiggle the edges of the remaining cobblestones experi-
mentally. "You'd need something to pry 'em up, though,
a crowbar or somethin'. An' a sack to carry 'em."

"Not if they were loose to begin with," Aiden retorted, drawn over despite himself. "You'd just pull 'em

up with yer fingers, one at a time. An' who'd notice or care if they saw someone walk by with somethin' that looks no more'n a rock in their hand."

"You'd need to know they were loose. Maybe you noticed the first one kicked up by a wagon an' thought, that'd do perfect for the pothole in front of my place. Catch it up and go. After that, you might start lookin' around for more loose stones, then finally, you might start prying up the rest 'cause you got away with it the first time."

Spotting a crowd of merchants beginning to gather on the pavement, Aiden straightened with a scowl. "Or maybe they were all just kicked up by wagons an' busted up or spun into an alley."

"Then there'd be debris littered about," Hektor insisted, ignoring the merchants, who'd begun to titter with amusement. "Nope, these have been lifted."

"So, what do you want to do about it? Wander Haven looking for new repairs?"

"We could post a guard."

"On a pothole? You've lost your mind."

"I s'pose. But this needs fixin' before someone actually gets hurt. Whose in charge of street repairs?"

"No idea. Get up before you get run over."

"I mean it, Corporal. Someone needs to get down here an' fix this."

"An' I mean it too, Sergeant. Get up now." Aiden jerked his younger brother to his feet just as an empty hay wagon lumbered past, the driver barely registering their presence. "You need to get more sleep."

"I'm fine." Hektor wiped his hands on the sides of his breeches. "I'll ask Paddy. He usually knows what's what on the street."

"Good idea, but Paddy's at the Watch House, where we should be. So, can we please get out of here before we lose what little respect this lot have ever accorded us?"

Hektor glanced over at the merchants, the oldest of which gave him a cheery, sarcastic wave in response.

"Um, yeah, I think that ship has sailed."

*   *   *

At the Watch House, the youngest Dann brother narrowed his eyes. "You wanna know if I've seen anyone repairin' the streets?"

"You'd have reported anyone *diggin' in* the streets, wouldn't you, Runner?" Hektor shot back.

"Well, sure, but I've never seen anybody actually doin' either repairin' or diggin'."

The older Danns exchanged a look. "Come to think of it, neither have I," Hektor admitted. "Have you?"

Aiden shook his head.

"But somebody must have made repairs at some time, shouldn't they? Or the streets'd be nothin' but potholes by now."

"Pavers Guild, maybe?"

"Do we have a Pavers Guild?"

"Dunno. Don't think so."

"How would you find out?"

"Records Hall?"

"Where's that?"

"Up by the Palace," Paddy supplied.

"That's a long walk in the fog," Aiden pointed out. "Couldn't we just ask someone, like Daedrus, maybe? He's an Artificer; he'd know if anyone would."

Paddy shook his head. "He's away, visitin' friends in Winefold."

"So, ask the Capt'n."

"Rather not," Hektor answered.

"Why?" Aiden asked with a grin. "'Cause you're afraid you'd look like a fool?"

Hektor opened his mouth, then closed it. "Somethin' like that."

"Good call. So, we need to ask someone old enough to have seen it done an' nosy enough to know who it was."

"Night sergeant's old," Paddy said.

"We can start with him."

Sergeant Jons handed Hektor the night reports before scratching his beard in thought. "I seem to remember it was the responsibility of the city shop owners to keep the streets in front of their establishments in good repair," he said after a moment. "Least ways, it was in the past."

"No wonder no one remembers it bein' done then," Aiden scoffed. "I can't see the shop owners around here forkin' out for somethin' like that."

"That's true enough," Jons agreed with a chuckle. "The citizens of Iron Street are . . . careful with their coin."

"But even if they were supposed to pay for it, they wouldn't be the ones doin' the actual work," Hektor pointed out.

"No," Aiden agreed, "but that answers the question about who to ask, anyway."

When Hektor gave him a blank look, he grinned. "Think about it. Someone older . . ." he prompted, clearly enjoying himself. "Someone nosier . . . someone closer to you . . ."

Understanding finally dawned. "No."

"'Fraid so."

"There's got to be someone else."

"There isn't. If the merchants really are responsible for street repairs, an' that means they have to pay for 'em, there's no one like your father-in-law for knowing it, an' throwing a complete fit if anyone ever tried to make him. He'd probably be out there with a measurin' tape trying to prove it was the responsibility of Willans across from 'im. Go ask Edzel."

"He won't answer. He hates me."

"He doesn't hate you, he just enjoys pretendin' he hates you. Take Ismy. For that matter, take the boys, there's nothing like a couple of grandbabies to soften a man's stance."

"I suppose."

"You wanna know what?"

Seated in the small workroom behind Edzel's Iron Shop, the master smith glared at his son-in-law suspiciously.

"Who's responsible for street repairs?" Hektor repeated in a stoic voice.

"Why?"

"'Cause someone's stealin' cobblestones, causin' potholes that're causin' traffic havoc, an' we need to get 'em repaired."

"Not here in Anvil's Close, they ain't."

"No. Mostly in Iron Street."

"And why should I give a rat's behind about traffic havoc in Iron Street?"

This was going about as well as Hektor'd envisioned. He turned a plaintive glance on Ismy, who gave her father an exasperated look. "Pa."

Her reproachful tone drew a scowl from her father.

"Don't Pa me," he shot back. "An' why's little Eddie snuffling like that?"

"He has a cold."

"Give 'im 'ere."

Edzel caught his namesake up in one heavily muscled arm, rolling his eyes as Ronnie opened his mouth to protest. "Yeah, yeah, you too. Honestly, yer as spoiled as they come." He caught the other boy up, tucking him easily into the crook of the other arm.

"They're a set," Hektor explained as the older man settled onto the corner of his workbench with a grunt.

"'Parently. Hmph. They seem a bit on the thin side. You feedin' 'em proper?"

"Pa." This time Ismy's voice held a note of warning, and he chuckled.

"Just askin'. Clearly they get scrawny limbs from their father's side." Edzel pursed his lips as his daughter crossed her arms. "All right, all right. Seems to me that the ward court what handles cases in this part of the city named four men from the Stonemason's Guild as street surveyors some years back. Let's see, there was . . . Dray Hennon. That caused some bad feelin's at the time. He was a foreigner. Came from Forchin originally. Older fellow. Been gone a decade or more now. Fell off a dock an' drowned. Some say his wife pushed him in, but nothin' ever came of it. She married a weaver a few a months later. Had a couple a littles without a lick a sense between 'em . . ."

Ismy sighed. "Pa . . ."

"What? Fine. Let's see, the second fellow was Simon Winsel, as I remember. His father owned a brickworks just south of town. Simon took it over after he retired. Died of some kind of fit last year. They say his face took on a terrible purple hue an' swelled up like . . . Stop chewing on them fingers, boy, I need 'em. Ismy, pass me that scrap a leather. I think your littles are teethin.'"

"They're too young," Ismy answered, but she handed it to him anyway.

"Tell my knuckles." Edzel folded the scrap and tucked the corner into Ronnie's mouth. "'Sides, you had teeth at their age."

"I did not."

"The other two surveyors?" Hektor prompted.

Edzel's lip curled, but then he shrugged. "Two of Linton's cousins. Barrin and Tam. A meaner pair of drunks you'd never find, but good stone men. When they were sober. Which weren't often. Twins like these two villains here," he added, glancing down at the boys in his arms with a surprisingly gentle smile. "Best keep the drink away from 'em as they get older, Daughter, or they'll bring you nothing but heartbreak, just as them two boys did to their own Ma."

"I'll keep it in mind," Ismy answered in a distinctly chilly tone.

"So where are Barrin and Tam now?" Hektor asked with as much patience as he could manage.

Edzel glared at him but cast his mind back. "Let's see. Barrin stumbled into the path of an oncoming wagon one night, drunk as usual, never saw it comin'. Nearly sent Tam off his rocker. That's the way it goes with twins most times. As one goes so goes the other, or there's trouble. You two best get used to bein' apart," he added glancing down, but when Ismy made to take Ronnie from him, he glared her away. "A year or two later, Tam took up with the sister of some priest at the Temple of Thenoth," he finished.

"That a Haven temple?" Hektor asked.

"Last time I looked."

"So Tam's still in the city?"

"How should I know? I said he took up with a priest's sister, not became a priest himself, boy. Pay attention. I got no idea if Tam's still in Haven. Go ask at the Temple. Maybe they know, maybe they don't. But I'd walk careful if you do find 'im," Edzel added with a cackle. "Tam never cared much for the Watch, an' he had a right mean temper on 'im in the old days. You might find yourself in a passel of hot water."

"So, where is this temple?" Hektor pressed, brushing off Edzel's warning with ease. He'd dealt with plenty of drunks in his time.

His father-in-law shrugged. "Couldn't tell ya. Ask yer sister. 'Parently they take in sick birds. Meantime, the one on the left here just messed himself. Take 'im off me."

Hektor accepted Eddie, who, separated from his twin and his grandfather, began to scream.

"Oh, sure, I know where t'is. I can take you," Kassie agreed, setting a small messenger bird back inside its coop in the Watch House aviary. "I've been there a few times with Master Aubrin, an' a few times with the Healer Trainees out of the Collegium to see to the in-jured birds in their loft.

"They care for creatures there," she explained when Hektor gave her a puzzled look. "The old an' the sick, tame an' the wild. Thenoth is some kind of Animal God or God of Animals," she amended. "I'm not too sure which. When do you want to go?"

"Now, if Master Aubrin can spare you."

"He's with the Capt'n, goin' over the monthly expenses." She turned to where Paddy was fixing a twisted hinge on the main coop. "Can you tell 'im where I've gone?"

He nodded without looking around, and she caught up her Watch House Messenger Bird tabard and pulled it over her head. "He won't mind," she reassured Hektor. "I've finished my chores an' tended the broody birds al-ready. We can call this Watch House business 'cause I always learn somethin' when I go there that helps with the birds here. Can you carry that sack?"

Hektor glanced at the burlap bag of grain she indicated.

"The Temple's right poor, so we always take a bit of food for their birds when we go. S'all right," she added, noting his uncertain expression. She picked up a charcoal stick and drew a line above the piled sacks. "Now, it's official. Come on."

Technically, the Temple of Thenoth was in the Water Street Watch House's district. Hektor'd never even been to this part of Haven before, but Kassie made her way through the winding streets with a confidence and authority he usually only associated with Paddy, until they came to a long, high wall, dotted with patchwork repairs and discolored by moss, a weather-worn gate set in the center.

Kassie pulled the bell, then smiled brightly at the old man who answered.

"Hello, Petrin," she said loudly. "It's Kassiath Dann."

He stared myopically at her, then broke into a toothless grin. "Oh, hello there, Hassien," he said. "You forget somethin'? Weren't you just here this mornin'?"

"Nearly," she answered easily. "Last week."

"A month gone by already, eh? My, how time flies. You here to see to the donkey, then?"

"I'll give 'im a brush down if you like."

"That'd be right kind of ye. Whose this then, yer beau? He looks a bit rough. You can do better."

Kassie laughed at Hektor's affronted expression. "This is my brother, Petrin," she explained. "And he's not rough, he's a Watchman."

"Huh. In my day Watchmen went clean-shaven, but I guess things have gotten lax all over. Yer name's Petrin too, is it?" the old man queried.

Hektor glanced at Kassie, who grinned.

"We need to see the Prior, Petrin," she said before Hektor could answer. "Can we come in?"

"What? Oh, sure, always welcome." Petrin stepped aside. "I'll jus' take yon sack up to the loft. It's for the birds, yeah?"

Hektor passed it over with a nod.

"Prior's in the kennels, seein' to a young stray what had a litter of pups last night. Mind ye both go quiet."

"We will," Kassie promised.

"Yer a good girl, Kether."

"Petrin's been here since he was a little," Kassie told Hektor as she lead him around the small chapter house toward a series of low stone buildings at the back of the temple complex. "He's deaf an' a bit muddled up, but no one knows beast tendin' like he does. All sorts of people come to ask his advice."

Hektor nodded absently, glancing about as they walked. He'd never seen the inside of any temple, let alone one dedicated to a god of animals, and he wondered if the sense of peace and safety he felt was common to all of them.

They found the Prior seated in a small, straw-covered stall, holding the head of a young, thin dog in his lap, eight puppies tucked into her belly, eagerly nursing. He nodded at Kassie's introduction, listening with half an ear to Hektor's question as he offered small pieces of bread dipped in milk to the mother dog.

"Tam married Brother Andel's youngest sister, Greda," he acknowledged. "He's a good man, if a bit rough around the edges. I hope he's not in any trouble."

"No trouble," Hektor assured him. "I just need to ask him a few questions. I was told he was in charge of street repairs years ago."

"It would have to have been some years ago," the Prior noted. "I've known Tam for over a decade, and he's never mentioned such a thing. He comes with Greda and her children about once a fortnight. She and the girls help Andel with the animals while Tam and her boy see to any stonework."

"Do you know where they live?"

"In a tenement house at the top of Water Street. Greda works in the laundry on the ground floor."

"Thank you." Hektor paused at the door. "So, what will happen to the dog and her puppies?"

"Petal will stay here," the Prior answered, stroking the

mother dog's ears fondly. "Her littles will either be found good, loving homes or they'll stay here too." He looked up, a speculative smile on his face. "Why, were you interested in a Watch House mascot or two, Sergeant?"

"Maybe, or a family pet."

"Well, come and see me in eight weeks' time. If Kassiath here gives you a good reference, I just might consider it."

After the promised visit to the Temple donkey, Hektor and Kassie headed toward Water Street in silence until Kassie glanced up at her brother with a grin. "You think Ma'll be all right with a dog in the flat?"

Hektor shrugged. "Probably not," he replied, looking a bit sheepish. "Don't honestly know what came over me."

She laughed. "It's the Temple. Somethin' about it makes folk wanna help out. They've placed a lot of animals that way. People come to get in with the god, or maybe just to feel good about doing a kind deed, and the next thing you know, they have a cat or a dog or some other creature in their care."

"Well, I hope the feelin' doesn't wear off once they get out and get 'em home."

"The priests follow up to make sure. You havin' second thoughts?"

"About the flat, yeah, but maybe the Watch House could use a guard dog. Breakneedle Street's got one."

"I don't see why not, then. The aviary's taken in plenty of birds, an' old Sammy comes from them."

"Does he? I always thought he just walked in one day and took the place over."

"No. Paddy say's Da brought him back one day after he'd gone to the Temple making inquiries about a horse theft."

"Huh. Well, remind me to keep my distance then, I don't think old Sammy'd appreciate another Watch House cat musclin' in on his territory."

"I'm sure he wouldn't mind. He mostly sleeps in the Capt'n's office these days."

"Still . . . the Temple seems like a place to keep clear

of." Hektor stopped at the entrance to Water Street. "You'd best head back now, Kas. Edzel say's Tam's got a temper on him, and I don't want you getting caught up in that."

"But—"

"You're a Watch House Messenger Bird Apprentice, not a Watchman," he said sternly. "But if it makes you feel any better, I'd have chased Paddy off, too."

"All right. I have chores to do anyway." She paused. "Be careful?"

"I will. You want me to bring home something from the Herbalist tonight?"

She blinked at him. "Didn't you go last night?"

"Yeah. 'Parently, we need more chamomile."

"Oh. Then yeah, thanks, you could bring me some red millet seeds."

Hektor found Tam sitting in the his tenement's inner courtyard, working a piece of sandstone into a small roundel. He was a thickset man with curly brown hair and a short beard covered in stone dust. He scowled at Hektor when he identified himself, the scowl growing deeper as Hektor outlined the reason for his visit.

"Street repairs," he spat with a derisive sneer. "That were years ago. An' nothing but a fight every time. Shopkeepers refusin' to pay up, an' court refusin' to do anythin' about it."

He slammed the chisel onto the small worktable, causing bits of stone to bounce off onto the ground. "We were supposed to get a weekly wage for the surveyin', an' that never came. Everyone claimin' someone else were in charge of it, an' no one payin' up at the end. So I chucked it all in. The streets can turn to mire for all I care. Where were they when Barrin died? They all said he was drunk, but I know different. He hadn't touched a drink for days. He got run over one evenin' in the dark, an' nobody did nothin'. Where was the Watch then, eh?"

"Tam? You all right?"

He turned to see a girl of about thirteen peering around the courtyard gate.

"I'm fine, Rasha."

"Want me to call Leon?"

"No. S'all good. Your brother's busy at his own work. The Watchman here was just leavin'." Tam returned his attention to Hektor, the scowl returning to his face. "I've said all I have to say. I left that life, and I ain't goin' back."

"Fair enough. Just one more question," Hektor said, his expression set, "Do you know any reason why somebody might be stealin' cobblestones?"

Tam stared at him incredulously. "No." He rose and stalked off, followed by Rasha, who glanced back at Hektor with a frightened expression.

"You think it's Tam what's stealin' the cobblestones?"

Back at the Watch House, Paddy handed his older brothers a mug of tea each before giving Hektor the avaricious look of a true gossip.

"No," Hektor answered. "But the girl did seem nervous."

"Sure, but the Watch makes everyone nervous."

"That's true."

"So now what?"

"Now, it's a long walk up to the Records Hall in the fog."

"I'll go." Paddy turned eagerly.

"No, I think I'd better go myself. This's turned into more'n a fact findin' mission. I've got to convince someone up there to appoint new surveyors." He glanced around. "Anyone seen where I left my tunic?"

His brothers exchanged a look. "Yer wearin' it, Hek, I mean Sergeant," Paddy answered.

"Oh, yeah."

"You need more sleep," Aiden grunted. "Paddy, go with him before he trips over his own feet."

The next morning dawned clear and warm. Both Eddie and Ronnie were enjoying a day of remarkable health and good spirits, so Ismy convinced Hektor to accompany the three of them to her father's for supper that evening.

"My brother an' Trisha'll be there, so that means Zoe

an' their new baby, Joanna, will be too. He'll be in a fine mood, you'll see."

Hektor gave her a sour look. "Yeah, well, a fine mood for Edzel Smith is a poor mood for anybody else."

"He won't even notice you're there. He dotes on little Joie."

"Everyone dotes on little Joie. I doubt she's ever had a colicky day since she was born."

"Don't be silly. All babies are colicky. Get your jacket."

Surrounded by grandchildren, Edzel's customary scowl was nowhere to be seen. After the meal, he leaned back with a contented smile.

"So, did the great cobblestone crime come to anythin'?" he asked, his voice more teasing than accusatory for a change.

Hektor shrugged. "Not yet. I've got a fella up to the Records Hall lookin' into whose in charge of namin' new surveyors."

"Don't hold yer breath. So, you never did find Tam, then?" Something in Edzel's tone made Hektor frown.

"I found 'im. He's not interested in comin' back to 'is old trade."

"Huh. Well, I guess you jus' don't have a way with people, does 'e, Jo-Jo?" Edzel chucked his youngest granddaughter under the chin, and she laughed.

The sound of the shop bell interrupted them.

"That'll be 'im now," Edzel stated, handing the girl off to Trisha before rising with a grunt.

"Who?"

"Tam, a course, who else? He an' I had a little chat yesterday."

Hektor glared at him. "You had a little chat," he echoed. "I thought you said you didn't know where he lived."

"He came to see me, if you must know. Askin' about you."

"Me? Why?"

Edzel waved a dismissive hand at him. "Wanted a

character, I suspect. I tol' him you could be trusted for all you weren't too bright."

"Trusted how?"

"To do what's right by everyone, fool. Honestly, I don't know what Ismy sees in you." Edzel paused at the kitchen door with a scowl. "Well, come on; 'e ain't here to see me. Get off yer arse and come see what 'e wants."

Hektor glanced over at Ismy, who shrugged, so, with a scowl growing on his own face, he followed him.

He found Tam and a boy of fifteen or sixteen who looked enough like the girl, Rasha, to probably be her brother, Leon. They were standing by the door, a rough burlap sack filled with something lumpy at their feet.

Tam gave him a baleful look and pointed at the sack.

"I ain't sayin' nothin' about where they came from 'cept that I didn't have nothin' to do with their pilferin'. If you're willin' to leave it at that, Leon an' me are willin' to do a bit of street repair work with 'em."

"Why the sudden change of heart?"

Tam studiously ignored the boy, who squirmed uncomfortably at his side. "Priests make for powerfully pushy family," he said finally, and the boy relaxed a little.

"Yeah, so do blacksmiths," Hektor agreed.

"I should tell ya," Tam continued, his tone no less belligerent, "they ain't all there. Some of 'em got … used before they was identified, but the mortar's set now, so they couldn't be pulled out without underminin' half the Temple wall."

"Temple wall. I see. Well, the bag seems pretty full. I guess that'll do. I'm happy to close the investigation if the potholes get filled up."

"Fair enough. We'll start first thing tomorrow mornin' if it stays clear."

They shook on it, the stonemason's huge, scarred fingers closing over the Watchman's like a vise.

"I've been to the Records Hall," Hektor told him. "If I can get your weekly wage reinstated, I will."

Tam snorted. "Yeah, well, I won't hold my breath."

"That's just what Edzel said a moment ago."

"Edzel's a wise man."

"Is he?" When Tam snickered, Hektor shrugged. "Yeah, I guess he is."

The sound of three babies crying pulled his head around. "Tomorrow, then."

"Tomorrow." Pointing Leon towards the sack, Tam took his leave, and Hektor returned to the kitchen to find Ismy's brother, Tay, bouncing little Joanna in his arms while Trisha set a packet of chamomile on the table and put on the kettle.

"She's colicky," the younger Smith said with a weary smile. "She set off the boys. Sorry."

"S'all right," Hektor answered, accepting his sons from Ismy and bouncing them the same way. "I'm used to it."

"I was gonna walk her out to the forge while the tea steeps. You wanna come?"

"Yeah."

Together, the two fathers maneuvered out the back door, their children slowly quieting in their arms.

Boggles and Spies
Louisa Swann

The evening breeze cooled Petril's face as he stared down at the waters of Lake Evendim. The wind had been hard out of the southwest instead of the east today, churning the surface into a cauldron of choppy waves, then ripping the tops off those waves. The spray cast an icy coating of mist over everything in the immediate vicinity, turning the jagged stones that made up the shoreline dark gray.

The breeze shifted, carrying with it the stink of freshly gutted bluegill overlaid with a hint of woodsmoke. It was still too early in the spring for the women to go sponge diving, but they'd gone out in the smaller skiffs and brought home nets filled with the silver-scaled fish.

Petril's stomach rumbled. There'd be fried bluegill tonight and crappie, along with a rash of early spring tubers Ani, his oldest sister, had found at the edge of a melting snowbank.

He wouldn't eat the fish, of course. Couldn't eat it. Not when he heard the wails and screams of dying fish in his head every time he took a bite. He'd taken to sneaking his portions underneath the table to the dog and then trying to fill up on vegetables and fried dough.

Not an easy task for an eight-year old who was always hungry.

Da said he let his imagination get the better of him, but Petril knew better. Imagination or no, the cries of the suffering creatures echoed in his head, bouncing around his skull like a swarm of angry bees.

He loved the water, loved the feel of the boat beneath his feet, the wind in his hair.

But he despised fishing.

Da and Petril's six older brothers had left five days ago, taking the fishing boats out on the first trip of the season, joining Petril's uncles and the men from the other longhouses. They'd be gone for another day or so if the weather held. Da hadn't argued when Petril said he didn't feel well enough to go out on the boat. He'd charged Petril with keeping the village safe. He took the duty seriously because he was the only man left in the village. Jem and Loni didn't count, as they were still in diapers.

The village was one of the smallest on the lake, pressed back against the forest, a furlong or so from the shore. A scattering of longhouses—one for each of the families—angled off a central firepit like spokes on a cartwheel that had been cut in half, leaving the lakeside open. The common area was busy with villagers gathered together to celebrate the coming of spring, women and girls weaving around each other, feeding the fire, chopping vegetables, mixing dough, and chatting as they worked to prepare the evening meal.

Petril turned away from the village, swishing a branch hard enough to make the air whistle. He brandished the branch like a sword. He wasn't a fisher who couldn't fish anymore; he was a soldier, battling a great army to protect his mum and sisters and the rest of the village from—

"I thought ye was a Herald?" a mischievous voice asked.

Petril lowered his branch-turned-sword and scowled at his little sister. She grinned up at him, her long nose wrinkled the way only Tinnie's nose could. Her dark, short-cropped hair stood on end, fallen victim to whatever his baby sister's newest "adventure" had been.

"That were yesterday." Petril whipped his sword-branch back and forth with an authoritative air. He hoped. "Today I'm protectin' the village."

Tinnie snorted. "From what? Mozzie bugs?"

The spring crop of blood-sucking insects had been particularly bad this year, not unexpected, given the relatively warm winter.

"Them what's tryin' t' snatch the women and kiddies." Petril stood tall and swished the sword-branch again. "Pirates 'n such."

Tinnie shrieked and her eyes went wide. She covered her mouth with her hands, then broke into a fit of giggles that sent tears running down her cheeks. Before Petril could grumble at her, she turned and raced back toward the longhouses.

Sisters.

Petril shook his head, swatting the wiry grass that somehow managed to grow between the stones with his sword-branch as he headed down to the lake. He had eight siblings, and Tinnie was the youngest of the lot, having just turned five. Petril was three years older, but Tinnie always found ways to make him feel foolish. His other brothers and sisters—even his mum and da—said that Petril was *imaginative*, but Tinnie . . .

He let the encounter fade, fighting off imaginary pirates as he wandered along the shore, dancing from stone to stone, jabbing left with his sword-branch, then right, driving the raiders back from the village.

He kept his eyes sharp as he fought imaginary foes, hoping to catch sight of something different, something special. There was magic hidden around the lake, if a body believed the stories and songs, as Petril did. Magic created by the Cataclysm—just as the lake itself was— and disguised as artifacts. He didn't know what these artifacts looked like, but he was going to find one, and then he'd be someone important. Someone who mattered. Someone who could make a difference.

A tern's haunting cry echoed overhead, the black and white bird's elegant wings slicing an arc across the pewter gray sky. As night closed in, light from the village fires would slowly start to twinkle, adding their light to the stars overhead. On a windless night, the lake waters became smooth as ice, mirroring the stars and turning the world into a sparkling wonder.

He liked being outside at night, with the stars overhead and the wind in his face. Being outside was better than sleeping.

He heard the screams of dying fish when he slept, felt the searing pain of the harpoon.

Better not to sleep.

Mum didn't get after him for going out at night. She seemed to understand that a man needed his freedom. She always saved him a little something when he missed the evening meal, something that became even littler after the dog got Petril's fish.

He took a vicious swipe at a stubborn clump of wiry grass sticking out from between two stones the size of a man's head, then paused, listening.

The unmistakable sound of voices drifted across the rock-strewn beach.

Strangers had come to his forest. Foreigners, by the sound of it.

Petril scowled down at the branch in his hand, then tossed it aside, trading in his soldier identity for that of a spy.

A spy who could help keep the village safe.

He needed to find out who the strangers were and then tell Mum. That would be the responsible thing to do.

Petril hunched over slightly to make himself a little smaller, then crept toward the tree line, hopping from stone to stone, barely making a sound.

Leaves rustled as he left the rocky shore behind, slipping into the forest like a creature of the woods. Even though he was a bit big for his age, he could be quiet as an owl hunting in the night, quiet enough to sneak up on folks and give them a good scare.

He loved the look of shock when he managed to surprise his sisters and brothers. He'd even managed, once, to sneak up on Da while he was napping, something Petril had promised never to do again.

He never thought he'd actually *need* to sneak up on someone, though. It just confirmed his belief that you never could tell when a particular skill would come in handy.

Maybe I will *be a spy someday*, Petril mused as he eased around a tree trunk as big around as five men. He'd travel to Haven, seek an audience with the King himself, or maybe the King's Own ...

He slid between the branches of a particularly thorny bush, imagining meeting the King's Own. There were always spies in the stories about kings and queens—

He froze.

He'd come to the edge of a small clearing. Three men stood in the clearing, but it wasn't the men who gave Petril pause.

It was the creature tied to a stake near the men.

At first, he thought it was a boggle, a monster that haunted the darkest night, whose sole purpose was to scare kiddies into staying in their longhouses and not go wandering about in the dark. The creature *looked* like a horse, but it was hard to tell in the fading light. It was *enormous*, with an oversized head, a neck as thick as a barrel, and a blotchy hide that could have been dirty gray.

Couldn't be a boggle though. Boggles had glowing red eyes and belched smoke. This creature's eyes didn't glow, and, so far, Petril hadn't seen any smoke. Not from it, anyway.

The men stood an arm's length or two away from the creature. The tallest one, lean as a fisher, kept running his hands through dark, shoulder-length hair.

The man nearest the horselike creature was shorter, though just as lean as the tall man, with close-cropped hair and a dark complexion that practically shouted "pirate," at least to Petril's mind.

The third man made Petril's blood run cold. A man who, judging by his girth and round cheeks, should be the lord of a grand manor, sitting by a warm hearth instead of standing in a forest clearing. Even in the dimness, Petril could tell the man's trousers clung snugly to his legs without any of the bag that came from wearing something over and over. Even his cloak looked to be fresh from the tailor.

He could have been someone's gramps, looking all friendly and jovial like.

Except the feeling Petril got every time he looked at the man wasn't friendly *or* jovial. More like the feeling one would get being out on the lake in a one-man skiff with bad weather coming on and realizing you'd lost your paddle.

The creature snorted and tried to look over its shoulder.

That's when Petril noticed what looked like a delivery wagon with four sides topped by a roof high enough to allow a man to haul crates inside without ducking his head and a rear door latched shut. The wagon had been tucked back among the trees on the far side of the clearing.

Something thumped in the wagon, a rhythmic, drum-like sound that set Petril's teeth on edge.

A wave of concern, followed by a sense of desolation, washed over him. Whatever was in that wagon was important, though he wasn't sure how he knew that.

He studied the creature with a growing sense of alarm.

The light was too dim. He had to get closer. Figure out what the creature was. And maybe, just maybe, figure out a way to help.

He eased back out of the bush and wound his way closer, mindful of the branches and leaves beneath his feet, the scent of damp soil in his nose. He turned when he thought he was close enough and followed a small animal path under a section of bramble brush, finally reaching a point where he could study the clearing once more.

The creature *was* a horse, he could see that now. A very big, very powerful horse. With intelligent brown eyes that seemed to *see* him through the broad bramble brush leaves.

The three men approached the horse, partially cutting off Petril's view. The tall man had a whip curled at his belt.

"It's time you learned some manners," the lordly man said, glaring at the horse. He stepped back, and the tall man unhooked his whip, letting the lash flow onto the ground.

Petril's breath caught in his throat.

He'd always had an affinity for animals. The village goats and dogs, the wild animals of the lake and forest, all were his friends. He'd volunteered to help with the horses when the carters arrived, men hired to haul dried fish and sturgeon roe north to Zoë for trade. The carters had welcomed his help, taking him in hand and teaching him how to care for the cart horses.

Until Da put a stop to it. "Ye'll be spendin' all yer wakin' hours on a boat soon 'nuf," he'd said, in that voice that sounded like thunder rumbling off in the distance. "No sense wastin' time learnin' somethin' ye'll naught use."

That had been *before* Petril heard the cries of the fish.

Now he watched the horse in the clearing as the tall man lay on the whip, feeling helpless and wishing he'd learned more about horses. A strange thundering filled the clearing, and it took a moment before he realized the sound was coming from inside the wagon. A high-pitched whinny split the air . . . and the enormous horse went mad.

It reared, yanking rope and stake free of the ground. The tall man snapped his whip, the crack of the long lash loud in the night air. At the same time, the lordly man reached beneath his cloak and pulled a long, dark object free. Then he stepped forward and whipped the object through the air with a deadly overhand swing.

Pain burst through Petril's head as a dull thud sounded in the air. He collapsed on the ground, knowing he wasn't the one who'd been hurt, but unable to stand the pain.

It was happening again.

First with the bluegill and the sturgeon. Now with an enormous horse.

Was he going out of his mind?

Petril didn't know how long he'd been on the ground. The pain gradually faded, but it was full on night before he rolled to his knees and checked the clearing.

He was surprised to see a fire burning in the center of the clearing and the horse tied to a stake. He'd half expected to find it stretched out dead on the ground. The animal stood quietly, head hanging low, as if still in pain.

Two of the men were in bedrolls on the far side of the fire. The tall man sat on a rock facing the fire, his back to the horse. He looked to be nodding off.

Petril could see by the light of the fire that the horse's nose was dripping, a dark, thick liquid that could only be blood. His heart skipped a beat.

One of the carters had told him if a horse was standing, it was still alive. And this horse was still standing.

But how much blood could a horse lose before it dropped over dead?

He crawled as close as he dared, hoping she'd be able to hear him. He wondered dully how he knew the horse was a *she*, then decided it didn't matter.

"Heyla," Petril whispered, struggling to remember how the carters talked to their horses. It felt strange talking to the animal, though he wasn't sure why. He talked to the dog all the time. And the fish. And the birds. And practically anything else that flew, crawled, or ran around on four legs. In fact, he did more talking to animals than he did to his own siblings.

Animals didn't talk back. They didn't tease, and they didn't say hurtful things.

But they could *be* hurt.

"Yer still livin' anyway. That's a good sign. I dunno what they're doing wi' ye, but I'll bring hep. I promise."

The mare didn't move.

It seemed as though he should say more, do more, but he didn't know what. He faded back between the trees and ran.

Petril woke his mum when he got home and told her about the horse and the men. And he felt like a widdle in diapers when Mum didn't think he'd seen anything important.

"Is this another one o' yer daydreams, then?" she asked.

Petril shook his head. "She's real as the 'air on me 'ead."

"Ye expect me ta believe ye? After tha last prank ye pulled?"

" 'Tisn't a prank, Mum. I swear it."

His mum sighed. "Ye said there's only the three?"
He nodded.

"Right, then. I'll let the others know first thing in the
mornin'. We'll be on the lookout for anythin' strange.
Three men passin' through ain't much cause for worryin',
though, and yer Da'll be home in a day or two."

"But wha' about the 'orse? She's a special one, I jus'
know it. And they be hurtin' 'er."

"Ye ken what a Companion is?" Mum asked, reaching
out to ruffle Petril's hair. He nodded.

"Men like yer talkin' about wouldna be stealin' a
horse o' the Heralds. And if'n it ain't a Companion, the
likes o' us got no call ta interfere."

Petril bowed his head. "She's not a Companion, Mum.
She's—" He stopped. He didn't really know what kind of
horse it was. "Could be a battle steed," he said in a rush,
then felt his face grow warm. He didn't even know what
a battle steed looked like, though he'd heard stories about
them. The stories also said that no one put their hands on
a Shin'a'in battle steed and lived to tell about it.

Mum gave him that *look*. "There's nowhat more ta be
said. Off ta bed wi ye."

Petril shut his mouth and went to bed, settling into his
place on the floor. With the other boys gone, Ani and
Tinnie got to sleep on the cot. But he didn't envy them.
Not really. More than likely he wouldn't sleep a wink.
Only this time when he started to drift off, instead of
hearing sturgeon cries, he heard a dull thump and remembered the pain.

No one—man or beast, Companion or battle steed or
carter's horse—deserved to be treated like that.

He tossed and turned, then tossed and turned some
more, feeling like a man caught in the throes of a fever.
Then he finally kicked off his blanket and tiptoed out of
the longhouse into the night.

A new moon lit the way, the tiny sliver reflected in gently
undulating waves. Normally, Petril would stop and watch
the way the waves caught the light and threw it back, but
tonight he was on a mission.

He was used to getting about in the dark, used to seeing without added light. On a night like this, with stars and a new moon, his surroundings were visible enough. It was only on nights that were blanketed with clouds that he had trouble.

Feeling exposed, he traded open sky for the shadowed shelter of looming trees, leaving the shoreline and staying just inside the tree line as he worked his way toward the mare.

What would he do when he reached the clearing?

Petril tried to think it through, but thinking wasn't really his strong suit. Imagining was.

So he *imagined* what he would do.

He'd sneak through the bushes, quiet as you please, and walk right up to the horse, who would immediately know he was there to help. He'd untie the poor thing quick as a white bass snapping a line, then lead her into the bushes and back to the village.

Easy peasy, bluegill breezy.

Right. Petril almost snorted. He was young, but he wasn't stupid. Imagining something was one thing; doing that thing was another.

He couldn't just do nothing, though. And he couldn't go back to the longhouse. He'd never sleep, never get the sight and sound of those men beating that poor horse out of his head—

A shout caught his attention.

Petril looked around. He was almost to the clearing. And judging from the intensity of the curses coming from that clearing, not only was the horse still alive, she was kicking.

He ghosted from tree to tree, staying as hidden as possible. The stench of sweat and blood mingled with the scent of trampled earth clogged his nose. He pressed his lips together, wormed his way through the bramble brush again, and peered into the clearing through a small gap between leaves.

The wagon had been pulled from the trees and now sat to the left of a blazing cook fire. The wagon's rear door had been opened and fastened flush to the side facing the fire.

The mare stood near the wagon. Her shadow—made monstrously huge by the flickering firelight—dominated the wagon's side.

As Petril watched, the mare reared and lashed out with her front hooves, striking a man-size lump crumpled on the ground at her feet. The lordly man stood nearby, left arm held at an odd angle. The tall man dodged the mare's hind feet as she delivered a kick that would have broken bones if it had connected. The tall man shouted and cracked his whip, laying the lash across the mare's bloodied back.

The lordly man moved, disappearing around the back of the wagon. He reappeared a moment later, leading something the size of a temple dog.

With everything that was going on, it took a moment for Petril to realize the newcomer was a baby horse, a newborn foal with spindly legs and eyes gone wide in fright.

The inside of Petril's head erupted as the mare let loose a scream filled with rage and terror. He crumpled to the ground, drowning in emotions so intense he could barely breathe.

The mare was furious. She was also terrified.

He curled into himself, frantically trying to move beneath the weight of her emotions. An overwhelming urge to stand up and run washed over him. He should have stayed in his bed, left the horse to take care of herself.

Instead, he'd pretended to be a spy. But the only way a spy could help was if'n someone *believed* that spy and sent in an army or something.

He couldn't even get his mum to believe him. She thought he was imagining things.

Just as he'd *imagined* cries coming from the bluegill and crappies and bass captured in their nets and by their lines.

Just as he'd *imagined* screams coming from the sturgeons when they'd been harpooned last fall.

But Petril knew now he hadn't imagined those things. They were *real*.

A line of reason fell into his pool of self-pity.

He grabbed the line and pulled himself up out of the pool, thinking frantically.

A Herald-Mage was the horse's best hope, of course.

What would a Herald-Mage do?

A Herald-Mage wouldn't hide from danger, that's for certain. A Herald-Mage would figure out a way to use magic to free the horse from her captors.

But magic couldn't be imagined into existence.

The thought chased the breath from his lungs and left his chest feeling as if a net filled with fish had just fallen on him.

He wasn't a Herald-Mage .

He was only an eight-year-old boy.

Panic lodged in Petril's throat like a broken fishbone, choking him with fear. Was the fear his own or the horse's?

Probably a bit of both, a tiny voice whispered in his mind.

Sweat soaked his tunic in spite of the icy night air. He shivered and swallowed hard, and suddenly Da's voice was in his head, soothing and calm.

"Fear'll send ye ta the deeps quicker than lightnin' if'n ye let it. Set yer mind on somethin' ye can do rather than sweatin' what ye cain't. If'n yer still breathin', set yer mind on that."

Petril blocked out the horse's screams and the men's curses and forced himself to take a deep breath. He listened to his breathing, felt the air rush in and out of his lungs.

And then he softly recited the lines of an old children's song: "Bluegills swimming, one by one, hurrah, hurrah. Come into the net, that's the fun, hurrah, hurrah."

Petril's breathing slowed. His mouth was dry as a sponge that had sat in the sun too long, but he could breathe freely again.

He listened for a moment, then his heart jump-kicked like a rabbit being chased by a dog. It was too quiet. All he could hear were gentle waves lapping at the shore and a bit of shuffling.

How long had he been curled up like a frightened kiddie?

Slowly, he rose to his knees and peeked through the hole he'd been using to spy on the clearing.

Firelight illuminated the mare, head down again, near the wagon. Otherwise, the clearing appeared empty—if he didn't count the tall man sitting by the fire, facing the opposite side of the clearing.

Petril chewed his lip, watching the mare and thinking. Realization washed over him like warm rain. The mare's head wasn't down because she was exhausted. Ropes had been lashed around her body from one end to the other, anchoring her head low to the ground and preventing her from moving.

Something else caught his eye, and Petril stiffened, feeling as though he'd been caught in winter's icy winds.

There was a net beneath all that rope.

Roped and netted.

Petril fingered the short-bladed knife at his waist. Would a netting knife be enough to cut through all that? He kept his knife proper sharp, as did all fisherfolk, but the blade was short, meant for cutting light nets, not sawing through heavy rope.

The hair on his arms and neck rose like the hackles on a dog's back, and the heavy weight returned to his chest.

Petril made himself take slow, deep breaths.

Bluegills swimming, one by one . . .

Time to move. Before the men came back.

He searched the ground until he found a large, club-like stick—just in case—then lifted his chin, pulled his knife from the sheath at his waist, and slipped into the clearing.

Petril was halfway to the wagon when a twig snapped beneath his foot. He froze, mouth gaping like a stranded fish, and glanced at the man by the fire.

The tall man didn't turn.

Petril dashed to the wagon and ducked beneath it, holding his breath and listening for an alarm.

No alarm sounded, only a loud snuffling that made his skin crawl.

It took a moment for him to pinpoint the sound. It was coming from the horse.

The angle of her head made it hard for her to breathe—

He needed to get to her, get her head free.

Heart thumping so loud he could barely hear anything else, he eased toward the enormous hooves an arm's length away. He stayed as low as he could, inching his way beneath the wagon, his back brushing the broad beams holding the wagon bed in place every now and again. It suddenly occurred to him that the lordly man— and the man who'd been stomped, if'n he wasn't dead— might be sleeping inside.

The thought almost froze him in place again, but Petril breathed through it. He reached the side of the wagon nearest the horse, paused between the wagon's wheels, and studied the horse.

She was *huge*.

He stared at the mare in dismay. He'd never been around an animal so large—except the sturgeons and they'd been, well, *fish*, swimming below him in the water and well on their way to dead. If he'd been betting with his brothers, he wouldn't have bet a fingerling that he could control such a horse. He was just a boy; she was as big as a longhouse *and* she was furious. He could feel the anger simmering inside her, just waiting to be released.

What *was* he thinking?

Not thinking, Petril reminded himself. *Imagining*.

Imagining he knew all about horses.

Imagining he was someone important.

Imagining he was a hero.

Petril took a deep breath.

Time to stop imagining and get on with it.

"Easy now," he murmured, fear cracking his voice. Someone was bound to hear him, but he had to let the

horse know he was here; convince her he was going to
help. Otherwise, she'd probably stomp him into the
ground when he got her free. "I'm a friend, now. Gonna
hep ye get quit o' this mess."

The horse snorted softly.

Without stopping to think, Petril darted out from under the wagon and fell to his knees next to the horse. He
peered at the stakes anchoring what amounted to a cocoon of net and ropes. He finally gave up trying to figure
out what rope went where, grabbed the nearest stake,
and yanked.

The stake didn't move.

Scowling so hard his cheeks hurt, Petril felt for the
rope attached to the stake, then used his knife and sawed
the rope through.

Just before the rope parted, memories of the mare
stomping the small man into the ground flashed through
his mind. She could stomp Petril, or kick him in the head
as she tried to get rid of the net.

Or she could get tangled in the netting—

The mare lifted her head with a soft sigh but didn't
move otherwise. She wasn't able to move her head far,
but it seemed to be enough to help with her breathing.
Her right front leg stiffened, and Petril realized she was
shifting her weight.

"All right, then," he murmured. "Let's see if'n we kin
get a bit farther."

One by one he cut through the lines, each rope taking
a bit longer than the strands of netting. He shook his
head, wondering at how he'd found himself cutting this
particular net apart instead of working hard to weave it
back together. Whoever owned this net was going to be
madder than an osprey robbed of its catch.

The mare rhythmically shifted her weight from side to
side, testing her bonds. Petril got the sense she was
preparing—

"Don't go doing nothin' stupid now," he quietly ad-
monished. "Lemme get this thing off'n ye first. Elsewise,
ye might get tangled and go down."

And then it was back, that strange connection between his mind and the horse's, only this time she wasn't in a rage—or panicking.

She was calm. And determined.

The mare wasn't *talking* to him, not exactly. But he understood what she was *feeling*. He could sense the dull pain still lingering in her head, the sting where the whip had ripped her hide open. But most of all, he could feel the sense of protection and panic at being separated from her foal.

Petril almost laughed out loud. He wasn't hallucinating or even imagining.

This was real.

"We'll get yer little 'un back. Jus' one last—"

He sliced through the final rope. Done. With one side, anyway.

Petril glanced at the man still staring into the fire. The man hadn't moved.

A good sign. Petril chewed his lip again, pondering his next move. He could go behind the horse and pull the net and ropes off, but that would put him too near her hindquarters and he didn't relish getting kicked.

He could go in front of her and risk getting run over.

Or he could crawl beneath her belly, which could get him stomped into a bloody pulp.

"Stand still, now. Jus' like ye bin doin'."

Smothering a groan, Petril swallowed the lump threatening to choke off his air and inched forward. He *imagined* himself underneath the horse, pulling the rope-and-net cocoon free. He kept that picture in his mind, going over it again and again.

And then he was *doing* it.

Without getting stomped or trampled or kicked.

He hooked his hands into the net and dragged it downward. At first, the weight of the "cocoon" was so great he could barely move it.

How had the mare stayed on her feet?

His arms ached and his fingers burned.

He should have brought help. Should have known he wouldn't be able to rescue the mare on his own ...

Petril gritted his teeth and pulled again, relieved to feel the cocoon slowly move. Over and over he pulled, ignoring the burn in his hands and arms. Inch by inch he dragged the heavy ropes and netting off the mare's back. It felt as though he'd never get the mare free. He'd still be here, hauling on the ropes and netting when the sun brightened the horizon—

He started as the cocoon slipped toward the ground instead of fighting him. Heart racing in anticipation, he snagged another section with his fingers, pulled . . . and ducked back under the mare's belly, barely reaching the safety of the wagon as ropes and netting fell to the ground with a dull whomp!

Freed of her prison, the mare leaped forward. Quick as a wink, she spun, rounded the end of the wagon, and skidded to a stop. Petril snatched his stick off the ground and followed her, feeling slow as a snail trapped in winter cold.

The tall man rose to his feet with a start, hand going to the whip coiled on his belt.

The mare screamed and charged the man, knocking him back toward the fire.

Petril didn't watch. He peered through the darkness at the back of the wagon, searching for the mare's foal. He doubled over, feeling as though he'd been thrust into heaving seas, when he saw the spindly legs sprawled on the ground.

One of the legs moved, and he sighed in relief.

They'd bound the baby, just as they'd bound the baby's mum.

He kept his movements calm and slow, moving close enough to see the ropes wrapped around the young foal's hooves. He set his stick down and went to his knees next to the baby.

A muffled thud shook the wagon just before a trousered leg appeared at the open door, followed by the rounded shape of the man who made Petril's skin crawl.

Petril grabbed his stick and rose before the man realized he was there. Without hesitating, he stepped on the wagon's rear wheel to gain a bit of height, gripped the large stick in both hands, and swung.

The stick connected with a satisfying *thud*, and the man dropped like a rock. Petril leaped after him, delivering another resounding blow, this time to the back of the big man's head. Petril winced. That was sure to raise a lump on the man's head. He carefully stepped over the fallen man's belly and climbed into the wagon.

Except for a few barrels, a crate, and a body-size lump under a bloodied blanket, the wagon was empty. He lifted a corner of the blanket and immediately dropped it. The short man wouldn't be going anywhere, at least on his own.

Quickly, Petril scrambled out of the wagon and dropped to the ground near the baby's hooves. One by one, he carefully sliced through the ropes. It took longer than he liked—the baby wasn't nearly as patient or still as her mum—but he finally cut the last rope free and stood back out of the way.

The baby lurched to her feet and stood for a moment, spraddle-legged, like a man on the deck of a heaving boat. Then she let out a bleat and bolted toward her mum.

Petril turned in time to see the mare swing her rump into the tall man, knocking him into the fire. He screamed as he rolled out the other side, writhing and twisting, attempting to put out the flames devouring his coat. The mare was after him in a flash, hooves raised.

Then she stomped the tall man into the dirt.

Once, twice, three times, her hooves pounded the still-burning body.

The screaming stopped.

For a moment, all Petril could hear was the mare's heavy breathing, then the baby bleated again. The mare turned as the baby trotted up and they touched noses, nickering softly to each other.

He had to get them out of here. Had to get them back to the village. But how?

More'n likely she wouldn't let him put a rope on her. *He* wouldn't, if'n it was him.

She'd listened to him so far, though. Would she listen now she was free?

"Come on, then," he said. He winced as his voice cracked. He'd meant to sound commanding, like distant thunder, and managed to sound like a kiddie who was too long for bed.

The mare lifted her head and looked straight at him, ears pricked and eyes intense.

Then she lowered her head, nuzzled her baby once more, and headed his way.

Petril watched an osprey rise gracefully on the morning currents, circling up, up, up, then soaring out over the lake. He imagined himself flying along with the bird, scanning the water far below, seeking the shadow that signaled a fish, then folding wings tight to his body, hurtling toward the lake's surface like a bolt from a crossbow, flaring his wings seconds before hitting the water, extending deadly talons—

"Ye ready, son?"

Petril turned from the lake, raising a hand to his da. He would miss watching the birds, miss the lake and the village, but he wouldn't be gone all that long. He skipped from rock to rock until he reached the grassy sand, then jogged to the waiting cart and climbed into the seat. Behind the cart, the mare and her foal waited patiently.

"Mind yer manners now. Do what old Fritz here tells ye."

Petril nodded as the carter, an ancient man with wrinkles as deep as the lake, heaved himself into the cart and took the reins.

Da had been quiet for a long time after he'd gotten home. He'd taken a few men and checked out the clearing. No sign of the three men—dead or alive—or the wagon, only a dead campfire and trampled ground. He'd clapped Petril's shoulder as they watched the big mare and her foal grazing on the wiry shore grass. "I'm proud o' ye, son," he'd said, and then he'd asked if Petril wanted to help the horses get back to their home.

Petril had solemnly nodded, trying not to show his excitement.

He didn't try to contain his excitement now. He'd already said goodbye to his family and the rest of the village. He'd miss them, but there was a whole big world out there, waiting to be explored. A world filled with adventures and mishaps and Heralds and Companions and Mages . . . and spies.

The world could always use another hero.

Couldn't it?

The Hidden Gift
Anthea Sharp

Tarek Strand shifted on the bench in the Healer's class-room, his skin prickling uncomfortably. His unease didn't come from the room itself, which was well-lit, with an open window letting in a breath of late summer air. Nor was there anything the matter with him. He might be one of the newest Healer Trainees at the Collegium, but he knew enough to sense that the discomfort was com-ing from a source outside his own body.

That source, in fact, seemed to be seated to his right, embodied in a girl named Lyssa Varcourt. As Master Adrun continued his morning lecture, Tarek gave Lyssa a sidelong glance.

She was small-boned and fair, a waif of a girl with big blue eyes, who was probably a half-dozen years younger than Tarek. Just like most of the class, some of whom only came up to his elbow. He tamped down a flare of resentment at his own Healing Gift, which had chosen to lay dormant for an abnormally long time before making itself known.

At least there were a few other Trainees closer to his own age, even if he was almost an adult. Lyssa, though, was the youngest of the First-Year Trainees. She'd come from a family of Healers, and Tarek often envied how easily she knew the answers to Master Adrun's ques-tions.

Today, however, there was definitely something wrong. Tarek felt an invisible vibration coming off

Lyssa's body at a frequency that set his teeth on edge. He closed his eyes a moment, trying to calm his mind and *see* past the discomfort.

Through the fabric of her long-sleeved tunic, he was shocked to sense that Lyssa's left arm was scored with cuts, some already healed, some newly scabbed over. Her entire forearm pulsed with a dim violet light, and he sucked in a dismayed breath. Why was her arm in such a state? Especially here, in the center of the Healers' Collegium?

She looked up, blue eyes scared, and met his gaze.

"No," she whispered.

The buzzing in Tarek's head stopped, as if a door had been slammed shut. The violet light around her arm disappeared, too. Strangest of all, the pain was entirely gone—the smarting from the cuts completely vanished, as if it had never even existed.

Tarek shook his head, and at the front of the room, Master Adrun looked over at him.

"Are you having difficulty grasping the lecture?" the Master asked in his deep voice.

"No, sir." Though, in truth, Tarek had no idea what the most recent part of the lesson had been.

"Excellent." Master Adrun folded his hands into the sleeves of his bright green robes. "Then please tell me about the healing properties of willow bark."

"Ah . . ." Tarek searched through his memory of the assigned reading. "It helps with, um, stomach aches?"

The Master lifted one brow. "Come see me after class, Tarek."

"Yes, sir." He bowed his head, feeling the heat of shame on his cheeks.

None of his classmates laughed openly, although he saw the pitying looks and hidden smiles. Bad enough to be the oldest one in the class, but to be thought stupid into the bargain was too much.

At least young Lyssa didn't seem to think less of him. In fact, she was ignoring him completely, seemingly intent on studying the herbal primer open in front of her.

The rest of the lecture crawled by until at last Master

Adrun released the class. The younger children bolted out of their seats, already hollering about the game they were going to play.

Lyssa was a bit slower. As she rose, Tarek saw a faint flicker of purple light on her left sleeve.

"Wait." He reached for her.

She jumped aside and snatched her book from the table. Without meeting his gaze or saying a word, she hurried out of the room.

Tarek stared at the doorway a moment, unease prickling through him again.

"Come to my study," Master Adrun said, pausing beside the bench. "And don't look so worried. This will be quick."

Spirits sinking, Tarek gathered his books and followed the Master. He didn't imagine a reprimand would take long, though he knew it would seem like an eternity. Every time he'd disappointed his father by not behaving as a lord should, he'd gotten lectures that had left him smarting, his ego bruised. Until he'd adopted the same arrogant manner and hard ways of Lord Strand.

It had been hard to shed that behavior, though his time at the Collegium had blunted it. And then, of course, everything had changed when Tarek's latent Healing Gift had burst out of him, and he'd had to face a far different future than what he'd planned.

Master Adrun held open the oaken door of his study, then closed it firmly behind them and placed his lecture notes on his desk. Instead of settling behind its intimidating expanse, however, he waved Tarek to one of the paired armchairs before the empty hearth.

Carefully, Tarek settled on the dark green cushions and waited. He'd learned from his interactions with his father that it never helped to begin the conversation with excuses. Despite the protests burning on his tongue, he remained silent.

Master Adrun sat across from him and smiled, lines crinkling at the corners of his eyes.

"You're learning," he said. "I commend you for it."

"I thought you were going to scold me."

"No." The Master's smile faded. "I need your assistance. And your discretion."

Tarek nodded, curiosity flashing through him. "I'd be glad to help."

Master Adrun's eyebrow twitched. "I would think a future jord would know better than to agree to anything without first hearing the terms."

"I trust you." The words surprised Tarek, even as he spoke them. It seemed the last of his anger with the Master Healer had dissipated. After all, it was not his fault that Tarek had been forced onto the Healer's path.

It was no one's fault, really, and though he thought he'd accepted the fact months ago, it was, finally, a truth he could live with. The knowledge gave him a measure of peace.

"I am much pleased to hear it," the Master said, and the dryness of his tone did not completely mask his approval. "There is a student in your class, Lyssa Varcourt. I believe you know who she is?"

"Yes." Tarek leaned forward. "In fact, and I know this sounds strange, but ... I think something is the matter with her."

Master Adrun let out a satisfied breath. "Your Gift serves you well, Tarek. Indeed, I've been sensing distress from her for some time, but when confronted, she refuses to admit anything's wrong. I was hoping that you might befriend her and perhaps gain some insight into the problem. You have a younger sister, I believe?"

"I do." Tarek dug the toe of his shoe into the thick carpeting. "But Lyssa's much younger than I am."

"Then think of yourself as a mentor or a champion. The girl needs help, but she refuses to turn to any of the Masters for it."

"Do you think there's a problem with her Gift?"

"Perhaps." Master Adrun rubbed his forehead. "I'm not quite sure where the problem lies. She comes from a family that's known for producing strong Healers, and she seems capable enough at her studies."

Privately, Tarek thought she was more than capable. It must be nice to come from a background where Gifts were accepted and supported. Where Healing was discussed openly, and information about it was freely available.

"I'm sorry I didn't know the answer to your question, today," he said. "I was distracted by Lyssa, in fact."

"Tell me."

"It's hard to explain." Tarek paused a moment, trying to put it as coherently as he could. "First, I felt a . . . well, it was an uncomfortable vibration, I guess. Then there was violet light on her left arm, and I thought I sensed cuts all along her skin. And then she noticed me looking at her, and all of that just vanished. She seemed perfectly fine."

Master Adrun frowned. "But you and I know that is not the case. This seems even more worrisome than I'd first thought."

"I'm not sure what I can do to help," Tarek said. "But I'll try and pay attention whenever I'm around her. And see if she'll maybe talk to me a little."

"Even that much is more than I can do," the Master said, rising. "Please keep me informed as to what you discover."

Tarek wasn't at all certain he could succeed where Master Adrun had failed, but he nodded anyway and let the Healer show him to the door.

Lunch in the Common Room was a noisy affair, full of the clack of dishes and babble of competing conversations. Herald Trainees in their Grays made up the majority of the diners, but there were a smattering of rust-clad Bards in training and, here and there, the subdued mossy tones worn by the Healer Trainees.

It didn't take Tarek long to spot Lyssa's pale hair. She was seated at a table in the corner, only a book keeping her company as she ate her serving of vegetable pie.

"Mind if I sit here?" Tarek asked, putting his plate down on the scuffed wooden table.

She gave him a cautious look. "Go ahead. I'm just studying."

"No wonder you always know the answers." He

settled on the bench across from her and nodded at the treatise on herbal remedies. "I need to spend more time with my books. Sometimes I feel like I'll never catch up."

She closed the text and dropped her left arm to her lap. Away from his gaze. He decided not to say anything; Lyssa was skittish enough already.

"I don't always know the answers," she said, something unhappy in her voice. "It can take years to master the Gift, my aunt says. She's the best Healer in Haven, you know."

Tarek glanced at her. "I'd heard you come from a family known for its Healers. My own family still doesn't quite believe that Gifts are real. It must be nice to have the support and understanding."

"It's horrible." She flushed. "I mean, not in the same way as your family, but I *have* to be good at Healing."

"You're one of the youngest Trainees in the class. Of course you're good at Healing."

She ducked her head and nervously thumbed the pages of her book. "Maybe I'm not."

Tarek gave her a close look. He wasn't particularly strong in Empathy, but he could sense the misery coming off her in waves. Something strange was definitely going on with this girl.

"Do you think . . . that perhaps the Collegium made a mistake?" he asked. "Have you spoken to Master Adrun about it?"

She shook her head.

He didn't want to push her, but he couldn't ignore that there was clearly a problem, and it seemed to do with her Gift.

The thought tickling the back of his mind emerged, and he smiled. Maybe Tarek couldn't do much, but he knew who could. Shandara Tem, the Bard whose quiet words had helped him face the truth about his own Gift.

And, honestly, he wouldn't mind the excuse to see her. Since he'd become a Healer Trainee, he'd chatted with her a few times and once even had lunch with her by a stroke of good fortune, but she moved in circles far beyond his own. Especially as he was now a First Year again.

"I know someone you could talk to," he said to Lyssa. "Someone who's good at helping people. Would you be willing to meet her?"

She shrugged, her shoulders, thin and vulnerable under the pale green fabric of her tunic. Tarek felt as if he were trying to coax a wild bird to take seed from his cupped hand. But it was worth a try.

"What's her name?" she asked.

"Bard Shandara. Do you know her?"

Lyssa gave him a blank look. "No."

Right. It seemed that the story of last year's Midwinter Recital had finally been buried beneath other gossip.

He scanned the room, looking for a smiling brunette wearing Scarlets. As usual, Shandara Tem didn't appear to be taking her lunch among the Trainees.

"She's not here," he said. "But after lunch we could go to her rooms and see if she's in. If you want."

"I'll need to let my floor manager know where I'm going," Lyssa said with an edge of aggravation. "Sometimes they treat us like babies here."

"How old are you, anyway?"

"Eleven. Practically grown up."

Tarek swallowed his smile. "When I was a Blue, they made us all check in until we were fifteen."

She looked over to a table filled with gray-clad students, and frowned. "Herald Trainees don't have nursemaids."

"They have worse." Tarek leaned forward and gave her a conspiratorial grin. "They have Companions, poor things."

A smile ghosted across Lyssa's face, and he was glad to see she was capable of some amusement, despite whatever shadow lay over her.

"Meet you at the Bardic Collegium in half an hour?" he asked.

"All right." Lyssa looked down and fidgeted with the pages of her book again, then picked it up and stood. "I'll be there."

"Don't worry—Shandara is really nice." *And pretty, and smart . . .*

As Lyssa left the Common Room, Tarek sipped his apple cider to distract himself. For one thing, he was way too busy to pursue anything more than friendship with Shandara Tem. And for another, she was a Bard and he was a Trainee, and he was fairly sure there were rules about those kinds of things—even if they *were* almost the same age.

Despite his resolve to think of Shandara only as a friend—and a distant one at that—Tarek couldn't help the knot in his throat as he knocked on the door of her rooms. Lyssa stood beside him, small and fragile, her left arm tucked down against her body.

He'd tried to get a good look at that arm, but his few glimpses at lunch and as they walked through the halls of Bardic hadn't shown him anything odd. The only thing, in fact, that made him certain there was something wrong was the way Lyssa was obviously trying to shield her arm from view. And in retrospect, it was a bit suspicious that she always wore long sleeves, even on the hottest days.

There was no response to his knock.

"Maybe she's not there," Lyssa said in a small voice.

"We'll give it a minute," he said. "And if she's not home, then we'll come a different time." Though, judging by Lyssa's tight expression, he might not be able to convince her to visit again.

He knocked one last time. After waiting at least another minute, while his heartbeat echoed the sound of his knuckles on the door, Tarek had to admit that Shandara wasn't in her rooms.

Swallowing his disappointment, he turned to Lyssa. "We can try again tomorrow."

"Maybe." She sounded unconvinced as they started back down the wide, wood-floored hall.

Windows set high in the walls let in beams of sunshine, and the portraits of famous Bards lining the hallway seemed to watch them as they passed.

Tarek frowned. He should have sent a note asking for an appointment instead of dragging Lyssa over on a fruitless quest for help. Now he'd probably lost his chance.

He glanced at the girl. "Is there anything you'd like to tell me?"

She chewed on her lip a moment, and hope sparked that maybe she'd confide in him after all. Then she shook her head, her pale hair falling over her face, and the opportunity was gone.

"Nothing," she said.

By all the rooftops of Haven, he'd bungled this one. And Master Adrun was counting on him. What kind of Healer would he make, or lord for that matter, if he couldn't solve the most basic of problems?

A flicker of bright red at the edge of his vision made him lift his head. Relief swept through him as he saw Shandara striding down the hall in their direction.

"Tarek!" she said, and the gladness in her voice gave his heart a treacherous squeeze. "What a nice surprise to find you roaming the halls of Bardic." Her gaze went to Lyssa. "And who is your young friend?"

"This is Lyssa Varcourt," he said.

"Of the Varcourt Healers?" Shandara came to a stop before them. The sunlight picked out the gold highlights in her brown hair and made her Scarlets glow.

"Yes, that's my family name," Lyssa said.

Shandara must have heard the sour note in the girl's voice, for one eyebrow went up. "Pleased to meet you, Lyssa. Can I help you two find something?"

"You already have," Tarek said, and he couldn't help smiling. "We were hoping to see you."

Shandara spread her arms. "What luck, then, that I am standing before you. Would you like to come to my rooms so we can talk?"

Despite the lightness of her tone, she shot Tarek a concerned glance. Clearly she could see this was not simply a social visit.

"Yes," he said, and Lyssa gave a sharp nod.

A few minutes later, Tarek and Lyssa were seated on a small couch in Shandara's cozy living room. She opened a window to let the clover-scented breeze blow through, offered them each a cup of cool water from the pitcher on her sideboard, then settled on the low-backed chair across from them.

A gentle silence filled the room. Tarek glanced at Lyssa, but she gazed at the floor and said nothing. It was up to him to get at the heart of the trouble—whatever it might be.

He cleared his throat and met Shandara's gaze. The quiet warmth in her eyes helped give him the confidence to begin.

"We're here because of your specialty with problem Gifts," he said.

Beside him, Lyssa stiffened and sent him a startled look.

Shandara nodded. "I suspected as much. I don't know if I can help, but if you tell me the trouble, we'll see what we might be able to do."

"But you're not a Healer," Lyssa said.

"No, I'm a Bard." Shandara gave her a quiet smile. "And yet, since my own Gift was a bit troublesome, it seems that I can offer insight and aid to others who are struggling."

She turned her smile on Tarek, and he vividly recalled the details of their first meeting. It had been awkward, conversing with her from his convalescent bed in the House of Healing. But her sincerity and kindness had won him over, even if he hadn't wanted to hear what she'd had to say.

"It's true," he said to Lyssa. "Shandara helped me accept my own late-blooming Healing Gift, and I know she's been able to assist others on their path."

Shandara waved her hand in dismissal, while a faint blush colored her cheeks. "Small things, mostly. But it seems I have some Empathy for sensing when people's Gifts are blocked or are giving them pain." She leaned toward the slight girl seated across from her. "As yours is, Lyssa."

Lyssa scooted back, her eyes widening. "There's nothing wrong with me."

"Truly?" Shandara tilted her head. "Tell me about your Gift."

"I'm a Healer!" There was a desperate edge to the girl's voice.

Tarek winced as a surge of buzzing discomfort rose from her body, centered on her left arm.

"What's the matter with your arm?" he asked, as gently as he could. "Can I see it?"

"No." She tucked it against her side, then sprang to her feet. "I'm fine."

Shandara held out her hand. "Lyssa—"

"Leave me alone," the girl said in a tight voice.

Before Tarek could say anything, she ran to the door and let herself out. The sound of her racing footsteps echoed down the hallway.

"Well." Shandara rose to close the door. "She's rather volatile."

Tarek groaned and dropped his head to his hands, running his fingers through his hair. "That was terrible. I promised Master Adrun I'd help, and now I've made matters even worse."

Shandara paused beside Tarek and set a warm hand on his shoulder. "Don't blame yourself. I've seen enough Gifts go awry that I'm fairly confident *that* is at the heart of Lyssa's troubles. One of the first steps is always acknowledging there's a problem. As you know."

"I do." He let out a rueful laugh. "I wonder what Lyssa's avoiding."

Shandara let go of his shoulder, and he tried not to lean after her.

"I think we can piece this out together," she said, settling across from him. "Tell me about her arm."

He did, recounting his fleeting impression of what seemed to be multiple cuts on Lyssa's arm, which had then mysteriously disappeared, plus the occasional prickling of his Healing Gift responding to her pain. A pain she always denied.

Shandara rested her chin in her hand, her face thoughtful, her hazel eyes watching him as he spoke.

"Anything else?" she asked when he'd finished.

Tarek tilted his head, remembering his conversation with Lyssa at lunch. "She doesn't like her family. Or, not that exactly, but she doesn't like being a member of the Varcourts."

"Hm." Shandara straightened. "She was awfully adamant about being a Healer, too. I wonder . . . This might sound strange, but what if she doesn't, in fact, have the Gift of Healing?"

"I thought of that, but then she wouldn't be in the Collegium. The Masters would never take bribes or succumb to pressure to accept an unGifted student — even one from such a prestigious family."

"Oh, I believe she does have a Gift," Shandara said. "But maybe it's not the one everyone thinks. Let me speak with Master Adrun on this. Meanwhile, how are your studies going, young lordling?"

She said this last in a teasing voice that made Tarek's pulse speed a bit.

"I don't relish being the oldest by far in all my classes," he admitted. "But since I know nothing of Healing, I have to start at the beginning. The Master did say that in a few months I'll be able to move more quickly, as I've already taken most of the other classes the First Years have to attend."

"And the Second, and Third, and Fourth . . ." She smiled at him. "You'll be in your Greens before you know it, Tarek."

"I hope so." He sighed. It was frustrating, having been so close to finishing his schooling, only to be sent back to the beginning again. Dratted Healing Gift.

Their conversation moved to less annoying subjects, and before Tarek knew it, half the afternoon had passed. The sound of bells drifted through the open window, and he jumped up.

"I'll be late for class if I don't go," he said. "Thank you, for everything."

She walked him to the door. "I'll see you soon, Tarek. I'm certain that between you, me, and Master Adrun, we'll find a way to help that poor girl."

*   *   *

Lyssa wasn't in class that afternoon, but as the rest of the students filed out, Master Adrun beckoned Tarek up to his desk.

"Come with me to my study," he said, rising. "I'm meeting with young Lyssa and her mother, and I'd like you and Bard Shandara to be there. It's high time we had some answers."

Tarek nodded. He couldn't imagine what those answers might be, but it was clear that something had to change. As he followed the Master down the halls of the Healer's Collegium, Shandara caught up to them and fell into step.

"Hello," Tarek said, grinning at her.

"Oh, I'm glad you're going to be there too," she said.

"Having been involved in whatever this trouble is, you both deserve to know the outcome," Master Adrun said. "I promise that we'll get to the bottom of this. Ah, I see that Lyssa and Lady Varcourt are already waiting for us."

A nervous-looking Lyssa and a woman with equally pale hair and a haughty expression stood outside the door of Master Adrun's study. They greeted the Master, who introduced Tarek and Shandara and then led them all into the room.

The armchairs before the hearth had been added to, along with a small couch. Lyssa and her mother settled there, with Master Adrun across from them. Silently, Tarek and Shandara took the remaining chairs on the side.

Master Adrun cleared his throat. "I asked you to come today, Lady Varcourt, because Lyssa seems to be having an issue with her Gift."

"I'm sure that's not the case," Lyssa's mother said. "The Varcourt Healers are all very accomplished." She shot her daughter a sharp look. "You're not struggling, are you, dear?"

Lyssa went a little paler than usual. "Of course not, Mother."

"You see? This is clearly some kind of misunderstanding." Lady Varcourt raked Tarek with her gaze. "Lyssa told me about you. Aren't you rather old to be a

Trainee? I believe you must be jealous of Lyssa's talent and are stirring up trouble for her."

The accusation made Tarek blink. Before he could say anything, Shandara spoke.

"I have a strong sense of Empathy," she said. "Trust me when I say that Tarek wishes no harm upon your daughter. In fact, he's trying to help."

Lady Varcourt sniffed. "Then he should stop spreading lies about her."

"What lies do you believe are being spread?" Master Adrun asked. Despite his mild tone, there was a steely look in his eyes.

"Clearly, someone here believes my Lyssa has a problem with her Healing Gift—which is patently ridiculous. Now, may we go?"

Master Adrun held up his hand. "Not yet. I'd like to hear what Lyssa has to say."

"It's all right," Shandara said to Lyssa, her voice warm with encouragement. "You can tell us whatever you need to, and no one will get in any trouble for it."

Lyssa chewed her lip and looked at the Bard for a long moment.

"Do you promise?" she finally asked.

"I do," Shandara said.

"And I do, as well." Master Adrun's deep voice was as gentle as Tarek had ever heard it.

Lady Varcourt gave an impatient *tsk*. "Really, now—"

"Lady Varcourt." Master Adrun gave her a hard look. "Please hold your tongue a moment and let your daughter speak for herself."

She sat back with an affronted expression but said nothing more. A tense silence filled the room as they all waited for Lyssa.

"I . . ." The girl lifted her head, tears sparkling in her blue eyes. "I can't do it. I can't Heal."

"But of course you can!" Lady Varcourt grabbed her daughter's hand. "That's foolish talk, and I won't hear another word of it."

"I *can't!*" Lyssa pulled out of her mother's grasp and yanked up the left sleeve of her tunic. "See?"

Her skin was scored with dozens of angry cuts, the newest ones barely scabbed over with fresh blood. Tarek winced as the pain hit him like a wave of purple wasps streaming into his head. Shandara sucked in a breath, and even Master Adrun looked surprised.

"What's this?" Lady Varcourt sounded horrified. "Is someone torturing you? I'll bring down the wrath of—"

"I did it, Mother. I cut myself."

Lady Varcourt stared at her daughter, her expression shocked.

"Why?" Shandara asked, no censure in her tone.

"To practice Healing. But . . . I couldn't do it." Lyssa's voice broke. "I can't Heal."

The buzzing pain was making it hard for Tarek to concentrate. He slipped out of his chair, going to his knees on the carpet before Lyssa.

"Will you let me help?" he asked.

"Can you?" Her voice was very small.

"He can," Master Adrun said, coming to stand beside Lyssa. "As will I. Now, hold out your arm."

The Master gave Tarek a nod, and gently, so gently, Tarek put his fingertips on Lyssa's wrist, just below where she was uninjured. He felt the bright push of blood through her body, the *wrongness* where her skin had been split by the blade, the violet shards of pain pulsing through her.

A blaze of emerald fire beside him signaled Master Adrun's presence. Trails of the Master's Healing touch flowed through Lyssa's arm, and Tarek watched, and followed, and helped where he could. Together, they coaxed the most damaged places to mend.

"Enough." Master Adrun's voice pulled Tarek out of his intense concentration. "We've done all we can for now."

Tarek lifted his hands, then blinked as a rush of dizziness swirled around him. The violet light surrounding Lyssa's arm had dimmed to pale lavender, the insistent buzz of pain faded to a muted hum. He took a deep breath in, and when he let it out, the last of the purple wasps flew out of his skull.

"Excellent work." Master Adrun gave him an

approving look. "That was Second, or even Third-Level Healing. I can see we need to move you up in several of your classes."

"Thank you." Tarek was too tired to fully appreciate the news. He summoned up a smile for the Master and crawled back into his chair.

Shandara reached over and squeezed his knee. Despite the fact that she wasn't a Healer, her touch provided a welcome burst of warmth and energy.

"Lyssa," Master Adrun said, "let me see if I have this correct. In order to practice Healing, you cut your own arm, but you were unable to mend it."

She nodded, her expression abject.

Lady Varcourt leaned forward. "I'm sure it's only a temporary block. My daughter is very skilled."

"While you are correct that she's quite talented, you're wrong about the nature of her Gift," Master Adrun said. "Lyssa isn't a Healer."

"But, that can't possibly be," Lady Varcourt said.

"How could the Collegium make that kind of mistake?" Shandara asked.

"Because her Gift is uncommon and shares facets with Healing." Master Adrun turned to Lyssa. "You, young lady, have the very special talent of Mindhealing."

"I do?" Hope sparked in Lyssa's eyes.

"Mindhealing?" Lady Varcourt asked. "Are you certain?"

Master Adrun ignored the question. "Lyssa, despite the fact that you injured yourself again and again, you seemed to control the pain most of the time. How?"

"I just told myself it didn't hurt," she said. "And sometimes . . . I almost thought I'd done it, that I'd Healed myself, because there wasn't any pain. But then I'd get distracted, and it would come back, and I'd know I'd failed."

"I sensed it," Tarek said. "Yesterday, in class."

He glanced at the scores of injuries on her arm, some of which went quite deep. It was amazing she'd been able to hide the pain from everyone—especially herself.

"By the bright stars," Master Adrun said, his gaze

going again to Lyssa's arm. "That much trauma, and you still were able to mentally manage the pain. You are talented, indeed."

"I am?" Lyssa straightened and pushed the hair out of her face.

"A true Varcourt Healer," Lyssa's mother said, her voice heavy with satisfaction.

"As for you, Lady Varcourt," Master Adrun said, "I advise you to look long and hard at the cuts on your daughter's arm and be aware that the weight of your expectation put them there. If Lyssa hadn't been afraid to fail as a Healer, we would have spotted the trouble much earlier. As it is, she will bear those scars forever."

Lady Varcourt's expression crumpled, and she raised one hand to her temple. "I am so sorry." She pulled out a kerchief and dabbed delicately at her eyes.

Tarek wasn't sure if she was apologizing to her daughter or was simply filled with grief that Lyssa was now permanently marked by the experience.

"I hope you know we are all very, very proud of you, Lyssa," she said. "A Mindhealer—who ever would have thought it?"

"Perhaps you should go share the news with the rest of your family," Master Adrun said, rising and offering her his hand. "I will, of course, keep you updated on your daughter's progress."

"Yes. Thank you." Lady Varcourt kissed Lyssa carefully on the cheek, then stood and let the Master escort her out.

Even Tarek, raised as he'd been by a hard father, could tell Lyssa needed more than that. He held out his arm just as Shandara leaned forward and mirrored his movement.

Lyssa darted up and flung herself at them, sobbing. Mostly tears of relief, he guessed—though now that she was no longer controlling her pain, he could sense the throbbing in her arm.

"There you are," Shandara said, gathering Lyssa into her embrace. "It's over now."

Tarek gently patted her back, recalling the times he'd

dried his sister's tears. After a few more gulping cries, Lyssa rubbed her uninjured arm across her face. Moisture darkened the fabric of her sleeve and still shone, smeared over her cheeks, but she was clearly trying to compose herself.

"I wish you were my family," she said.

"In a way, we are," Shandara said. "Everyone at the Collegium is."

"But you especially," Lyssa said, then glanced at Tarek. "Both of you."

"Then I will be," he said. "You can be my honorary little sister. I promise to look out for you, and help you, and probably tease you a bit, and steal your pocket pies."

She turned a smile on him that blazed like the sunshine outside. "I'd like that."

"And you can always come to me," Shandara said. "Whatever the trouble is, know that I'll be there to help."

She held out her hand, and Lyssa took it. Then Shandara nodded at Tarek, and he cupped his larger hand around them both. The truth of her words rang through him. The Collegium was family. Closer than family.

No matter if they were Healer or Bard, Herald or Mage, the Gifts of Valdemar ran through them all—a shining silver cord binding them together.

Secrets and Truths
D Shull

The crackling flames in the inn's hearth were a merry counterpoint to the whistling wind outside, and though the inn was mostly closed down, the Avelard Family Traveling Show was gathered at a largish trestle table near the hearth and bar to discuss the night's performance.

Ella mainly stared at the table, listening to how her family was speaking more than their words, but it wasn't until Ronnet said the thing they'd all been avoiding that she finally looked up.

"This is the first time Zanner's missed a performance, isn't it?"

Hesby flattened his hands on the table. "But it's not the first time this season Zanner's been late to practice or rehearsals. Ever since Jayin was scooped up by the Healers—"

Ella spoke up, wanting to stop *that* thought right in its tracks. "Hesby. You've been around longest, barring my husbands and I. And as I recall, you were just as enthusiastic about welcoming Serril to the family as any of us. Are you blaming him, then, for what Jayin plainly said she needed to do?"

Hesby hung his head. "Sorry. I'm just not the juggler Zanner is, and you can only play being fumble-fingered for comedy if you're actually much better than I am." He blew into the empty bowl in front of him. "My upset is because I wasn't ready for Zanner to not be here."

Ella nodded. "Thank you. Yes, we miss Jayin, but that's why we're wintering here in the Tipsy Gryphon, even if you can't pry her away from the Collegium for more than a few marks at a time. And she at least seems relieved that she's getting the training she needs."

Hallen tapped the back of his spoon on the table. "I'm fairly sure that Zanner's not been up visiting Jayin. And under most circumstances, what you all do with your time is your business. But not when it interferes with the Family."

At the end of the table, a serious face peered out from beneath black hair and a spoon balanced on the tip of his nose. "This didn't exactly interfere, did it? We were able to change our routines, and despite Hesby's upset, the act went well enough."

Wenn brushed strands of reddish-brown hair out of his eyes, muttering something about a haircut before saying, "Finn, I know you're trying to be diplomatic about this, but Zanner's been a lot more moody lately. Maybe our young romantic's got a sweetheart in town?"

"If Zanner fancies someone, you get over the moon, not sullen silence," Conna replied. "I've seen it happen enough, mostly when we're out on the road." She paused, then continued, "In any case, we're very definitely not talking about what we're really worried about, which is that Zanner wasn't here."

"And that's not normal, whatever you'd call 'normal' for our Zanner." Ella sighed and tugged at her braid. "Before we discuss what to do with our missing sibling's share of the take, has anyone heard from Zanner? Any note or message?"

Before anyone could respond, the door of the inn bounced open, and Serril, in full Greens, practically dragged Zanner in behind him.

"With timing like that, is it any wonder Serril's an Avelard?" Wenn whispered to their newest Family member, Lisbet, who giggled in response—only to stop when one of the City Watch followed close behind the two of them.

Serril rolled his eyes in front of his family before

turning to the man behind him. "Constable Farris, I swore to you that Zanner's family would be here at the Tipsy Gryphon, and there you see them. I'm sure you'd much rather be back at the Watch House on a night like tonight, rather than waiting around an inn where they've likely shut down the kitchens because it's after the middle of the night."

"Not a chance, Healer Serril. Your charge there's still been charged with malicious vandalism, and nobody's provided proper proof that he's—" The Watchman paused, blinking in confusion when he heard Zanner growling, and then he realized that nearly everyone at the table was also glaring at him. He started again, stubbornly. "You've vouched for this person, sure enough, and I hear you're trusted up at the Collegium, but we still have no proof. And with all the burglaries in the area, we haven't really had the chance to send for a Herald."

"I've sent for a Herald myself, but if you're bound and determined to wait here instead of getting that Herald's testimony in the morning like a sensible person, then take a seat. Just not with the Family."

"Funny looking family, if you ask me," the constable groused, but he found a chair near enough to the fire to warm his boots. He paid more attention to the flames than the renewed round of grumbles and mutters coming from the entire Family, clearly doing his best to ignore the pointed stares.

Zanner plopped down between Conna and Ella, shaking so much that Ella reached out to hug Zanner, only to be stopped by a hissed, "No. Please don't."

After several long moments, Ronnet ran a thick hand through short blond hair and said, "Well, it's clear there's a story here. Likely more than one, and I'm thinking that maybe our Healer should start. What say you, Serril? It's a long winter night, and a story would help us all, I'm thinking."

The Healer sighed and nodded at the rest of the Family. "I can only share my part, of course, but I'll tell it. But to reassure you, Jayin is doing well enough with all the work we've put on her shoulders. I think she'll be one of the better Healers to come out of the Collegium, once she's gotten through the training. And she's in bed at this hour, so no surprise visits tonight.

"I was just finishing dinner with a couple of friends when the messenger knocked on the door. . . ."

Serril looked up at the knock; it wasn't Jayin, because he knew she'd gone to bed after dinner in the refectory, and he was in Tessa's sitting room with Ostel, the latter practically tearing his hair out at the latest of Brone's antics.

Serril had been about to tell Ostel that it was his own fault for antagonizing the man—never mind that everyone who met Brone was antagonized by him and wanted to return the favor—but instead he called out, "Come in?"

One of the Palace messengers poked her head in, cornsilk braids in a crown around her head, and said, "Is one of you Healer Serril? I was told you'd be here."

Serril stood, frowning. "I'm Serril. Who told you I'd be here?"

"One of the Trainees, sir. There's a summons from the city, from one of the Watch Houses. A person's invoked your name to come and free them from the Watch." The messenger paused. "I don't know the details, as the person from the Watch didn't stay, but it didn't sound like anything as serious as a murder."

"I'm not the only Healer who can determine the cause of death."

Ostel smiled faintly. "But you're very good at it, you know. Go, go; I can complain about Brone just as effectively without you here." The smile faded. "And I shouldn't complain, at least not in front of you. I wish you'd told me sooner how much pressure we were putting on you."

Serril snorted as he headed toward the door. "Brone wouldn't have stopped, and you did. That's why you're the Dean and not him."

"You'll need to know which Watch House to go to, sir, but after that, I've got three more messages to deliver."

The messenger gave Serril the directions and then sprinted off toward the Palace.

Half a mark later, he stood in the front room of the Watch House, listening to the wind wailing outside while waiting for the sergeant to finish giving instructions to a group of constables. Apparently, there had been a rash of burglaries with some broken heads and broken teeth, and all the Watch for the neighborhood had been called up to deal with it. Once the constables were out the door, however, the sergeant turned a frown on the Healer.

"What're you doin' here?"

"I'm Healer Serril, and I was told someone in your jail had called on me to stand for them. But I never got the details."

The sergeant shook his head in confusion but picked up a sheet of paper, and slowly his face cleared. "The name he gave is Zanner, and he's accused of vandalism and some destruction of property. Nothing too expensive, thank the Havens, and he'd nary a weapon on him, which is why he's in with the drunks and others and not in a cell of his very own." The sergeant ignored the storm cloud on Serril's face and said, "We also haven't had a chance to call up a Herald and make sure of his guilt or innocence, so I can't let you have him without that."

Serril took a deep breath and exhaled just as slowly. "I will vouch for Zanner's innocence, and if you give me a pen, paper, and a messenger, I'll send for a Herald myself."

The sergeant got a relieved look on his face. "That'll make my job that much easier. Th' Herald, that is. 'Course, I'll still need to send a constable with you until the Herald shows. No offense, Healer, but you don't look like you could stop a breeze, much less someone who decided to run."

"I'll keep that in mind," Serril responded dryly as the sergeant handed him the requested pen and paper, then called out for a Constable Farris.

*   *   *

"And that's the extent of it. I had hoped we could get here before the food was gone, because as far as I know, Zanner hasn't eaten since breakfast."

Ella was up and across the room before anyone else, and back again with a wooden bowl and some bread balanced on top. "Zanner. If you can, please eat."

Zanner just stared at the bowl, rocking slightly back and forth.

"*Zanner.*" This time it was Ronnet's deep voice rumbling across the table. "You're innocent, but you're also clearly upset. Put some food in you. We'll square this away once the Herald has left." He put a hand across the table, careful not to touch Zanner but just as clearly inching the bowl closer to the shaking person across from him.

Zanner glanced up, nodded, and very carefully picked up a spoon. Once the first mouthful of stew was consumed, Ronnet looked back over to Serril.

"What's this about a Herald?"

Serril smiled half-heartedly. "In cases where there's any kind of doubt about the guilt or innocence of a suspect, a Judge has the right to call in a Herald to perform the Truth Spell. Things are very much up in the air, and I didn't want to leave Zanner in the jail. I do know a Herald or two, and this one is definitely in Haven. So I anticipate she'll be here fairly soon."

Once again, the door opened onto the wild wind, and a woman in Whites walked in, her black hair in twin braids in stark contrast down her front.

"Serril, I swear, you must be an Avelard with that kind of timing," Conna teased, and she was relieved to see the Healer's answering smile.

"Serril! On a night fit for neither man nor beast nor Companion, I get a note from you with an urgent summons to the Tipsy Gryphon and not a word of explanation past that? You couldn't possibly be setting up an assignation with me, most especially not in front of an audience, could you?" The Herald grinned wickedly as she strode toward Serril and kissed him firmly on the mouth. "Well, I for one am glad you've unbent enough for a more public display of affection."

Serril gaped at the Herald, who laughed and kissed him again, this time on the cheek. "I'm Herald Kerina, and I know full well why I'm here. But I must say I've never been able to tease Serril in front of his family before. The other ones are all worse than toads, and he's never quite gotten around to introducing me to his proper family."

"Mostly because I *knew* you'd do something like this!" Serril sputtered. "One night as Trainees, out in Companion's Field—"

"You enjoyed it too, even with half the Companions studiously not paying attention—"

"And the other half apparently offering suggestions! *And* you never let me forget it! Even after you paired off with nearly every eligible person in the Collegia!"

"I had to test them all, to compare them."

While Serril sputtered, Wenn said, "It's a shame neither of you would consent to do *that* in front of an audience." At that, the Healer blushed crimson while the Herald burst out laughing.

"What the good Healer can't tell you at the moment is that we stayed good friends even through all the horrible embarrassments I could concoct, and there's nobody I trust more for Healing. I'm sure there's some good reason that Serril tolerates me, though it escapes me at the moment." Kerina grinned, only to be surprised as Serril kissed her back.

"Your insistence on embarrassing me is vastly outweighed by your better qualities, among which is that you still let me kiss you. That, and if I send you an urgent message, you *do* pretty much drop everything and respond." Serril was still blushing as he spoke.

"You hardly ever send me a message like that. I take it this has something to do with the constable over there by the fire, and the young person staring at me like I've got a second head?"

Without waiting for Serril's answer, Kerina walked

over to where Zanner was staring and bowed. "As I've said, I'm Herald Kerina. I understand you're a suspect in a series of crimes, and while my dear friend is convinced of your innocence, that's not enough for the Watch or a Judge. Do you consent to me casting the Truth Spell on you? It's only going to be the most basic form, to determine whether your answers are true or not, but I prefer to get permission before doing it, especially in situations like this."

Zanner put the spoon into the bowl and nodded. "Please, cast this on me so everyone knows I didn't do this."

"Very well. Constable Farris, I'll need you to tell me what the crimes are, so that I can properly ask the questions." While the Watchman cautiously walked over, Kerina quietly chanted until a blue glow surrounded Zanner's head.

"Constable Farris, please tell me what this person is accused of doing?"

"Malicious vandalism, several times over. People have had their houses and shops defaced with some very nasty things written and items destroyed. This has been happening for a couple of weeks."

Kerina nodded. "Zanner, please tell me the truth. Have you defaced anyone's home in the past three weeks?"

"No." The answer was short, and the blue glow remained.

"Have you defaced anyone's business in the past three weeks?"

"No." Again, the blue glow did not change.

Kerina narrowed her eyes. "Why does the Watch suspect you? Your best and most truthful guess, please."

"Because people reported that I was at all of the places that were vandalized." Zanner paused. "I was, but not because I did any of it."

It was clear Zanner was telling the truth, and Kerina turned to the Watchman. "Is this sufficient for your needs?"

Farris frowned, and said, "No, I have a question my

sergeant will want an answer to: If you didn't do it, why were you there?"

Zanner paused before responding, "Because they're all friends of mine, and I had this idea I could figure out who *did* do all those things."

"Truth in every word, Constable Farris. Anything else you'd like to ask?" Kerina had not dismissed the spell, but the Watchman shrugged.

"Nothing I can think of. I'm sure my sergeant will have a lot of other questions, but it's late, and I'm more or less done. I'll let my sergeant know you're innocent, and we'll just have to figure out who might have done all that." With that, he stomped back to the inn door and let the wind slam it shut behind him.

Everyone in the Family could see the blue glow still surrounding Zanner, but Kerina was silent until it was clear the Watchman had gone. Only then did she quietly ask Zanner, "You know who did all this, though, don't you?"

Zanner's face twisted. "Not for sure. If I'm right, it's going to mean a lot of heartache." And still the blue glow remained steady.

The Herald nodded, and just like that, the blue glow went away. "Come over here, toward the door. I'm going to ask you about that, and while everyone here but me is family, I have the feeling you'd rather keep this part private."

Zanner stood, a study in upset and unhappiness, but followed the Herald.

"Well, that's a thing you don't get to see hardly ever," Finn said from a way down the table. "Truth Spell and all that."

Serril looked over at Hallen, Ronnet, and Ella. "I'm not going anywhere. Zanner's innocent, like I guessed, but the rest of it is Family business, yes?"

"It is, and you're Family, so of course you're not going anywhere." Hallen shook his head. "I'm sure Zanner has some very good reasons for not telling us all this."

Ronnet looked over at where Zanner was standing

with Herald Kerina and shook his head. "It doesn't necessarily matter whether those reasons were good. The
reasons got Zanner in trouble, and if Serril hadn't been
part of our Family, we might still be wondering where
Zanner was tomorrow. Or the next day, or until the
Watch had been able to send for another Herald."

Ella sighed. "Zanner's not the happiest person at the
moment, so let's be gentle." She looked as though she
was going to say more, but Kerina was already halfway
to the door, and Zanner was walking back to the Family
with an unhappy expression.

Serril glanced at the rest of the Family, and everyone
nodded. He moved over to make room for Zanner, who
instead stood facing the Family, eyes firmly fixed to the
floor.

"You want to know what's going on, right?" The normally cheerful performer seemed more like the person
Ronnet had rescued years back from the Holderkin family who would not unbend enough to understand their
child. Without waiting for anyone to respond, Zanner
continued, "I have friends here in Haven, and a couple
of weeks ago someone started painting nasty things on
their homes, and then businesses, and then breaking
things. Last night it was Bren's business. Oils, soaps, perfumes, that sort of thing. It's going to take money Bren
doesn't have to replace the stock."

Serril waited a moment, but Zanner didn't continue.
The Healer sighed and said, "You're leaving out a lot,
but I think the most important thing for everyone here
is why you didn't mention this to anyone."

Zanner looked up and started pacing around in front
of everyone. "My friends are different like I'm different.
They're not ashamed of it, but it's still safer if they're not
open about it. We do what we can to take care of each
other, and because I've got a family, I can help out when
I'm here."

Ella very gently said, "We love and accept you. Why
should your friends be any different?"

"Because they *are* different!" The anguish in Zanner's
voice was plain to everyone there. "Because you don't

know them like you know me. I know we adopted Serril, but he put his heart out there for all of us to see. He trusted us, and we all accepted him. But they don't know you, and the one thing I do know is that my friends have tried trusting before, and they've been pretty badly hurt. They trust me, but they don't know you."

Hallen stood up with a bit of a grunt. "And trust is not something given lightly, or carelessly. I do understand, Zanner. It's why we do what we do. Because there are too many people in this world who've trusted and had that trust betrayed—me included. But I'm not as worried about your friends trusting us as I am about *you* trusting us. We don't ever ask any of you what brought you to us; we let you decide how much of your past you share. But we Avelards need to trust each other, and keeping secrets from the Family that could affect the Family—that's where I get worried."

"But the vandalism wasn't affecting the Family!" Zanner cried, finally looking everyone in the face. "They're my friends, not part of the Family!"

Ronnet's smile was bittersweet. "You care about them, so by extension they're Family too. I know you're protecting your friends, and they have no reason to trust us, but I swear to you that because you care about them so much, by the Lady, I'm going to care about them too. Even if the only thing I can do is give your friend Bren the money to replace what was broken."

Zanner paled. "That's a lot of money! Do we even have that to spare?"

One by one, each one of the Family pulled out their coin purses and put some of their share on the table. "It's not much, true, and it may not be enough. But it's more than your friend has, right?"

Zanner took one look at the pile of coins and sat down heavily, sobbing. "Why do you care so much?"

"Because it's clear you care so much, Zanner." Serril had also put coins into the pile in the middle of the table. "Now, tell us your story."

It took some time before Zanner nodded and began, "I got up this morning like I usually do and headed out before any of the rest of you woke up. I had a feeling that the vandalism was going to continue, and I wasn't wrong. . . ."

Zanner stared at the front of Bren's shop. *Scents and Wonders* wasn't a big shop, and it wasn't in the higher rent district, but everyone in the neighborhood knew Bren could talk with a person for a few minutes and then pick out or make a soap or an oil that the person would fall in love with. Even the men who worked labor-intensive jobs found that Bren's soaps were the best at keeping them clean *and* keeping their lovers happy.

Everyone in the neighborhood was fond of Bren, at the very least, even if the merchant had some oddities. Or that's what Bren would say. Up to this point, Zanner had believed it. But the window had been shattered, and oil bottles and equipment had been smashed. The door to the shop had the word *FREAK* painted on it as well.

Bren came out of the shop with a sad smile. "I've salvaged what I can, but I think I may need to limit my soap-making to the less expensive scents for a while. I won't be able to make perfumes either; the vandal got that equipment as well."

Zanner asked the first thing that popped to mind. "How's Nessa?"

"She's fine. I'd moved her to my spare bedroom, so she missed all the excitement. But she knows it happened. And she's beginning to suspect that whoever is doing this is targeting her."

"But how would they find her?"

Bren just shrugged in response and moved back into the shop, clearly distracted by all the damage.

Zanner thought back to all the other attacks. It was true. Each place Nessa had stayed at was vandalized in short order. And because each of those people was a good friend, Zanner had come by to see if there was anything that could be done. Well, that and maybe try to find out who had done this. The first time it could have been random, but the second time, then the third, and the ones after that? It couldn't be random at that point, especially because it seemed to be following Nessa, who had figured out she was different.

Nessa's family had disowned her and thrown her to the street, where it was by sheerest luck she had run into Zanner while trying to figure out what she was going to do and where she would live. Zanner had the story out of her very quickly; he introduced her to a number of people who understood what Nessa had been through and would take care of her. Only now, it seemed that they could no longer protect her.

Zanner looked at the window and the word on the door, and thought for a while; there was something in all of this, something obvious, something that would point out who had been doing it. Zanner knew it, just as Ronnet knew his accounting. And Zanner was on the edge of figuring out who did this when a voice said, "Turn around slowly."

Zanner did as the voice had ordered and saw two Watchmen standing there, looking very serious, hands very close to their swords.

Zanner swallowed. "Is anything wrong?"

"You've been spotted at every single location where there's been this kind of vandalism, but all you've been doing is watching, according to witnesses. Please come with us." The taller of the two Watchmen took a step forward, clearly ready for Zanner to make a break for it, while the shorter one was just as clearly watching to make sure he knew which way Zanner would run.

Zanner realized that the only thing to do was go with the Watchmen. This was Haven; there'd be a Judge, so Zanner could demand a Herald and then go free in time to perform tonight. Trying to look as innocent as possible, Zanner responded, "I'll come with you. I didn't do any of this, and I want to see a Judge and a Herald."

The shorter one frowned. "We have other problems at the moment; you're going to have to wait in the jail."

"Wait, what? You're arresting me but telling me that we can't get this cleared up?"

"Look, kid, vandalism isn't nearly as big as the other stuff we have to deal with. But you fit the profile of a suspect, and I'm not going back to my sergeant to tell him that we let a suspect go."

Zanner swallowed. "How long?"

The taller Watchman shrugged, and gestured for Zanner to go with them.

"They stuck me in the common jail cell and forgot about me. Eventually I got someone's attention and asked him to get a message to Serril, so Serril could at least get me out of there." Zanner looked up from the floor. "It was so late by that point that I knew I'd missed the performance, but if I could get out, I could at least try to explain. I didn't really think any further than that."

Ronnet had sat on the floor during Zanner's story. "It's late enough that I think maybe we should all get some sleep. We'll figure out what to do, if anything, in the morning. Do you want a hand up? A hug?"

Zanner fell into Ronnet's arms, and the strongman held Zanner close while Zanner sobbed some more. "That'll be a hug, then."

But none of the Family could sleep after Zanner's story. Ella and Hallen huddled together over the pile of coins, quietly discussing ways to make it bigger. Finn told stories about life on the road to Lisbet, who had pulled out costumes and was busy mending and adding embellishments. Conna and Wenn listened as Serril talked more about how Jayin was doing, and the kind of training she was getting at the Collegium. Soon, Serril had the entire Family gathered around him, telling stories about anything and everything he'd experienced, mostly around being a Healer and the sorts of things that Jayin could expect once she became a full Healer. He even — at everyone's demand, even Zanner, who'd finished weeping by that point — told the story of his fling with Kerina.

Serril was just at the point where he and Kerina had finally found a private place out in Companion's Field when the door opened, this time more carefully, to reveal Herald Kerina entering, her earlier smile completely gone now.

"Avelard timing," Zanner managed, while Conna and Wenn laughed a bit.

"Zanner Avelard, I'm sorry to say that we've caught the vandal."

Zanner blinked. "Oh, no."

"Yes, you were right. Do you want to come with me? The person in question is, well, not being polite about a number of things, but your suspicions helped identify her well before any of the Watch would have considered her. I think you deserve this vindication, but it's up to you." Kerina offered a weak smile now. "I understand if your answer is no. But if it is a yes, you can bring a few of your Family along with you."

"Serril, Ella, and Ronnet," came Zanner's instant response.

The sergeant who'd been there when Serril came to get Zanner just gaped when the five of them came in, and he bowed to Herald Kerina. "Yes, Herald. She's in a private cell as you requested. She's not violent or anything, but she is a bit young to be kept in with the drunks." As the Sergeant turned to lead them, he said over his shoulder, "She's got a mouth, though, and no mistake. My da would have had soap in that mouth right away."

The private cells were empty save for one at the very end. A teen girl, skirts clenched in her hand, looked up and saw the five of them, but she immediately stared with blazing eyes at Zanner. "You! You did this to my brother! You're the one that corrupted him!"

The target of her anger paled, but Serril and Ronnet both put a protective hand on Zanner's shoulders. "That's not the truth, and you know it."

"My ma and da told me you'd lie about my brother—anything to save your own skin!"

Kerina looked at the raging girl and asked, "Why, though? Why did you do it?"

"Because my brother doesn't know what it's like out there. He's in danger if he's not with his family, because we'll take care of him and make sure he's safe!"

Zanner said with some acid, "Oh, safe? Like kicking

her out of the house and telling her never to come back?"

"*HIM!*" screeched the girl. "Stop lying! It was only for the night, then Ma or Da would have come out to get him and bring him home, where he belongs!" Now, tears were flowing along with the anger. "If you hadn't come along and taken him away, he'd be home safe in bed by now!" The girl turned away, sobbing into the mattress.

"Elly," Zanner said, "Jeck wouldn't have taken your sibling back. Liah, either. Or, if they did, your sibling would have been very unhappy. Trust me, my parents are very much like Jeck and Liah."

"NO! They love us!" She grabbed the lone pillow and put it over her head.

Zanner turned to Herald Kerina and asked, "What's going to happen to her?"

Kerina frowned. "She's just under the age of majority, sadly, so back to her parents she goes. And they'll be made to pay the damages where possible, within reason." She blew air past her lips. "Zanner, Serril, can you come with me? I've only just met you two—" she said to Ella and Ronnet, "—but please come with us? There's a bit we need to discuss."

Outside, the sky was finally going pale, and they heard the sounds of a working city waking up. "She's very, very upset, and I wouldn't be surprised if there was more trouble brewing. I'll ask someone to check in on Elly and her parents to make sure they won't do anything rash. But that's not really why I'd like to talk with you, Zanner."

Zanner shrank a bit but nodded.

"You and your friends have suffered quite a bit, and I'm sure with more than just the damages. There's probably been talk in the neighborhoods as well, yes?"

"Some. Bren is probably safe, but I'm not sure of the rest." Zanner looked away. "And Nessa. . . . This is going to break her heart."

Kerina snorted. "Well, yes, but I'd say it's safer for Nessa to not be with that family. And that leads at least partly into the next thing I need to ask: You and your friends, you don't have anyone to keep watch over you, make sure that you're not in danger, or have some kind of support, do you?"

Zanner's eyes got wide. "No. It's . . . not anything any of us had ever thought about because it's been easy for people not to believe us about other things." Zanner glanced briefly back at the Watchhouse. "Like Elly. She won't believe Nessa, but she will believe her parents."

"So you need someone to believe you all, right?" Kerina grinned. "I've been at loose ends for a couple of months now; something about riding Circuit doesn't agree with me, and most of the other things I could get involved in already have Heralds working on them. Would you be willing to introduce me to your friends? We can start small, maybe with Bren, and then go from there."

Zanner's mouth fell open. "Just like that? Why?"

"Because someone believed me years ago. Granted, that someone was an interfering, nosy, busybody of a Companion, but Errol is one of the best things that happened to me. Maybe I can pass that on, be one of your best things." She smiled and shook her head, apparently "listening" to her Companion. "Errol says he's seen some very odd things in his time as well, so your friends aren't likely to be all that different. He's also quite interested in meeting Bren, especially if your friend makes anything for a Companion's mane."

"I'll say yes, tentatively," Zanner offered to Kerina, "but first I think we all need to get some sleep." Turning, Zanner grabbed Ella's hand, then Ronnet's. "I'm sorry I hid this from you."

Ronnet just smiled. Ella was the one who pulled Zanner into a hug, and said, "I understand why, just don't do it again?"

Serril beamed and then yawned hugely. "I love you all, but it's been years since I pulled an all-nighter, and Jayin isn't easy to keep up with even when I've had plenty of sleep. I'll come by in a few days, check on you all." And he headed off toward the Palace, whistling.

"Your own bed awaits, young Zanner," Ronnet said,

295 *D Shull*

"and so does ours. New day, new dawn, more people to amuse and entertain. And there's money to be earned to help your friend—after all, Bren's your friend, and a friend of yours is a friend of the Family's. And thank you, Herald, for your help here."

Kerina smiled and said, "I'll visit in a few days as well!"

With that, the three Avelards turned back toward the Tipsy Gryphon, and the rest of the Family.

Ordinary Miracles
Rebecca Fox

It is said in certain circles that the first of many miracles heralding the return of a true Son of the Sun to Karse occurred near the country's northernmost border, in the tiny village of Sunswatch, a place so small that its ramshackle Temple is tended by a single Sunpriest, and the village blacksmith also serves as horse marshal and mayor. The particulars of the miracle vary depending on the teller, but all the stories agree on two points: that it happened in the fifth year that Radiance Lastern sat upon the Sun Throne and that it began, as so many miracles do, with a dream ...

The dream belonged to Kip, the blacksmith's boy, an utterly ordinary looking lad with bony elbows and skin the color of toasted almonds and dark curly hair that always seemed to be an inch too long, and it was a dream he very much did not want. In it, young Kip knelt before the altar of an echoing temple built entirely of some sort of pale stone, in a pool of rainbow light that poured through a vast stained-glass window depicting the Sun in His Glory. He could smell incense and woodsmoke. In the dreams that came true, he could always taste and smell. It was how Kip knew them from the others, the ordinary kind.

As he knelt there, a veiled woman robed in white stepped from the shadows behind the altar. Silver bangles on her wrist chimed softly, like little temple bells. As she drew closer, he could see the blood that stained her robe. She was limping badly.

Kip stared at her. The woman reached up to push aside her veil. As she did so, there was a flash of clear, cold, silvery light.

Kip awoke sweating. It was still pitch dark in the little hayloft where he slept. With a sense of relief, he breathed in the familiar dusty golden scent of hay and sleeping horses. Somewhere outside a single cricket chirped languidly, the song of waning summer. The boy felt rather than saw the cat that jumped onto his pallet to lie beside him, and he automatically reached out to rub the notched ears and rough, dirty fur.

"I had another dream, Spot." He hadn't had one of the coming-true kind since that one last summer about the Temple olive grove burning, and Kip had begun to let himself hope they'd stopped for good.

"*Mrow*," said Spot, rubbing his cheek against Kip's wrist.

"You don't understand," Kip said, as if the cat had just voiced his approval. "If anyone ever finds out about my dreams, they'll put me to the Fires just like my ma."

Spot just wriggled closer and kneaded Kip's thin coverlet with contentment.

"Of course you don't understand," the boy sighed. "You're a cat. I'd trade you places if I could."

Eventually Kip must have slept again, and far too deeply and too long, because the next thing he knew the weak light of dawn was peeking through the cracks between the boards of the barn. The entire household would already be at morning prayer!

Swearing under his breath, he pulled his boots on over bare feet, yanked his tunic over his head, and ran a hand through his tangled hair before scrambling down the hayloft ladder and pelting across the packed-dirt courtyard separating the barn and the smithy from the blacksmith's dwelling.

He slid onto the rock hard kneeler at the back of the smith's Sun Shrine, in between the housemaid and Sen, the smith's apprentice, just as the smith was lighting the incense. Sen glanced at him and gave him a nasty smirk. Kip had been missed, and there would be punishment waiting.

Kip ignored him and tried instead to focus on the sound of the smith chanting the Morning Office, on the tendrils of incense smoke rising from the thurible. He wished he hadn't. For a just a moment, he seemed to see the shape of the veiled woman outlined in the curling smoke.

Heart pounding, he shut his eyes tightly. When he opened them again, there was nothing more extraordinary about the incense or Sun Shrine than there had been on any other morning of Kip's life. He breathed a tiny sigh of relief.

When the time came for them to make their private petitions to Vkandis Sunlord, Kip knew what he should pray for—that the Sunlord would take his dreams and make him Clean, so that he might be spared the Fires. But that wasn't the prayer that he whispered in the secret depths of his heart.

Lord of the Morning, if there's something you want me to do, I wish you'd tell me what it is. He closed his eyes and bowed until his forehead nearly touched the floor, breathing in the scent of incense and wood polish.

But the only answer he got was the smith's wife hauling him roughly to his feet and propelling him out the door of the Sun Shrine and into the courtyard.

"Lazy wretch! I hope you aren't expecting breakfast after that. Did you think I'd miss you sneaking in after we'd already said the first canticle? And with your tunic stained and your hair uncombed. Sloth's a sin against Vkandis Sunlord, you know. Honestly, boy, you're no better than your heretic slut of a mother." The smith's wife was a plump dark-haired woman with rosy cheeks who looked perfectly motherly as long as one didn't bother to look in her eyes.

The color rose in Kip's face, but he hung his head in what he hoped was an adequate show of meekness. No sense in starting the morning with an empty belly *and* a beating.

The smith's wife went on, as she always did. It was a familiar refrain. "If it weren't our bounden duty to Vkandis Sunlord to shelter the orphan and the destitute, I'd have turned ye out to starve years ago."

Why go to the trouble of turning me out when you can starve me right here? he thought bitterly as his stomach growled. By this and other acts of pious charity did the blacksmith and his wife win the favor of Sunpriest Aram and the Voices of Vkandis.

Kip muttered something about having to sweep and open the smithy and darted across the courtyard before he had the chance to say something he knew he'd be given cause to regret.

Just before the midday meal, Varelian the chandler brought his jenny mule to the smithy to be shod. The animal liked to bite and kick anyone who handled her, so naturally Kip was summoned to hold her while the smith trimmed her hooves and fitted her shoes. Still, dodging the mule's teeth for a half-candlemark was not without its compensations. Varelian was also the village gossip, and he liked to stand and talk to the smith while the man worked.

"That Old Man Dunnett's spinnin' his crazy stories again, Smith," Varelian said as he tamped a bit of pipeweed into the bowl of his battered old corncob pipe and lit it with a coal. "Las' night 'round sunset, that old half-broke pasture fence of his on the west side come down, and out came all them half-starved cows of his, all over Garal's cornfield. Garal says the old man came a-runnin' after them, wavin' his arms around and yellin' how it wasn't his fault."

"Never is." The smith held a shoe against the jenny mule's left fore hoof, regarded it critically, and took the shoe back to the anvil. "What was it this time? A Firecat hunting for his supper?"

Every story Old Man Dunnett told was wilder than the last. He'd once gone to Sunpriest Aram claiming he'd seen the spirit of the last Son of the Sun walking the gardens of the village Temple at twilight.

"Better. Says he saw a White Demon come galloping down out of the hills faster'n' anything natural could possibly run and plow right through that old fence of his."

The smith's laugh was rough. "Old Man Dunnett is half blind and can't be bothered to keep his fences in good repair. Probably it was that old white bull of his who broke that same fence last winter. Garal find anything?"

"Some white hair on his fence, which could've come from one of the cows, and a bunch of trampled corn and cow prints. Only place the thing could've went and not been seen is the arroyo, and Garal sent his eldest on down there to check. Wasn't so much as a rabbit. Bah!"

"Dunnett's trying to get Garal to pay some to fix the fence, no doubt." The smith bent over, took the jenny's leg between his knees, and started nailing on the shoe. "Still, if Sunpriest Aram sends word to the Hierophant like he ought to, things might get a bit interesting around these parts before long. I heard there were Voices of Vkandis riding circuit up near Jainstown."

"Ain't nothin' the Voices like better than stirring up trouble for other people," Varelian agreed gruffly. "Sorry, Smith, I know that's blasphemy. But it's also true."

Varelian's story had stirred in Kip an odd, inexplicable restlessness that lasted through midday prayers and into the afternoon. So when Sen came from the smithy with the empty kindling sack over his shoulder, Kip took the bag from him and said he'd do the gathering, even though the day had turned dark and windy with intermittent spatters of cold rain. Sen gave him an odd look but handed the sack over without complaint.

Spot joined him as Kip picked his way through Garal's cornfield along the path Dunnett's White Demon was supposed to have taken. If nothing else, the greasewood and thorn choking the arroyo to the west of the village would provide more than enough dry twigs to fill his sack. The cat seemed to simply melt out from between the cornstalks between one breath and the next. After all these years, Kip was so inured to its sudden appearances that he didn't even jump. "I suppose it's useless to ask you where you came from or where you've been."

"*Mrow*," said Spot, as usual.

"You should have been born a dog, Spot. Sunlord knows you follow me everywhere like one. And I should have been born ... well, just about anything else."

Kip wondered what he would do with a White Demon if he found one. Maybe it would eat him for its supper and put an end to his troubles.

Kip, with Spot sauntering along in his wake, was halfway down the slippery gravel-strewn track that led to the stream at the bottom of the arroyo when he heard it: the sound of something big—as big as a White Demon, maybe—crashing around in the thorn thicket on the far side of the stream. Kip froze and turned to run, but then the crashing was followed by a horse's whinny, high and desperate and terrified.

He let out the breath he hadn't realized he was holding, feeling shaky with relief. Surely no Demon would ever sound so frightened. It was just someone's horse that had gotten loose and blundered into the arroyo in a panic, the way the gelding that pulled Thuril's plow had last spring. Whoever owned the horse would undoubtedly be grateful to have their wayward animal back, perhaps grateful enough to speak well of Kip to the smith. And if the beast had broken its legs, well, at least Kip could go back to the village and bring someone with a bow to end its suffering.

"You stay here," he said to Spot, who gave him a withering look. "Horses are stupid when they're scared, and I don't want you getting kicked." He spared a moment to wonder why he felt the need to explain himself to a cat, and then he slid the rest of the way down the path and plunged into the thorn thicket with a faint pang of regret for what was about to happen to his only tunic. At least he'd have a good excuse when he came back to the smith's house with his clothes in tatters.

By the time he found the horse, tangled in a great mass of green thorn branches and desert mistletoe, Kip was bleeding from dozens of stinging scratches, and it was raining in earnest. He blinked the cold droplets from his eyes and regarded her.

From what he could tell, the mare was a fine little animal, gray underneath the patches of mud and bleeding thorn scratches and green stains, and powerfully but gracefully built. She wore what looked like the tattered remnants of a very fine bridle, though the bit was apparently long gone. He could only hope it hadn't done too much damage to her mouth when it ripped free of the bridle. He walked forward carefully, afraid of startling her into trying to bolt, but she just stood there as he approached, head low and flanks heaving.

Hesitantly, Kip put a hand on her neck. The little mare flinched a bit but didn't try to run. "Well, clearly you belong to someone," he said softly, soothing her. "I wonder who. You're way too nice for anyone around here, and the Voices don't like grays. You don't really look like a Sunsguard horse, neither. Guess it doesn't really matter. We need to get you out of here regardless. There's a stream a little way away where you can drink, and there's some grass to eat. 'Fraid it isn't very *good* grass, but it's better than an empty belly." Kip knew something about empty bellies.

It took what must have been the better part of a candlemark to extract the little mare from the thorn thicket and coax her into the open, while the wind howled and the rain turned into an icy drizzle that beaded on his skin and ran in rivulets under his collar and down his back. Scared as the horse must have been, not once did she try to fight him or to turn and run.

"You're a rock-solid little thing, you are," he told her. "Whatever it was that made you bolt must've been something pretty bad. Is there a White Demon around here somewhere after all? I sure hope your rider's okay."

Kip would have called the noise the horse made a sob if she'd been a human. He'd never heard its like from an equine throat, and he hoped to never hear it again. It raised all the hair on the back of his neck. But perhaps it had only been a grunt of pain. As soon as the mare stepped onto level ground, Kip could see she was terribly lame.

The cause was immediately apparent: a wicked gash on her right hind leg that had just barely missed the tendon. The edges of the wound were too clean to have been the product of an accident, and the leg, when Kip ran his hands gently down it, was hot and swollen.

"Someone did this to you on purpose. No wonder you bolted." In that first rush of terror, she probably hadn't even felt the pain of the wound. She was lucky she hadn't injured herself further when she'd stumbled into the ravine. Kip sat back on his heels. The gash looked as though it might have been made by a long knife or even a sword. If the mare had come from the hills as Old Man Dunnett had said, she might have come from up near Jainstown, where the Voices on circuit were supposed to be staying. But why would the Voices, or the men of the Sunsguard, who always accompanied them, hurt a horse?

As Kip sat pondering, the rain stopped and the sun peeked out from behind the clouds for just a moment. It was then that Kip realized that the little mare wasn't gray at all but *white:* the clean pure white of Sunpriest Aram's festival robes. And her hooves weren't black like the hooves of a natural horse. They were *silver.*

Kip scrabbled back so fast that he caught his heel on a rock and sprawled backward into a patch of thistle. "Oh, no. No no no no no." The words poured from his mouth without conscious volition. This was no horse that he had just helped.

This was Old Man Dunnett's White Demon.

Kip could be sent to the Fires of Cleansing just for having *touched* her, even in ignorance.

The mare hobbled a few steps forward, lifted her head slowly, and looked at him. Her eyes were the clear deep blue of a midsummer sky. And overlaid on the figure of the Demon-mare, as if he'd hit his head and was having some strange sort of double vision, Kip could see the image of the veiled woman from his dream. He sat up gingerly.

Just that morning he'd prayed for Vkandis Sunlord to

show him the meaning of his dream. But this couldn't be the Sunlord's answer, could it?

"I don't understand," he whispered. "Oh, Sunlord, I don't understand."

The mare met his gaze. Her look was filled with a grief so profound that it brought tears to Kip's own eyes. And then . . . there was something like an instant of startled recognition, and he felt as though he were tumbling into the blue depths of her eyes.

Right up until the moment that Spot, who had apparently been waiting among the rocks in the rain just as Kip had instructed him to, leaped down to land between the boy and the Demon-mare and yowled authoritatively.

The spell was broken.

The mare dropped her head, nuzzled the cat with an air of something like apology, and whickered. Spot quirked his tail in a funny little 'S' shape and rubbed against her legs, purring so loudly Kip could hear it from where he sat among the thistles.

It was the strangest thing he'd ever seen, but in that moment he was as certain of one thing as he was of his own name: that the white mare with the blue eyes was no more a Demon than he was himself.

So he got to his feet, coaxed the mare into the chilly waters of the stream, and washed out her wound. She flinched and grunted when he touched her leg, but she stood as still as if she were rooted.

Kip whistled softly. "Even the best-trained horse I know would've tried to kick me for that. But you're not really a horse, are you? I'm sorry it hurts. The cold water will help with the swelling."

She nuzzled his shoulder, and he reached up automatically to stroke her muzzle. It was soft and warm and velvety, and she smelled like warm horse and fresh hay and sunlight. Unaccountably, he felt as safe and loved as he had when his ma had used to hold him and sing to him, and he swallowed hard against tears. That had been a very, very long time ago. The mare's breath was warm against his ear.

There was a patch of heal-all growing on the near bank of the stream. Kip chewed a few of the leaves, grimacing at the bitter, astringent taste, and packed the wound with the mess. "This is the best I can do for now. The smith has horse medicines, though. I'll come back tomorrow with some of them and a proper bandage, I promise. Just . . . stay here and hide and try not to let any real demons eat you, okay?"

The mare studied him as gravely as any human patient listening to her Healer and nodded her head vigorously up and down.

Kip went without supper that night and endured a beating from the smith's wife on account of his half-empty bag of kindling and the wet, ragged mess he'd made of his tunic. He'd muttered a half-truth about having tripped and fallen into the thorn thicket while gathering wood and promised himself that he'd ask Vkandis's forgiveness for lying in his morning prayers. The smith also lectured him on the sin of ingratitude.

Eventually Kip slunk up to his hayloft and fell onto his pallet without bothering to remove his boots. He was asleep almost before he managed to drag the thin coverlet up over his shoulders, drifting in and out of uneasy dreams in which he sat in the darkened Temple, listening as a deep-voiced man and a woman with a soft contralto conversed in low voices. The speakers were in the shadows somewhere just beyond Kip's line of sight, and their conversation made no sense.

:*So, he's the one?:* The woman sounded resigned.

:*One of them, yes. So I'm very much afraid that you can't have him, Portia. I'm sorry.:* The man's voice was at once apologetic and amused.

:*Well, if I'm to agree to leave him here with you, you're going to have to promise me you won't let* THEM *get him. I know perfectly well how* THEY *feel about Gifts, and that's without them knowing he's had a hand in helping me. Even leaving aside the other thing, I owe him now.:*

:*It would mean a lot of wasted effort on my part if I let the bastards take him at this point, now wouldn't it?:*

The woman sighed heavily. *:I suppose. I still don't have to like any of this.:*

:I'll look after him, Portia. You have my solemn word. When all has been set right in Sunhame, you may even be able to see him again.:

:If you let anything happen to that boy, mark my words, I will personally make sure that beautiful fur of yours gets made into a cloak for some pretty noblewoman in Haven. You see if I don't.:

It was Kip's job to tidy the smithy and the barn, so the next afternoon it was easy enough for him to slip a mostly empty bottle of arnica, a little pot containing the last remnants of a batch of wound-heal ointment, and one of the most ragged standing bandages underneath his tunic. If anyone missed the items, he could simply say they were beyond their usefulness and he'd tossed them into the garbage midden.

He told the smith's wife that he'd do without his midday meal to gather sage to burn in the Sun Shrine. Kip left her with the impression that he was trying to do penance for his behavior of the day before, so she was willing enough—even eager—to let him go.

With the rest of the household at table, Kip shoved the medicines into an empty kindling sack, slipped into the barn so that he could add a small bag of grain to his inventory, and headed back to the arroyo with Spot trotting along at his side.

The Demon-mare's leg was a bit better, though she still couldn't bear much weight on it. Still, Kip thought it probably wouldn't be much more than a sevenday before she was well enough to make her way home. The border was close by to the north, and Sunsguard patrols in this poor, rocky, sparsely populated bit of the countryside were usually small and uninterested.

Kip washed the mare's wound again and dried it, then rubbed the leg with arnica and wound-heal and wrapped it tidily with the standing bandage before spreading the grain on the ground before her. "Now don't you go chewing on that bandage or trying to rub it off or anything," he scolded, just as if she were any other horse. "It's for your own good."

She snuffled his hair with what he could only imagine was amusement.

Kip stuffed his bag with as many sage branches as he could find and climbed back out of the arroyo.

After another three days, Kip was almost willing to let himself breathe again. The Demon-mare's leg was healing steadily, and it had proven simple to find excuses to slip away with Spot while everyone else was at their midday meal. Firewood to be gathered. Hopelessly broken tools to be taken to the garbage midden at the edge of the village. A patch of heal-all he'd seen growing near Old Man Dunnett's cow pasture. While the smith had lectured Kip and Sen about being more sparing with the costly horse medicines, threatening beatings for both if they continued being so wasteful, it hadn't seemed to occur to him that anyone might be *stealing* the medicines. In another three or four days, the Demon-mare would be safely on her own side of the border, and no one would ever be the wiser.

Just before dawn on the fourth day, Kip woke sweating from uneasy dreams of flickering torchlight, red-robes, and the jangle of men in armor marching. He told himself it was just a nightmare born of his worst fears and the strain of hiding the Demon-mare, but even in his own mind the words rang false.

He was gathering stray horseshoe nails from the barn aisle when he knew for certain his luck, and the Demon-mare's, had run out. At the unmistakable sound of a horse pelting into the packed-earth courtyard at a full gallop, Kip started violently, dropping his handful of nails so that they scattered across the barn floor like a shower of sparks. An instant later, a man's unfamiliar voice shouted for the smith. Heart pounding, Kip left his work and went to see what was the matter, even though in the depths of his soul he already knew.

In the courtyard, he found a messenger, tall and stern,

in the livery of the Hierophant's household, astride a dark bay gelding foamy with sweat.

"You," the messenger said. "Boy. Go and tell your master to prepare for the arrival of the Voices of Vkandis and a contingent of the Sunsguard. For your safety, no one is to leave the boundaries of Sunswatch until they arrive. The Voices have tracked a White Demon here. It is hiding somewhere in the countryside. Do you understand?"

Kip must have managed something that looked like a credible nod, because the messenger wheeled his poor sweating horse around and galloped off the way he'd come. Kip prayed that his horror didn't show on his face when he repeated the messenger's words to the smith.

The little mare! He had to get away and warn her!

Kip didn't get his chance until after evening prayer. By then the sun was setting, and the little packed-earth courtyard that lay between the smith's house and the barn and the smithy was so crowded with men and horses that surely no one would notice a skinny boy and a cat slipping away in the chaos. In addition to the usual two black-robed circuit riders, another Voice had come as well. This one wore red robes and carried himself with terrifying authority. The Sunsguard men accompanying them all wore full armor.

Kip had stuffed an entire pot of numbweed in his tunic. He'd think of a lie to cover the missing pot later, assuming he survived this.

At the edge of the village, he hesitated. No sane Karsite ventured abroad after sunset for fear of the Demons roaming the countryside. Sunpriest Aram said Vkandis had made the Demons on the eighth day to punish the disobedient. But then Kip thought of what the Voices would do to the Demon-mare if they found her.

He remembered his ma screaming as the Voices gave her to the Fires of Cleansing.

Spot pressed himself tightly against Kip's leg. Kip wasn't sure what help a scrawny, filthy, notch-eared barn cat would be against the horrors that roamed the night, but Spot's presence was somehow comforting.

Clutching the pot of numbweed against his chest, the boy broke into an awkward run.

The journey to the arroyo in the swiftly gathering twilight was like something out of a nightmare, even with Spot loping alongside him. Kip ran as fast as he dared, trying not to look over his shoulder. In the gloom, he caught his toe on the root of a scrub oak and went sprawling. The pot of numbweed bounced out of his tunic, fetched up against a stone, and cracked.

Somewhere in the distance, something terrible howled, and he felt his insides grow cold as he gathered up the pot. Just cracked, not broken, but he didn't dare drop it again. He wasn't sure if he heard hoofbeats behind him in the distance or if it was merely his heart thundering in his ears. His chest felt as though it might burst. He went on.

A rustling at the edge of Garal's cornfield made him freeze with terror, but it was nothing more than a half-starved rabbit looking for a meal. Spot bit him insistently on the ankle as Kip stood for a moment longer, trying to catch his breath, and all Kip could do was shove the pot back inside his tunic and force his tired body back into a shambling run. By now he was certain those were really hoofbeats he heard nearby.

When he finally slid down the gravel path to the floor of the arroyo with Spot behind him, he almost wept with relief. He didn't have breath enough to whistle for the little mare, but somehow she came to him anyway, slipping out of the deep purple shadows like a sliver of moonlight come to life.

Kip didn't bother to explain. There wasn't time. It was almost completely dark, and the hoofbeats were getting closer. Much closer.

He tore the bandage from her injured leg, being as gentle as he could in his haste, and started smearing the leg with numbweed. It should stop her from hurting long enough to run across the border into Valdemar. If she went up the far side of the ravine, it shouldn't take her more than half a candlemark at a gallop. It was said the White Demons could outrun any mortal horse. Kip offered up a prayer to the Sunlord that the stories were true.

"You have to go!" he whispered. "Run as fast as you can. Before they get here. Your border's not far. Just head north."

The mare leaned down and delicately lipped at his hair. Spot pressed himself against Kip's side and purred.

And then it was too late.

Horses and Voices and Sunsguard men in armor, carrying lanterns and torches, poured over the side of the arroyo. "There!" someone shouted.

The mare somehow melted into the shadows of the thorn thicket, but Kip wasn't fast enough. He got to his feet to run, but a soldier slid from his horse and grabbed him roughly by the upper arm. Spot hissed and spit and showed his teeth, but the soldier just kicked the cat out of the way.

"Holiness," the soldier called. "I've found the boy."

The horse carrying the red-robed Voice detached itself from the crowd and strode toward the soldier and Kip. The soldier shoved Kip to his knees. "Kneel before your betters," the man said, twisting his arm hard.

Kip didn't dare look up, but after a moment, the heavily embroidered hem of a fine red robe came into his line of vision.

"The boy had this, Holiness," the soldier said. "Numbweed."

"So." Red-Robe's voice was oily and cold. Thick, beringed fingers reached down and plucked something from Kip's tunic. "And what's this? White hair, eh? The Fires of Cleansing will burn bright this Equinox."

Kip closed his eyes tightly and felt his guts turn to water. Better that they should just kill him now!

"The Demon seems to be gone, Holiness," another voice said from somewhere outside the circle of torchlight.

"No," Red-Robe said. "We'd have seen her run. These White Demons are as sly as any man. But no matter. This should draw her out."

And Red-Robe began to sing. The words were in no

language Kip had ever heard, but the sound made his skin crawl with a sense of utter wrongness.

With strength he didn't know he had, Kip wrenched his arm out of the soldier's grasp and lurched to his feet. He threw himself between Red-Robe and the thorn thicket.

"*Portia,*" he screamed, "*RUN!*" He didn't stop to wonder how he knew the White Demon's name.

Everything seemed to happen at once.

Something heavy and impossibly sharp struck him square in the chest, knocking him to the ground, and Kip felt something inside him give way in a burst of incandescent pain. He struggled for a breath he could not draw. A horse whinnied. Someone screamed.

Then there was the sound of bells and hoofbeats that rang like a hammer on hot metal. And over it all, the deep angry yowling of a furious cat.

And then the smell of ozone and a flash of light, brighter than high noon at midsummer, and a crack so loud it was as though the sky itself had been rent open!

After that, Kip of Sunswatch knew nothing more.

When Kip opened his eyes again, the sky was streaked pink with dawn. He was lying on his back at the bottom of the arroyo. A sharp rock pressed painfully against his left shoulder, and chilly dew covered his entire body. A warm, furry, purring mass was curled beside his right ear.

With shaking hands, Kip reached up and touched his breastbone. His tunic was torn and stiff with blood, but the skin beneath it was whole.

:*That was well done, lad. Very well done indeed. If I still had hands, I'd applaud.*:

"I'm not dead," Kip breathed, staring up at the thorn branches that crisscrossed the brightening sky.

:*Not anymore, no.*: The warm baritone voice in his mind was rich with amusement. :*I'm very much afraid you're going to need a new tunic, though.*:

It was just about then that Kip realized the voice he was hearing was coming from . . . the cat. He sat up, then stared. Because the creature unfolding itself beside him was easily the size of a large dog, and it was covered in a luxurious coat of cream-colored fur, save for a mask, tail, and paws the color of flame. And yet the creature was somehow also unmistakably ... Spot.

"I—I—" Kip stammered. "You ... you're a ..."

:*Yes,*: the Firecat agreed. :*I am.*: He sounded rather smug. :*There is a true Child of Vkandis coming to the Sun Throne. She will have need of those, like you, who can See truly.*:

Memory came rushing back. "Portia!"

:*Oh, I'd imagine Companion Portia is safe and sound in Valdemar by now, no doubt being fussed over by an entire bevy of Heralds and Healers. And those Voices have gone home with plenty to talk about, at least the two who are left. Imagine, a Red-Robed Voice of Vkandis, struck down by a bolt of lightning out of a perfectly clear night sky. Ha! I'd like to see them try to deny that Vkandis is on the move now. Bloody old fools.*:

Kip clambered stiffly to his feet. "And I bet they'll think twice before they go hunting any more White Demons."

:*That's the spirit, lad. Now come along. It's a long way to Sunhame, and we've got a lot of trouble to make there, you and I, before the One Who Is To Come can stretch out her hand and say, 'In Vkandis' name.'*:

The Firecat trotted off with a jaunty flick of his tail, but Kip hesitated.

"Um ... sir? Master Firecat? What'm I supposed to call you now? 'Spot' seems awfully ... undignified."

Kip could have sworn the Firecat *smiled* at him. :*Oh, lad, the day is coming when all of Karse will know who I am, but that day isn't yet. 'Spot' will do just fine for now. I find, somewhat to my embarrassment, that I've grown rather fond of the name. Now, are you coming or not?*:

Five days and what seemed like a thousand years ago, Kip had knelt in the smith's Sun Shrine, and prayed for Vkandis Sunlord to show him what it was he was supposed to be doing. Now, he couldn't help smiling. *Ma always did say a body ought to be careful what they prayed for. She wasn't kidding.*

And according to Spot, somewhere out there there
was an even greater purpose waiting for one orphan boy
from Sunswatch. Though hopefully they'd find him some
new clothes before they got on with the whole 'greater
purpose' business. Kip squared his shoulders, straightened what was left of his tunic, and fell in step beside the
Firecat.

Cloud and Sparrow
Michele Lang

Hidden by night, Sparrow met her heartmate in the plane of dreams, and together they flew. It had been far too long. She held Cloudbrother's hand, and they rode the astral breeze that blew lightly and steadily over them.

"After Tis was born and you were in Haven with Abilard," she said, "I couldn't dreamcast to save my life. I couldn't find you up here because I couldn't get up here at all, not without your help. I started out at ground level, and now that I am a mother, it's as though I've grown deep taproots. I didn't think the air would receive me anymore."

She kept her voice light, but both of them knew serious trouble was afoot. Sparrow had just emerged from a terribly crowded moment in her life. Within a short span—only six months or so—she had lost her beloved father, Hari, been separated from her heartmate, and given birth to her son, Thistle.

Flying with Cloudbrother now comforted her tremendously. It reminded Sparrow of who she really was at the core, in the center of her being, beyond the reach of the external circumstances that always changed. It was like hearing her heartbeat, sure and steady, pulsing underneath the noise and chaos that rose and passed away on the surface of her life.

But this comfort did not erase the elemental fact ... their flight now was meant to establish their next moves

in a larger battle. Normal was still gone, flown away over
the horizon.

Cloudbrother's hand tightened over her own, and he
pulled her closer to him and tucked her under his arm.
Her heartmate interrupted her unsettled thoughts with
a low chuckle.

"You are named Sparrow for a reason, you know,"
Cloudbrother replied, his voice easy. "You were meant
to fly here, and even the mightiest cedar tree waves its
branches in the sky. You have the benefit of both places,
and nobody else I know can really say that. Most people
are like me, of one realm or another."

A childhood fever had robbed Cloudbrother of his
sight, and subjected him to bouts of disconnection from
the earth. Sometimes Sparrow marveled that he ever
had the strength to leave the clouds and return to earth,
blind and distant.

A shadow passed over his face and away. The shadow
leaped to Sparrow, and tension shot through her body
like a bolt of heat lightning. "What is it, my love?" Sparrow asked.

His voice remained calm, but Cloudbrother's expression was wary, now, confirming her own train of thought.
"The entity I seek is of the air, and of the earth as well.
At the Council, we tried to find the answer to what I'm
hunting, and the closest we could get was that it may well
be that only water can stop him."

Cloudbrother had returned from Haven only a few
weeks ago, just in time to help save Sparrow from a grim
invader of the Vale itself. They both knew he had been
called to Haven for momentous business indeed, but it
was clear that the danger was close to home.

"The many attacks on us, in Longfall and even within
the safety of k'Valdemar Vale—Sparrow, we have to stop
them. You and I, the locals. We grew up here in the
North. The Council at Haven believes that only we
northerners will find a way to stop these attacks. Because
of our connection to the land."

"But how?" Sparrow asked. "I'm not a Mage, and
while I helped you earn your Whites, I am not a Healer,

only your love. I will do anything I can to help you, but how is this my quest as well as yours?"

"I need your help, Sparrow," Cloudbrother said, his voice quiet. "I don't think I'd ever have made it through the Collegium without you by my side. The only way I can complete my mission now is with you, as always."

"But everything's changed now . . . what about Tis?"

Cloudbrother's intent expression didn't change. "Tis will either have to ride with us, or . . ."

The implications sank into her slowly, like a slice from a blade. Tis. Their baby. He was not even three months born, and Cloudbrother wanted—no, needed—her to ride away with him. The safety of the Vale, the northern reaches of Valdemar, all were threatened by the pattern of strange attacks. Tis was in danger, too.

Sparrow couldn't bear to leave the rest of Cloudbrother's sentence unspoken. "You're saying I will have to leave him." She spat the words out like poison.

Cloudbrother sighed, knowing how much the truth hurt her but honoring her strength by delivering it undiluted.

"This is the thing, my love," he said. "You and I have been having trouble on and off for years, since the day Abilard and I found you in the Forest of Sorrows. Three times over we have been assailed by foul Adepts, Change-Wizards that seek to destroy k'Valdemar Vale. And Valdemar too."

Sparrow gulped, then shared her deepest fear. "It's me, isn't it?" she whispered. "Something about me—my weakness, my smallness. They see me as a portal into greatness since because of you I travel among the brightest stars of Valdemar."

Cloudbrother drew her close and protected her within an all-encompassing embrace, one that wrapped her pain and fear in a warm mantle of complete acceptance and love.

"No, it's not you, my darling," he said, his voice hoarse now. "The Council saw to that. We did as much as we could to isolate the source. It's me. I am the draw, and it is because of who I am. What happened to me."

Their progress over the tops of the clouds halted, and together they hovered in the clear starlight. His words vibrated painfully in her chest. Sparrow hugged him back, tried to send the protective warmth back to him even though her magic, such as it was, did not manifest on this plane.

"It can't be, Brock Cloudbrother. There is no one like you — Healer, Herald, or Queen — in all of Valdemar. I've always said your blindness is a strength, not weakness. You can see patterns from the sky, patterns of magic and behavior, that we all miss on the ground. How could someone so strong prove to be a liability?"

Cloudbrother kissed her gently, and Sparrow melted into that connection, grateful to express her love for him in a language beyond words, beyond conscious thought. Together they floated, connected through their heartbeats in a place beyond ordinary time. A place where Sparrow had always felt supremely safe and protected.

:*Strength is weakness, and weakness strength,*: Cloudbrother whispered into her mind. :*My strength, the power that got me through my Herald training, the aspects that convinced Abilard to Choose me, this is where the danger lies. I must go back to where the Cloudwalker clan first discovered me when I was a five-year-old kid who loved to find trouble. That is the place of entry. It is where the bad magic has been slipping in. It is chasing after me.*:

Their kiss faded away, and Sparrow pulled back to look into Cloudbrother's beautiful, pitted face. "So tell me. Finally."

His gaze pierced her. "Tell you?" he asked.

"What happened to you. When you disappeared from Longfall."

Cloudbrother's jaw set, and his nostrils flared. The expression of a man going into battle.

She gulped. "If we are going to hare off into the wilderness with a baby strapped to my back, we better both know what we are facing, right? I know it hurts to go back in your memory, but I need to know the truth."

A low wind began to blow, scudding off the surface of the pillowy clouds billowing below where they hovered together. Sparrow looked up, into the inky black, star-sprinkled sky.

They were alone. They were still safe.

Cloudbrother sighed, gave in.

"I was sure a handful," he began. "You did your best to help me stay out of trouble, but you could only do so much. We were only five years old, right? I remember the time I got you to jump out of the hayloft and onto the mule's back."

The memory made Sparrow laugh. "That was a stupid thing to do. Old Farley was not amused ... that was the shortest ride I ever took before he kicked me right off."

"I was always looking for the excitement, the rush of the unknown. And you were the only one who could ever keep my feet on the ground."

"I guess that was always our way. I used to worry that I was holding you back."

"Never. You were keeping me alive."

Sparrow laughed again. Up here, the touch of his skin against hers whispered like an updraft, soft and rising heat along the length of her arms, the curve of her back. He held her so surely, so deftly, that she knew nothing could hurt her here.

He sighed, his smile fading. "The day I disappeared, I followed a dancing spirit in the woods. A wood maiden, maybe, or some kind of Change-Beast that disguised itself as a pretty wisp of mist. I fell into a terrible nightmare ... tangled up in something I didn't understand."

The thought of it almost stopped her heart; Brock led into such danger, at the edge of the familiar. It could have been her. It could have been any of the children in the village.

Sparrow had to remind herself to breathe as her heartmate continued. "By the time the Cloudwalkers found me," he said, "I was already deathly sick, my hair had already silvered. Only the wisest and bravest Adepts could rescue me ... and one of them lost his life in the saving of mine. He was Silver Cloud, my father in the clan, and my family took me in. I owe them an everlasting debt."

She knew the bonds she and her heartmate shared with the Cloudwalkers went deeper than blood, and she understood that Brock saw his current mission as part of the debt he owed to his adoptive family.

It didn't change the truth of what she had to do.

"I . . . can't go," she whispered. "I can't risk . . . whatever snatched you . . . grabbing Tis. It's too much. I can't sacrifice my baby, not even to save Valdemar."

He sighed. "But this is my charge. At Haven, it became clear that I was the right Herald to follow this to the end. Not the most renowned, not the most powerful. But I was born to see this through. And I am afraid that without you, I will fail."

"I'm so sorry," Sparrow whispered past the lump in her throat. "But I can't risk Tis. And there is nobody else to take him." Rork, her best friend and the kindest and bravest of all the *hertasi* folk in the Vale, still could not serve as Tis's mother. And her own parents were gone.

"The Healers would take him."

"I couldn't bear to leave him, my love. I'd be useless to you."

The silence hung heavy between them, but there was no foreboding or anger in it. He was too great-hearted to try to force her to change her stance, because he felt the need to protect Thistle as keenly as she did.

The weight of all their obligations pulled on Sparrow's ankle like an anvil on a chain, and she began to slip out of her heartmate's grasp, back down into the world of cares below. The falling sensation made her stomach clench.

"Hey, now!" Cloudbrother said, such a note of command in his voice that her fears and worries scurried back down to earth. "You stay with me. I will help you!"

She wrapped her arms around his shoulders and held on, knowing he would protect her, and Thistle too, with his last breath. She hoped with all her heart that it would not come to that.

They both awoke in their narrow bed, no closer to the solution to their dilemma.

Sparrow rose up on one elbow in the darkness of their

little ekele, squinting into the silvery, moonlit shadows to see Thistle, sleeping like the mellow little Adept he was, tucked into his cradle alongside them. She wanted to trail her fingers down his round little cheek, but she didn't dare wake him.

"He's good," she whispered to Cloudbrother.

:Yes he is,: Cloudbrother whispered back into her mind, his Mindspeech resonant as a bell sounding on a mountainside at dawn. *:He's perfect. And so are you.:*

In the midst of her confusion and trouble, with her worries roosting around her like crows, Sparrow still fell deep into sleep by her sweetheart's side, knowing they would face it all together in the morning.

Trouble always looks less scary by daylight. It looks even more manageable after getting served breakfast in bed by a thoughtful, clever *hertasi* who enjoyed baking.

:Scones!: Rork announced from the doorway to the bedroom. *:Scones and hot tea coming in! Good morning!:*

He made Sparrow laugh every day of her life. He announced his scones like the coming of the Queen.

The door swung slowly open. "Good morning, dear sir," Sparrow said.

She was awake, and Tis was nursing, tucked in among the pillows. Cloudbrother was awake, in a sense, but tranced, soaring through the clouds of his mind. He would not be interested in breakfast ... Sparrow knew he floated far away, searching for patterns, clues in how to solve the puzzle of his mission and of the reality of Tis.

:You are rosy and refreshed, my dear child. Your heart-mate does wonders for your looks!:

Sparrow tried not to laugh. She knew she looked a fright; hair tangled into a nest, half asleep, frowzy in the bed. But she understood what Rork meant. She looked happy and rested.

The turmoil underneath still clung to her ankles, pulling her down. But now she had the counterweight of Cloudbrother here once again, lifting her up.

Rork advanced from the doorway, his tail held high, his eyes glittering as he carefully placed the carved rosewood tray heaped with scones across her lap. *:I made lingonberry, your favorite. Spiced with cinnamon and beer-root for your health, little mother.:*

"They're still warm," she said with delight. "No more talking, I'm going in." And she did, having perfected the art of holding Tis one-armed and doing any manner of work with the other as she held him.

The scones were perfect, of course, rich and buttery and light, the beer-root sharp and sweet at the same time. She ate two without speaking, washing them down with warm, milky tea.

"Thank you so very much," she said a while later.

:My pleasure, my dear,: Rork replied.

Her gratitude ran to so much more than the scones. Rork had tended to Sparrow's every need from the moment Cloudbrother had left for Haven, and he had only heaped more loving care on her since her heartmate had returned.

"Can I do anything for you, dear Rork? Anything at all?"

:Why, yes. Eat another scone. Quick, try the lingonberry! Before they get all cold and vile,: he replied, his tone so dry that this time Sparrow did laugh out loud.

She gratefully obeyed his command and demolished the plate of scones and drained the daintily painted pot-bellied teapot dry.

Once she was done, she looked across the room to where her friend waited, his amber eyes bright and clear. "We're leaving very soon, you know."

His gaze faltered for a moment, but only for a moment. *:Oh, you Valdemarans,:* he said, his voice light. *:So restless, so like the gryphons' flight. High flyers so quick to dart into the sky. But like the gryphons, you will always return, my dear. Because you know you are so dear to me.:*

Even his endearments and unspoken dismay made her smile. "You flatter me shamelessly, Rork, but I'm no gryphon. I'm a little gray sparrow, and I dart in the dust and the underbrush, right near the front door. No great ballads will ever be sung for me. And I don't care."

Rork's wide mouth tipped open, and his iridescent

cheek scales sparkled in the morning sunlight streaming in through the half-open window near her bed. The *hertasi*'s toothy grimace of a smile would have frightened Sparrow's mother, and maybe even her father, but his reptilian face was dear to her now. She had no fear of him and his profound and homely magic.

:The world needs gryphons, it needs hertasi, *and it needs sparrows too,*: Rork said.

Tucked safe in her bed, filled with Rork's scones and tea, his words Spoken in her mind echoed and sang like chimes. "You've got something there, my friend," Sparrow said in growing wonder. "I think you've solved a puzzle that's been troubling me sorely."

:It isn't me, but the power of the scones,: Rork replied. *:Scones and sparrows—the foundation of the world.:* And with a flourish, he swept forward to claim the tray full of crumbs and tea service and was out the door with a single fluid movement.

She watched him go in a blue and green iridescent flash. And she nestled Tis closer to her heart, wishing she could trap this moment in amber and keep it like a jewel on a silk thread, forever.

The plan was hatched while they all rode with Abilard at midmorning—Cloudbrother, Sparrow, and Tis strapped to Sparrow's back—taking the air together. The Vale was warm, lush, and gorgeous as always, the vines, trees, and flowers effusing pure life all around them, the air scented with herbs and sweet nectar.

:We cannot risk Tis, and if you cannot leave him, there it is,: Abilard said.

Cloudbrother was having a bad day. They rode bareback, and Sparrow clung to him, holding on as if he might slip out of her grasp and fly into the sky at any moment.

"So, dear Abilard, how shall you complete your mission?" she asked. "On a good day, Cloudbrother and you would be fine without me. But on a day like today . . ."

Sparrow trailed off, not willing to talk about her heartmate's condition when he was not necessarily going to be able to participate in the discussion. She held him tight, knowing the pressure on his skin would keep him oriented, even if he could not stay verbal today.

"I've been thinking," Sparrow ventured. She was always half-shy around Cloudbrother's magnificent Companion. He was so powerful, and brilliant, and nearly overwhelming. He had always treated her with the utmost respect and friendliness, and yet she felt keenly the fact that he had Chosen Cloudbrother long before he had ever known of her, long before she and Brock had become heartmated.

She respected him too, profoundly. But she could not relax into their friendship the way she had, almost instantly, with Rork.

:Your common sense is a deep magic, Sparrow,: Abilard whispered, his Mindspeech like sun-warmed honey in her mind, golden and sweet. *:I suspect you will find the key for us.:*

"This is what I'm thinking," she said slowly. She took a deep breath, fortifying herself with the heady perfume of the Vale before leaping into her idea. "Cloudbrother first encountered the evil at the edge of Longfall, right? And, on top of that, the entire village was bespelled a few years back. This was the first point of contact."

Abilard hummed into her mind, an encouragement to go on.

"So we could go to Longfall, and I could visit the home village, stay there with Tis. It could become our home base. And I would bet you a thousand of Rork's scones that the evil would come to us there."

:But would that not mean that Tis was unsafe in the village?:

Sparrow's heart sank. It was so obvious . . . she should have recognized the danger instantly. It was just that even after her experience there a few years ago, she still associated Longfall with boredom and ordinariness, not with magic of any kind. It was just her hometown, after all.

But Brock had been snatched from that very place.

The safety she always assumed had never existed at all.

Sparrow sighed. "Well, it's not safe. Clearly. But it is

safer than diving into the Forest of Sorrows. It's the
safety of the familiar, after all. I think it is very different
with you there, and Cloudbrother there as well. Tis and
I would not be undefended."

*:All safety is relative ... even the Vale was not safe for
you. It is too dangerous for us to hide and pretend we can
keep you safe.:*

Sparrow sighed again, then sat a little taller. Sometimes admitting the worst was a relief over pretending.

"I'd always thought an ordinary girl would go unno-
ticed in a forgettable place like that. The whole place felt
positively invisible growing up, so I never imagined that
it could attract the notice of great and fell powers."

*:Nobody is ordinary if you truly know them, Sparrow.
And yet ... :*

Sparrow sensed his hesitancy as well as heard it ... a
faint ache in her joints, a tightness across her chest, con-
stricting her breath. But she waited for Abilard to follow
his thoughts wherever they led.

The stone path they followed turned to a rough track,
and they plunged into the jungle foliage. Somewhere far
above, a Bondbird shrieked in delight, looping in and out
of the canopy crown. A creature unseen rustled the
leaves in the thick, droopy vines to their left, sending
cascades of flower petals tumbling onto their heads.

Cloudbrother's Companion sighed, his ears twitching
backward toward Sparrow. *:Perhaps you're right. Maybe
the uncanny stands out more in a place like Longfall,:*
Abilard finally said.

He picked up his pace, and Sparrow swayed with his
gait, her legs still aching a little as she held on to Cloudbrother and sat extra straight so Tis and his carrier
wouldn't tweak her back muscles. Bluish shadows and
patches of sunlight filtered through the intricate weave
of branches and leaves, and Sparrow once again considered the varied patterns of energy in Valdemar, how very
different Longfall was from a place like the Vale.

They rode in silence a bit longer.

*:You've convinced me, despite the dangers. We leave for
Longfall tomorrow morning,:* Abilard said.

Sparrow knew Cloudbrother would approve . . . this was as close as they all could get to his abduction and as close to the ground near to where it first happened. She would stay with Tis in the "safe" part of the village, and hope that Cloudbrother and Abilard could chase the menace while keeping her and the baby clear.

It was the best they could do.

"I'll be ready. Here's hoping Cloudbrother has a better day tomorrow," Sparrow replied. Her right hand let go of her beloved long enough to pat Abilard's flank in thanks.

Unfortunately, Cloudbrother was a little worse the next morning. His skin, waxy pale, was cold to the touch. With a shiver, Sparrow remembered how very ill he had been the day Abilard had first brought him back to her. She worried that the closer they drew to the place of his disappearance, the worse his old symptoms would reassert themselves.

She drew back from her foreboding and lost herself in the minutiae of packing diapers and sun hats, long-sleeved shirts and baby slippers. It was amazing how much effort and preparation it took to dress such a tiny person.

After packing as lightly as she possibly could, Sparrow slung their single pack across Abilard's withers. He wore a special traveling saddle designed to hold Cloudbrother on his mount even when he wasn't fully conscious, with space for Sparrow to perch on the back.

Cloudbrother stood shivering in the clearing outside their ekele, drooping in the crisp morning light. Sparrow had given him an infusion of trefoil to drink on waking, but it didn't appear to have done much for him this morning.

"Are you up to this, my love?" she murmured.

Cloudbrother didn't answer at first, and she feared that he was altogether gone into the plane of the spirit.

But with a great effort he cleared his throat, licked his lips. "Not really ready," he whispered, almost too quiet for her to hear. "But I can hunt him better this way."

Sparrow put her worrying away ... there was no more time for it. Instead she reached up and hugged him close, inhaling his sandalwood and trefoil scent. "Tis and I will come with you, close as we can."

Almost on cue, a ruckus rose from inside the ekele. Tis was making his displeasure known ... Rork was saying goodbye, and the baby was getting impatient for his mama. "I'm being summoned," she said. "We're ready to go."

Inside, Rork dandled Tis on his bony lap, careful to keep his hooked claws clear of the child's ruddy, sensitive baby skin. Tis squirmed and kicked his chubby legs, looking for a place to push off.

:Ah, he's a handful.:

The words, evoking her heartmate's description of himself as a child, sent a cold prickle of fear down Sparrow's spine. "He's my handful, Rork dear. And yours, too. We'll be back after this visit, just as you said. I can't wait to come back home."

Rork didn't smile this time. He tilted his head, considering her. Knowing she had not told him all the details of her trip back to Longfall ... Cloudbrother had sworn her to secrecy.

:Go in peace, honey. Sometimes the past is a battlefield, sometimes it's a lost country. But it's always a wild ride. Don't try to hoard the scones either ... they'll get stale instantly.:

"You always give the best advice, dear Rork." And Sparrow meant her words with all her heart. She could not bear to say the word goodbye.

"Someday we'll tell Tis all about this trip. We'll tell it like it's an adventure," Sparrow said, a little desperately, about three candlemarks later.

By now it was midafternoon, and the little band had left the Vale and traveled the thick, almost impenetrable Forest of Sorrows. Longfall was still a long, arduous ride away.

And it was pouring rain outside the Vale, an unremitting, soaking downpour.

Soundless, Cloudbrother hunched over Abilard's

mane. Other than shivering occasionally, he gave off few measurable signs of life. Tis, protected from the rain by the brim of Sparrow's sun hat, squeaked every so often when an errant raindrop sneaked down the back of his neck.

And between nibbles of Rork's farewell scones, Sparrow was left alone to contemplate her galloping thoughts, never a good situation.

The heavy rain spattered through the hardwood forest as Abilard's silvery hooves trampled the slippery dead leaves underfoot. He was completely silent, so present that to Sparrow it seemed that he was bigger than the entire forest. His presence was huge, like the sun.

Since the actual sun was hidden behind sullen cloud mountains and torrents of cold sluicing rain, Sparrow was grateful for his calm, warm constancy.

Abilard snorted, and after a small eternity replied to Sparrow's observation. *:It could be an adventure now, dear soul. In this moment, which is all we ever have.:*

:Worry is a form of time travel,: Cloudbrother Mindspoke in both her and Abilard's minds, startling her.

"And that travel is to a future that hopefully never comes," Sparrow replied, thrilled to hear his voice amid all the mud and drudgery.

Abilard came to a giant puddle that had formed in a small clearing and splashed through it, mud spraying up along his flanks. The rain slowed, and Sparrow almost reflexively glanced up at the branches above their heads, scanning for crows.

Crows had served as harbingers of danger to her time after time, and she was grateful for their intercessions in the past. But today, not a single crow could be found in the forest surrounding them.

Somehow, their absence was more sinister than their looming presence had ever been.

Abilard doggedly pressed on, refusing to rest, and Tis, the little enlightened one, slept. Almost imperceptibly, the forest track gave way to a wider, more delineated way, then to a broad, gravel path that met with other, smaller trails.

"We're almost to Longfall now," Sparrow said, excitement creeping into her voice. Who knew what to expect once they got there . . . but she and the others could hope for at least a little shelter from the rain.

None of them expected to take a wrong turn.

The first sign their travels had gone amiss was the mist.

Longfall was set in the mountainous region of the border district of northern Valdemar. They traveled the main pathway, an extension of the north track road that led to the villages beyond the larger town of Errold's Grove. At this point, the way was clear.

And yet they were lost.

The mist danced up from the puddles, refracting the low light in weird and fantastic ways. It looked like ladies, dancing inside the smoke. Sparrow gasped, remembering her heartmate's description of the dancing, alluring mist maiden that had led him to his near destruction.

"I don't like this," she said, her voice flat and hard to her own ears. It sounded as if somebody else were talking, somebody annoyed beyond composure.

Abilard stopped walking. He took in the suddenly trailless forest and whinnied. His voice echoed forlornly among the trees.

:Mama,: Tis spoke into her mind, so quietly she didn't realize it was him until he had finished.

Goosebumps prickled up and down the length of Sparrow's bare forearms. "Hush," she said, her voice shaking. "Sweetie, just hush."

:Papa needs me.:

By the Mother, Sparrow was in trouble—they all were—and she knew it to the bottom of her toes. Tis was speaking in her mind, clear as any Companion. And with the impulsivity and innocence of youth, he wanted to leap into the unknown after his hero, his daddy.

And who knew how far away her beloved Cloudbrother walked in the sky now, hunting his nemesis. Sparrow was trapped between mud and sky, not sure where to turn.

"Help me, Abilard!" she finally said aloud. "Keep Tis here with you! We're surrounded."

In all her misadventures, never had Sparrow found herself so far from home, any home. She and her beloved ones were swallowed up by wilderness, with no pathway to escape.

In a city like Haven, the denizens could romanticize the northern wilderness, the wild winter wastes, as a frontier, a place to prove your mettle. But the natives of this region had no illusions about the primeval forest that surrounded them, hungry to swallow them whole. Like the ocean a continent away, the forest was immense and intrinsically wild, untamable.

Forget the Change-Circles, the Change-Adepts, or strange creatures that hunted easy human prey ... the very land itself was a threat as much as a place to find firewood and wild herbs.

That same forest held them in its grasp now.

The forest was haunted, saturated with magic. Sparrow had lived at the edge of this forest for her entire life, and she had never sensed its menace as she did in this moment.

It was the forest itself that had sought Brock Cloudbrother. The forest that sent the mist maidens to tempt a little boy deeper into the wild. The forest itself was enchanted, alive, hungry. The forest wanted to claim its sovereignty over the people, the rocks, the creatures both magical and mundane.

The forest was aware. It had a name, and it demanded its dominion. A sickness in the magic here waxed powerful.

Sparrow slid off Abilard's back and crouched under his belly, in the mud. She crabwalked sideways to get clear of his nervously dancing hooves, to a damp, horizontally striped boulder. She leaned against it, Tis snuffling fussily against the nape of her neck.

She could not send to her baby or to her heartmate. But with Cloudbrother's help, she could fly. Abilard would hold Tis back from flying with her.

She closed her eyes, took a deep breath. Snuggled deep into the loamy, leaf-soaked earth.

And leaped into the ether, desperately searching for her heartmate before she tumbled back into her body.

It made her think of the kite festival held at Longfall each autumn, the only frivolous thing the sober little village ever undertook. She tossed herself into the wind, then crashed into her body again. She tried it again and again, each time slamming back into her head, her skull screaming in protest.

One more time . . .

And Cloudbrother's fingers grabbed her, squeezed.

"It's dangerous!" he half yelled.

She saw him, her beloved. Clear and white as a bolt of lightning. "How can the forest hurt you here?"

He grabbed at her fiercely. "It's like I told you, branches in the wind all reach into the sky. Air and earth, remember? Not so easy to ride clear."

She fluttered in his arms like a sparrow in the storm. "It's the Forest of Sorrows, Brock. It was the forest itself that took you. Once you have the name, you have the power."

Cloudbrother scissored his legs, and they shot higher, much higher. The trees swayed under their feet. Sparrow could never recall flying so far in the daylight.

Cloudbrother was speaking to her. It cost her an effort to focus on his words. "No, love. That is the name the people of the land have given to this place. We need the name in the ancient language. And even then . . ."

Before he could finish, clouds of steam rose to enclose them. Tendrils reached for them, twined around them, between them. The forest was hungry, would remain hungry.

Fear lashed at Sparrow like a vicious, unceasing wind. She fought to think through it, to where Tis huddled on the ground with her, far below. Abilard could not ride the ether, could not help them from the ground.

She had no power, no magic to hurl. Her magic, the humble one of love and hearth, seemed infinitely out of reach. She feared that this time, the forest would finish the job of devouring her heartmate and would take her and Tis for good measure.

Sparrow and Cloudbrother climbed even higher, desperately leaping away from the forest's grip. Ever more
distant from their lives on the ground.

The air grew thin, so high. The trees receded so far
below that the mist could not reach them. Sparrow
clutched at Cloudbrother, terrified.

The only thing that kept her from unraveling was a
deep sense that somehow the key to their salvation traveled with them, was with them at this moment.

She forced herself to breathe, to slow down the torrent of her thoughts.

She remembered what Cloudbrother had told her.
And what she knew of this place.

And it all became clear.

"Water," she said.

"Water?"

"You told me your captor owned the air and the
earth."

"Water . . ."

"We have to go to Lake Evendim."

"What? You've never been to Lake Evendim, my
love!"

And Sparrow's heart sang then, for Brock Cloudbrother began to laugh, despite the siege. "Really, the
lake? It's pretty far away."

"I don't know the details. But the lake holds great secrets. My mother, of all people, used to tell me so."

"Your mother never went to Lake Evendim, either."

Now Sparrow was laughing, mixed with her tears and
with the rain. "I know! But somehow she knew, and she
made sure to tell me. She said it was my inheritance."

The memory sobered her a bit, but it softened and
steadied her too. "The Bitter Sea would do, my love. It is
a mighty water. But the Lake is closer."

"How do you know all of this, my darling?"

Sparrow stopped to consider the logical and obvious
question. And the answer floored her. "Because my
mother used to sing to me the lullaby:

Higher than the Peak of Thurlos
Deeper than the secrets of Lake Evendim

Stronger than the Forest of Sorrows
Is the love you have for him . . .
Is the love you have for him . . ."

They floated together, and considered the words of
the long-ago song.

"Did your mama ever sing you this lullaby, Brock?"

"No, ma'am. She used to sing me songs about pirates
and dragons. Maybe they were also about Lake Evendim. But never this. Never this."

"So what do we do now?"

They floated above the tops of the trees, like two in-
tertwined kites escaped from a long-ago Longfall Kite
Festival. Cloudbrother peeked down, way down, to the
forest bed below.

"We get you and Tis back on Abilard's back. And
Abilard calls to his brother Companions, and we head to
the Lake of Evendim as fast as we can. I'm thinking the
Change-Circles hacked a hunk out of this forest—it's
missing something that keeps it in balance.

"This forest is terribly out of balance. I learned from
my clan brothers how important it is to keep the balance,
to keep the magic from turning to harm. The forest needs
healing. It's sick. And something we are doing is making
it sicker. We need to restore the balance."

"So can we outrun the forest now?" Sparrow was terrified to go down, and she also was terrified to stay up
here, leaving Tis alone with Abilard.

"We can't outrun the forest, no," Cloudbrother said,
his voice filled with power and excitement. Sparrow had
never seen him so centered in his own power. "Running
won't fix this. We have to face the forest head on. I came
here to do this."

He paused. "I might not make it, love. But you will.
And Abilard will. And that is enough to keep Tis safe."

Sparrow surrendered to his lead and refused to think
about the risk. Her fear hid deep in her heart, where she
could no longer feel it. "Let's go down to Tis, then," she
said, her voice shaking only a little. "You show me the way."

She closed her eyes, and they descended slowly, more
like gently falling leaves than crashing kites now. She

didn't want to see the branches reaching for her, didn't want to see the darkness closing in all around them.

Instead, she hopped down the last little way to where Tis waited for her.

:Mama,: he Spoke into her mind.

"Sweetie," she said out loud. "Mama and Daddy are here."

She opened her eyes. Cloudbrother still clutched at clumps of Abilard's thick, blue-white mane. He was smiling.

Abilard whispered into her mind. *:Cloudbrother has told me of your mother's lullaby. The simple wisdom is the best. It is of a piece with the predictions of the Council in Haven. The Council was right ... only Cloudbrother can reach the forest now. They are linked by pain and blood.:*

Sparrow climbed on the striped boulder to reach the saddle and sit behind Cloudbrother. The leaves overhead rippled and rustled with a hiss like snakes.

Brock Spoke to the forest, not to Sparrow, but she could hear him in her mind just the same. *:I swear to you that I will ease your pain. The Changes have sheared away your connection to Water. I will seek that energy and return it to you. The answer is hidden to the west, where the great Lake lies. You know me. I am yours. Allow us to go, and we will heal you.:*

Sparrow finally understood. The forest wasn't their enemy. It hadn't sought to destroy Brock, but to absorb his energy, to heal. The forest was lashing out in pain.

She held her breath, straining for an answer.

When it came, she could not believe it.

YES

The forest spoke directly into her mind, so loudly that pain spiked from inside her eyes. Tis began to cry, but she didn't try to hush him. She just held on to Cloudbrother with all her strength.

GO. AND RETURN. OR ...

Sparrow let her breath out slowly, her lips trembling.

:I will come, I will heal your pain,: Brock said.

And all at once, the rustling stopped, and before them lay the track to Longfall.

"We'd better go to Evendim through Haven," Brock whispered, so softly that Sparrow could hardly hear him. "We'll follow the road south. And report to the Council before we go west."

Together they flew, racing with Abilard through the Forest of Sorrows.

The nature of their quest had changed, from a battle to the death to a mission of healing. But that made their mission no less dire. The Forest of Sorrows was out of patience.

They had no time to lose.

The lullaby was a fragile thread connecting Sparrow to the past, and pointing their way forward. They would ride into the future together, Sparrow and Cloudbrother and Thistle, and that was everything.

Clay and Fire
Angela Penrose

Warm sun shone down on the knee-high grain fields to either side of the wide road, and a cool breeze ruffled the green shoots, making them rustle and wave. The breeze carried the grassy scent of the wheat to Herald Arvil, along with a pure whiff he recognized as water. A few puffy clouds drifted here and there across the rich, blue sky. The fluff of treetops fuzzed the horizon beyond the fields scratched out of the rock-hard soil native to the area. A gap in the trees marked the place where Elmdale lay.

It'd been almost four years since Herald Arvil had last been to the village and eight since his first visit. He remembered the place with a smile, despite having humiliated himself horribly that first time, falling flat on his face in the middle of the tavern, his attention caught by a gorgeous man.

The same man riding next to him, in fact.

Smooth brown skin, a handsome, angular face, and broad, muscular shoulders had drawn Arvil's attention on that evening eight years ago. Humor and kindness had led them down the path to love and then marriage.

Usually a glance at his husband was enough to get Arvil smiling. The circumstances of their trip back to Elmdale were grim, though, and Embry's expression was tight with pain.

Arvil wanted to fix everything, to put the world back

the way it was supposed to be, but he couldn't, and that knowledge gnawed at his gut.

No one, not even a Herald, could bring back the dead.

They rode into Elmdale, Arvil on his Companion, Graya, and Embry on his bay horse, Rusty. The village was barely a ten minute walk from end to end, all timber and plaster houses with neat thatched roofs, most two or three stories high. The shadows stretched clear across the road, and the air was full of supper smells — roasting pork and sizzling peppers and the yeasty scent of the flatbreads folk made in that area.

The buildings facing the main road all had shops on the ground floor, shuttered for the evening. They rode past them all to the far end, where one building had become a blackened pit with a few broken timbers stretching upward like fire-cracked bones.

Embry took a sharp breath. When Arvil looked over, his eyes were squeezed closed.

Arvil reached out to squeeze Embry's hand and got a squeeze back. Another breath, and then Embry opened his eyes again and stared at the wreckage of what had once been his brother's home and workshop.

"I suppose I was hoping it'd all been a mistake," he said, his voice low and rough. "I knew it wasn't, but my gut was still hoping."

"It often does take longer to convince your gut," said Arvil. He'd seen grief over death time and again since becoming a Herald. He never knew what to say to the sorrowing survivors, and this time, even with Embry, was no different.

Before Arvil could think of something comforting to say, a new voice called from up the road. "Embry Smith! That you?"

They both turned to see a gray-haired woman in a leather apron come striding toward them.

"Nan Turner, hello," said Embry. "I hope you've been well?"

"Well enough," she said. "Would I could say the same of yourself. Terrible thing, terrible loss."

"Thank you," murmured Embry. "This is my husband, Arvil."

Arvil bowed from the saddle and said, "Well met, Mistress Turner."

Nan nodded to Arvil and said, "And yourself," then turned back to Embry. "Imagine you'll want to go to Gilly, then. She's at the Two Hares. Sarry took her in, bundled the babe right up with her own."

"Thank you, yes," said Embry.

Nan nodded at him, then turned and headed back up the road.

"This way," said Embry, and nudged Rusty into a walk. Arvil would usually have teased him, reminded Embry that he hardly needed directions to the tavern where they'd met, but his husband was clearly running on his last thread, so Arvil kept silence and followed.

They'd actually passed the Two Hares on their way in. It sat at the western edge of the village, where travelers from Tindale—the largest settlement nearby—would go by it on their way into town. It wasn't big enough to call an inn, only two stories and the upper floor taken by the host's family. You could buy a space on the plank floor if you wanted to stay the night, and Arvil imagined they'd be doing that, for however long it took Embry to settle his brother's business.

Loud talk and the clunking of tankards spilled out when Embry opened the broad, iron-banded door. It took only the space of a few breaths for their arrival to quiet the room.

The hostess wound her way across the floor, wiping her hands on a long apron. She walked right up to Embry and pulled him into a hug. Arvil couldn't hear what she said to him, but whatever it was made him tighten his arms around her and kiss her on the cheek.

She took a step back and said, "Come, Gilly's upstairs. She's that turned around, the poor mite, sad and confused and striking out when it's too much for her. Seeing family will help some, we can hope."

Arvil touched Embry's shoulder and said, "I'll see to Graya and Rusty. You go on."

Embry gave him a quick nod and a twist of the lips that was doubtless meant as a grateful smile, before following the woman, likely Sarry.

Back out on the street, Arvil took Rusty's reins and led him around the back of the building, where he recalled there was a decent enough lean-to stable. Graya followed close behind. Arvil removed packs, saddles, bridles, and blankets, stacking the packs along the back wall where Graya could make sure they didn't walk away with someone, then gave each of them a good brushing and left them with hay and water.

The sun finished setting while he worked, and by the time he re-entered the tavern, lamps burned all around. He collected a trencher of pork stew and a beer from a young man who resembled Sarry quite a lot, then settled down at a trestle table with a half-dozen locals.

"Herald," said the man across from him. He was lean and wiry, with some gray in his beard. "You escorting Embry?"

"He's my husband," said Arvil, taking a big bite of the stew. It was thick and flavorful, with mushrooms and peppers and generous chunks of pork.

"Ah, aye, I remember you now," said the man. "You're the one measured your length on the floor some years agone."

He chuckled, and a few of the others, clearly listening, laughed along. It didn't sound mean-spirited, so Arvil just shrugged and gave them all a smirk.

"I'm Todd, since you likely don't remember, traveling around as you Heralds do," said the wiry man. He swept his own tankard around the table, adding, "Burn, Ulf, Young Hender, Kat, and Meg."

"Good to see you," said Arvil, nodding at each. "I wish it were for a better reason."

"Aye, that's bad business," said Todd. "After midnight, when folk are sound in their beds, and then a fire with none to see nor hear until the whole place has caught. I live across the way a piece and knew nothing of it till I heard shouting."

"I live next to Nilly and Corden," said Meg. "I heard

the cracklin' an' then a roar, and I raised the cry. Nilly was hanging outa the window screamin', and when I ran over, she dropped little Gilly like a laundry bundle. I caught her and ran, thinkin' Nilly'd be right behind. I handed Gilly to Annabet by the bakery and ran back, thinkin' Nilly mighta broke something on the fall and need help, but she weren't there in the road and weren't in the window no more. All I could see were flames and smoke and timbers falling. I reckon a fallin' timber got her afore she could jump. Never did see Corden."

She nodded gravely before taking a long drink of her ale, then added, "You can wager I take extra care to bank the fire afore bed. Roll up the hearth rug, too. Can't be too careful." The others around her nodded back, lifting their tankards before drinking.

Arvil had heard enough witness tales to recognize one that'd been told many times. It sounded as though the fire had blazed up suddenly if it was already out of control by the time anyone heard or smelled it. He remembered Nilly as a serious woman, a little shy, a quiet shadow to her more boisterous husband. She was a sensible woman, not one given to dithering. If the fire blocked the stairs—and surely it must have, for her to drop her child out the window with what sounded like no hesitation at all—then Meg was right that Nilly herself should have jumped immediately after.

She must not have had the chance.

After some silence, the other folk at the table turned the conversation to local matters—whose pig had rooted up a neighbor's garden patch, who else was missing chickens, which young man or woman was driving their parents to drink. Common stuff in small villages, and Arvil hoped they'd not think to bring any of the messes to him.

He scraped his trencher clean, drank the last of his beer, bid his companions a good even, and dropped the crockery off in the tiny scullery before asking the way upstairs.

The way was clear, of course—there was only one staircase, and that in plain view—but it was polite to ask. The young man who looked like Sarry led the way up and took him to a small, dark room under the eves lit by a single lamp. Three large pallets lay in the three corners of the room, the fourth being where the door stood. There were eight children in nightclothes, plus Embry.

A small girl with a tear-streaked face had her arms wrapped around Embry's neck, hanging on as though she were dangling over a cliff. And come to think of it, she might well have nightmares of falling for some time, poor mite.

He threaded his way through the children, likely Sarry's. He managed a smile for each of them, although they just stared at him with huge brown eyes.

Arvil lay a hand on Embry's shoulder, then knelt beside him. "How is she?" he whispered.

"She had a good cry," Embry whispered back. "Demanded I take her home, to her mam and da, and threw a royal fit when I said I couldn't. She exhausted herself, I think."

"The sleep should do her some good," said Arvil, keeping his voice low. "She's too young to understand but young enough to recover well."

Embry shot him a scowl. "She lost her parents and her home and everything she's ever known, and we're going to take her away from her village to a big, noisy place full of strangers. She's not going to just forget so easily."

"That's not what I meant, love," said Arvil. He rubbed Embry's back, massaging tense muscles. "She won't forget them soon, and perhaps never at all. But young children are resilient. The Lady protects them from great sorrow if they're taken care of after. We'll take fine care of her, and she'll find her way. She'll be happy again. Not tomorrow, nor next week, but she'll find things to smile about again."

Embry buried his nose in Gilly's dark curls and huffed out a sigh. "I suppose you would know."

"I do," said Arvil. "I've held my share of crying children who've just lost everything. Gilly is special because she's yours, and I hope will be ours soon. But she'll get past this. We'll see to it."

Embry nodded, and they sat together for a time. The

other children shuffled about, dividing themselves
among the pallets. It was crowded, and it was soon clear
there'd be barely enough space for Embry to stretch out
on the floor with Gilly. Arvil fetched Embry's bedroll
and pack, then said goodnight and took himself back
downstairs.

There was no sense trying to sleep until the locals had
left, so Arvil got another beer and sat down with a different group of villagers. After greetings and the obligatory
retelling of the story of the fire, the locals settled in to
discuss whose pigs were the fattest and whose carrots
would be the sweetest that year.

Arvil thought he might actually get through a whole
evening without having to take on his official persona,
but his luck gave out when two men came up behind
him. One coughed to announce himself, then said, "Milord Herald? Might we have a word?"

Arvil smothered his sigh and gave them a courteous
smile. "Of course." He got up and followed them to a
chilly corner of the room where they had at least the il-
lusion of privacy.

They introduced themselves as Hobbert and Eldric.
Both men were pig farmers, which was the common oc-
cupation in the area for anyone who didn't farm wheat
or practice a crafting trade. They were both brown
skinned—some from the sun and some, like Embry, from
birth—and looked to be around Arvil's age, midthirties.

They gave each other a tense look, then Hobbert said,
"We were wonderin' whether you might've heard any
word of our children. My daughter, that is, Bayla, and
Eldric's son Mort."

"Mort said he'd have none o' pig farming," said Eldric.
"Said he'd go to Haven and join the Guard."

"And Bayla," said Hobbert, "she were that sweet on
him and determined to marry him an' none other. She
said she'd wait on him, but when he left for Haven, she
went too. Likely she knew there'd be a branglin' about it
if she'd been honest."

"They knew nobody in Haven," said Eldric, "so Mort,
he said he'd find Embry the smith and ask fer some

advice, maybe some space on the floor fer a bit, till he could find a place of his own. And he promised he'd write, so we knew he'd landed on his feet."

"But he never did," said Hobbert. "Nor did Bayla. We heard nothin' at all from neither of 'em, these two years now."

"Two *years?*" asked Arvil. He felt his spirit sink. After two years, any trail would've gone cold.

"Nearly," said Eldric. "It'll be two years come harvest."

"Did they turn up?" asked Hobbert, and both men looked at him, fear and hope in their eyes.

Arvil kept his expression neutral and said, "I haven't seen them, but I'm away from home much of the time, riding Circuit. I'll ask Embry whether they turned up. He's asleep with the children now, but I promise I'll ask him in the morning."

The men looked at each other again. Hobbert frowned and looked away, while Eldric said, "Thankee. I 'preciate it."

"Did you ever send a note to the Guards?" asked Arvil. "Ask whether Mort ever did join up?"

"I did," said Eldric. "Sent a note with Danil last year. He grows wheat, takes it to Haven to sell himself. Says he gets a better price than selling it to the jobber. He took the note, but we never heard nothin' back."

Arvil's first thought was that the young couple hadn't made it to Haven. Or had changed their minds and gone somewhere else? But why not let their families know they were well? Unless there was more of an argument before their leaving than their fathers were willing to own.

"I'll ask Embry in the morning," he repeated. "And if he heard nothing from them, I'll inquire with the Guards when we get back to Haven."

"Thankee," Eldric said again. Hobbert nodded, and the two men took themselves off. Arvil watched them exchange a few words by the door, then they left the tavern together.

The place emptied out, first slowly and then more quickly. Arvil was the only guest staying the night, aside from Embry, and Sarry said Arvil could have the place

before the fire. He thanked her and soon enough was
lying snug before a very carefully banked fire.

Something about that bothered him, but he was too
tired to ponder it. He set it aside for later and slept.

Arvil was seated on a hard wooden bench with a mug of
tea and a hunk of hot bread and toasted cheese on the
table before him when Embry came downstairs carrying
Gilly. Embry had pulled on his shirt and trousers, and
Gilly wore a loose dress, plain white and about knee
length. Both were barefoot, and both sported uncombed
hair that stuck out all over, looking exactly as though
they'd only just rolled out of bed. Arvil thought it was
adorable, but he was smart enough to stifle a grin.

Sarry's son, who'd introduced himself as Samal when
he came to stir up the fire, bade Embry good morning
and set about making more toasted cheese.

Embry walked over to stand by Arvil, who stood up
and gave a wide-eyed Gilly a smile. "Good morning," he
said. "Did you sleep well?"

Gilly blinked at him, then buried her face in her uncle's shoulder.

Embry rubbed her back and said, "This is your Uncle
Arvil."

She peeped up at Arvil with one eye, then hid her face
again.

"You don't remember me," said Arvil. "But I saw you
once before. You were just a tiny baby. You've grown
into a big girl since then."

She gave him another suspicious look, then yawned
and looked up at Embry. "Cheese?"

"Yes, we're having cheese for breakfast," said Embry.
"And bread. And maybe some milk?" He looked at Samal, who nodded.

"Good." Embry sat down next to Arvil with Gilly on
his lap. Arvil leaned into him, shoulder to shoulder, and
Embry leaned back, then leaned farther and stole a kiss.

"Missed you last night," he whispered.

"Same," murmured Arvil.

"I'm sorry." Embry looked down and bounced Gilly

in his lap. "I know this isn't how you meant to spend your off-Circuit time."

"No, it's not," Arvil admitted. "But family comes first. I'm just glad I was home to come with you, that you didn't have to come by yourself."

"I'm glad too."

Samal came over with Embry's trencher of bread and cheese, with a bit extra for Gilly, plus a mug of tea and a mug of milk. Arvil was nearly done with his own breakfast, so he watched Embry supervising Gilly, making sure at least part of her breakfast ended up in her mouth rather than slopped down the front of her dress.

What now? Gilly seemed attached to Embry, which was good. Embry'd come visiting without Arvil a time or two, so she knew him, if not well. He was somewhat familiar, though, and he looked a lot like his brother Corden, so she'd have that to hang on to when they left. They should probably give her another day or two to become accustomed, though, before whisking her away.

Whisking her away reminded him of his conversation with Hobbert and Eldric the night before, so he asked, "Embry? Did a young man from the village here, a Mort, visit you in Haven? About two years ago? Or any time since then?"

"Mort?" Embry looked up for a moment. "Eldric's son? No, I haven't seen him. I didn't know he was coming to Haven."

"His father said he wanted to join the Guards. He meant to contact you, get a leg up. They haven't heard from him or the young woman who went with him."

"That'd be Bayla?"

Arvil nodded.

"Aye, they've been sweet on each other since they were children. Huh. I wish I could say I'd seen them, but I haven't. After so long...." He frowned and stared off into space.

"Exactly." Arvil sighed and finished his tea. "When we get back, I'll see if he ever enlisted. If they ran into bandits or some such, though, I'm afraid we'll likely never know what happened, not after all this time."

Embry shook his head. "I need some good news right now." He tore off a piece of cheesy bread and held it up for Gilly. "In your mouth, Princess, not on your dress."

Arvil didn't have any to give him, which felt like a failure on his part, even though he knew that was unreasonable. He clapped his husband on the shoulder and stood. He took his trencher and mug to the scullery, then went to the stable to wash and dress and tend to Graya.

He cleaned out the two stalls—which were just spaces bounded by strung ropes—and brought their breakfast, adding a scoop of oats to each flake of hay. While working, he told Graya about Mort and Bayla.

"It's too bad they didn't raise the alarm sooner," he said. "But then, they didn't know anything was wrong until too much time had already passed."

Graya nodded while munching her hay.

"Something's bothering me about the fire, but I can't put my finger on it." He flopped down next to her and looked up into her big blue eyes. "By the time anyone knew, it'd consumed enough of the building that the ceiling was caving in. That's very fast. I know fires can spread quickly, especially with a thatch roof, but still . . ."

He stared out into the morning chill. The back door of the tavern gave onto the stable yard. To the left was another building, a bakery. The lane between them was too narrow for him to be able to see the road from where he sat, but he could hear folk walking along, calling good morning to one another. To the right, in the gaps between Graya's legs, he could see the hard-packed dirt of the yard, then the road. A small river ran by the village, and the road passed over a bridge. Elm trees grew thick along the river, before giving way to the wheat fields he and Embry had ridden past the previous day.

Birds calling, butterflies fluttering, and the scent of baking bread in the cool air all made it feel like morning.

The lean-to stable was open on three sides, and he could see canvas through the gaps in the boards of the roof. It might actually be watertight, although he was glad not to have to worry about that, in midsummer. There was a decent supply of hay, but if they hadn't brought their own oats, Graya's diet would've been rather boring for a while.

On one of the posts that supported the lean-to's roof there was a spike meant for a candle. Arvil could care for Graya blindfolded, but not all travelers were so skilled.

Wait, the candle . . .

"Why was everyone so sure the fire caught from the hearth?" he wondered.

Graya snorted and cocked her head at him.

"That's what they said. Meg said she takes extra care to bank her fire now. And Sarry was especially careful with the fire last night. How did they know it was the fireplace?"

Graya cocked her head in the other direction.

Arvil nodded and rose. "I'll ask. Maybe they were just assuming. But if not, who would've known about the fireplace?"

He went back into the inn to find Sarry, who was in the back room cooking hops for a batch of beer. He asked her, and she turned to frown at him.

"Why, I don't know. 'Tis just what everyone says. A coal popped out of the hearth and started the fire."

"How would anyone know?"

"I suppose they wouldn't, would they? Someone must've just assumed."

"I suppose," Arvil echoed. "Thank you. I was just curious."

He left her to her brewing and went to find Meg, who was working in the vegetable patch behind her house. She said the same, that she'd just heard it from someone, but didn't remember who'd said it first.

"Just a guess, then," she said. "It seems likely."

"But it could've been a lamp overturned, or a candle too close to the bedclothes?"

"Could've been, I suppose." She shrugged and looked away. "I don't like thinking about it. We only just kept the fire from spreading here. It makes me shudder to imagine it."

Arvil apologized and took his leave, but he didn't go far. The charred ruin of Corden's house lay a few steps

away. The side of Meg's house was scorched black, and
the earth between them rutted up from being soaked
and then trodden by dozens of feet before drying. The
smell of burned wood hung in the air even now, more
than ten days after the fire.

Arvil circled the ruins, scanning the charred beams
and cracked tiles. A huge oven squatted in the center of
the wreckage—Corden's kiln. Made of thick firebrick, it
wouldn't burn, of course.

Before he could go inside to investigate further, he
heard Embry calling him from the road.

He jogged around to the front of the ruins and found
Embry, holding Gilly, who had her face buried once
more in his shoulder.

"Gilly wants some clay to play with. We were going
to walk to the river and dig some for her. Would you
like to come?" He then lowered his voice, "She needs
to get to know you. Come with us?"

Arvil looked over his shoulder at the burned-out
building, then nodded and fell into step beside Embry.
The ruins weren't going anywhere, and Embry was
right—Gilly needed to get to know him.

"You know where Corden dug his clay?"

Embry nodded. "I helped him haul it back to the shop
a time or two."

"Good," said Arvil. "It's a fine morning for a walk."

They strolled out of the village toward the river,
pointing out trees and flowers to Gilly.

"Listen to the bird singing," said Arvil. He pointed to
a blue and brown bird perched on an elm branch to one
side of the path. "Do you know what kind of bird that is,
Gilly?"

She craned her neck, staring, then said, "Swooper bird!"

"Really?" said Arvil. "I didn't know that."

"Everbody knows!"

"I don't live here," said Arvil. "The birds are different
where I live. So are the flowers."

"Nuh-uh!"

"They are too," he said with a laugh. "We'll show you
when we get there."

She turned away and waved a hand toward the river. "Wanna dig."

"We will, Princess," said Embry. "Almost there." He picked his way down the bank and along a narrow track, careful of his balance while carrying Gilly.

"Not *here!*" she said, her little voice dripping scorn. "No clay here. Da said. Used it all up. He digged *there!*" She pointed farther upstream, leaning as far as she could out of Embry's grasp and waving both hands.

"Whoa, look out!" Embry laughed and shifted his grip on her. "All right, show us. We'll follow you." He put her down, and she dashed off, bare feet nimble on the muddy, pebbly riverbank, both men striding after her.

She led them through thickets and around boulders for a good half-candlemark to another gentle but long curve in the river, where a wide stretch of bank was exposed. There were signs of digging, a shallow trench in the bank revealing fine red clay.

Gilly was already on her knees, digging in with a stick. Arvil looked at Embry, who smiled and shrugged.

"Might as well let her," Embry said. "She's already as muddy as a little pig. She'll need a good wash no matter what, so no harm letting her have fun."

Arvil read what Embry didn't say, that the child had had little enough fun recently.

Gilly dug a blob of clay bigger than her two fists, then sat down right on the wet ground to squeeze and knead it. At her urging, Arvil and Embry dug out clay for themselves too, and they all settled in for a morning of making clay bowls, and getting incredibly dirty. Arvil had never worked clay before, and his bowl turned out laughably lopsided, but it was fun, and it made Gilly smile at him.

Well, all right, she was laughing at him, but that was a good beginning.

After washing up as best they could in the gentle river, they went back to the tavern to have some dinner. Some few of the villagers came for the same purpose, mainly younger folk who took the opportunity to get away from their families for a bit and chat among themselves.

Gilly was getting cranky, so as soon as she'd eaten her bread and drunk her milk, Embry took her upstairs for a nap. Arvil settled down to chat with some of the younger people and find out what they knew about Mort and Bayla.

As Embry had said, Bayla'd been sweet on Mort for years, and everyone knew it. Mort had been sweet on Bayla since she'd grown into a woman, which was perhaps not quite so long, but his affections, once attached, hadn't wavered.

"Were any of you particular friends with them?" he asked. "Secret-sharing friends? Maybe Mort wasn't off to the Guards after all. If they'd actually had something else planned, who'd know?"

The young folks looked at each other and shrugged. "I were Bayla's best friend," said a young woman named Annik. "She told me he were going to the Guards and that she meant to wait for him. He wanted to earn some money first, then marry her when he came home on leave some time. That's what she said, then she was up and gone. Whatever they were up to, they didn't tell nobody."

A young man who claimed to be Mort's best friend said the same.

"They weren't close to anyone else? You're sure?"

Annik and two other girls looked at each other and giggled. "Well," said Annik. "There's Danil, o'course. He was sweet on Bayla, swore he were her soulmate, like. Tried to woo her to him. He were kinda stupid over her, aye?"

"But she rejected him?" Arvil asked.

"She weren't mean about it," said Annik. "But, aye, it were always Mort for Bayla, and she never made no secret of it."

"So she wouldn't have told Danil about any secret plans, then."

The whole group laughed at that and shook their heads.

"Well, if you think of anything else, come find me?"

They all agreed, then turned back to their food and their chatter.

Arvil took Graya with him when he went back to the burned-out house. "Maybe you'll see something I miss," he said. "Or smell something." She tossed her head in a nod and followed him up the road, her hooves ringing on the rocklike dirt.

"I remember the shop," he said. "The floor was laid with tiles, not boards. There weren't even any rugs." Stepping carefully through the mess, sure enough he found no charred floorboards. The only blackened wood had been timbers and furniture. And he seemed to remember . . .

He walked around the kiln, and there it was. A smaller opening on the opposite side to the larger one, where the pottery went. "There," he said. "There's a smaller oven here on the other side of the kiln. That's where Nilly cooked and baked, in the back room. The chimney's fallen, but it went up to the second floor and heated the bedrooms in the winter. Very thrifty. And very safe. There was only one fire, here in the kiln, with tile all around it—nothing to catch."

Graya reared up and propped her forefeet on a fallen timber to get a good look. She wouldn't try navigating the uneven tumble inside the building unless she had to, he knew, but she looked in from various angles.

"It wasn't a hearth fire because there was no hearth, not like the other houses have. So perhaps it was an overturned lamp or a carelessly placed candle after all?"

Graya kept circling the building, looking and snuffling. When she reached the back of the building, she whinnied and stamped.

"What is it?" Arvil made his way over to where she stood, kicking against the remains of the back door. "What are you looking at?" he asked, wishing for the thousandth time the Lady had blessed him with Mindspeech.

Graya tapped her hoof along a curving band of darker

wood in the door, then pointed with her nose at a similar band running up one of the still-standing timbers.

Arvil frowned at the markings for a moment before it hit him. Oil.

His trainer, Herald Jinnia, had shown him markings just like that in a fire they'd investigated. A merchant had found himself deep in debt and burned his own house down, hoping for sympathy and to have his debts forgiven in light of the tragic "accident."

Someone had deliberately set Corden's house on fire.

Well, of course they had. That was what he'd been thinking all along, wasn't it? Even if he hadn't thought it in so many words. Someone had doused the house—the back of the house, hidden from the street—with oil, then set it afire. With the timbers soaked with oil, the fire would've spread quickly and hot, which was exactly what'd happened.

But why? No one had mentioned Corden or Nilly having any enemies. Why would anyone want to kill them? Hate them enough to try to murder the whole family?

Then he thought of where he'd heard Danil's name before that afternoon, and everything slotted into place.

Arvil gathered a half-dozen men with shovels and went back to the riverbank to dig, while Embry stayed behind with Gilly. It was nearly sunset before they found the bodies of Mort and Bayla.

The grim men and weeping women of the two families saw to bringing the bodies up and arranging for a more respectful burial, while Arvil and Graya took six men to find Danil Farmer. With two men holding him and under a Truth Spell, Danil eventually admitted to the murders.

"He didn't deserve her," Danil spat. "A Guard? What kind of husband would he make, never two coins to rub together? I have a good farm, a house, I'd have taken care of her, of our children. He turned her head, made her foolish."

"You murdered him *for her*?" Arvil wanted to be

shocked, but he'd heard too many similar self-righteous justifications.

"Yes! But she came looking for him, they were supposed to meet, I didn't know ... She started screaming, and I had to quiet her." Danil finally broke down and sobbed. "I didn't want to kill her. I had to. I buried them by the river, and everyone thought they'd run off together. Everything was fine until Corden started digging there. I couldn't let him find the bodies, so ..." He shook his head and looked down. "I'm glad Gilly is alive."

Arvil left the village men to do what they did with murderers and went back to the village to find Embry.

Four days later, Arvil, Embry, and Gilly stood over two fresh graves. They all had bunches of flowers, and Gilly divided them up carefully between her mam and her da.

Arvil was pretty sure she didn't understand that her parents' bodies were buried there, but when she was older, she'd remember laying flowers and would maybe take some comfort in it.

"So much death, and for love," murmured Embry as they watched Gilly switch flowers around in some arrangement that made sense only to her. "Such horrible things done because he wanted to make a family with her."

"He never loved her," said Arvil, his voice just as low. He slid an arm around Embry's waist and hugged him close. "He wanted her. She wasn't a person to him, not really. She was just a thing he wanted to have, like a fine coat or silver bowl. He didn't care what she wanted, what would make *her* happy."

"I don't know how you stand it, being around people like that all the time."

"It's not always like this. But, yes, it can be hard. I think of the people I'm helping, I do it for them."

"For Gilly," said Embry. "And for me. We have justice, and I suppose that's something. It doesn't feel like much, though."

"No. But it's the best we can do right now." Arvil turned and pulled Embry full into his arms. "Let's go home. We're Gilly's family now. We'll love her and take care of her. And we'll make sure she remembers her parents."

Arvil felt a little arm go around his leg, and Gilly cried, "Hugs!"

Embry gave a watery laugh and picked her up. They all three of them hugged for a few minutes, standing there by the two graves, then they turned away and started for home.

Bootknife
Stephanie Shaver

The Ferryman's House hadn't changed much, and neither had its primary inhabitant. Both were a little grayer, a little weathered; his face had more lines, and the roof had a few loose shingles. But both persevered, so intrinsically a part of Cortsberth that the town couldn't exist without them.

"Papa," Herald Wil said to the old ferryman.

"Wil," Langfirch said. He craned his head to look at the small figure riding pillion behind the Herald. "Ivy, yes?"

The child peeked out, waving shyly.

Langfirch then nodded at Carris, who rode the other Companion accompanying Wil. "This my grandchild, too?"

Wil squinted. Silver laced Carris's faded red hair and her face carried its fair share of crow's feet. No one would mistake her for a youth.

Did he just tell a joke? he thought.

:I think . . . yes?: His Companion, Vehs, seemed equally astonished.

"This is Carris," Wil said. "She's a Master Bard under arrest for high treason."

Langfirch scratched his cheek slowly, clearly thinking over an array of responses.

"I have questions," he said at last. "Many questions."

"I have answers," Wil replied.

"And I need to pee," Carris said.

"When I was a little-little little, I liked snails," Ivy said.

:I feel like I should interject something, too,: Vehs said.

"Snails you still like?" Langfirch asked his grand-daughter.

"They're okay," she said, looking everywhere but at him.

"My garden, would like to see? Many snails. All you can have."

"Yee!" Ivy hopped off Vehs faster than Wil had ever seen her. "Oh! I need a jar!"

"Help with that I can, too." Langfirch put his hand out to her but kept eye contact with Wil. "Where outhouse is, you know."

"Yes, sir." Wil dismounted. "C'mon, Carris."

"Yee," the Bard said dryly.

"Meet in house when done," Langfirch said. "And then, answers."

"Answers," Wil agreed. *But for your sake, not all of them.*

"So ... a Karsite."

Carris said it with just the faintest hint of disdain, but Wil knew better. Bereft of her physical weapons, the Bard had turned to the ones her Circle had trained her on. Insinuation, intonation, *words*.

"Is he from the brigand or the bad weather side of the country?" she asked.

"Says the traitorous murderer with a bladder the size of a teacup." He gave the privy door a meaningful look.

Her mouth twisted. "Now I must wonder how far the apple fell from the tree, or if it fell on Valdemaran soil at all."

"Some of our finest weren't born here. Have you *met* Alberich?"

She rolled her eyes. "Typical Herald nonsense," she half-muttered.

"Do you think you've figured something out, Carris?" Wil asked, steering the conversation toward broader waters. "Does it matter where I was born, or what color my mother's hair was?"

"With Selenay selling our country out to other countries, I'd say yes, resoundingly. A foreign Weaponsmaster. A foreign Herald Captain. Not one, but *two* foreign spouses, one of who plotted against her. And let's not forget about Elspeth's disaster of a betrothal."

"That's just a fraction of the Heraldic Circle you've named, and the Council is almost entirely Valdemar-born. You're a *Bard;* you *know* royalty marries into foreign families all the time. It's politics."

"Selenay's incompetence is staggering, and the only reason you defend her is because there was a Companion stupid enough to Choose her and that little traitor-born brat of hers."

Words, Wil reminded himself. *They're all she has left.*

"You can call me traitor if it helps you sleep at night," she said. "I know who the true Valdemarans are."

Wil pointed to the outhouse. "Pretty sure my father built this on Valdemar's soil." He tapped his feet against the scrubby grass. "In fact, I know the caves under this Valdemaran earth better than you ever will. Which ones go down to the river, which ones drop you down a hole where you'll scream in the dark until death comes."

"Is that a threat?"

He sighed. "Everything's a threat to you, Carris. Right now I just want to keep you from wetting my father's guest bed." He pointed to the outhouse. "Please."

She obliged, leaving him staring at the tree line.

Something flickered in his belly. A little tremor that some people would call gut instinct but that Wil knew to be his Gift.

:We're being watched,: he thought to his Companion. *:Is it—:*

:Yes. They just arrived.:

:Good.:

When Carris reemerged, he bound her wrists and threw a light Truth Spell on her. "Did you do anything in there to attempt escape?"

She glared at him. "No." The glow over her head said she didn't lie.

He pointed to the house. "Let's go."

*   *   *

Wil herded his captive into the one spare bedroom. She sat down on the bed as he crossed to the room's one window. Aubryn, the Companion that wasn't Wil's, had already taken up guard duty outside.

"You know," he said, "if you'd just tell me where Lord Dark's stashing his weapons—"

Carris let out a shriek of laughter, cutting him off. He'd brought this up multiple times in their three weeks together. He kept hoping her answer would change, but—

"That's the only bargaining chip I've got, Herald," she said. "And so far, you haven't given me a good reason to give it up."

"Atonement."

She snorted. "I have nothing to atone for."

"Ferrin's dead because of you."

"Ferrin, the vacuous fopdoodle missed by precisely no one?"

"Murder is still murder."

Aubryn turned her head in their direction. *And if you think Lord Dark is going to reward your loyalty, you're mistaken,:* she said. From the surprise on Carris's face, Wil knew the message hadn't just been for him.

"Yes, well," Carris said. "There are worse things than death. If I keep my mouth shut, he may make mine swift."

"And too bad if my family might be collateral damage," Wil said, half-growling.

"That's on you, Herald," Carris shot back. Then she rolled over, turning her back.

:Thanks for trying,: Wil thought.

:It's a lost cause,: Aubryn said, with her usual brick-to-the-head bluntness. *:Give her to the Mindspeakers and Mindhealers. They'll get a confession.:*

:I'm trying.:

The building the locals called the Ferryman's House had started as a one-room, dirt-floor hovel but had been built up and out over the years. First a separate room for sleeping in, then one for storage, then another. The original room was still the largest, with a hearth and a hatch leading down into the basement and cave passages below, one of which let out by the river and the ferry landing. The whole structure hid within a small forest, so only the locals knew about it. The house and its ferryman's role had been passed down in one family since before the Last Herald-Mage.

Until fifty years ago, when the childless ferryman had taken in a Karsite refugee and her son, Langfirch.

Wish they'd worked a little more on his language skills, Wil thought as he took a seat at the big trestle table.

"Where's Ivy?" Wil asked.

"Collecting snails under your Demon-horse's watchful eye," his father replied in Karsite. "I suppose she doesn't speak the mother tongue."

"*Your* mother," Wil said, obliging his father by switching to the language he was more comfortable with, and ignoring the jab at Vehs. "*My* mother was born in Cortsberth, thank you very much. And neither of that girl's parents ever lived in Karse."

The old man grunted. "Lucky them." He lifted a brow and inclined his head toward the hatch leading down to the basement. "Wouldn't the cellar be a better place for the criminal?"

"I have other plans for that. Speaking of which, I don't suppose you have anything in the pantry for us?"

"In fact I do. Eggs and cheese, some bread and butter. And handpies from Addy."

Wil drew a small quarrel from a pouch hanging around his neck, then rolled it around on the tabletop.

"What I'm about to do is massively unfair to you," Wil said, "but I'm running short on options, and this is the only safe place I could think of."

Langfirch shrugged. "It's the job of parents to protect their children."

"The very short version of the tale is that she's a Bard who's turned against the Crown and is in collusion with someone trying to start a civil war. I should have taken her to Haven by now to be formally charged and questioned."

Langfirch raised his brow. "But instead?"

Wil hesitated. Not many knew about the assassination attempt on Elspeth, and he wasn't sure his father should, either.

"We got . . . diverted," he said. "An incident in Haven. It gave her accomplices time to send assassins. They've been following us for a few days now."

"How many?"

"Not sure. At least three tried to ambush us at a Way-station on the way here." *And thank the gods for Gifts, or they'd have caught us, too.*

"You say the woman is a traitor and a Bard, but I see you have *two* Demon-horses." Langfirch lifted his brows. "Is your daughter to be a Demon-Rider?"

Wil grimaced. The Karsite words that revolved around Heralds weren't particularly kind—there wasn't even a word for Herald—and hearing them come out of his father's mouth after the conversation with Carris about foreigners. . . .

But then Langfirch grinned, lips splitting to show hard, white teeth. "I jest, *liebshahn*." The Karsite word for "beloved son" didn't slip out of his father's mouth often. That jarred Wil almost as much as the Demon-Rider epithet.

"Aubryn is . . . she's kind of a nanny," Wil said and braced himself for—

:I am not *a nanny,:* Aubryn interjected with sour-apple annoyance.

:Yeah, Chosen. She's really more of an eavesdropper,: Vehs said.

:All Companions *are busybodies,:* Wil replied. *:And do you both mind? I'm trying to have a conversation here.:*

"That's how I managed to convince everyone that I wasn't completely insane for wanting to take a child on Circuit with me," Wil continued, focusing back on his father. "Aubryn watches Ivy when I can't."

"She could . . . stay with family."

A small blurt of strained laughter escaped Wil's lips before he could strangle it into submission. "Papa, you hate kids."

The old man shrugged. "Other people's kids, yes. This one is. . . ."

"Safest with me. Companions are good at keeping people alive."

His shoulders tightened as the words dropped out of his mouth. The wrong words, and if this were twenty years ago, with his sister Daryann's death still fresh in their hearts—or even ten years ago—he had no doubt Langfirch would have torn into him.

Wil struggled to overcome the misstep. "We—you and I—we haven't always—"

"Gaaah." Langfirch waved his hand. "Stop with the touchy-feely sentimental crap." He got up. "So. What next?"

"I want to do some exploration. The Companions did some scouting to make sure no one followed us, but I'll feel better if I take a check, too." That was mostly true, but it sidestepped his real reason for wanting to go off alone into the woods. "Can you watch Ivy?"

"Watch my only grandchild decimate the entire snail population of Cortsberth? Hm." He grinned. "Such a burden."

:Is it me, or has the old man softened?: Vehs asked.

:Downright cordial,: Wil replied as he quit the house and crossed the broad swath of green toward the forest ringing his father's home. *:For him.:*

Wil had grown up hunting these woods, following game trails that led seemingly nowhere and everywhere, or exploring the caves that pocked the hillside.

I think I liked walking in the woods better when I didn't have a Gift constantly reminding me that I'm being stalked, he thought. And, yes, there it was, twisting in his gut, that little alarm of unseen surveillance.

He saw a flash of white, and a Companion—not Vehs or Aubryn—trotted into view. The stallion dipped his head and danced playfully in place before gliding deeper into the green gloaming.

Follow me, he seemed to say, and Wil did.

They came to a clearing, where a figure shrouded in a

patchwork of earth-toned cloth sat on a fallen log. The
Companion ambled up to the log, and the stranger patted his neck before looking at Wil and saying, "Have you
ever heard of the blue-heart butterfly?"

"Hello to you, too," Wil replied.

The Herald wore a mantle with a deep hood and a
scarf wound around the lower half of his (her?) face. The
muffled voice didn't convey gender definitively. "It's very
beautiful," the voice went on, as if Wil hadn't spoken.
"And rare. Doesn't show up around here. The Herald I
trained with told me the story of it once. Last we spoke,
he had hoped to capture one. Not sure if he ever did,
though."

Wil knew from experience that this Herald indulged
in rambling non sequiturs. This one seemed to be over.

"So . . . here we are," Wil said. "We were followed,
right? The farmer on the road?" He saw the person in
question again in his memory—a squat man in home-
spun, with a flat nose and a wagon full of clay jars.

"Good eye. You sure you're not the Herald-Spy?"

"All the spying I ever wanted in my life fell to Lelia,"
Wil said. "It doesn't suit me."

The Companion issued a wistful sigh, and the Herald-
Spy patted his neck affectionately. "My Companion says
Lelia always brought the best apples to the Field."

Wil swallowed around a sudden knot in his throat.
"For a Bard, she did all right."

"The Companions adored her." The Herald-Spy's
Companion nodded, agreeing. "On to more cheery
subjects—yes, the so-called 'farmer' turned about the
moment you were around the bend."

"Really hoped we'd lost them."

"Irrational. You're a Herald traveling on the main
roads with a child and a prisoner."

And you cannot hope to travel off *the main roads
when transporting a prisoner and a child. Not at enough
speed to escape pursuers.* Wil had thought their options
through before deciding to stay on the road: Outpacing
their pursuers was more important than obfuscating
their journey. Not to mention the risks of moving

through unknown territory—flash floods, drop offs, beasts of the Pelagiris. . . .

"I've traced them to a large cave outside town," the Herald continued. "Six so far. They keep sending people to buy handpies at the village inn."

"Be careful watching them. I don't want my bootknife getting caught."

A chuckle. "Bootknife? I like that. And while we're handing out monikers—don't worry about me, Herald-Dad. I'm nowhere near them when watching. I'm probably safer than you for now. They don't know about me. Yet."

No one knows about you, friend, Wil thought. *Though I just figured out you must have Farsight.*

"What's next?" asked Bootknife—it was as good a label for his anonymous assistant as any.

"Preferably Haven." Wil rubbed his forehead, trying in vain to massage away a blooming headache.

"We can't go back to Haven yet."

"We could try cutting through the forest. I know this region. If Ivy stays tucked up against me, and with you keeping an eye out. . . ."

"Or we hole up here, call for help, and hope they don't find you in the meantime. There's a garrison a day from here as the Companion rides."

Wil shook his head. "Trusting a garrison is why Carris is my prisoner and not Ferrin," he said. "Give me to-night."

"Risky."

"I don't want to rush a decision."

Bootknife sighed. "Fine. I'll be back in the morning."

"We'll be here," Wil said, turning back to the house.

Langfirch squinted at Ivy, then at Wil. "Does she chew?"

Chew? I'm not sure she breathes, Wil thought as he watched her turn on the sourstalk pie, mouth and hands covered in buttery crumbs and alternating smears of brown gravy and golden custard. Not that he blamed her. Addy made amazing pies.

"I can see you've invested many candlemarks in

teaching her manners," his father added, lapsing back into Karsite. Ivy didn't seem to care.

"You know, I didn't *have* to pay you for these," Wil reminded him.

"But you did. Because I raised you right." Langfirch took a big bite of his own custard handpie, looking pleased.

Wil picked up a spare chicken pie, leaving the last two apple ones on the table. He'd give Carris dinner but no dessert. Traitors didn't get dessert.

He found her stretched out on the bed, hands bound in front of her, eyes closed. He'd cleared the room of anything useful before putting her in here—that meant no pottery she could break into sharp pieces, no mirrors, nothing metal.

"A cup of wine or beer would be nice," she said as he set dinner down on a dresser.

"My father doesn't drink, sorry."

"Of course he doesn't." Her eyes opened. "Karsites outlawed happiness centuries ago."

Not for the first time he found himself reminded of Ivy's mother, the Bard Lelia. Carris had some of the qualities he'd loved in Lelia—offbeat humor, direct wit—but held up to a mirror, in shadow. Lelia had held on to her youthful hope and optimism even when her own body turned against her; Carris had abandoned it without a fight. He wondered sometimes what the gods were thinking, whisking someone like Lelia to the Bright Havens and letting Carris live.

"He's the ferryman," Wil said. "People come through at all times, and being drunk on the job isn't good for business."

As Wil rejoined his family, he glanced up at the bell hanging from the house's central rafter. Slightly larger than an adult's head, it had been hanging there since the house had been built, and it rang without need of a rope. Not unlike the Death Bell, but for a decidedly less grim reason—it rang whenever anyone needed the Cortsberth ferryman to take them across the river.

"And that's one of the reasons the Ferryman's House

stays on the hill," his father had told him once. *"Because no one knows how the damned bell works, and we're too afraid to move it."*

"Has the bell rung today?" he asked.

"This morning," Langfirch said, wiping crumbs and custard off Ivy's cheeks. "Lea and Xendar from Horn. And a stranger who I took to be a trapper. Smelled like one. Asked me if I'd seen a Herald with a child. Then he asked if I knew a Herald named Wil."

Wil's breath hissed out through his teeth.

"To be clear, I said no," Langfirch added dryly.

"Dear gods."

"That's when I figured to expect you soon." Langfirch spread his hands. "And here you are."

"You *were* awfully calm when we rode up," Wil said. "I just assumed you had manifested Foresight in the last ten years."

"Not me. Just an old ferryman. I blame your mother for all that." Langfirch grinned, then switched to Valdemaran and looked at Ivy, fussing over something in her lap by the hearth. "Ho, little. You two sleep tonight in big bed made by grandpapa, yes?"

"Papa—" Wil said.

Langfirch flailed his hands at him. "Shush, you. Don't question gift."

Ivy lifted the toy in her lap, a yarn-haired cloth dolly wearing a yellow dress adorned with embroidered flowers and suns. "My poppet wants a pie."

"Did you give that to her?" Wil asked his father.

Langfirch shrugged. "Eh."

"Did you *make* that?"

"Ehhhh." He turned to his granddaughter, avoiding Wil's astonished look. "Pie your poppet wants, hmm?"

Ivy nodded.

"Is you who wants the pie, I think!"

She grinned.

"Get crumbs all over my big, beautiful bed!" Langfirch said, shaking his fist in mock rage, eliciting a full belly laugh from Ivy.

"And then what would Vehs and Aubryn eat?" Wil

asked, ruffling her hair. "I think they deserve a treat, don't you?"

"Ooh! Can I help?" she asked.

"Of course."

The Companions greedily gobbled their handpies, gave Ivy snuffling kisses, and then went back to their guard duty while Wil escorted her to her grandfather's bedroom.

The bed dominating the middle of the room was as tall and sturdy as he remembered. The old man had hand carved it decades ago as a wedding gift for his bride. Curling flowers and vines adorned the sheets and blankets, also his father's handiwork. Wil couldn't remember if his mother had had a knack for needlework; his memories of her all revolved around a woman who made berry jams and iced buns, a woman who had sung to him every night before bed. The first important person he'd lost.

Stacks of Wil's letters sat on the bedside table. Wil wondered if his father read them before sleep. He traced the bedframe's swirling lines while thinking of his father bent over the wood, laboring to finish in time for the wedding. He knew now that Vkandis hid amidst the lines—as a child, he'd simply thought the faces fanciful.

Langfirch and Elain had had eight years together. The bed's size and intricacy suggested Langfirch had expected more time with her than that.

Physical objects kept a memory that his Gift allowed him to witness. If he wanted, he could reach out and maybe see the moment his father had given the bed to his mother . . . but no. He felt the weariness of the journey in his bones; he didn't need to compound that by extending his Gift.

Ivy fell asleep with ease—full belly and lots of exertion equaled sleepy child. But he couldn't sleep, not yet.

He found Langfirch sitting by the fire, a bit of cloth and needle in his hands.

"Need more blankets?" the old man asked, not looking up from his work.

"We're plenty cozy. Papa. . . ."

His father looked up then. "Hm?"

Wil stood silently, feeling awkward and oddly embarrassed. "It's hard raising children alone."

Langfirch grunted. "Try doing it with two."

"Yeah." He took the chair next to his father, watching as the needle slid silently in and out of the crisp cloth, a spray of white flowers growing with each stroke.

"At least you have the nanny Demon-horse," Langfirch said.

Wil burst out laughing, slapping his hand over his mouth to keep from waking up Ivy.

"Only Demon-horses I got took them away completely," Langfirch went on. "Raising children is hard, yes. Losing them?" He glanced up at Wil. "No parent should outlive their child."

Wil swallowed around a knot in his throat. "Papa—"

Langfirch made a shooing motion. "Go to bed," his father said. "Sleep. You need it more than me."

"Wish I could." Wil went over and pulled the cellar hatch open. The firelight illuminated only the first two steps down, the rest lost to a yawning darkness. He retrieved a lantern from a hook by the fire and lit it with an ember.

"Going for another stroll?" Langfirch asked.

"Keep an eye on things," Wil replied, descending into the cellar.

"Which first? Good news or bad news?" Bootknife asked as Wil approached, the nameless Companion once again acting as escort. Wil had decided to name him Sashay, to compliment the Companion's light, dancing step.

"There's good news?" Wil asked.

"They still don't know where you are, and they're getting frustrated that they haven't figured it out yet."

Wil nodded. "That *is* good."

"More good news. Addy made wagonwheels with cinnamon today."

Wil sighed wistfully. He'd grown up on wagonwheels, delicate dough swirls basted in honey as they cooked. They emerged from the oven a burnished gold, sticky, chewy, and buttery all at once. "I always liked the anise ones."

"Blech."

"It's an acquired taste."

"Cinnamon is superior."

"You must be from Haven."

"Oh, I might be. Never stop trying to figure out who I am, Herald-Dad. It amuses me."

Wil allowed himself to smile a little. "I've only been trying, what—three weeks, now?"

Bootknife took a deep breath. "And now the bad news. They're confident that you're in the area and that they're going to find you. They have watchers on the road. They're well over six now."

"They also may be armed with those weapons of Madra's."

"Uh-huh. Something funny about their leader, too. Lower your shields. Let me show you."

Wil eased them down and felt the brush of a mental hand. A picture unfolded in his mind: a group of men crowded around a fire by a cave, somewhere in the woods. The darkness made their bodies and faces a muddle of shadows, but none of them were Madra. He wondered which had crossed on the ferry....

The mental image had both motion and sound, playing out against his mind's eye like a hyper-real lucid dream. Its focus turned on one figure, who looked up and said, "Lord Dark speaks."

The circle of people—already silent—seemed to somehow grow even more still.

"Carris is near," the figure said, his voice taking on an odd reverberation. *"We will sever her from this world. But more importantly: the Herald. Turn his Whites red, shatter the heart that compels him. He cannot be allowed to live."*

The others shrunk back as he spoke, nodding. The speaker blinked, shook himself a little, and then looked back down, one hand on his forehead.

The vision melted away, leaving Wil wondering.

Shatter the heart that compels him. In other circumstances, the odd turn of phrase might be considered weirdly laughable, but the implication made him sick. If he had to guess, it meant Ivy.

"I think he allowed this 'Lord Dark' to speak through him," Bootknife said.

"Is that a thing?" Wil asked. *:Vehs?:*

:How would I know?: his Companion said. *:I'm not Myste. But whoever or whatever Lord Dark is, he has access to the Gifted, so—maybe?:*

"It's time to muster the Guards," Bootknife said.

"Guards aren't a guarantee of safety. We know there are Bards working for Lord Dark. Hellfires, Madra's a former Healer. She can *control* people. Not easily, but—"

"I know this is going to seem a touch ironic coming from me, Herald-Dad, but we can't go down that rabbithole."

"I—what?" he asked.

"If you start to see spies and assassins around every corner, you're going to drive yourself crazy. The temptation is to only trust Heralds, but take it from someone whose job it is to question everything—not everyone is out to get you. In fact, most people just want to mind their own business and get on with their lives."

"All right, but—it'll take the Guard at least three days to get here."

"I know. That's why I already sent my Trainee to get them." And at Wil's startled look, said, "You think Alberich only sent me?"

"Wil!"

Langfirch's voice called from the edge of the forest. Bootknife made a shooing motion and slipped off. Wil hurried back to find his father standing a few feet within the tree line, crossbow in arms.

"We've got a visitor," he said.

Margot, Addy's daughter, sat at the trestle table, face drained of color. When she saw Wil, her eyes went wide.

"You *are* here!" she said.

"Margot," he said. "It's been too long. What—"

"They hurt Ryland," she said, tears boiling up out of her eyes. "They broke his arm!"

Wil dug around in his memory. Ryland—Addy's son, Margot's brother. Always a bit of a loudmouth. Apparently it had finally gotten him more than he bargained for.

"I'll put on tea," Langfirch said.

"Who did, Margot?" Wil asked.

"Those strangers what've been asking about you. His arm, Wil!"

Wil's heart sank. "What—"

"They said we had to know where you were." She dabbed her eyes with a handkerchief. "They said they'd burn the inn down if we didn't tell them where you were hiding."

"Did one of them have a deep voice? Black hair, green eyes?" Carris asked from the doorway of her room. Wil turned to glare at her, but the Bard ignored him.

Margot nodded.

"Fent," Carris said. "The Eternal Journeyman, if you want to get him spun up." She smirked, but a moment later her mouth melted into a troubled frown. "Madra's goon. Not what you'd call a negotiator."

"So much for your loyalty," Wil said.

The Bard opened her mouth to answer, then closed it again.

:*Vehs,*: he thought. :*We have a big problem. Can you communicate this to Bootknife?*:

:*Yes . . . and your problems are bigger than you know.*:

Wil felt his stomach twist, and in that instant, he knew without his Companion needing to say it.

:*They followed Margot,*: he thought.

Fent wanted to yell, but he couldn't just yet.

They'd been careful, and now the gods had rewarded them. The locals had done what he knew they'd do—one threat, and they'd run off to the Herald, to this house hidden on a hill in the woods. The temptation to do something the moment they'd spotted the Companions hanging around the Ferryman's House had been powerful, but he'd reined it in. He'd even been generous and let the woman go back to town without intercepting her. They'd watched from the forest as she ran home. They didn't want her anyway.

So they waited, poised to do something if anyone else left the house. No one did. Sometimes the Herald would come to the front door and peer out, or the Companions would wander by, but the house stayed silent. And the more they waited, the more of his men Fent mustered. By nightfall, all of them had arrived.

The gods lavished more praise by putting clouds over the moon just for him. He would use that darkness to their advantage. The Herald had escaped them at the Waystation. He'd escaped them on the road. But he couldn't escape anymore.

Skulking wasn't Fent's thing. He had a big voice, the kind that could thunder over a battlefield. Some of his fellow Trainees had named him the War Bard, and he'd loved that so much he'd embroidered it on his handkerchiefs. That name demanded respect, and should have elevated him above the rest of the dreck.

Instead, he'd watched as the Bardic Circle promoted them all to Master, while he kept getting passed over.

They'd found a new name for him then: the Eternal Journeyman.

Well, no one shunted him to the back anymore. Lord Dark and Madra found him useful, even if the Bardic Circle didn't. They'd given him men to command and big, *important* things to do. No one asked him to write stupid songs about boring things like royal appointments or trade agreements or who married whom. His voice had a use. It had power, and someone finally recognized that.

Lord Dark certainly seemed impressed by it—that's why he borrowed it sometimes.

Not that Fent liked that much. Being Lord Dark's mouthpiece took its toll—every second *he* spoke through Fent felt like someone had swapped his blood for ice water, and he always felt a bit muzzy-headed and disjointed afterward.

But yelling helped clear it out. Fent intended to turn that Herald's bones to jelly with his voice.

Fent kept glancing at the small building where the Herald stabled his Companions. Two of his men had orders to tackle that. Madra had given them all clay flasks filled with a special oil she said could burn anything down, and certainly the demonstration she'd given them had convinced him of the weapon's potency . . . but still. Companions were tricky.

The last light in the house flickered out. They waited one more candlemark, and then he could wait no more.

"Now," Fent said. He lit the wick on his flask and closed on the house.

One flask arced through the night. It hit the door and bounced, landing on the grass, the wick still burning but the oil inside contained.

Need to throw hard, Fent thought, pulling his arm back —

He heard a hum and felt something cut across his cheek. Gault, who'd been behind him and slightly to the left, collapsed. And now that he looked around, some of them were missing — where'd Lim and Drekker go?

Someone screamed, then someone else. He froze, turning in circles to find the threat. He heard the thunder of hooves —

The clouds split off, spilling moonlight down on them. He saw the glow of blue eyes and a shining white coat and started to raise his arm, but the club speeding toward his face got there first.

"The other reason the Ferryman's House stays on the hill," Wil's father had also told him once, *"is the caves under it. No matter what the weather, the ferryman can always get to the landing, and get there fast."*

Wil's whole reason for coming here hadn't just been because he knew the land. It was because here, he had an exit. And he'd been relatively certain Fent's crew didn't know that.

His father, Carris, and Ivy hadn't been in the house since noon. Wil had used the caves to get them out, then to leave the house and come back around. He and Boot-knife had quietly disabled two of Fent's men before the assassins even launched their attack.

Now Heralds and Companions—Vehs, Aubryn, and Sashay—circled the captives. They'd killed two, an unfortunate side-effect of the skirmish, but at least Fent lived. Wil's sap had left the man with fewer teeth and a broken nose, possibly a fractured jaw. Maybe he wouldn't be able to talk right again, but he'd live.

"I'm still amazed that worked," Bootknife said.

"We caught them by surprise," Wil said, pulling a set of manacles out of Vehs's saddlebags. "Same trick that worked on Ferrin. You helped with that. Thank you."

Bootknife did a little half-bow. "You're wel—"

Fent suddenly jerked forward, gripping something that Wil hadn't seen half-buried in the high grass.

He threw—

Wil leaped forward—

The flask hurtled through the air and burst against the Companion's chest, exploding with a deafening *BOOM*! Flames engulfed the stallion.

"Shatter the heart that compels him!" Fent shrieked as Wil collapsed on top of him, punching him in the face with a fistful of manacle chain.

Fent's screams turned high-pitched and his eyes rolled into his head. Around him, Wil heard the *thud* of not one, but two bodies.

"No . . ." he said, twisting around.

Sashay had collapsed, blue eyes darkened, chest stove inward. Bootknife convulsed on the ground, handspans away from the Companion.

"No!" Wil yelled, running over to the Herald. *"No!"*

:Move aside!: Aubryn's Mindvoice compelled him like a physical force, and he danced away as she bent over the Herald, nose to face.

Wil held his breath, manacles dangling uselessly from his fists.

Aubryn looked up.

:I'm sorry,: she said. :I tried.: Her head bent down. :I tried.:

And as it always did with Wil, possessor of a Gift that served simultaneously as blessing and curse—he knew in that moment a Herald had died, without having to be anywhere near the Death Bell.

Wil sat at the trestle table, drinking tea and rolling the quarrel around. They'd buried Bootknife and Sashay and had handed the gang of assassins over to the Guards and Bootknife's Trainee. Carris hadn't been wrong about Fent. "Goon" was high praise. If he knew anything, it would take weeks of healing to get it out of him anyway.

"So then," Langfirch said. "You'll leave again soon, hm?"

"Off on another adventure," Wil said. "The faster I leave, the better." He cleared his throat. "When you said Ivy could stay with you. . . ."

Langfirch lifted his brows. "Hm?"

Wil closed his fist on the quarrel. "Nothing."

His father's gaze went over Wil's head to a point behind him. "Ho, traitor-Bard," he said. "Going for a walk, maybe?"

Carris shuffled over, then sat down next to the old man, bound hands in front of her. She didn't look either of them in the eye, instead watching the quarrel as Wil batted it about.

She licked her lips, took a hesitant breath, and said, "The cache is in a cave on the Baireschild estates. If you bring me a map, I'll mark it for you."

Wil froze. "Really?"

"I've had some days to think about it, and I've decided there's no point in being loyal to someone who'd burn down a house where they thought a child and an old man were sleeping inside." She put her fists on the table. "Besides, Androa . . . Madra . . . whatever she calls herself. She's not an idiot. She'll have moved everything by now. My information is useless." She shrugged. "And it'll probably get you killed. So I have that to look forward to."

Wil started laughing, setting his tea down as deep, convulsive belly laughs spilled out of him. She watched, bemused.

"What?" she asked.

"One moment." He went and retrieved his map along with a quill and a pot of ink. "First, mark the location."

Carris studied the map a few minutes, and then did so.

"Are you going to tell me?" she asked as Wil slid the map away, setting it closer to the fire so the ink could dry.

"Do you really think Madra would have gone to all this effort if she could easily move her cache?" he asked.

Carris opened her mouth, then closed it.

No more words, Wil thought.

At long last. He'd disarmed the Bard.

Ivy should have been asleep, but poppet was afraid of the dark.

"It's okay," she whispered to her, "I'm here."

The door opened, and her dada came in. She pretended to be asleep, throwing in a few very convincing snores for good measure.

"Why aren't you asleep?" he said, climbing into bed.

Drat, she thought. *How'd he know?* "Poppet got scared and woke me up."

Her father sighed. "Of course. I guess it's better than snails."

"The Bard-lady said the same thing."

He chuckled. "Did you talk to her while you were out on the ferry?"

"Yeah. I think she was crying. I told her it was going to be okay because you wouldn't let us get hurt. Are we leaving tomorrow?"

He didn't answer. He just kissed the top of her head.

"Go to sleep," he said. "I love you."

"I love you, too, Dada." She kissed her dolly. "Poppet says she isn't afraid now."

"I'm glad."

After a while, his breathing deepened. In the stillness, Ivy closed her eyes and concentrated.

Good night, Aubryn, she thought.

:Good night, dear one.: The Companion's voice felt
warm and sweet—like fresh wagonwheels—in her mind.

Ivy snuggled down, wrapping herself in her grandfather's blankets, and drifted into dreaming.

To Catch a Thief
Mercedes Lackey

Herald Arville perched comfortably on the sprung seat of his caravan and clucked his tongue at the two horses pulling it—the unimaginatively named "Ruddy" and "Brownie." They were, he'd been assured, excellent specimens of a breed of horse called "Zigans." The one on the right was a bay gelding with a white nose, the left was a chestnut mare with a white blaze. Both had one white foot and heavily feathered fetlocks. Both had stocky bodies, about a hand taller than the average riding horse, and both were about eight years old. Their manes and tails were shaggy and long, and their coats were too rough to ever be glossy, but they were mild tempered and willing and disinclined to be spooked by anything.

What Arville cared about was that they were old friends. He had driven and cared for them for the last twelve months as he and his three human friends— Trainees Rod, Laurel, and Alma—undertook their Journeyman year under Herald Elyn.

The four former Trainees had been absolute best friends *before* they had all been Chosen. They were all from Haven; Rod was the son of the Goldsmith Guild's Guildmaster, Alma the daughter of a highly respected Artificer, Laurel the daughter of a talented Healer at Healers' Collegium, and Arville's father was the Chief of the Watchhouse that covered the part of Haven that contained many of the most expensive mansions. He was the Chief of that Watchhouse for good reason; their family *owned* one of those mansions, and he could be counted on to be diplomatic where the feelings of the rich and highborn were concerned.

As a result of living on the sides of the Hill, once Arville, Rod, Alma, and Laurel were out of the nursery, their parents had all taken advantage of their rank or wealth to have their children educated at the Palace, at the school that gave Healer, Bard, and Herald Trainees their basic educations. They were the only four of the same age who were *not* Trainees, and while that fact alone wouldn't necessarily have meant much, somehow they'd become inseparable. No one could have been prouder of his friends than Arville on the day when three Companions turned up over the course of a single day and Chose first Alma, then Rod, then Laurel—

Although he'd gone down to the river after congratulating them to bawl his eyes out. Not because he was envious but because it meant he'd be left behind while they went on to become Heralds, their new lives taking them far away from him.

And no one was more surprised than Arville when his own Companion, Pelas, had tracked him down there and assured him that no, he wasn't about to be abandoned and, yes, he was never going to be alone again.

So he and his best friends in the entire world had been able to stick together through training. Then, instead of being broken up for their Journeyman Circuit, because the Heralds had been so short-handed for mentors, they'd all been assigned to Herald Elyn.

Arville sighed. Everything had to come to an end, of course. And once they passed their Journeyman Year ... well, there was no way they were going to all be assigned together. It was rare for *two* Heralds to take the same Circuit. Unheard of for three. Four? Well, the only time there were four Heralds together was on the battlefield.

:You're still not alone, you know,: Pelas reminded him kindly, trotting up alongside the caravan. *:You not only have me, you have Ryu.:*

As if he had sensed his name being mentioned, the *kyree,* Ryu, bounded back from where he'd been scouting ahead, causing both horses to snort. "Rall rear!" the *kyree* told him. "I round a rood ramping rot!"

Arville cheered up a little. Ryu had a knack for not only finding "good camping spots" but ones that were safe from predators, scavengers, and unexpected problems. He'd stopped counting the number of times Ryu had picked a place that was *near* water yet above the waterline in a flash flood. Or the ones where the tree they'd parked under provided shelter from a blizzard rather than coming down on top of them.

The other three were off on Circuits where they were doing things the way Heralds normally did—staying at Waystations. But there were no Waystations on Arville's Circuit; because of Ryu, he'd been given one that skirted the edge of the Pelagir Hills. These lands that had only recently elected to join Valdemar were so newly acquired that they didn't have Waystations yet. In fact, they barely had roads. So Arville had been given the sole use of the six-person traveler's caravan that Rod's father had given to the Heralds when all four of them had gone off on that Journeyman's Circuit.

Repainted, of course. Arville missed the way it used to look—sky blue painted with flowers. But he supposed it was probably just as well that it had been sanded to bare wood and was now the regulation Herald's White. Besides, white reflected heat now, in the summer, and would blend in with the snow in the winter, giving him camouflage of a sort.

"You should be really comfortable," Elyn had said as she helped him load the considerable amount of supplies he would need, given there were no Waystations. Four of the six bunks had had their mattresses removed and had been turned into storage units, holding bags of grain for the horses and Pelas and food for him. And, he supposed, he probably was going to be more comfortable than the others. The caravan had a little heavy iron stove he could cook over, which would also keep it warm in winter; he just needed to bank the fire before he started each day's journey, saving him the tedium of starting a new one every night. The caravan would not have to be cleaned or

have insects smoked out before he could use it, either—
Waystations were *supposed* to be kept in readiness for a
Herald at all times, but not every village kept that end of
their bargain very well. He already knew the roof was
sound and there were no drafts. But he would have
traded every bit of that comfort to have just *one* of the
others along.

It wasn't just, or even mostly, that he was lonely. Arville was afraid he wasn't going to be a very good Herald.

The "joke" (which Arville didn't think was all that
funny) had been that with the Gifts and other talents
each of them had, combined with their faults, the four of
them made *one* really outstanding Herald. Laurel's vari-
ant on Empathy meant that virtually everyone she met
liked her and wanted to help her. Like most Heralds,
Rod and Alma could Mindspeak only with their Companions, but they both made up for that by being logical
and practical. In Alma's case, her ability to reason to a
swift answer and her Artificer training amounted to genius. Rod was a natural leader; whenever things were
going wrong, everyone, even those who didn't know him,
looked first to him for guidance.

But Arville . . .

He sighed. *What* do *I have? I can run really, really fast.
I'm not all that smart. Nobody ever wants me to lead. I've
got Ryu, but a lot of people would mistake him for a monster. And I've got Luck as my Gift, which is nice for me but
doesn't do much for anyone else.* Now he wished Elyn had
flunked him and made him do a second year as a Journeyman. He felt woefully unprepared for all of this.

:And so do the others,: Pelas assured him. He looked
up from where he'd been glumly contemplating the rear
ends of Ruddy and Brownie. *:And they miss you.:*

Surely his own Companion wouldn't lie, would he?
"How do you know that?" he demanded. Well, not demanded. It came out a lot more plaintive than a demand.

*:Because I keep in touch with their Companions. Why
wouldn't they miss you? You're still all best friends, right?:*
Pelas tossed his head and gave Arville a sideways look.
:Distance isn't ever going to change that.:

Arville sighed again. Pelas wasn't lying to him, but Arville couldn't see how the Companion could possibly know that was true. Or it might be true now, but how long would it continue to be true?

The imagination that all too readily populated the world with ghosts, demons, and monsters was just as good at picturing how his best friends would discover how much better their lives were without him.

And as if that wasn't bad enough, tomorrow morning he was going to be pulling into his first village as a Herald on his own. He couldn't make people like him the way Laurel did. No one *ever* looked at him—in his uniform that always looked too big, even though it had been fitted exactly to his size—and saw a leader or someone they could respect. If they had some sort of problem, he'd never be able to reason his way through it the way Alma could.

If it hadn't been for Pelas trotting alongside, radiating confidence in him, he'd have turned the caravan around and gone straight back home to Haven, and ... what, then? He couldn't have Pelas if he wasn't going to be a Herald. If he wasn't good enough to sort out a tiny little village's problems, how could he expect to handle the bigger problems in Haven? And he certainly wasn't any kind of a teacher!

So there it was. All this had seemed doable back when he'd been one part of four, but now he was on his own. And there was no turning back.

:The only way out is through, Chosen,: Pelas said cheerfully.

He sighed. At least he'd be able to camp tonight in peace, make himself a good meal. Maybe break out one of those honeycomb travel cakes. By this time tomorrow, he probably would be so sick with stress he wouldn't have an appetite anyway.

The first thing that Arville heard when he approached the tiny village of Sternbridge was shouting. Angry shouting. Alarmed, he decided to pull the caravan in under the shelter of some trees beside the river that stood between him and the village, tether the horses out, and ride in on Pelas. *I'm not going to make much of an impression regardless, but I'll make less of one if they think I'm a trader and not a Herald.*

"Ryu," he said as he unhitched Brownie and Ruddy, put halters on them, hobbled them, and tethered them in the midst of a lush patch of grass. "Will you stay here and keep an eye on the horses? I don't want them wandering off *or* somebody stealing them."

In reality he didn't want anyone seeing Ryu before he had a chance to find out what was going on over there — where there was *still* angry shouting. And, depending on what he found, maybe not at all. Even though *kyrees* were native to the Pelagir Hills . . . or, at least, to the Pelagiris Forest . . . they weren't all that common, and he didn't want people to panic and think Ryu was some sort of monster.

"Rure, Rarrille!" Ryu said cheerfully and flopped down beside the horses, who were perfectly accustomed to him at this point. Arville went inside the caravan and changed out of the old working clothes he was wearing — a *very* worn set of Whites that were . . . technically white . . . and into a set of his brand-new and unworn Whites, picked up from the seamstress before he left. It wouldn't matter, of course. He would never look like a proper Herald, like Rod, say, or Laurel. But at least he'd be in Whites and not Smudgeds.

Then he got Pelas' working tack out of the storage box built into the side of the caravan and onto his Companion. This wasn't as fancy as formal tack, but it did come with bridle bells, so as the two of them cantered over the hand-hewn wooden bridge to the little cluster of houses that called itself Sternbridge, the bells rang out cheerfully, announcing their arrival.

And, apparently, just in time . . .

There was the tiniest of tiny squares in this village, really little more than a common pump and watering trough surrounded by some turf where, presumably, people set up stalls during seasonal fairs. And it was there that Arville and Pelas found the heart of the commotion:

what looked like everyone in the village either keeping custody of a young girl bound and weeping or attempting to erect what looked like the scaffold for a public hanging.

Their arrival distracted everyone enough that the girl managed to break away from her captors, stumble to them, and fling herself down practically underneath Pelas' hooves, crying, "Herald! Herald! You must save me! I have done nothing!"

A few of the bolder members of the group started to rush forward to grab her again, but Pelas reared and lashed out with his forehooves as Arville hung on, desperately trying to look as if he were as confident and imposing as Rod. The villagers backed right off when Pelas uttered a challenging scream that put the hair up on *Arville's* neck.

In fact, that alone was enough to stop all activity and babble dead and focus the attention of the entire group on Arville and Pelas.

Arville pulled himself up out of his usual slouch and set his face in a frown. "What's going on here?" he demanded, and he felt rather proud of himself when the words came out with some authority.

Unfortunately, that only unleashed the babble again. All Arville could make out from the angry shouting was that the girl was accused of being a thief and that she had stolen some valuable objects, including jewelry, silver spoons, and some unidentifiable trinkets. Within minutes, his ears rang, and he began to get a headache.

:Let them yell themselves out, Chosen,: Pelas advised, stomping a warning hoof whenever anyone ventured too near. *:Just sit there looking annoyed.:*

That wasn't hard at all, given that "annoyed" and "experiencing a splitting headache" invoked practically the same expression.

Finally, as Pelas had suggested they would, the villagers ran out of accusations to make. And faced with a Herald frowning silently at them from the back of a scary big Companion, they, too, fell silent.

"Did anyone see her take *any* of the things you claim

she did?" Arville asked, the first question to pop into his head, along with the thought that Alma would certainly have demanded to know just that.

The villagers exchanged wary looks. Finally the one who seemed to have appointed himself to be in charge of the hanging admitted, "Well, no, but—"

Arville didn't get him get any further. Now using Rod as his example, he barked, "And were your things found anywhere on her or in her possession?"

The head man was clearly taken aback. Obviously he wasn't used to being cut off by anyone. And it surprised another "Well, no, but—"

"She hid 'em somewhere!" someone else shouted, which started up another chorus of yelling. Arville waited that one out, too.

Meanwhile, he thought of another question Alma would have asked. "Didn't any of you *look* for a hiding place?" he demanded in Rod's voice. "She's just a girl! You mean to tell me she was smarter about finding a hiding place than *all* of you are?"

As he had hoped, the implication that they were a bunch of wooden-headed boobs invoked a torrent of claims that "they had looked everywhere!"

To which Arville responded, "Then you looked everywhere, looked completely and thoroughly, and found no hiding place for the stolen goods, and you didn't find them among her possessions or on her person. So what are you suggesting? That she stole them and threw them in the river or down a well? Is that's what you think? But those aren't the actions of a thief. Those are the actions of someone with something wrong in their head. And you can't hang someone for that. Not in Valdemar, you can't."

The man who seemed to think he was in charge got all red-faced at this challenge to his authority and shouted, "We aren't in—"

Pelas cut him off this time, with another trumpeting neigh, giving Arville time to think of exactly what Herald Elyn would have said to the claim that this village wasn't in Valdemar. "Oh?" he asked, slyly. "You're saying you're going back on that petition you sent the Crown to be included inside Valdemar's borders? Well, good, I'll just send a message to intercept the platoon of the Guard that was on its way here to give you that garrison of protection you were asking for. That will save us a lot of money and trouble. I'll just be on my way then." And he picked up the reins as if to head back across the river.

It wasn't only the terrified girl who wailed in protest at that—it was a good half of the villagers. In fact, they sounded downright panicked about it. Arville waited for a bit until they quieted down, then dropped his hands to the saddlebow. "Do I take that to mean you've changed your mind, and you *are* in Valdemar now?"

The man who considered himself in charge opened his mouth, closed it, opened it again, looked around at his fellow villagers, and closed it once more, this time for good.

"All right, then," Arville said into the silence. "So . . . here I am. And from everything you've told me, nobody *saw* this girl stealing anything, nobody *found* anything that she allegedly stole, and you've really got no evidence she did anything wrong. All you *do* have is a bunch of missing stuff and no idea where it went. Right?"

Mutters. Exchanged looks among the villagers, some baffled, some sullen, some exasperated, but no one denied the truth of what he had just said.

"All right, then. You untie this girl and let her go," he ordered. "This is not how we do things in Valdemar. I'm here, and I will conduct an investigation. Who lost the silver spoons?"

A cross-faced woman standing next to the man in charge raised her hand.

"All right," Arville said. "Since those are the most valuable of the missing things, I'll start with you. Now untie this girl. If you want to lock her up in a shed with some food and water and a bedroll until I'm done, that's fine. But there won't be any hanging today."

After everyone had dispersed and the girl had been locked up in a *nice* shed—one in the shade, with a bedroll, a clean pail of water, and the first food she'd had in

more than a day—Arville spoke to the woman with the
stolen spoons, who turned out to be the wife of the local
miller. They were the most prosperous couple in the village, her husband was the one that had done most of the
talking, and she had clearly egged him on to this hanging.

He wished he were a strong enough Mindspeaker to
set a Truth Spell; if he were, the problem would be
solved a lot sooner. He was just going to have to think
like Alma and Rod: be logical, walk through this mystery
step by step, and be patient. Well . . . being patient was
not something he needed to imitate. He was always patient. He was the most patient of the four of them.

"So, Dame Eller, this girl—" he began.

"Yulia," the miller's wife almost spat, as if she hated
the name right along with the girl.

"Yulia. She's your servant? For how long?" Patiently,
he extracted the story. Yulia's parents had been traders
whose caravan had been attacked by . . . something . . .
just outside the village; ten-year-old Yulia had been
found hiding in a chest inside it and was taken in by the
Ellers to be their servant. Arville found that Dame Eller
actually had no reason whatsoever to suspect the girl of
being a thief except that during her first year as their
servant, like any child, she'd snitched bits of food in the
kitchen. And that had stopped once Dame Eller had
beaten her for it.

In fact, there had been no apparent reason for Dame
Eller to be so hateful toward the girl in the first place . . .
no reason, that is, until the Ellers' eldest son, *Morten*, had
started meandering in the direction of the shed where
Yulia was being kept, and his mother called him back in
a tone of pure rage. It was easy enough to read *that* little
story, even for someone as normally dense about people
in love as Arville was.

It was Dame Eller's insistence that Yulia was a thief
that had gotten everyone *else* who'd had things go missing decide that she had taken their things as well. When
he questioned the others, they all admitted that while
there had been occasions when they had shown Yulia the
object, or she'd had occasion to see it, they hadn't seen

her anywhere nearby on the day it went missing. And once he gently pointed that out to them, they started losing their enthusiasm for a hanging. And at that point, that was his main concern; it was pretty obvious that he needed to get to the bottom of this thing, but he wasn't going to be able to keep Yulia safe *and* conduct an investigation at the same time.

By the end of the day, he had everyone but the senior Ellers in a somewhat chastened frame of mind, and some of those who hadn't lost any valuables volunteered to make sure "nobody gets hot-headed again." That was good enough for Arville, and he and Pelas went back across the river to the caravan around sunset, with enough time to fix a meal, water and feed the horses, and give Ryu a chance to go hunt for his own dinner before they settled into the caravan for the night.

He'd taken one of the bunks along the side for himself. He was tall, and the most comfortable one, across the front wall, just behind the driver's seat, was too short for him. Ryu had that one. They both settled in, and Arville blew out the lantern so bugs wouldn't be attracted inside and opened the windows so fresh air could come in before climbing up into his chosen bunk. He'd considered taking the bottom one, but on second thought, having several hundred pounds of grain above him while he slept didn't seem like a good idea.

:So what are you thinking?: Pelas asked, as he tucked his hands behind his head and closed his eyes to think better.

:I can't see how it's Yulia. There's no reason for her to steal those things. She can't use them or wear them. There's nowhere for her to sell them.:

:She could be taking them for revenge and throwing them down a well,: Pelas pointed out. *:Or this could be a conspiracy between her and Morten Eller. She* and *he could have been stealing things, planning on running away together and selling it all in another town.:*

Arville thought about that for a moment. *:Well, if they're going to run away together, Morten'll find a way to distract the guard on Yulia, they'll collect their loot, and*

*escape tonight. If he's in on it with her, he has to be getting
nervous about me sniffing around. I dunno how we'd figure out if she was throwing things down a well or into the
river, though — wait, I wonder if I could scare her into it,
making her* think *I could put a Truth Spell on her?:*

He sensed Pelas' approval. *:That can work, but if she's
innocent, as we both think, we need to consider other possibilities. So who else were you thinking might be our cul-
prit?:*

Arville had a good answer for that. *:Hoarder rat.:* He
knew from his Circuit with Elyn that the things were all
over the Pelagiris Forest, and they were master thieves.
Usually they stole food, but sometimes they stole shiny
or colorful things and hid them in their nests. *:I figured
Ryu could literally sniff around tomorrow and see if he
could smell one or more of them around where things
went missing.:*

Ryu's Mindvoice was perfectly clear, as opposed to his
speaking voice. *:Wowsers!:* he replied with enthusiasm, a
nonsense exclamation he'd picked up from Alma. *:Sure!
Great idea!:*

:Do the sniffing first,: Pelas advised. *:If Morten, Yulia,
or both are guilty, it will give them more time to get nervous. Well done, friends, we have a plan. I think we've
earned our rest.:*

He'd introduced Ryu to the villagers as his "Rethwellan
mastiff." Most of them knew a mastiff was a very big dog,
none of them had ever seen a *kyree*, and Rethwellan was
just the name of a foreign land to them, so they accepted
the name — and Ryu himself — as being what the Herald
said he was. Arville hated to lie . . . but he needed Ryu to
be able to move freely around the village and see if he
could sniff anything out.

Yulia was still where she'd been locked up last night.
Morten was still moping around, staying within sight of
the shed but out of sight of his mother. So unless they
were extraordinarily timid (in which case, how had they
been brave enough to steal anything in the first place?)
or stupid (in which case, how had they been smart

enough to steal and get away with it?), the idea that the two had been building a nest egg to run away on seemed to be a washout.

So that left Arville with his second-to-last card: sending Ryu around to every place things had been stolen from to see if he could sniff out one of the little purloining pests. They started at the site of the latest theft, figuring any scent would be fresher there. Dame Eller had just finished polishing her spoons and rinsing the polishing grit for them, laying them out on a towel in the sunlight on a table by a window to dry. Ryu went straight to the table in question, under Dame Eller's gimlet eye, and began sniffing. And sniffing. And sniffing. With a very puzzled expression on his face.

:Well?: Arville asked.

:Not a rat,: Ryu replied. *:But . . . something. Just tell her that the scents are too faint to read, and let's get out of here.:*

Dame Eller's response was a disdainful sniff, and she turned her back on them as they left the house. And the moment they did, Ryu stuck his nose high in the air and began drinking in the scents. *:Got it,:* he said after a moment. *:Let's go.:*

A candlemark later, winding in and around through the forest as Ryu followed the scent, Ryu suddenly stopped. *:It's very strong now,:* he said. *:Time to sneak. We don't want to disturb it. Slowly.:* And suiting his own actions to his words, he got down on his belly and crawled toward a thicket.

Arville followed him, moving just as sneakily. And as Ryu's nose parted the grass and he stuck his own head in just above Ryu's, he felt his eyes nearly pop out of his head.

"Now you've *got* to be really, really quiet," Arville cautioned the group of three people he'd brought along as his witnesses. "This is a dangerous situation if what we're looking at is startled. I mean that. Someone could be killed."

Dame Eller looked both impatient and momentarily

taken aback. But to her credit, she went down on hands and knees and sneaked in toward the thicket along with the others, moving as silently as only people who depend on their hunting skills to eat can do.

And finally she, along with the rest, carefully parted a few stems of the thick grass around the thicket—and Arville heard her swift intake of breath as he made his own little peephole.

There, in a space burned clear in the center of the thicket, was an arch made of the stems of very green grass. Arrayed in a pleasing pattern in front of the arch, along with bright pebbles and bits of metal scrap, was every object that had been stolen from the village.

And under the arch was a firebird, critically eyeing his handiwork and moving the objects tiny bits at a time until he was completely satisfied. And only then did he spread his tail, spread his wings, raise his head to the sky, and begin his dance.

It was obvious why he had stolen what he had and why the arch was made of fresh green grass. Sparks and even tiny droplets of fire shook out of his feathers with every stamp of his delicate feet, and things like berries and petals wouldn't have lasted a moment. All of his stolen treasures shone in the light and reflected the glory of his feathers, until it almost seemed as if he had two tails, one spread out on the ground, and one raised high in the air.

Eventually his song was answered. The female firebird—almost as glorious as her mate, but lacking the spectacular tail—answered his call. That was when Arville tapped each of the villagers on the back in turn and motioned for them to crawl away. No need to urge them to caution now—everyone in the Pelagiris knew you didn't frighten or startle or challenge a firebird, not if you wanted to escape being burned to a crisp.

As they got to their feet where Pelas and Ryu were waiting, far enough away from the dancing bower that it was unlikely the firebirds would be disturbed, Arville saw to his surprise that Dame Eller had tears in her eyes. Unashamed, she wiped them away with the back of her hand. "That was the most beautiful thing I have ever seen," she sniffed, obviously affected to the point of tears. Arville thought about pointing out something about love always being beautiful or asking her if she was sorry now that she'd accused Yulia unjustly and very nearly gotten the girl killed, then thought better of it. There was a time to keep his mouth shut . . . and besides, there was probably at least one spiteful neighbor who would never miss a chance to remind the woman she'd nearly caused a murder.

"But . . . when can we get our things back?" the village tailor and shoemaker, who had lost several valuable small tools, asked plaintively.

Fortunately, Ryu had told Arville just that detail. "Once they start a nest, they'll abandon the bower," Arville told him. "Keep sending someone to check on it— carefully! When you see the grass has dried out, that means he's abandoned it, and it's safe to collect your things. And next year at this time, don't leave shiny things near windows or outside. You might collect broken bits of shiny pottery, or pretty stones, or even *paint* stones in bright colors, and pile them up in a tray on the edge of the village. Chances are he'll take things from there and not go into the village itself."

"Well, *I* for one am very glad you came here when you did, Herald Arville," declared the third person, a woman who had lost a silver chain to the thieving firebird. "When you are ready to leave, let me know. I'll make a tray of pocket pies for your travels."

:Wowsers!: said Ryu in his head. And Pelas licked his lips.

With a basket full of pocket pies stowed in the caravan and the morning sun at his back, Arville clucked to the horses and waved to the people of Sternbridge who had come out to see him off. Pelas trotted alongside as they drove out of sight, on their way to the next village about three days away.

Arville was feeling very cheerful about—well, everything. Not only had he had a fabulous breakfast of warm pocket pies, he'd spotted Yulia and Morten holding

hands as they waved goodbye, right in front of Dame
Eller. It looked as if even that had sorted itself out.

:*I suspect Dame Eller suddenly realized that if she
wanted to be a grandmother any time soon, she had better
bow to the inevitable and get over the fact that her son is
in love with the servant girl,*: Pelas remarked as the village vanished into the distance. :*And how are you feeling,
Chosen? Good, I hope. You do realize that you solved this
entire problem all by yourself, right?*:

"I—uh—what?" he said, startled. "But I didn't! I just
tried to think like Rod and Alma and Elyn, and—"

:*And none of them were there to tell you* what *to think.
You took the* how *and came up with answers on your
own. Maybe a little of it was Luck—that probably kept
the firebirds from attacking you and the people that were
with you—and that's a good thing. And most of it was you
being* kind, *and thinking about what you said before you
made angry people even angrier. But when it all is put
together,* you *are the one that did everything.*: Pelas'
Mindvoice was warm with affection. :*Didn't he, Ryu?*:

"Rye roo roo rould," Ryu said with satisfaction. "Roor
a real Rerald!"

And to his astonishment, Arville realized they were
both right. He wasn't "a fourth of a Herald."

He was all of one. And it felt . . . right.

About the Authors

Nancy Asire is the author of four novels: *Twilight's Kingdoms, Tears of Time, To Fall Like Stars,* and *Wizard Spawn. Wizard Spawn* was edited by C.J. Cherryh and became part of the Sword of Knowledge series. She also has written short stories for the series anthologies *Heroes in Hell*, edited by Janet Morris, and *Merovingen Nights*, edited by C.J. Cherryh. Other short stories of hers have appeared in Mercedes Lackey's anthology *Flights of Fantasy*, as well as in the previous Valdemar anthologies. She has lived in Africa and traveled the world but now resides in Missouri with her cats and two vintage Corvairs.

For as long as he can remember, **Dylan Birtolo** has always been a storyteller. No matter how much other things have changed, that aspect has not. He still tells stories, in whatever format he can. He currently resides in the great Pacific Northwest, where he spends his time as a writer, a game designer, and a professional sword-swinger. His thoughts are filled with shapeshifters, mythological demons, and epic battles. He has published a few fantasy novels and several short stories in multiple anthologies. He has also written pieces for game companies set in their worlds, including *BattleTech*, *Shadowrun*, *Vampire*, and *Pathfinder*. On the game designer side, he's worked on *Dragonfire* as well as his first game, scheduled to release in 2017. He trains in Systema and also with the Seattle Knights, an acting troop that focuses on stage combat, performing in live shows, videos, and movies.

Endeavoring to be a true jack of all trades, he has worked as a software engineer, a veterinary technician in an emergency hospital, a martial arts instructor, a rock climbing guide, and a lab tech. He has had the honor of jousting, and, yes, the armor is real—it weighs over 100 pounds. You can read more about him and his works at dylanbirtolo.com or follow his Twitter @DylanBirtolo.

Jennifer Brozek is an award-winning author, editor, and tie-in author. Two of her works, *Never Let Me Sleep* and *Last Days of Salton Academy,* have been nominated for the Bram Stoker Award. She was awarded the Scribe Award for best tie-in Young Adult novel for *The Nellus Academy Incident,* a *BattleTech* YA novel. *Grants Pass* won an Australian Shadows Award for edited publication. In between cuddling her cats, writing, and editing, Jennifer is an HWA volunteer, SFWA Director-at-Large, and an active member of IAMTW. She keeps a tight writing and editing schedule and credits her husband, Jeff, with being the best sounding board ever. Visit Jennifer's worlds at jenniferbrozek.com.

Brigid Collins is a fantasy and science fiction writer living in Michigan. Her short stories have appeared in Fiction River, *The Young Explorer's Adventure Guide,* and *Chronicle Worlds: Feyland.* Books 1 through 3 of her fantasy series, Songbird River Chronicles, are available in print and electronic versions on Amazon and Kobo. You can sign up for her newsletter at tinyletter.com/Harmon icStories or follow her on twitter @purellian.

Ron Collins is the bestselling Amazon Dark Fantasy author of *Saga of the God-Touched Mage* and *Stealing the Sun,* a series of space-based SF books. He has contributed 100 or so stories to premier science fiction and fantasy publications, including *Analog, Asimov's,* and several volumes of the Valdemar anthology series. His work has garnered a *Writers of the Future* prize and a CompuServe HOMer award. His short story "The White Game" was nominated for the Short Mystery Fiction Society's 2016

Derringer Award. Find current information about Ron at typosphere.com.

Dayle A. Dermatis has been called "one of the best writers working today" by USA Today bestselling author Dean Wesley Smith. Under various pseudonyms (and sometimes with coauthors), she's sold several novels and more than a hundred short stories in multiple genres. She is also a founding member of the Uncollected Anthology project. A recent transplant to the wild greenscapes of the Pacific Northwest, in her spare time she follows Styx around the country and travels the world, all of which inspires her writing. She loves music, cats, Wales, old houses, magic, laughter, and defying expectations. For more information and to sign up for her newsletter (and get free fiction!), go to dayledermatis.com.

Rebecca Fox always wanted to be John Carter of Mars when she grew up because of the giant birds. Unfortunately the job was already taken, so she got her doctorate in Animal Behavior instead. She makes her home in Lexington, Kentucky, where she shares her life with three parrots, an evil canine genius of a Jack Russell named Izzy, and a big goofy gray thoroughbred gelding. When she isn't writing or on a horse, she works as an associate professor of biology at a liberal arts college and spends a lot of time in the great outdoors spying on the private lives of house sparrows for professional reasons.

Michele Lang grew up in deepest suburbia, the daughter of a Hungarian mystic and a fast-talking used car salesman. Now she writes tales of magic, crime, and adventure. Author of the Lady Lazarus historical urban fantasy series, Michele also writes urban fantasy for the Uncollected Anthology series.

Fiona Patton lives in rural Ontario where she can practice bagpipes without bothering the neighbors. Her partner, Tanya Huff, and their two dogs and many cats have taken some time to get used to them, but they no longer run when she gets the pipes out. She has written seven fantasy novels for DAW books as well as over forty short stories. "Cobblestone" is her tenth Valdemar story, the eighth involving the Dann family.

Diana L. Paxson is the author of 29 novels, including the Westria series and the Avalon novels, nonfiction on goddesses, trance work, and the runes, and ninety short stories, including "Weavings," which features some of the same characters in the 2014 Valdemar anthology *No True Way*. Many of her novels have historical settings, a good preparation for writing about Valdemar. She also writes nonfiction on topics from mythology to trance work. Her next book will be a study of the Norse god Odin. She also engages in occasional craftwork, costuming, and playing the harp. She lives in the multi-generational, multi-talented household called Greyhaven in Berkeley.

Angela Penrose lives in Seattle with her husband, seven computers, and about ten thousand books. She's been a Valdemar fan for decades and wrote her first Valdemar story for the "Modems of the Queen" area on the old GEnie network, back in the 1980s. In addition to fantasy, she also writes SF and mysteries, sometimes in combination. In the last year, she's had stories published in the anthologies *No Humans Allowed, Last Stand, Haunted, Alien Artifacts, The Year's Best Crime and Mystery Stories 2016,* and of course *Tempest,* the previous Valdemar anthology.

Kristin Schwengel lives near Milwaukee, Wisconsin, with her husband, the obligatory writer's cat (named Gandalf, of course), a Darwinian garden in which only the strong survive, and a growing collection of knitting and spinning supplies. Her writing has appeared in several previous Valdemar anthologies, among others. Any resemblance of this story to William Shakespeare's *Twelfth Night* is purely intentional.

Growing up on fairy tales and computer games, *USA Today* bestselling author **Anthea Sharp** has melded the two in her award-winning, bestselling Feyland series, which has sold over 200,000 copies worldwide. In addition to the fae fantasy/cyberpunk mashup of Feyland, she also writes Victorian Spacepunk and fantasy romance. Her books have won awards, topped bestseller lists, and garnered over a million reads at Wattpad. She's frequently found hanging out on Amazon's Top 100 Fantasy/SF author list. Her short fiction has appeared in Fiction River, DAW anthologies, *The Future Chronicles*, and *Beyond the Stars: At Galaxy's Edge*, as well as many other publications. Her newest novel, *Star Compass*, is now available at all online retailers.

Stephanie D. Shaver lives in Southern California with a prepositional-phrase-crushing spouse, two rambunctious children, and a very patient cat. By day she works for Blizzard as a program manager, by night she's probably trying to catch up on sleep. You can find her full bibliography at sdshaver.com, along with occasional ramblings when she isn't sleeping or chasing the kids off the cat.

Having gotten both a BA and an MA in Communication, **D Shull** now gets to answer emails for a tech company and dream of bigger things, like working for workplace diversity. D manages to find some time to read for fun, as well as run the odd tabletop RPG, and would love to get out to the ocean more. D was born, raised, and still lives in California, with very good reasons for staying there, thank you very much.

Growing up in the wilds of the Sierra Nevada mountains, surrounded by deer and beaver, muskrat and bear, **Louisa Swann** found ample fodder for her equally wild imagination. As an adult, she spins both experiences and imagination into tales that span multiple genres, including fantasy, science fiction, mystery, and her newest love—steampunk. Her short stories have appeared in

Mercedes Lackey's *Elementary Magic* and *Valdemar* anthologies (which she's thrilled to participate in!); Esther Friesner's *Chicks and Balances*; and several Fiction River anthologies, including *No Humans Allowed*. Her new steampunk/weird west series, Abby Crumb, debuted this summer. Find out more at www.louisaswann.com.

Elizabeth A. Vaughan is the *USA Today*-bestselling author of fantasy romance novels. She has always loved fantasy, and has been a fantasy role player since 1981. This story is dedicated to Kandace Klumper and Patricia Merritt, both fans of Valdemar. You can learn more about her books at www.writeandrepeat.com.

Elisabeth Waters sold her first short story in 1980 to Marion Zimmer Bradley for *The Keeper's Price*, the first of the Darkover anthologies. She then went on to sell short stories to a variety of anthologies. Her first novel, a fantasy called *Changing Fate*, was awarded the 1989 Gryphon Award. Its sequel, *Mending Fate*, was published in 2016. She is now working on her short story writing, in addition to editing the annual *Sword and Sorceress* anthology. She also worked as a supernumerary with the San Francisco Opera, where she appeared in *La Gioconda*, *Manon Lescaut*, *Madama Butterfly*, *Khovanschina*, *Das Rheingold*, *Werther*, and *Idomeneo*.

Phaedra Weldon grew up in the thick, atmospheric land of South Georgia. Most nights, especially those in October, were spent on the back of pickup trucks in the center of cornfields, telling ghost stories, or in friends' homes playing RPG. She got her start writing in Shared Worlds (*Eureka!*, *Star Trek*, *Battletech*, *Shadowrun*); she has written original stories for DAW anthologies and sold her first urban fantasy series to traditional publishing. Currently she writes three series (The Eldritch Files, the Grimoire Chronicles, and the Zoe Martinique novels) as well as busting out the occasional *Shadowrun* novel (her most recent one is *Identity Crisis*).

Through her combined career as an author and cover artist, **Janny Wurts** has written nineteen novels, a collection of short stories nominated for the British Fantasy Award, and thirty-three contributions to fantasy and science fiction anthologies. Best known for the *War of Light and Shadow* series, other titles include the *Sorcerer's Legacy, the Cycle of Fire* trilogy, and standalones *To Ride Hell's Chasm, Master of Whitestorm,* and the Empire trilogy written in collaboration with Raymond E. Feist. Her paintings and cover art have appeared in exhibitions, including: NASA's 25th Anniversary exhibit, Delaware Art Museum, Canton Art Museum, Hayden Planetarium in New York, and have been recognized by two Chesley Awards and three times Best of Show at the World Fantasy Convention. She lives in Florida with three cats and two horses and rides with a mounted team for search and rescue. Life experience as an offshore sailor, wilderness enthusiast, and musician is reflected in her creative work.

About the Editor

Mercedes Lackey is a full-time writer and has published numerous novels and works of short fiction, including the bestselling *Heralds of Valdemar* series. She is also a professional lyricist and a licensed wild bird rehabilitator. She lives in Oklahoma with her husband and collaborator, artist Larry Dixon, and their flock of parrots.

MERCEDES LACKEY
The Valdemar Anthologies

In the ancient land of Valdemar, beset by war and internal conflict, justice is dispensed by an elite force—the legendary Heralds. These unusual men and women, "Chosen" from all corners of the kingdom by their mysterious horselike Companions, undergo rigorous training and follow a rigid code of honor. Bonded for life with their Companions, the Heralds endeavor to keep the peace and, when necessary, defend their country in the name of the monarch.

With stories by authors such as Tanya Huff, Michelle Sagara West, Sarah Hoyt, Judith Tarr, Mickey Zucker Reichert, Diana Paxson, Larry Dixon, and, of course... stories and novellas by Mercedes Lackey.

To Order Call: 1-800-788-6262
www.dawbooks.com

DAW 157

MERCEDES LACKEY
The Novels of Valdemar

To Order Call: 1-800-788-6262

www.dawbooks.com

Mercedes Lackey & Larry Dixon

The Novels of Valdemar

"Lackey and Dixon always offer a well-told tale."
—*Booklist*

DARIAN'S TALE

OWLFLIGHT
978-0-88677-804-2

OWLSIGHT
978-0-88677-803-4

OWLKNIGHT
978-0-88677-916-2

THE MAGE WARS

THE BLACK GRYPHON
978-0-88677-804-2

THE WHITE GRYPHON
978-0-88677-682-1

THE SILVER GRYPHON
978-0-88677-685-6

To Order Call: 1-800-788-6262
www.dawbooks.com

MERCEDES LACKEY
The Dragon Jousters

JOUST
978-0-7564-0153-4

ALTA
978-0-7564-0257-3

SANCTUARY
978-0-7564-0341-3

AERIE
978-0-7564-0426-0

"A must-read for dragon lovers in particular and for fantasy fans in general." —*Publishers Weekly*

"It's fun to see a different spin on dragons...and as usual Lackey makes it all compelling."—*Locus*

To Order Call: 1-800-788-6262
www.dawbooks.com

MERCEDES LACKEY
The Elemental Masters Series

"Her characteristic carefulness, narrative gifts, and attention to detail shape into an altogether superior fantasy." —*Booklist*

"It's not lighthearted fluff, but rather a dark tale full of the pain and devastation of war, the growing class struggle, and changing sex roles, and a couple of wounded protagonists worth rooting for." —*Locus*

"Putting a fresh face to a well-loved fairytale is not an easy task, but it is one that seems effortless to the prolific Lackey. Beautiful phrasing and a thorough grounding in the dress, mannerisms and history of the period help move the story along gracefully. This is a wonderful example of a new look at an old theme." —*Publishers Weekly*

"Richly detailed historic backgrounds add flavor and richness to an already strong series that belongs in most fantasy collections. Highly recommended." —*Library Journal*

To Order Call: 1-800-788-6262

www.dawbooks.com

DAW 23

MERCEDES LACKEY

Gwenhwyfar
The White Spirit

A classic tale of King Arthur's legendary queen.
Gwenhwyfar moves in a world where gods walk
among their pagan worshipers, where nebulous
visions warn of future perils, and where there are
two paths for a woman: the path of the Blessing,
or the rarer path of the Warrior. Gwenhwyfar
chooses the latter, giving up the power she is born
to. But the daughter of a king is never truly free
to follow her own calling...

978-0-7564-0585-4
Hardcover
978-0-7564-0629-5
Paperback

To Order Call: 1-800-788-6262
www.dawbooks.com

DAW 135